Donegal
Irish Justice

Donegal

Irish Justice

by

JAMES LOWER

LITTLE MIAMI PUBLISHING CO.
Milford, Ohio
2010

Little Miami Publishing Co.
P.O. Box 588
Milford, Ohio 45150-0588
www.littlemiamibooks.com

Copyright ©2010 by James Lower. All rights reserved. No part of this book may be reproduced or transmitted in any form or by any means, electronic or mechanical, including photocopying, recording or by any information storage and retrieval system without written permission from the author, except for the inclusion of brief quotations in a review.

Printed in the United States of America on acid-free paper.

ISBN-13: 978-1-932250-74-9
ISBN-10: 1-932250-74-3

Library of Congress Control Number: 2009935168

*For Lynne, the love of my life and my
coauthor in everything*

*In memory of
Reverend J. Paul O'Brien, SJ
and
William M. Lower*

Contents

	Preface ix
Prologue	*January 1897* *Donegal, Indiana 1*
CHAPTER 1	*April 1922* *Donegal, Indiana 13*
CHAPTER 2	*May 1922* *Indianapolis, Indiana 25*
CHAPTER 3	*June 1922* *Logansport and Donegal, Indiana 41*
CHAPTER 4	*September 1922* *Donegal, Indiana 59*
CHAPTER 5	*September 1922* *Donegal, Indiana 75*
CHAPTER 6	*October 1922* *Donegal, Indiana 87*
CHAPTER 7	*November 1922* *Donegal, Indiana 109*
CHAPTER 8	*December 1922* *Donegal, Indiana 127*

CHAPTER 9	*Christmas 1922* *Donegal, Indiana*	*143*
CHAPTER 10	*January 1923* *Donegal, Indiana*	*159*
CHAPTER 11	*February 1923* *Donegal, Indiana*	*179*
CHAPTER 12	*March 1923* *Donegal, Indiana*	*195*
CHAPTER 13	*April 1923* *Chicago, Illinois*	*215*
CHAPTER 14	*April 1923* *Donegal, Indiana*	*229*
CHAPTER 15	*May 12, 1923* *Donegal, Indiana*	*241*
CHAPTER 16	*May 13, 1923* *Donegal, Indiana*	*257*
CHAPTER 17	*May 13–14, 1923* *Donegal, Indiana*	*271*

Preface

THE KU KLUX KLAN BECAME A METEORIC MOVEMENT in America between 1915 and 1925. The climate was perfect for such a strange phenomenon. People suffered from poor health, a bad economy, and an indifferent government. The Klan offered hope to certain citizens who had been excluded from the riches produced by industrialization. Once the economy strengthened in the middle of the Roaring Twenties, the attractiveness of the Klan with its annual dues waned. In Indiana, a murder conviction of its leader hastened the Klan's demise.

My research uncovered evidence of the Klan actions described in this story, but not in Indiana. The only malevolent steps I noted in my home state were the ostracism and hate letters directed at my grandfather and others.

My thanks to the many people and institutions who helped create a story from family legend. My wife, Lynne, kept my drafts from wandering off course and proofread the manuscript several times. My children, Carrie and Dan, offered support. And Carrie graciously performed the last edit. My father, Bill, offered encouragement from the very beginning and provided key information concerning the legend. My siblings, Bill, Barbara, and Tom, read the manuscript and offered corrections and advice.

Thanks also to my editors, Heather Weber and Kim Peet, who bravely took on this project from a novice storyteller. I am extremely grateful to my publisher, Barbara Gargiulo at Little Miami Publishing Company, for her support and efforts to bring this story to print.

I must also acknowledge the help I received from the Cass County Historical Society and Mr. Bryan Looker, the wonderful people at the Indiana Historical Society in Indianapolis, the Iron Horse Museum and its curator Carl Simons, All Saints Catholic Church of Logansport, the Logansport Public Library, the Fulton County Library in Atlanta, the Auto Heritage Museum in Kokomo, and Lee and George Naftzger, our hosts at Inntiquity Inn in Logansport.

The story of *Donegal: Irish Justice* is my own, formulated after research from many different sources. Any errors contained within this story are mine alone.

Prologue

January 1897
Donegal, Indiana

On the dresser in his tiny sparse bedroom, Father Thomas O'Brien methodically arranged the few possessions he had brought with him to his first parish assignment, St. Mary's Catholic Church. Only twenty-three years of age, he was excited but nervous about bringing his innate love for people, shaped by his education, to this small farming town in central Indiana.

Adding to his anxiety was the intimidating presence of the senior pastor at St. Mary's, Father William Grady. Father Grady was large of stature and much older than even Tom's father. His demeanor was more stern and reserved than any of Tom's professors at St. Meinrad's. During their discussions after Tom's arrival this morning, Father Grady had seemed nothing like Tom's idea of a pastor caring for the members of his flock. His new mentor appeared callous and worn down by the struggles of this parish.

As Tom placed family photos and books on his bedside table, there were footsteps in the hallway and then a sharp knock on his door, followed by the gruff timber of Father Grady's voice.

"Father Tom, are you awake? There is an emergency. I need you to visit a dying member of our congregation."

Tom crossed his room and hurriedly opened the door. "What can I do, Father?"

"Thomas, Dr. Davis is downstairs with young John Conner. John's mother, Bridget, is at home gravely ill. The doctor fears it may be pneumonia. He is on his way over to the Conner home and stopped to see if I would come along to administer Extreme Unction, if it is necessary."

Tom realized Mrs. Conner may be on her deathbed. One of seven sacraments for Roman Catholics, Extreme Unction or Last Rites was offered to those who were thought to be dying. It was also performed on those who had recently expired in hopes they were still cognizant of what was taking place around them.

"Do you want me to accompany you, Father?" asked Tom.

"No," explained Father Grady. "These winter nights are not good for me in an open buggy. Your predecessor, Father Gordon, handled these emergency calls. I know this is your first day and you have not had a chance to meet many of the parishioners, but I would appreciate it if you would go."

"Of course, Father. I'll put on a sweater and bring my kit. I think my hat and coat are still downstairs."

Father Grady held up his hand to slow Tom's preparations and frowned. "I must caution you, Tom. Mrs. Conner is a widow with five young children. If she is about to be taken from this life, a decision will have to be made about the well-being of the children.

"We have recently received a letter from Monsignor Ryan, the bishop's administrative assistant. There are no places available at the diocesan children's home. The typhoid and influenza attacks over the past few years have stretched their capacities to the limit."

"What about the local children's home?" asked Tom.

"We cannot let them be taken to the county home. The conditions there are abysmal," replied the elder priest with a look of dismay in his eyes.

"Mrs. Conner and her late husband moved here from back east six or seven years ago. There are no other family members in the area. I fear there are no neighbors who would be willing to take in the children. The eldest, Joseph, is around fifteen. If his mother dies, he will have to serve as temporary guardian until other arrangements can be made. I'm sure he will be upset and overwhelmed. In that case, it will be your duty to advise and direct Joseph as to the disposition of the children. Maybe the younger children can be sent east to live with relatives."

The older priest paused and ran his fingers through his full head of gray hair.

"This is quite a burden to lay on your young shoulders. We must believe that the Lord has great confidence in your abilities," said Father Grady as he patted Tom's arm and turned toward the stairway.

For a moment, Tom stood dumbly, watching the older priest descend the stairs, and thought again how indifferent he seemed to his parishioners' concerns. Then the full weight of his forthcoming task washed over Tom, and he felt a moment of panic. In a quick prayer, he asked for the presence and help of the Holy Ghost. He picked up his new minister's kit and set off, determined to do the best he could to help the Conners.

His slight build, sandy brown hair, and fair features gave him a boyish look, and he knew this sometimes was not an asset. He had received excellent grades in his studies and had considered continuing his education in advanced theology. But he was most at ease when he worked with people, who were naturally attracted to his straightforward intelligence.

He had been raised in the urban environment of Indianapolis, which lay sixty miles south. Recently ordained into the priesthood, he had obtained his education at St. Meinrad's Seminary in southern Indiana. All of his pastoral training and school vacations had been spent at parishes and hospitals in Indianapolis. He was more than a little anxious about his duties at this new rural farmland church, St. Mary's.

Tom had arrived at St. Mary's late that morning. After meeting the housekeeper and sharing a small lunch consisting of lamb, beets, thick bread, and strong tea, Father Grady had spent a good part of the afternoon educating Tom on the economics of running the small church of almost two hundred Roman Catholics. The church had been established to serve the large influx of faithful immigrants who had come west to build the Wabash and Erie Canal during the 1830s. Irish workmen who built the canal lock needed to bypass the rapids at this point in the Wabash River started a camp they named after their home county, Donegal. But many of the canal builders had moved on to the west. The settlers who replaced them were mostly Protestant farmers from the eastern states. The early community grew from a trading post and lumber production site to a small town, and eventually it became the county seat. Nearby farms on both sides of the river brought their produce to the town, and commerce thrived.

By the 1850s, the canal gave way to the Lake Erie, Wabash and St. Louis Railroad, which became the major source of transportation through the area. The railroad made Donegal a crew change point and established a car repair facility and freight yard east of town along the river. These developments brought jobs to a region that had been primarily agrarian in nature. These positions couldn't be filled from the farm-based population of the area. However, the Europeans who were leaving the Northeast slums for the promise of a better life in the Midwest were the perfect candidates for the various jobs required by the railroad. Unfortunately, the mostly unskilled positions in maintenance and yard operations did not pay well. Thus, donations to the church were not substantial. The Fort Wayne diocese had to subsidize the meager programs of the parish. Tom perceived this to be a major irritant to Father Grady.

Father Grady hurriedly introduced Tom to Dr. Eugene Davis and young John Conner in the hallway at the front door of the rectory. Tom was still buttoning his coat as they climbed into the doctor's buggy outside. The night air was frigid, and a light dusting of snow had fallen onto several inches that had accumulated over the past month. Dr. Davis took control of the horse and buggy, and it was apparent that he was a skilled horseman. They rode east along the muddy track of Broad Street with the boy sandwiched between them on the front seat.

Dr. Davis concentrated on directing his horse to their destination.

He seemed like a kindly middle-aged man to Tom. He wore a string tie with his suit and sported a pencil-thin mustache. Father Grady had introduced him to Tom as a good friend but a Methodist. Dr. Davis had been pleasant enough during introductions, but Tom sensed he was leery of having a young newcomer along on this emergency call.

Tom was content to talk with and attempt to comfort the young boy. John was obviously worried about his mother. He volunteered that he was ten and would soon be eleven. Young John talked of strong memories of his father's death three years earlier while he was working on a track repair gang at the rail yards. Mr. Conner had been the only casualty when a string of boxcars had been misrouted onto a track being repaired. As John told the unfortunate tale of his family, it was clear that he was not ready to relive such a difficult and sad time, especially without the comfort of his dear mother.

Bridget had fallen ill several days before but refused to see the doctor because of the expense. She had continued to work at Coleman's Laundry in the center of town during the day even as fever and persistent coughing racked her plump body. Today, she had been unable to get up from her bed, and toward evening she had held conversations with her two eldest boys, Joseph and Paul, before lapsing into a semiconscious state. A neighbor, Mrs. Miller, had been summoned, and it was she who made the decision to send John to fetch Dr. Davis.

The east side of Donegal had become an Irish shantytown for the immigrants who came to work for the railroad. The proximity to the rail yard and maintenance facilities had made this area perfect for conversion from open meadows to a small village that had little in common with the rest of the town. The cold air would have been bearable but for a fierce wind that raked the flat open lane, lined by small low hovels on either side. The north central part of Indiana contained abundant rich farmland. But in winter, the absence of trees or growing crops allowed the winds to sweep over the fallow ground and accost any person who dared to stand against these zephyrs. Tom shivered with each blast that overtook them from the north.

As they approached the Conner home, Dr. Davis spoke over John's head to Tom in a manner that suggested he hoped the boy did not understand his message. "I don't know why some people wait until they are at death's door to summon me. I've never been one to charge much for my care, and I've never pressed anyone for payment she couldn't afford. But they are proud people who don't like to ask for help if they can't pay for it."

Tom nodded to the doctor and considered that his Irish ancestry qualified him for inclusion in the doctor's analysis of "proud people." He contemplated some sort of explanation for this behavior but felt powerless to explain an attitude that was to him quite normal.

The doctor brought the horse and buggy to a stop in front of a wood and tar paper shack, where a couple of men huddled, smoking rolled cigarettes at the front door. John bounced down from the seat on the heels of the doctor, ran to the door, and pushed it in while calling out that he had brought the doctor. The doctor made his way to the door and stepped in after a brief greeting to the men outside. Father Tom stopped and introduced himself to the two men. They shook his hand and quickly showed him into the Conner home.

Inside, Tom found a warm, dry room with a pot-bellied stove in the middle. One side was devoted to a kitchen area with shelves, a cabinet, and a large table with several chairs. There were some adults seated. One woman held a young girl. The other side of the room contained makeshift beds in various states of disarray. Clothing hung from pegs on the walls, and toys and other children's items dominated the floor on that side of the dwelling. At the back of the room was a doorway that led to the rear of the home.

The woman holding the child rose from the table and greeted Tom. "Hello. You must be the new priest at St. Mary's."

"Yes," said Tom. "I'm Tom O'Brien. I've just come up from Indianapolis."

"Do you like to be called Father O'Brien or something else?" inquired the woman.

"Father Tom will be just fine with me. I'm still getting used to the idea that I'm now an ordained priest."

"Well, Father Tom, I'm Ginny O'Rourke and this is my husband, William." She motioned to a man who stood up from the table. "Here also are Sara Combs and Amy Fitzpatrick. Their husbands are outside having a little nip before they fetch some more firewood for the stove. We are all members of St. Mary's. 'Tis a sad time to be having to greet you, Father."

Tom gave a wan smile to the occupants at the table and focused on Mrs. O'Rourke and the child who stared up at him with a look of indifference. "And who might this be?" inquired Tom as he brought up a gloved hand to within inches of the girl's small fingers.

The girl said nothing, but reached out and touched Tom's glove.

"This is Maureen," said Mrs. O'Rourke. "She's only three, . . . Bridget's youngest. She's a tad shy about all the commotion in the house today. Can you say hello to Father Tom, my little one?"

Maureen only looked at him and then turned her head to bury it into the shoulder of the woman who, at the moment, took the place of her mother. From the dark corner opposite the kitchen area, a child's voice broke the silence with a formal greeting. "Hello, Father Tom. I'm Matt, and I suppose you've come to see our Ma."

Tom turned to seek out the source of the greeting and found a young boy approaching him with an outstretched hand. At first Tom thought the boy meant to shake his still gloved hand, but the child merely took his wrist and guided Tom toward the rear doorway. He looked up into the priest's eyes and stated in a serious, adult tone, "The doctor is back in Ma's room with Mrs. Miller and my brothers. I've got to stay out here, but I'm sure you're allowed to go in."

Tom uttered a quiet "Thank you, Matt," and walked through the doorway. The room was lit by a hurricane lamp turned down low to produce a hazy golden glow. On the bed lay a deathly still woman while Dr. Davis felt for her pulse and used his stethoscope to search for her heartbeat. A woman sat on the other side of the bed, while John and two older boys stood at the opposite end of the room.

After another minute or two of forced silence by those present, Dr. Davis finished his examination and turned his attention first to the seated woman and then to Tom. His look told Tom the worst had taken place. As the doctor removed his stethoscope, he addressed the young priest. "Father, I'm afraid it's too late. Mrs. Conner is in need of your services now." He then turned to the children, who had stepped forward. "Boys, your mother has quit breathing, and I can find no heartbeat. She has succumbed to the bronchial pneumonia she developed." His shoulders drooped, and his head moved slowly from side to side. "I'm sorry, but there is nothing that I can do."

As Tom moved to the doctor's place next to the woman, he heard the oldest boy tell the doctor, "It's all right, Dr. Davis. Ma won't have to suffer anymore." Tom was struck by the courage of the strapping boy, who must be Joseph. However, young John appeared shocked by the news, and there were tears in the eyes of the other brother, Paul. The woman rose and walked over to the young men and put her arms around them one at a time, holding each for a moment. Tom began to take off his outer garments and open his kit. He was suddenly struck by the solemn thought that he was no longer in school. He now had responsibilities in dealing with human suffering that were much more profound than he had ever experienced during his years of study and training.

After Tom had finished with the prayers and ritual anointing of Bridget Conner, he straightened up as the woman brought the bed sheet up over the deceased's head. The children had left the room with Dr. Davis and were talking with him just beyond the doorway. "I'm Katy Miller, Father," she whispered. "I try to lend a hand with all the young families in the area. I attend Mass every morning on my way to work, so you'll be seeing a lot of me."

"I'm Father Tom O'Brien, from Indianapolis, Mrs. Miller. I look forward to talking with you on happier occasions."

"There's nothing more to be done here tonight," said Katy. "Ginny will take little Maureen to her place. Joseph and the boys can take care of themselves here tonight. I'll make arrangements for the undertaker before I start work in the morning. If you would be kind enough to arrange for the funeral Mass, Father O'Brien, then things should be in good order."

"Yes, of course," said Tom. "But we need to consider the long-term living arrangements for the children. Father Grady has told me that there are no other relatives in the area. Do you know if that is true? Are there perhaps family members back east?"

Katy Miller gave him a thin, tolerant smile. "Bridget had no kin who would be wanting this brood, Father. She was instructing Joseph and Paul earlier on what they must do. Go, talk with them, and I think you'll find their plans are pretty well made."

Tom finished packing his kit and picked up his hat and coat before gazing again at the covered form of his departed parishioner. He glanced at the table next to the bed and spotted a well-used Bible near the hurricane lamp. He picked it up and tucked it under his arm while bowing his head. "Lord," he whispered, "have mercy on this faithful servant and grant her the heavenly reward she deserves. Grant also unto me the wisdom I need to deal with her unfinished responsibilities."

As Tom stepped into the other room, Mrs. Miller turned out the bedroom lamp and came behind him, shutting the door after her. Joseph and Paul were talking quietly to Dr. Davis in the main room. John and Matt were adding more kindling wood to the stove. The other adults had left, and the little girl was gone as well.

When Joseph saw Tom, he came toward him. "Tell Father Grady that Ma should have a High Mass on Thursday afternoon. Folks can come after work, and we can still have a graveside service before it gets dark. There'll be money for the church, so Father Grady don't need to worry about the cost. Both of you are welcome to come for the wake tomorrow evening."

Tom was taken back by the forcefulness of the young man's bearing. Tom perceived that the boy had to be hurting inside, but his duties, real and imagined, had caused him to adopt the role of head of the family. The younger boys appeared to be in great pain as well but kept silent in deference to their older sibling.

Tom took a moment to organize his thoughts and to look at each of the four boys before speaking. "Thank you, I'm sure Father Grady and I will stop by tomorrow evening. And whatever your wishes are for the funeral Mass and graveside service, I will make sure that they are carried out.

"What are your plans for the care of your brothers and sister,

Joseph? Will you discuss them with me?"

"I've just been speaking with Dr. Davis about them," said Joseph. "Ma agreed with me and Pauly. This town has been bad luck for us. We need to move on to Chicago, where we can get jobs and take care of each other. Pauly can mind John, and I'll take care of Matt. We can get a room in a neighborhood where they look after our kind."

Tom looked at Dr. Davis and saw a look of resignation on the man's face. Tom was perplexed, but he perceived that to argue with such a plan would be futile. He tried to approach the problem from another angle. "And your sister, Maureen. What will you do about her?"

"Ma said that there was a convent in Chicago that would take care of Maureen, if we could pay for it. Do you know if it's true? Will you help us to find it, Father?"

"I know that there is an order, the Sisters of St. Francis, who look after young girls like your sister. I can contact them for you. But what about John and Matt? They're too young to be out in the world. You can't believe that you can take care of them and also hold down jobs in that big city. Wouldn't they be better here at home with friends? Can't you get jobs here and also get a decent education?"

Joseph looked at his brother Paul and then to Dr. Davis before he turned back to Tom. He stared at the floor as he spoke and his voice had a hard, bitter tone. "There are no good jobs in Donegal for Irish lads. The railroad can get grown men to do the work that they have here. Farmers and storekeepers don't pay nothing. In Chicago there are lots of jobs . . . even Matt can work, and he's only seven. It's what we are going to do, Father," he said emphatically.

Tom felt defeated and wondered how he had failed to discern a better solution. He meekly nodded his consent and put on his coat. "All right, Joseph. I'll do whatever I can to help you boys get settled." He took a couple of steps toward the door before he stopped and held up the Bible he realized he still carried under his arm. "This is your family's Bible, Joseph. It belongs to you now."

Joseph stepped forward and took the book. Turning, he handed it to his little brother, Matt. He looked back at Father Tom and Dr.

Davis. "Matt should keep it. Ma used to read to us from it at night, but Matt was the only one who listened and asked questions. Ma hoped he would become a priest someday."

"Well, maybe he will in the future. I'd be happy to see about getting him into a Catholic school in Indianapolis," Tom offered.

"That's not likely to happen," replied Joseph. "We're orphans now, and we have to make our own way in the world. No offense, Father, but the priesthood is for those who can afford it."

As Tom and Dr. Davis climbed into the buggy, the doctor caught Tom's eye. "It's for the best, Father. I've seen more than a few of these young men leave here for the adventure of the big cities or the western frontier. Some come back and settle down with their families. Most find new lives and start new families of their own. I'm sure some fall victim to bad company or bad luck. But I have found that there is only so much one can do to help our fellow Christians. This world is full of suffering, Father, and we have to accept that fact."

Tears came to Tom's eyes and turned cold on his cheeks. He kept his gaze on the horse in front of them as it stepped slowly toward its home. "I'm sure you offer good advice, Doctor. And your experience far outweighs my own. But I feel a terrible sadness at the thought of a boy at the age of seven or even twelve having to go out into that world of so much suffering. What chance do they have of growing up and leading useful lives? Will they ever get the education and training they'll need to survive and start families? Or will they be doomed to lives of poverty and drunken sorrow?"

The horse made its way back to the rectory next to St. Mary's. Neither man spoke during the remainder of the cold, sad trip.

CHAPTER 1

April 1922
Donegal, Indiana

MATT CONNER TRUDGED DOWN THE STEPS from the upper floor of his house with his Bible, the only keepsake from his boyhood. He felt tired, and now with the two children tucked into bed, he was hoping for an hour of quiet contemplation of John's First Epistle. It was one of his favorites, and it always helped to calm his spirits before bed.

As Matt reached the parlor, he caught sight of his wife, Annie. He cherished her, and his partnership with her was the most important thing in his life. But her appearance on the living room sofa warned him that his hour of meditation would have to be postponed. Annie had finished her kitchen chores and had already dressed for bed. Her long dark hair hung down around the shoulders of her white robe. She held an issue of Collier's magazine, but her facial expression signaled that something was on her mind.

Matt slowly walked forward, admiring her features more with each step. She was the most attractive woman he knew. Her long fingers delicately closed the magazine. She placed it on her lap as she raised her head and peered at him with her unusual emerald green eyes.

"You look as though we need to talk, pretty lady," said Matt as he collapsed into his favorite chair across from her.

Annie didn't reply but only smiled as she contemplated the significance of her news. This was one of those moments a woman cherished, and Annie knew she would always remember for the duration of her life. She took in the exhausted features of her husband. Matt was of normal height and weight. He parted his brown hair just off center, and his brown eyes and fair features were decidedly Irish. Outsiders considered him a hard man. No one wanted to cross him; even her father had grudgingly come to respect him.

But her loving husband could be as friendly as a saint when he relaxed around friends and people he loved. Annie was thankful he treated her with respect and even devotion. Such was not the case with many couples with whom they were acquainted.

Finally she reached over, and took his callused hand and placed it between her own. "I had some tests done by Dr. Nash last week. He's the one who practices here and at St. Joseph's hospital in Logansport."

"What tests . . . what's wrong?"

"Nothing's wrong," answered Annie in a soothing tone as she smiled at him.

She looked into his eyes and savored the moment until she could hold back no longer. "We're going to have another baby," she whispered as tears rose in her eyes.

Matt looked stunned, and his jaw tightened while his mouth worked into a scowl.

Annie waited, and when Matt didn't reply, she released his hand and wiped her eyes. "What's the matter?" she asked in a reproachful tone.

"Nothing."

"You don't seem to be very happy with the news."

For Matt it was a private joke between them that Annie could see into his thoughts even before he could sort them out. No one else could read his features the way she did, and it left him anxious to explain himself before she drew the wrong conclusions.

After a moment he came over to sit next to her on the sofa. He placed his arm around her and drew her close to him.

"I'm relieved that your health is good," he stated matter-of-factly. "I'm also surprised by your good news. We both come from large families, and we certainly have room for more children. But I've had no warning, dear. The country's in another depression, and I'll need to find a way to pay for this. The doctor and the hospital are going to require funds I don't have at the moment.

"But don't worry. You concentrate on bringing us another healthy baby, and I'll find a way to increase our funds." He kissed her on the cheek, and she held him more tightly.

Annie released Matt and gave him her smile of approval. It was so like her husband to worry about money. They had gotten by with less when she had delivered Brian and then Katy just a few years earlier. But they had sunk all their capital into this home and the bakery when they settled here in Donegal. And sales had declined just as crop prices had dropped over the last two years. If it weren't for the wages earned by the railroad workers, the town would have little to support itself.

She looked up into his eyes and saw the familiar sparkle that came to them whenever she examined them closely. She knew that they would get by and even prosper. Her faith in God and in her husband was absolute.

At 3:40 on the following Monday morning, Matt quietly pushed the lever to turn off his alarm clock and slid from bed. The alarm was set to ring in another five minutes, but he almost always woke up in time to stop it from disturbing his family. He dressed slowly and silently in the work clothes he had laid out on the chair next to his bed. The house was cool because the coal furnace had been shut down for the spring season. He kissed his sleeping wife on the cheek. She stirred, mumbled "good-bye" and continued to doze. Matt then moved deliberately across the floorboards of the upstairs of their house, making no noise as he checked on his children. Three-year-old Katy was sleeping peacefully in her room. A moonbeam crossed over her bed, illuminating her features and giving her a cherubic appearance. Matt smiled to himself as he felt the joy of a father for his daughter. Next, he tiptoed to the end of the hallway and looked into the room of his eldest child, Brian. The room was very dark, but Brian's breathing indicated that he was in a deep sleep. Matt thought how the boy was still very innocent, unlike himself at the age of six. Matt was resolved to protect him from the harsh realities of the world for a few more years. He then made his way to the bathroom to prepare for the day ahead.

Downstairs, Matt donned his corduroy jacket and his straw boater hat and departed through the front door of his comfortable two-story house. He strode quickly and with purpose on this early morning walk to his bakery. The neighborhood was dark and still slumbering through another chilly spring night. The full moon lit the concrete sidewalks except where the shade from the towering hardwood trees blocked the light. The streets were paved with large smooth red bricks that appeared black in the semidarkness. Unless it was raining, Matt always strolled down Tenth Street to Broad Street and west on the main boulevard to his bakery on Seventh Street. Matt usually liked the six-block walk to work. It gave him a chance to organize his day and develop new ideas to promote his business. It was on such a walk that Matt conceived the idea to advertise his fresh warm breads in the newspapers in Donegal and in nearby Logansport. He had created interest in his products among the readers of the papers. They, in turn, had requested the bread from their local grocers. And many of these grocers had contacted Matt and offered to carry his products at a price only slightly less than his retail prices. It had doubled his sales, and they continued to rise until the current economic depression threw everyone's business into a slump.

But today Matt felt uneasy about the future. Another baby would enter their world by the end of the year. It wasn't that he disliked the idea of more children, but he was apprehensive about the responsibility for their welfare. He was keenly aware of the misfortune that could befall a family. His regular visits to his parents' graves since his return to Donegal two years ago constantly reminded him of the trag-

liked to have good bread without the laborious effort required baking it. Matt reasoned that what was true in large cities could also work in small towns. Instead of taking hours once or twice a week to bake their own bread and dinner rolls, homemakers might be tempted to spend some of their money for quality breads that he could provide. The country was growing, and the economy was putting more money in the hands of the people. Farmers complained about the low prices for their goods, but Matt felt that even farmers would soon benefit from the overall upsurge in prosperity.

As another advantage, Matt had memorized the recipes for several kinds of baked goods he had helped prepare in Chicago. He was terrible at remembering people's names, but his memory served him well with other things. He could even recognize people just by hearing their voice in another room. So he was easily able to reproduce Italian loaves, breadsticks, and even a brioche-type of holiday bread. Such staples should generate a steady stream of customers. He was sure he could offer people products they couldn't make for themselves.

Matt had one other advantage he thought would push him ahead of the other bakeries already established in most communities. People loved warm fresh bread and baked goods. By starting very early each morning, Matt could offer his products to customers straight from the ovens by seven o'clock. Even the goods he would transport to grocery stores in the area would exude a fresh aroma that lingered for a time. No one else started baking so early in the morning. This concept would give him the edge he needed to establish his bakery as the best in the area.

The opportunity seemed genuine, and from his travels Matt considered Donegal to be the ideal location, even though it already had a bakery. Besides, it was the locale of the only real home he had ever known. As the county seat of Fairview County in the Wabash River valley, it had a growing economy for banking and law practice. The roundhouse, freight yard, and crew change facility for the Wabash Railroad provided transportation-related activities. But the backbone of this rural commercial center was the rich farmland, tended by many small families, that surrounded the town. While they had always needed the basic supplies of farm life, these families were purchasing major consumer items, such as automobiles and radios. Fresh bread at ten cents a loaf might be tempting for a mother who already had too many chores to accomplish during the week.

And so Matt and Annie moved to Donegal and bought an empty one-story building on Seventh Street between Railroad Avenue and Broad Street. They also purchased a nice brick house northeast of the center of town. Matt had been able to pay cash for the house, but the building, ovens, and special equipment he required for the bakery had necessitated a large loan from the First Bank of Donegal. The monthly payments were a constant reminder to Matt of the precariousness of his situation.

Matt refused to let Annie work at the bakery. Her job was to manage the house and raise the children. He provided her with a good household allowance and asked that she not buy anything she couldn't pay for from her weekly cash stipend. That allowance would soon have to be increased, and there would be additional bills for the birth of the new child. Matt was losing just a little more control over his life. That thought scared him more than meeting someone here on the shadowy streets in the hours before sunrise. He was going to have to find a way to generate more income at the bakery.

As he turned onto Broad Street, he caught sight of the dark form of Officer Billy Harris of the city police force. The young officer was out patrolling the downtown area in the wee hours before dawn. Billy Harris was a local boy from a farm south of the river who had joined Chief Paul Johnson and his other four officers last year. Matt suspected the boy had little intelligence and less motivation. As the least senior patrolman, Billy drew the night watch four times a week. Matt assumed Billy spent much of the evening at the jail and only came out to patrol when he knew Matt would be walking to work. Matt had gone to the bakery at other times during nights when special preparations were required for holiday treats, and he was nowhere to be seen. Because Matt enjoyed a friendship with Chief Johnson, he speculated Billy was clever enough to try to stay on his good side.

Matt waved to the young policeman as he approached Seventh

Street and the entrance of his shop. Billy gave Matt an informal salute as he came abreast of the baker on the opposite side of the street. Matt smiled and walked on toward his store.

The lights were on in the rear kitchen, and the exhaust fan hummed. Davy Krebs was up and busy with the day's preparations. Davy lived in the back room of the bakery and handled many basic functions for Matt. Davy was a tall, lanky young man who liked to slick his hair sideways. He dressed in ill-fitting overalls and an undershirt while he worked near the hot ovens. He had a charming smile, but his brown eyes remained dull, as if they could never focus on who or what was before him. Davy was probably retarded or at least slow enough to need supervision for most employment. He had said factory work and even many farm jobs were too dangerous for him. But Matt kept things simple, and Davy had become a loyal assistant.

As usual on Mondays, Davy would have awakened at 3:15 A.M. and had a quick snack while he started the coal-fired ovens. Then he would have begun mixing the bread dough in the quantities which had been measured for him on Saturday.

By the time Matt arrived, Davy would be busy kneading the balls that would be the first into the ovens. Davy was always consistent with his actions. He'd push the heel of his flour-covered hand into the ball. Then he'd take the far edge of the now flattened ball and fold it back on top of itself. Then Davy would give the ball a quarter turn and repeat his actions. When the dough developed a satiny, elastic texture, Davy would place it in a mixing bowl lined with butter and roll the dough to coat it with the slippery substance. Then the bowl was covered with a towel and set on a shelf near the ovens. The bread dough would now need about ninety minutes to complete its first rising.

Matt walked past the empty display cases in the front room of the bakery and stood in the doorway of the kitchen area. "Good morning, Davy," he called as he surveyed the young man's work. "How is everything going for the start of the week?"

"Morning, Mr. Matt," Davy called out. "I've got six bowls on the shelf."

Matt went over and inspected each bowl to ensure the yeast was active and the dough rising. Next he checked the fires to be sure they were heating the ovens properly. Finally, he removed his jacket and hat, donned his apron, and rolled up his sleeves in order to help Davy get the rest of the bread dough into bowls. There would be many customers today who needed to replenish their bread tins after the weekend. Matt quickly became too busy to worry about his economic position.

Matt and Davy worked methodically through the first rising in the bowls and then through the second rising in the baking pans. Davy would now clean the bowls in the big sink while Matt began preparing biscuits and dinner rolls that generated a smaller portion of his sales. Later in the morning, they would bake cookies to round out his choice of goods for the day. Matt got great joy from making these smaller treats. He would experiment with recipes customers brought him so as to have a different selection for each day. He'd also prepare various types of bread once his primary loaves had been baked for the day. He made a fine white bread he sold for ten cents. His special breads, like the quality Italian loaf, sold for fifteen cents. None of the other four bakeries in Donegal and nearby Logansport would have fresh bread available before ten o'clock. His first customers would arrive by seven, and he would have his truck making deliveries two hours later.

Matt kept a Ford Model T truck in a shed he rented in the alley behind the store. He employed different men to deliver his baked goods to several grocery stores in Donegal and the much larger town of Logansport, six miles to the west. Later, Matt would drive the truck home for lunch and a short nap before running his afternoon errands.

He learned he could depend on selling two hundred loaves a day plus more on Monday and Saturday. This produced the basic income he needed to pay his bills. It was the "special treats" he added to his display cases that generated the bonus money. These additional sales let him provide for his family a level of comfort that would have been unheard of for most second-generation European immigrants.

He was reminded of this fact daily when he went home for lunch and a nap. The women of his neighborhood, who were so pleasant to deal with when they were in his store, were less so when they encountered him on the streets. The local baker was considered an outsider who did not belong in their neighborhood, even when he cleaned up and donned a suit for his afternoon of work. Annie received similar treatment but didn't let it bother her. She made her friends at church and stayed active in the affairs of the parish.

As it came time to put the bread pans into the ovens, Matt turned his attention to the rest of the day's activities. There was no unsold inventory from yesterday, as the bakery had been closed on Sunday. He had dispersed last week's unsold goods to the orphanage, jail, and hospitals on Saturday afternoon. As usual, certain baked items had been given to the needy of the community who knew to visit the back of the shop before closing.

Mrs. Ginny O'Rourke, an old friend of his Ma, would arrive by eight o'clock. Her husband had to quit the railroad when his arthritis became unbearable. William O'Rourke did odd jobs around town, including maintenance at Matt's house and the bakery. But to survive, it was necessary for Mrs. O'Rourke to work, and handling customers at the bakery was as good a job as a woman in her fifties could expect to find in this small town.

Matt relied on Mrs. O'Rourke to deal with customers, almost all of whom were attracted to her motherly manners and her slight Irish brogue. In addition, she would measure out many of the ingredients for the next day's preparations during the afternoon when customers came less frequently. This arrangement allowed Matt to better handle the added traffic in the morning and to enact his business outside the store in the afternoon. Today, he would make his rounds buying supplies for the week ahead. He would pay his account at the flourmill and Hendrick's Emporium, where he obtained many of his spices and other ingredients. He also needed to send a telegram and money order to Gambini's in Chicago to obtain the olive oil and garlic cloves that went into some of his Italian baked goods.

Davy would continue to bake and then clean up the kitchen until

Matt arrived back at the store in the late afternoon. Once the supplies had been unloaded, Davy was relieved from his twelve-hour shift to wander about town until he came back to sleep in the early evening. Mrs. O'Rourke would leave around four o'clock, and Matt stayed until he closed at five and finished making his preparations for the next day.

As the sun rose over the oak and maple trees on one of those beautiful spring days that radiated over the Indiana countryside, the initial stock of loaves came out of the ovens and was left to cool on the counter behind the display cases.

"It looks like we're going to have a good week, Davy," Matt said.

"It's always good when the bread smells like this, Mr. Matt," replied Davy.

With that, Matt realized his earlier anxiety had dissipated, but his mind was still working on how to increase his profits. And like a flash of lightning on a stormy afternoon, the solution came into his head. The key to increasing his profits lay in expanding his selection of "special treats." It was time to augment his offerings with pastries and desserts. In order to do that he would need the help of his younger sister, Maureen. Fortune may still be favoring him and his endeavors. Maureen had unique baking skills that probably did not exist anywhere in Indiana.

He would write her this evening.

CHAPTER 2

May 1922
Indianapolis, Indiana

LUCAS CRAWFORD EXAMINED HIS CUTICLES for the tenth time in the past hour. The hard bench in the waiting area of the Highway Department had become uncomfortable. He was used to waiting in outer offices for his chance to speak to someone, having spent more than ten years making sales pitches for a variety of products, ranging from laundry soap to farming implements. But this was different.

In good health for someone over thirty years of age, he nevertheless was not as fit as when he had done farm work in his youth. He had hated manual labor and believed his superior intelligence would free him from the hard farm life of his parents. But the life of a salesman was tedious, and cigarettes and booze did not keep one in shape. Actually his life had not been much easier than when he had labored on the farms of his parents or neighbors. The drudgery of trying to make a sale or getting a better job was a constant problem. He just couldn't get a break that would let him exercise his talents. Those breaks always went to someone who had a connection he didn't have.

Lucas had finally awakened to the idea that a steady income could make him more money than the commissions that came all too infrequently from sales. And nobody provided steady employment better than the government. So Lucas had completed an employment application for the Highway Department a few weeks ago. Yesterday, he received a notice to report for an interview with a Mr. Stanley as soon as possible. Lucas continued to rehearse lines that would accent his abilities for the management job he hoped would be available. Lucas was sure his best asset was his declared affiliation with the Republican Party. As long as they controlled the Statehouse, then Republican rank and file would get the jobs.

Lucas felt an ironic smile play over his features as he realized that this "great revelation" was due directly to the constant nagging of his now absent wife. After he lost his last position, she ranted for days about the insecurity his career had brought them. When he went out for a night of drinking, she left for parts unknown. A note told him he should get a divorce, but he saw no reason to spend any more money on a woman who no longer mattered to him. Now if he could land a position with a good salary, he might even look her up and buy her dinner. But he didn't want her back.

At last the buzzer sounded at the clerk's desk, and the young man looked over his wire-rimmed glasses at Lucas. "Mr. Stanley will see you now. Just go down the hall to the second door on your left."

"Thanks." Lucas made an effort to rise slowly, to appear comfortable in front of this minor constituent of the bureaucracy. He had no idea why he wanted to make a good impression on a mere clerk, but for nothing more than practice, he intended to carry out the act.

He carried his derby in one hand, and straightened out his brown wool suit as he walked, hoping the wrinkles were not obvious. He should have had it pressed, but he couldn't afford it. Had he the money, he would have bought a lighter weight suit for the warm weather. Fortunately, May was normally mild in Indianapolis, and many businessmen wore wool suits.

At the second door, Lucas found Mr. John Stanley's name stenciled on the opaque glass. He took a deep breath, knocked lightly, and opened the door with as much confidence as he could muster. Inside, he found a large middle-aged man in a starched white shirt and bow tie seated behind a dark walnut desk examining Lucas's application.

The man wore black-rimmed glasses and was almost entirely bald. His girth indicated he must have a good appetite—and the means to satisfy it.

"Mr. Stanley, I'm Lucas Crawford. I'm responding to your notice regarding employment here at the Highway Department." Lucas made an effort to sound confident and at ease.

"Yes, Mr. Crawford, please come in and sit down. I'd like to ask you some questions."

Lucas stepped forward and held out his hand for Mr. Stanley to shake as a preliminary to taking a seat in the wooden chair opposite. He had learned that to project confidence, you had to appear comfortable in any surrounding.

But Mr. Stanley upset this strategy by ignoring the offered hand. "I see that you've had trouble keeping a job."

Lucas was stunned. His aura of confidence drained away. He sat down, balancing his hat upon his knee. After a moment, he managed to stammer, "Salesmen get hired and fired depending upon whether or not there are buyers for what they've got to sell."

Mr. Stanley looked down at the application and then looked at Lucas once more. "I notice you were born in Donegal. Did you get your education there?"

Lucas had only stayed in school through tenth grade but considered the best response was a brief "Yes, sir, I did."

John Stanley gave no indication of where this conversation was leading. "Do you still have friends up there?"

"Sure," replied Lucas. "There are a bunch of guys who know me. I got along with most of the folks in the area." Lucas began to perceive that the Highway Department needed someone for the Wabash Valley. He began to stroke his thick mustache, a habit he fell into when nervous.

Stanley made a note on the application with his fountain pen and, without looking up, asked, "Do you go to church very often?"

Lucas had prepared himself for this type of question. He calmly explained that he was raised in a Baptist church but had been accompanying his wife to her Methodist church near their home. He had visited the church yesterday in order to familiarize himself with it. He had never been inside it before.

Mr. Stanley next focused on Lucas's references. "Are these men business or social acquaintances?"

"Well, I have done business with each of them," replied Lucas, "but I consider them to be good friends. Once I've sold something to a customer, I believe I've made a friend, and I treat him that way from then on."

John Stanley made another note on the application and then reached inside his top desk drawer and brought out a plain piece of paper and a large brown envelope. As he began writing a letter, Lucas began to feel encouraged that there might be an opening for him. He broke the silence and Mr. Stanley's concentration. "What sort of positions do you have open in your department?"

Stanley looked up and stared across his desk for a moment and then a thin smile developed on his face. "We don't have anything available for someone with your experience, Mr. Crawford."

Silence stretched on for several seconds. Even in his dismay, Lucas was conscious of the automobile traffic on Senate Avenue four floors below.

"However, I know of an organization looking for someone like you to set up an office in the Logansport area. Let me finish this note, and I'll give you directions to his office. It's only a few blocks away."

Lucas was confused and speechless for one of the few times he could remember. On the one hand, he was crushed that his hope for a secure government job was gone. But on the other hand, he was intrigued with the idea of running his own office.

Mr. Stanley finished his letter and put it and the application in the brown envelope. He sealed it with glue from a bottle in his drawer and wrote a name and address on the front of it. Then he offered it to Lucas.

"Take this to the address I've written down for you. Ask to see this man, Clarence Carpenter. You are to give the envelope directly to him and don't open it. If you qualify, he'll explain to you the nature of the job he has available. Think over his proposal; it's a very good opportunity to get in on the ground floor of what is becoming a major political movement in this country.

"That's all I can say, but you would be wise to visit with Mr. Carpenter as soon as possible." John Stanley rose and now offered his hand to Lucas. Lucas stood, took the envelope with his left hand, and placed his derby on his jet-black hair before shaking Mr. Stanley's hand with his right. He read the name and address and nodded to the gentleman before turning and retreating through the door.

Once outside in the hallway, Lucas had a chance to absorb what little information had been imparted from this unusual interview. He focused on the address and recognized the location. Since he was dressed properly, and not getting any younger, he decided to walk the three blocks east to the center of town in hopes of finding this Mr. Carpenter. Lucas believed in luck, and right now he wasn't sure if his was turning or not. His optimistic nature gave him hope.

Several blocks to the north, Father Thomas O'Brien waited anxiously. He had requested a meeting with the bishop of the diocese. Tom was dressed in his best black suit and held his black brimmed bowler in his left hand as he sat in the parlor of the residence. He'd known and worked for Bishop Green for several years. Tom had been a parish priest when the bishop came to Indianapolis twelve years ago. Having worked in different positions for the diocese, he was currently superintendent of the Catholic schools.

The bishop's secretary, Father Digby, entered and led Tom into the bishop's study, which was richly appointed with burgundy upholstered chairs and a couch in blue fabric that matched the draperies. Bishop George Green stepped forward and greeted him with a warm smile and hearty handshake. The bishop was a small man with closely cropped gray hair except for a small bald area on the top of his head. He was dressed in his casual cassock, and his gray eyes sparkled with the intelligence Tom greatly admired. "Hello, Tom. It's good to see you. Please accept my congratulations on the completion of another fine school year."

"Thank you, your Grace," replied Tom with some modesty. "I have to give all the credit to my staff and the wonderful principals and teachers who make our program work. The Lord has been kind to us."

"That is quite true," seconded Bishop Green. "Now, to what do I owe the pleasure of this visit? Have you concocted some new program to drain more funds from our beleaguered treasury? You always know how to get my support for your expanding empire."

"No, your Grace, the plans are set for the coming year, and we will stay within our budget."

"Well, that is good to hear. I hope you took no offense at my attempt at humor," he added with a smile.

"Not at all, your Grace." He paused. "Actually I've come to you with a personal request. I'd like your permission to step down from the school system and transfer to the Fort Wayne diocese."

The bishop appeared stunned but recovered his calm demeanor with the ease that comes from years of experience in dealing with human emotions. "Come, my friend, let's sit down and discuss this request. Can I offer you some coffee or perhaps some lemonade?"

"I'm fine, your Grace, and I don't wish to take up your valuable time." Tom allowed himself to be directed to the small couch.

After they had seated themselves, the bishop placed his fingertips together. "Are you unhappy with your current duties?"

"No, your Grace. It's just that I feel I could be of greater service to our Lord by getting back into parish work. I've missed it, and quite by accident I've learned there is a vacancy in my first parish in the Logansport area. There are some fine people whom I know there, and I feel that perhaps I could be of service to them. An old friend wrote to me recently to tell me of his father's death. He talked of how the town, Donegal, was growing and changing but that the old parish was stagnant. It lacked vitality. St. Mary's Church has long been in dire need of physical repairs. My friend also added in his letter that Father Egan, the pastor, was ill and would retire this year."

Bishop Green studied Tom for a long moment before he spoke. "I'm confused, Tom. Do you feel your current duties, that benefit the entire diocese, are less important than dealing with the people of a single parish? You have a splendid future in front of you. You must know you will probably be made a monsignor in the near future. You are still young and perhaps will become a bishop before your career is done. Such responsibilities are of great benefit to the church."

Tom lowered his gaze to his bowler resting on his lap. He chose his words carefully. "I know that the administrative work I have been given has great importance, and I do it gladly. But as I've grown older, I've come to miss the close relationships a parish priest forges with his own congregation. Being of help and comfort to people is the reason I became a priest." He glanced at the doorway and then turned toward his bishop before adding in a hesitant tone, "I've written Bishop LeFranz in Fort Wayne and asked if it would be possible to be appointed pastor at St. Mary's. His secretary has replied and said the position was mine if I obtained your approval."

Bishop Green smoothed the wrinkles in his cassock and appeared to contemplate the gravity of the situation. Tom knew his superior did not like being confronted with such a request without warning, and that only his many years of experience kept him from becoming angry. The bishop needed more information before making his decision. Tom prepared himself for further exploration of his request.

"Tom, if you really feel the need to be back in a parish, I can find one here in your hometown. I can rearrange some positions, which would actually be healthy for our diocese. You could have your choice of just about any parish. Then, in time, if you wish greater responsibilities, it would be easier to arrange for you to transfer again. There are many more opportunities to serve the Lord in this city than you will find in the farmland to the north. Would you be willing to take a position in any of the fine churches we have here?"

Tom looked into the gray eyes of his superior and felt strangely calm about what he was about to say next. "Your Grace, I took a vow of obedience when I was ordained, and I will do whatever you deem best for the Church. But I must tell you that I did not make this decision without much prayer and contemplation. You may think it was my imagination, but when I read of Father Egan's retirement, I could almost feel our Lord's hand on my shoulder. It was as if He were guiding me toward this path."

A fan hummed in another room, and the bishop rose from his wing chair and paced the length of the room and back. Tom watched with calm resignation, for he had seen the bishop pace back and forth before he delivered his valued opinion on subjects that concerned the diocesan schools. Finally the bishop stopped, placed his hands on the back of his chair, and looked down at Tom with a benevolent smile.

"Tom, I also took a vow of obedience. It would be a sin if I were to place my interests above those of our Lord. At my age, I try not to commit many sins. I should warn you that as one is given greater responsibilities in the Church, it becomes easier to commit sins of omission. We must be careful to consider all sides to an issue before selecting a course of action. In this case, I believe you are needed in Donegal. I'll write my colleague in Fort Wayne and tell him that you are available immediately.

"You will go with my blessing and my prayer that our Lord will be with you," concluded the bishop as he came forward and reached for Tom's hand.

Tom rose and shook the bishop's hand with great enthusiasm. The last doubt he harbored about his decision had just vanished. It felt good to know where his future lay.

Just before noon, Lucas stepped off the elevator onto the fifth floor of a modern bank building overlooking Monument Circle, the center of the downtown business district. The tall stone Soldiers and Sailors Monument, which was dedicated to war veterans from Indiana, was a grand idea for honoring those warriors who had fought for the republic. There was talk of adding a museum to the bottom of the monolith. Lucas had always considered the circle area a good spot to have lunch and watch the tourists from the farms come to climb the tower. The only problem for both diners and tourists was the traffic that rushed around the brick streets enclosing the monument. Situated in the center of the crossing of the two main roads that reached out to the four compass points, the monument was not an easy place to reach on foot. Trolleys, trucks, and autos drove around it in great numbers. Policemen helped the pedestrians at regular intervals, but it was still dangerous. A pedestrian tunnel crossing under the street was needed, but Lucas didn't think he'd get the chance to suggest it to the mayor and certainly not to the State Highway Department.

Lucas walked down the corridor, looking for Room 515. He straightened his tie and was glad he hadn't become hot from his walk from the government building. He didn't like being rejected by Mr. Stanley. Experience told him that the available position working for this Mr. Carpenter was probably a dead-end. More than likely, they needed some unlucky guy like himself to sell washing machines to the farmers around Donegal, who didn't have electricity to run the motors. Still he would listen and act positive; he knew his luck had to turn. He needed to be ready when opportunity came knocking at his door.

The door to Room 515 was open. A breeze blew into the corridor from open windows inside. A young man sat at a desk that guarded the gate of the light oak railing separating the entrance area from the rest of the office. As the clerk looked up, Lucas approached and bluntly stated, "I'm here to see Mr. Carpenter. Mr. Stanley from the Indiana Highway Department sent me over."

The young man inspected Lucas with bright blue eyes framed by shaggy blond hair. He stood, and Lucas decided that his shirt and bow tie were more fashionable than his haircut. His mother probably bought his clothes for him, but she obviously didn't go to the barbershop with him.

"Just a moment. I'll see if Mr. Carpenter is available," he said enthusiastically as he headed through a door to the right of where Lucas stood.

Lucas was happy to get such attention. Maybe he'd have a reason to celebrate this evening. Like most people who lived in this town, he knew where he could find a drink or two and enjoy some good conversation with gentlemen like himself. The prices were higher than before Prohibition, but the atmosphere was better. He didn't know if doing something illegal was more fun or if he just liked to thumb his nose at the proper Baptist ladies behind the law.

The young man came back into the outer office and approached the wooden railing. "Mr. Carpenter will see you now. Right this way, please."

Lucas strode first through the gate and then the door the young man held open for him. Inside he found a tall slender man with a dark thin moustache and dark brown hair combed back from his face. He appeared to be ten or more years older than Lucas. Mr. Carpenter wore a fashionable lightweight suit and a crisp white shirt. A gold chain and watch fob hung from the front of his vest. He held out a bony hand and stated rather formally, "I'm Clarence Carpenter, and I believe that envelope is for me."

Lucas shook the man's hand and then deposited the brown envelope into it. "Hello, I'm Lucas Crawford. Mr. John Stanley asked me to visit you. He said you might have a position that required someone with my talents."

The tall man just smiled and waved Lucas to a chair on the opposite side of his desk. They both sat down. Lucas removed his derby and waited in silence as the other man extracted the letter and the application and studied both for a few minutes. Lucas always felt uncomfortable sitting in the presence of someone and not making any conversation. He had to will himself to be quiet and not interrupt the other man's perusal of the papers. He concentrated on the office walls, which were light green in color. A rather large painting of an English hunt scene covered most of the wall on one side of the man's desk. Four partially opened windows filled the opposite wall. The tile floors were rather ordinary, but the man's enormous walnut desk was impressive, as it dominated the room.

Mr. Carpenter absently reached for a cigar that burned in a large glass ashtray to his left. He took two short drags from it while he read. The bluish gray smoke billowed around his head before ascending toward the high ceiling of the office. After another minute, he looked up and smiled across the desk at Lucas. "I do have an opportunity for someone like you. Would you be willing to move back to

Donegal?"

"Sure, for the right job," answered Lucas.

"We are looking for someone to recruit the good citizens of that area into our organization," offered Mr. Carpenter. "We need someone who is comfortable dealing with farmers, railroad workers, shop keepers, and other men who are Christian and of good character. We are not interested in Catholics, Jews, immigrants, or darkies; so you wouldn't have to deal with any of them. We will provide you with a car and an allowance that we deduct from your share of the membership dues you collect. Does any of this sound interesting to you?"

Lucas was having trouble absorbing so much information at once. He could concentrate only on the basic facts. "What kind of organization are you talking about?"

"I like to call it a fraternal order dedicated to the improvement of its membership," replied the tall taciturn man. "We are also dedicated to keeping this country secure for democracy and guided in a manner consistent with the ideals of our forefathers."

"Does it have a name?" asked Lucas.

Mr. Carpenter hesitated and glanced at the ceiling before leveling his gaze on Lucas. "Yes, Mr. Crawford. Our organization is known as the Ku Klux Klan or more precisely, the new version of the Ku Klux Klan."

Lucas was stunned, and he knew it showed on his face. He didn't have anything against the Klan; it was more an item of history to him than anything else. But he had read in the newspapers how it was making a resurgence in the South and even the Midwest. There may be an opportunity for him here, but he needed to proceed cautiously.

Shifting in his seat Lucas said, "I thought the Klan was outlawed by the government."

"The *old* Ku Klux Klan was banned by federal law in the South during Reconstruction," replied Mr. Carpenter. "Those men were uncontrollable and committed certain excesses that cannot be tolerated by any civilized society. But many of their noble ideas had merit, and now men of integrity have banded together to revive the best of that experiment. Our group obeys the laws of this state. Some of our membership even have positions within the state government."

Lucas thought of Mr. Stanley and realized he may be dealing with something greater than he imagined. He couldn't think of a delicate way to phrase his next question so he merely blurted, "Do you still go around dressed in sheets and meet in the middle of the night?"

Mr. Carpenter gave him a tolerant smile as he folded his arms across his chest. "Our organization is private. We find the custom of meeting in uniform to be appropriate. All our gowns are specially made. They symbolize the armor worn by medieval knights who maintained law and order in England. We are able to conduct business and support our membership yet still protect the privacy of individuals within the group. We meet at times and places that are convenient and ensure this privacy. We believe the most effective way to advocate for the rights and ideals of true Americans is to work behind the scenes in our own cities and communities."

Lucas was impressed more with Clarence Carpenter's demeanor than anything else. Yet he was reminded of Mr. Stanley's advice about being in on the ground floor of this movement. Any enterprise that promised a good income was a worthy concept to Lucas. He began to stroke his mustache. "What kind of duties would I have, and how would I get paid?" he asked.

Carpenter unfolded his arms and leaned forward on his desk. "We would like you to organize a chapter, or a klavern, in the Logansport area. It is a developing region, and there are many potential recruits in the towns and farms throughout the Wabash Valley. Membership, called a klectoken, costs ten dollars."

"Whoa. That's a lot of money for farmers. It will be a tough sell."

Carpenter nodded in agreement. "Yes, it is, but it can be collected over time. Four dollars must be paid up front to initiate membership. You keep two dollars as a commission, and the other two go to Headquarters. The rest can be collected over the balance of a year's time. An additional four dollars must be sent to us here in Indianapolis to support our efforts within the state. You would have the title of Kleagle, which is what we call all our recruiters. You retain the remaining two dollars of each member's dues as a final commission. There are also annual membership taxes such as the Realm Tax and fees for robes. Each member will probably pay an additional six dollars each year, and you would share in those proceeds.

"At first, you will submit your portion to us until your salary and car have been reimbursed. After that has been paid off, you keep your share. If you work hard, and successfully organize a klavern of perhaps five thousand members, you can make a good living. There will also be opportunities to make money from activities that you will set up for your klavern."

Lucas made a quick calculation in his head and decided this was more money than he had ever had the opportunity to earn. He was hooked, but he tried not to show it. "But how do I go about recruiting members?" he asked more to himself than to his interviewer.

"You go about it the same way we've been recruiting members for the last couple of years," Carpenter explained. "People are fed up with the way this country is being run. You promise to give them membership in a group that understands their problems and gives them a means by which they can work to correct the injustices that have befallen them.

"Good American boys sacrificed their health and some even their lives during that European war, and what have we gained from it? The poorest of the poor from that continent continue to come here and take our jobs and keep wages low. The Jewish bankers in New York have infiltrated the federal government, and they are conducting a campaign to keep commodity prices low, while they make more profits for the corporations they own. We know America's labor leaders have corrupted the railroad and the labor unions. The economy has been a disgrace for the past three years. President Wilson did nothing his last year in office, and Harding is just as bad. He thinks Congress should lead the country, but they never have and never will initiate the laws required to put America back on the road to prosperity. A president must lead the country and Congress. It takes a tough, smart man to keep commerce running smoothly in America. We haven't had such a president since Roosevelt occupied the White House.

"We are in the third economic depression to befall this great land since 1900. This one looks worse than the Depression of 1893. A free-market economy is fine, but it needs leadership from the government to keep the robber barons from manipulating it to their advantage.

"We intend to elect powerful leaders to government positions who will represent us. People need fair wages, and farmers want fair prices. We just have to recruit enough members whose votes will put the right men into state and federal office."

Carpenter took a breath, puffed on his cigar and then went on. "Here around town, we draw our members from the factories and the trades. We're also getting more members from the shops and other retail establishments in the center of town. Good men who know they have been disadvantaged by the rich and powerful elements of our country are looking for a force that will support them.

"You'll find that the same thing is true in the rural parts of our state. That's why we're willing to support you and others to increase our membership and power in Indiana and across the country. We have a Kleagle doing quite well in Kokomo. His territory would border yours. Our goal is to return this country to the heirs of the people who created it. That's the only way we know to make it great again. It won't happen over night, but in time we will dominate state and national elections and turn our government around. Lucas, is it all right if I call you by your first name?"

Lucas nodded, pleased that he had gained a small measure of familiarity.

"You won't have any trouble finding a thousand or more good Christian American men waiting for you to come into their hometowns and give them the chance to join such a movement. You start by approaching the prominent citizens of town. Then you cultivate the workers and farmers. We hear the Logansport roundhouse workers are ready to strike over their right to unionize. If the Pennsylvania Railroad won't let them organize, then we can become their surrogate union. Get them to join us, and we'll represent them."

Lucas looked down at his hands that held his derby and thought for a moment. He looked up to make eye contact with his interviewer. "Mr. Stanley mentioned something about my working at an office."

Clarence Carpenter nodded and a sly grin formed below his thin mustache. "We'll set you up as a life insurance agent in Donegal, but make your home elsewhere, like Logansport. Approach your friends and acquaintances in town and let them give you leads as to the judges, doctors, clergymen, and businessmen who would be amenable to our cause."

Lucas shifted in his chair and scratched his chin. "I want to be sure I understand. Who exactly is eligible to join the movement?"

Clarence Carpenter stiffened and sat back in his cushioned desk chair. "Eligibility to the Ku Klux Klan is limited to native born Christian males who owe no allegiance of any nature to any foreign government, ruler, person, or sect. We obviously eliminate the Negroes, but they aren't a problem. They know their place, and they make good maids and janitors. There aren't many Jews you'll confront, either. No, your problem will be the Catholics who have settled all through the area. There's a Catholic church or two in just about every town along the river. And Roman Catholics pledge their allegiance to the Pope in Italy. They cannot become members. Plus, they are the biggest impediment to returning the country to its Protestant heritage. You will need to learn some of our tactics for ridding the valley of papists and other immigrants."

Lucas Crawford leaned forward in his seat and looked into the eyes of Mr. Carpenter. Lucas could sell this concept. Even better, he could make good money from this enterprise.

Lucas relaxed his features and tried to project an image of sincerity. "This sounds like a very important enterprise, Mr. Carpenter. I believe I am the man to help you. I'm sure that in a short time I can build up your membership in the Logansport area. When do I start?"

Clarence Carpenter smiled and offered his long slender hand to Lucas. "We'll need to arrange for you to take some training sessions on our rules and procedures. Also, we'll need to teach you about life insurance sales. But you should be able to travel north in a couple of weeks."

"Fine," replied Lucas. "I'm looking forward to going home."

CHAPTER 3

June 1922
Logansport and Donegal, Indiana

ANNIE CONNER DROVE THE BLACK ELCAR SEDAN down freshly paved Market Street, the main boulevard through Logansport. Most streets were covered with bricks, but more recently asphalt was being used as an overlay on main roads, making the ride noticeably smoother. She enjoyed the freedom of driving her car, and it annoyed her that soon she would have to forgo driving for the duration of her pregnancy. Her doctor considered it too strenuous for a woman during late pregnancy.

Matt had insisted they buy the expensive six-cylinder, five-passenger vehicle because it gave them prestige among their neighbors. More important, the Elcar automobile contained a self-starter that allowed Annie to motor around on her own. Matt's Ford truck had a crank starter, which was difficult and dangerous even for a strong man. A woman would have found it nearly impossible to operate. As it was, Annie wore white driving gloves to protect against blisters as she held tightly to the steering wheel.

The late spring day was glorious, and the drive along the Wabash River from Donegal had been rewarding. Fields of growing crops were interspersed with stands of hardwood trees that towered over the road. Oak, hickory, walnut, and poplar trees were leafed out in various hues of green and covered the land north of the river, which rose up thirty or more feet above the water into a series of rolling hills. She had rushed past fields of ripening wheat and others with young corn stalks. The land was different from the south side of the river, where the rich brown soil was devoted almost exclusively to corn.

Logansport was the commercial center of the Wabash Valley, and Market Street was filled with automobiles. Just as many people hurried along the sidewalks toward shopping or business engagements. Annie turned south on Fourth Street and drove to the Pennsylvania Train Depot. She pulled to a stop in the dusty parking area next to the two-story brick train station. The massive rectangular windows of the large building gave her the feeling that she was on display for the many railroad workers who labored here. The area was noticeably quieter than the center of town, which lay two blocks north. That would soon change, as several passenger trains were due to pass through town by mid-afternoon.

It was not quite eleven o'clock, but the heat was becoming uncomfortable. Annie set the parking brake and slid out from behind the wheel of the car. She wore a light gray cotton dress that came down to her buttoned shoes. It was one of the maternity dresses she had stored away from her last pregnancy, and she was pleased she finally felt stylish in it now that dresses with shapeless waists were in vogue. Her long brunette hair was pinned up under a white straw hat adorned with a navy ribbon.

It was too hot to stay inside the vehicle, even with the windows rolled down. She was finding she had less tolerance for temperature extremes now that she was in her fourth month of pregnancy. She was in good health according to Dr. Nash, whose office at St. Joseph's Hospital she had just left. But as before, while carrying her second child, Annie was irritated by minor things such as the weather.

Annie was also annoyed by the changes in her life that were hurtling at her all at once. She was prepared to cope with the new baby and its impact on her family life. But here she was waiting for the train from Chicago that would bring her sister-in-law, Maureen, to live with them. Maureen would share Katy's room until she could find a proper place to board.

Her stay in their home was not the problem, Annie admitted to herself. She had always gotten along well with her sister-in-law and enjoyed her company. The real issue was how Maureen's entrance into their family would change the relationship she and Matt had enjoyed for the past seven years. While Annie was sure of Matt's love and faithfulness, she couldn't shake the twinge of jealousy she felt at having to share him with his younger sister.

Annie had supported Matt's efforts to make the bakery successful. She had accepted the role of managing their family life while he devoted so much time and energy to the business. She unreservedly gave him her advice on problems encountered in the business. But she stayed away from the bakery and left Matt free to run it. Now he wanted to embark on a significant expansion of the business, and to help with that expansion, he was bringing in his sister to work side by side with him. For the first time, Annie felt Matt did not fully appreciate and respect her efforts as his partner.

Maureen was still considered the baby of the Conner family. Paul had died tragically in Chicago in 1912. One of his frequent visits to the saloons that occupied the north side of Chicago had resulted in an argument and the fatal beating and robbery of the young man. Joseph was thought to be settled somewhere on the west coast. Thus, it fell to Matt and John to look after Maureen, and eventually she had moved into her brother John's house in Chicago. John was the stable, dependable one. He had joined the Chicago police department and had risen to the rank of sergeant.

However, Maureen Conner was no child. Now twenty-eight, she had matured into a confident and independent woman. She had been privileged to receive an excellent education from her years at the convent. While she had seriously considered becoming a nun as a teenager, her curiosity about the commercial world and her interest in material possessions apparently convinced her that she did not have a religious calling. Yet she remained a staunch Catholic, and her convictions probably inhibited her marriage prospects. Catholics were encouraged by the church to marry other Catholics, and Irish families encouraged marriage to other Irish descendants. Annie knew that an Irish Catholic woman in America had a hard time attracting acceptable suitors, since many Irish men were reluctant to marry and be burdened by families.

In any case, it was a talent that Maureen developed during her formative years at the convent that now brought her to Donegal. Maureen had worked in the convent kitchen, helping to prepare meals for the sisters. She had learned to bake sweets, such as pies and pastries, and had become quite talented at it. Recently she and Matt had discussed the opportunity to market these delicacies in this rural area of Indiana. Matt thought the time was right to expand into such goods for his growing clientele. Annie had to agree that delicious baked desserts would be a tempting addition to the store, even as it galled her to defer to Maureen's obvious expertise.

And so here she was, a pregnant woman out in public to greet her younger relation while the children stayed with a friend from church. At least she had been able to take advantage of her morning out to arrange an appointment with her new doctor.

Feeding Annie's irritation were Dr. Nash's comments about her advanced age for having another child. Dr. Nash was well regarded in Logansport, and Annie had found his advice to be good concerning the children's health. But the family doctor from her hometown of Huntington had delivered Brian and Katy, and that made him special to her. Dr. Nash suffered in comparison. Now this relative stranger, a Protestant, advised that she should avoid another pregnancy. At thirty, Annie was the same age that her mother had been when she had her fifth and last child. Annie wanted more children, even though Matt was not in favor of a large family. Matt was the cautious one; he worried about how to feed the four of them. Yet, he was all for bringing Maureen to live with them. All this upset Annie.

She checked the schedule board inside the station and saw the chalk notation of the 11:09 expected arrival time of the #97 train from Chicago. The station clock showed that she would have a seven-minute wait. She nodded to the station agent in the cage and took a seat near an open window, avoiding the sun shining in. Fewer than a dozen people lingered on the polished oak benches in the large waiting room. A distinguished looking gentleman in a dark suit sat in the next row reading the morning newspaper, *The Press*, and smoking a cigarette. A colored man dressed in blue dungarees shined the shoes of another man at the end of the room, and a uniformed janitor polished the brass on the doors leading to the parking lot.

Various advertisements decorated the walls above the benches. She focused on a sign at the newsstand across from her that advertised Chesterfield cigarettes for eighteen cents for a pack of twenty. Cigarettes were becoming popular with young women, but Annie disliked them. It bothered her that they cost more than a loaf of Matt's best Italian bread.

Reflecting on her morning, Annie mulled over her greatest fear pertaining to the doctor's advice. Matt and Annie enjoyed sexual relations in a way that made their marriage magical. The physical pleasure was something neither of them professed to have felt in any other part of their lives. Moreover, the intimacy that was part of their lovemaking brought them the happiness and contentment that they never reached in their other daily activities with each other. They did not have relations frequently; there were few opportunities for such activity. Yet when they did make time for themselves in their bedroom, they met again as soul mates.

If they could no longer pursue their sexual activities, Annie feared their shared intimacy would be gone as well. Without such closeness and the physical profession of their love, Annie wondered if their marriage would suffer. She had seen evidence of this happening with friends. She knew that some women continued to have sexual intercourse with their husbands without producing children, but she had been taught that birth control was forbidden. She didn't think her faith allowed members to engage in sexual relations that were not for the procreation of children. Annie wasn't certain of the religious regulations that governed this part of her life; it wasn't a topic discussed in church. The talks Matt and she had with their parish priest prior to their wedding were now a vague memory to her. Annie knew she needed to have a better understanding of the church's law before she discussed it with Matt. As with most Irishmen she knew, social and religious matters that restricted his freedoms quickly irritated Matt. And yet, her dear husband would not want to do anything that would jeopardize her health.

The new pastor at St. Mary's, Father O'Brien, was an educated man. Annie presumed he could explain the regulations to her. It was not the type of subject one discussed with a stranger, but it might be easier to speak with him than with a priest who was also a friend. She would have to make an appointment with Father O'Brien as soon as he had a chance to settle into his new duties.

A train whistle interrupted her thoughts, and Annie realized that Maureen was arriving at the platform outside. It was time to put aside her personal concerns and welcome home her sister-in-law.

The steam locomotive braked to a halt just past the passenger platform. Uniformed attendants descended from each car and placed stools beneath the stairways. Several passengers descended from the three cars, then one of the attendants climbed back into a vestibule and returned with two suitcases and two hatboxes. A beautiful young woman followed him, dressed in a stylish blue suit that hid her waist and stopped six inches above her ankle. An attractive large brimmed dark hat accentuated her red hair. Annie smiled as she watched her younger sister-in-law tip the attendant. Maureen always managed to make a grand entrance on any stage.

Annie stepped forward to greet Maureen. "Well, sister, welcome back to your birthplace."

"Oh, Annie, it's so good of you to meet me here. You look terrific. Motherhood agrees with you," cried the breathless Maureen.

"You are too kind, but I'm afraid I no longer have the girlish figure that you hide under the latest fashions. You are more beautiful than when we last met in Chicago four years ago."

They hugged and exchanged pecks on each other's cheeks. A blue uniformed porter approached with a cart, and Maureen pulled a baggage slip from her purse. "I have two trunks that were in the baggage car. Can you get them along with these bags? Annie, how will we get all of my things to your house? I'm afraid I brought everything I own except the furniture."

Annie smiled and gave Maureen a maternal look. "We are not all that primitive here in Indiana. We'll just arrange for the baggage agent to send your luggage to the house. The hatboxes and your personal case can come with us in the car."

Annie nodded to the porter who began to load the suitcases onto his cart. The two women then strolled to the end of the platform and waited while the porter retrieved the trunks.

"Did Matt tell you? I learned to drive when we bought our car last year. I hope you're prepared to be transported home by a woman."

"It will be my first time, ever." Maureen laughed, sounding excited. "Will we be safe?"

"I believe so," answered Annie. "It's only a short drive through the country, and we'll stop at the bakery. Matt's very anxious to see you, although he has been trying not to show it."

"Oh, how wonderful. I'm anxious to see the place where I'll work."

As Annie parked the car in front of the store, Matt came out with his arms outstretched and a broad smile on his face. From the bakery's front window he had seen the car pull up. He went to the passenger side, opened the door, and embraced his sister. "Welcome home, young lady. You look gorgeous. I'm going to have to keep the lads in line or else you'll have no time to help me with my business!"

Matt stepped back to find Maureen inspecting him from head to toe.

"You look well," she offered. "Annie has taken good care of you, and I believe family life agrees with you. I can hardly wait to see the children, but first I had to see the bakery."

"Well, come on in, and I'll give you the grand tour. There aren't too many customers at the moment, but some folks will soon be stopping by to purchase a fresh loaf or some biscuits for lunch. I'll introduce you to our help."

Maureen strolled toward the doorway as Annie came around from the far side of the big sedan and greeted her husband with a kiss. "How did it go with Dr. Nash?" he inquired as he hugged her and ushered her to the shop.

"Everything is fine," she said as she preceded him through the doorway.

Inside, Maureen was scrutinizing the display cases and the counter to the right of the doorway. She then turned and viewed the two sets of tables and chairs placed against the opposite wall. While the bakery did not function as a restaurant, Matt had set aside space for customers to sample his goods and to enjoy a cup of coffee.

The couple stopped and observed Maureen's examination. He and Annie followed her as she moved pointedly through the doorway to the kitchen area in the back of the building. Again Maureen became absorbed in her inspection, this time of the baking area. Both Davy and Mrs. O'Rourke had stopped working and were staring in silence at the young intruder who seemed to be unaware of their presence. Matt gave her a moment to complete her observations, and then he broke the spell.

"Mrs. O'Rourke, Davy, this is my sister, Maureen. Maureen, let me introduce you to the other two members of our staff."

Maureen smiled and approached them with her gloved hands outstretched. "Hello, I'm so glad to finally meet you both. Matt has written to me about how invaluable you both are here at the bakery." She went to Ginny O'Rourke and grasped her hands with her eyes full of anticipation. "Mrs. O'Rourke, this is a pleasure for me. I believe you were a friend of my mother and took care of me on occasion."

"Yes, that's true," replied the older woman, smiling broadly. "Oh Maureen, you've grown into such a beautiful lady. Your mother would be so proud, God bless her." Matt saw tears come to the eyes of both women, and then they embraced.

After a moment they separated and each reached for their handkerchiefs. Maureen walked over to Davy, who was wiping his hands on his apron. "Hello, Davy. My brother tells me that you are a good friend. I hope you'll be my friend as well."

Davy took her hand and pumped it several times. "Yes, ma'am, I'd like that, and I was hoping that you'd teach me to make one of your pies."

"Certainly," she agreed. "I plan to make several different desserts, and you shall learn to make each of them, if you want to."

Davy's eyes grew wide, and he shook his head affirmatively, apparently at a loss for words.

Maureen turned and addressed Matt. "The ovens are larger than I'm used to, but I think the facilities are adequate. We'll need a selection of different pans and tins, plus a collection of mason jars for canning fruits."

Matt walked over to his sister and gave her a confident look. "We can get most of your baking equipment from our local store. If necessary, we'll order any special items from Chicago. The mason jars we can purchase from the Ball Brothers Company in Muncie. What do you want to make first?" he inquired.

"I think we should start with some fruit pies. Are the strawberries coming to market yet?"

"They're not a big crop in the valley, but I know several farms that have small fields of them," he offered. "We can buy a bushel basket and test them for quality. If they make a good filling, then we'll offer to buy up the remaining crop. We can get them cheaper by avoiding the market here in town."

Annie interjected, "Most folks I know enjoy cream pies and desserts that rely on dairy products. Why wouldn't we want to produce what they are used to making for themselves?"

Maureen smiled knowingly, but Matt looked at both women, puzzled. Maureen seemed to enjoy her superior knowledge. "Oh, we will produce some excellent cream pies and pastries, in time. But we need to establish our reputation with local fruits while they are in season. Then we can preserve the best fillings and continue to bake them during the winter. People will be more eager to buy our goods if the quality has been established."

Matt's eyes widened as he grasped the market potential of his sister's plan. "Plus, we can raise our prices for out of season items," he speculated. "I was thinking of charging thirty cents per pie, but we could price them as high as fifty cents in the winter. That will more than offset the extra effort in preserving the fruits."

Maureen nodded her agreement and seemed to beam with excitement. But Matt sensed that Annie was uncomfortable. Perhaps this morning's events had tired her.

The bell over the front door tinkled, announcing a customer. Mrs. O'Rourke walked past them and went into the store area.

"Matt," Annie said, "I must take Maureen home to rest, and I need to retrieve the children from Mrs. Fitzpatrick's care. Do you want to come along with us and eat an early lunch?"

"Yes, of course," he replied. "Over lunch we can develop a plan for which fruits we want to use this year and make a list of the farmers we'll need to visit."

"And I can draw up a list of supplies I'll need," added Maureen.

"Maureen, maybe we can experiment at the house," added Annie. "I have some baking pans we can use to make your first creations. I'm sure the family will enjoy sampling anything sweet."

The trio left the kitchen area, leaving Davy to his work of mixing ingredients for tomorrow's bread.

As Matt steered the Elcar sedan up Broad Street, Lucas Crawford stepped out of his Chevrolet at the other end of the main thoroughfare. Stewart's Mercantile Store stood in front of him, looking smaller than he remembered it. He stepped over the curb and entered the nine-foot double doors. Mr. Stewart had once told him that big doors impressed customers. Privately, Mr. Stewart's son Tom had revealed to Lucas that the doors enabled them to carry out odd-sized items such as lumber. Tom had been Lucas' schoolmate and best friend. Lucas was intent on making Tom his first recruit in the new klavern he was organizing.

Once inside, Lucas noticed the old, worn wooden floor that gave slightly as he stepped forward. Lucas didn't believe the floors had ever been cleaned in the ten years since he had last visited Donegal. When his parents had sold the farm and moved to Iowa, there was no longer any reason to return to this poor part of the country. Now with prohibition, the one entertaining aspect of small town America, the saloons, were gone.

Lucas ignored the young man behind the closest counter and wandered back among racks of fabrics waiting to be turned into dresses or shirts. Lucas spotted Mr. Stewart helping a small older woman select cooking utensils at the rear of the store, and he moved toward them. After a couple of minutes of conversation, the woman opened her purse and handed over a dollar. Mr. Stewart wrapped the purchase in brown paper and handed the woman her package and her change. They exchanged farewells, and the woman moved away. At that point, the proprietor scanned his store and focused on Lucas, who had been standing in the next aisle.

It took only a moment, and then recognition crept into the man's features. "Well, I'll be damned. The prodigal son has come home to visit. How are you, Lucas?"

"I'm fine, sir. I wasn't sure you would recognize me."

John Stewart chuckled. "You spent so much time underfoot here and at home that I'd have to be blind not to recognize you. What brings you back to Donegal?"

"I've been sent here by my employer to open up a branch office," boasted Lucas. "I thought I'd stop by and look up my old friends. Would Tom be living in the area?"

"Sure, he still lives at home with me and his mother. He'll be in after lunch to work the afternoon spot."

"That's great," enthused Lucas. "I was hoping he'd be here. It will be nice to catch up on what he's been doing and what he knows of our other friends."

The older man's face clouded, and he hesitated before he spoke. "Lucas, you probably don't know it, but Tom was in the Great War. He was injured at the front in France. The Krauts gassed him. He still isn't well."

"Oh, damn," blurted out the startled Lucas. "I never heard about him or anyone from here going to Europe. Is he going to be all right?"

The older man looked down and hesitated momentarily. "We don't know, but the doctors are hopeful. Tom has trouble with his breathing periodically, and sometimes he can't sleep because of it. But at other times, he's like his old self, except he's lost some of his weight. Maybe it'll be good for him to see you. He gets moody, and you may be able to cheer him up."

"Yes, sir," replied Lucas. "I'll do anything I can to help."

"I'm sure you will," said Mr. Stewart. "Listen, why don't you head over to the house and have lunch with Tom? He'll be glad to see you, and you can visit before he has to come to work. He relieves me so that I can take a late lunch with his mother. Ruth will be glad to feed you and pry a little into what you've been up to for the last ten years."

"Well, thanks, Mr. Stewart." Lucas had hoped to talk to his old friend in private, and it would be easier to do so away from the store. "I could use a bite to eat, but I don't want to keep Tom from his work."

"You go along, and I'll call Ruth and let her know. I'll tell her to keep your secret so you can surprise Tom when you get there."

"I appreciate it." Lucas shook hands with the old storekeeper. "It has been good to see you again, sir. I'll be sure to stop by for my supplies once I get the chance to set up my office. And maybe we can talk about your insurance needs."

"You do that, young man," said the storekeeper. "If we don't have it, I can order it from Chicago or Indianapolis."

Once outside on the street, Lucas observed the traffic and gauged that there were maybe twice as many people in town since he had left ten years before. It dawned on him that while there were more potential recruits for him, there were also more undesirables to deal with. He knew there were plenty of Irish "micks" who had been in town for years, but there seemed to be a new wave of European immigrants that now lived here. He wasn't sure if this was true, but the clothes some people wore didn't resemble anything made in America.

He got in his car and headed up Broad Street to Third Street and turned north, remembering the way as he went. The north/south streets were numbered from one to twenty-four, while the east/west streets were named after trees. The exceptions were Railroad Avenue, which paralleled the Wabash rail line and, one block north, Broad Street. This appropriately named wide thoroughfare was the commercial boulevard that connected the highways leading east to Peru and west to Logansport.

The street names had not changed, but the town was different. There were more shops and commercial buildings on Third Street, in place of the single story bungalows that existed during his childhood. Two blocks north, the once vacant fields now contained large houses with mature landscaping. Sycamore and maple trees bordered the brick paved roadway. A gentle breeze blew through the branches, and Lucas wished he had a touring car rather than the practical hard top he had been given by his new employer.

Lucas approached Maple Street, spotted the red brick two-story home and pulled up to the curb in front. As he ascended the porch steps, he recalled the times he and his friends had sat on this very spot, passing away hot summer days. If they were lucky, Mrs. Stewart would bring them lemonade to drink. If not, there was always water to quench their thirst. Since most days they would have already put in five hours of farm work before lunch, anything wet tasted good.

Lucas knocked firmly on the screen door. Mrs. Stewart came quietly from her kitchen, opened it, and held out her arms for a hug. She said nothing, and Lucas took this as his cue that the surprise reunion had been set up for Tom.

"He's in the kitchen, just sitting down for his meal. You go ahead, and I'll follow," she whispered.

Lucas moved slowly down the hallway, the floorboards squeaking under his weight. He passed through the doorway and stared at his friend, who sat on the other side of the breakfast table at the end of the kitchen. Lucas was probably the more surprised of the two men. Tom glanced up at him with a distant gaze and a gaunt face that looked much older than Lucas would have thought possible. He scarcely looked like the apple-cheeked boy whom Tom had known as a teenager.

"Howdy, Tom," said the subdued Lucas. "Do you mind if an old friend joins you for lunch?"

"Howdy, yourself," replied his friend. "Where did you come from, and what the hell brings you back here?"

"I've taken on a new job in the area. I'm moving back home, and when I visited the store, your pop told me to come up and have lunch with you."

Ruth Stewart had followed Lucas into her kitchen. She ushered him to a chair and brought him a plate with some cold ham and a cucumber salad on it. "Here," she said. "Take off your coat and relax. Can I get you some of my lemonade, or would you prefer coffee or water now that you've grown up?"

"Lemonade would be fine," Lucas replied. "I haven't grown up all that much."

"Well, it's good to have you back in town." She poured a glass of the tart beverage and brought it and the pitcher over to the table. "I'll let you boys catch up, but I'll be wanting a report from you, Lucas, on your wanderings and how your folks are after lunch."

"Yes, ma'am," said Lucas. Ruth departed, and Lucas began to eat. Tom didn't say anything, which concerned Lucas. He couldn't think of any reason why his boyhood friend wouldn't be receptive to his visit, but something clearly was wrong.

Finally Tom swallowed and took a drink. "I had a bad night," he whispered. "I kept waking up out of breath, and it would take a while to get back to sleep. I'm a lot slower these days than when we were kids."

Lucas looked at the emaciated man who only vaguely resembled his friend. "I understand you fought in the Great War. Was it as bad as I've heard?"

A thin smile lined Tom's face before he spoke. "It depended upon where you were. I was with the First Division east of Paris. My outfit, the Eighteenth Infantry, occupied a quaint town called Villers-Tournelle in early May. We hadn't seen any combat, but the Krauts knew we were there and started shelling the town. Some of their ordinance contained poison gas, and a lot of us were overcome before word came to don our masks. I was evacuated before I could even fire my rifle. All of that training went for nothing." Tom took another mouthful of the salad and ate in silence. His face brightened as he looked across at Lucas. "At least I didn't have to charge across no-man's land into the Kraut's machine guns or do anything else that was brave and daring. I saw a lot of cemeteries started for British and French troops who met that fate."

"It must have been awful," stated Lucas.

Tom stared at his plate for a few seconds and then replied, "Yeah." He ate a bit of bread from his plate and then swallowed some lemonade. Tears formed in his eyes as he relived his only ordeal of the war. His voice became shrill as he fought his emotions. "We were hunched down next to some buildings, trying to get some cover from the exploding shells. None of our officers had warned us that the Germans would mix gas in with the barrage. We had masks, but we didn't get them on until it was too late for some of us. My throat started to burn, and then my lungs ached, and I thought I was going to suffocate. Somebody got a mask on me, and the next thing I knew I was in a hospital with a lovely nurse hovering over me. Some of my pals didn't make it that far, and you know what, they were the lucky ones."

"Don't say that," interrupted Lucas sympathetically. "Your pop says that you have good days."

"That's what he wants to think," snapped Tom. "The truth, as I see it, is that you never get better. A chunk of my lungs has been burned up, and I think what's left is slowly being eaten up. The doctors said that the tissue would grow back like new skin, but I don't think that's the case."

Lucas ate some more and stared at the table. Finally he said, "You're a hero, Tom. You went to war and helped protect what's great about this country. No kaiser or foreign king will ever mess with us again. You're braver than I am."

"If I'm a hero, why am I rotting away here in the home of my parents?" asked Tom flatly. "Why doesn't the government give me a pension and a job to compensate me for my injury? I'm not sick enough to be hospitalized, but I'm not well enough to support myself."

Lucas saw his opening. "That's why I'm here, Tom. I've been sent to the valley to recruit loyal, God-fearing Americans like you into a new political party that's going to correct these things. Join with me, and we'll get the help that you and thousands of our fellow countrymen deserve."

"What are you talking about?" Tom looked skeptical.

"I'm talking about the Ku Klux Klan," whispered Lucas. "The movement for the preservation of the values that made this country great has come back to life. Members of the Klan are running part of the state government down in Indianapolis right now. My job is to get it started up here so we can control things at the local level."

"I've read about the Kluxers rising up again in the South, but I'm not one to run people out of town or lynch them on some oak tree while I hide under a sheet," groused Tom.

"No, you've got it wrong," replied the impassioned Lucas. "I wouldn't do that, either. But all these European immigrants keep coming over, taking our jobs and working for low wages and paying little or nothing for the food we grow. We've got to band together to preserve our jobs and our way of life. We can get decent prices for our crops. And we can deport those foreigners who don't belong here. People who can't afford our standard of living need to be sent back to their own countries.

"Let me ask you something. Did you and your buddies fight that war in order to free the poor slobs who were living under tyrants just to have them come over here and take our jobs?"

"No," Tom said, sounding confused. "They should be able to live well in their own country."

"Then join me and let's organize the rightful owners of this town to help do something about it. Without a saloon, where do the solid citizens meet to relax and discuss the important matters of the day?"

Tom's brow furrowed and then his eyes brightened. "Higgins' Funeral Parlor is open for drinks and conversation on evenings when they don't have a service. Even undertakers are having trouble making a living these days."

The two friends chuckled together at Tom's humor.

"Good," Lucas said, relieved. "Why don't you get ready for work? I'll have a talk with your ma, and when you're ready, I'll drive you to the store. When it's time to quit work, I'll take you out to supper. Then we can go over to Higgins's, and you can introduce me to some of my old neighbors."

Tom appeared to ponder this plan for a few seconds and then forked up his last bite of ham. "All right," he said. "It sounds like this could be an entertaining day after all."

CHAPTER 4

September 1922
Donegal, Indiana

THE BEDROOM WINDOW STOOD OPEN, and birds chirped as the first signs of daylight crept into the room. It had been a warm Saturday evening, but the house had cooled quickly during the night. The sun was slow to creep over the trees, foretelling the end of the summer.

Annie Conner was awake early, as she was most days this far into her pregnancy. The baby did not let her sleep late even on Sundays. Yet she refused to get up, because she treasured being in bed with her sleeping husband. Sunday was the only day Matt could sleep past 3:45, and Annie loved to cuddle up next to his muscular frame and revel in the wonder of her situation.

Annie's parents had a wonderful life together. Her father was a locomotive engineer for the Erie Railroad in Huntington, Indiana. He had always been able to provide for his family, and economic hardship had not been a problem for them. He spent four days a week pulling trains between Huntington and Chicago. The rest of the time he spent at home helping Annie's mother raise four daughters. Their home had been happy and full of love, and Annie modeled her own family life after that of her parents.

When Matt first came to her attention, Annie was playing the organ at Mass in her parish church. Her watchful sisters informed her of the young man who spent as much time turning in his pew to watch her in the rear loft of the sanctuary as he did focusing on the priest celebrating Mass at the front of the church. Months passed before Matt found the occasion to introduce himself to Annie at the county fair, of all places. Annie's father had a reputation for making sport of any of the young men who came to court his daughters. Matt had vowed to friends that he would not come around the Murphy home to have amusing limericks composed to rhyme with his name.

But Annie's mother, Rose, came to the rescue by inviting Matt to supper on the evenings when her husband was in Chicago. Annie shifted in bed and smiled to herself at the realization that she had so many things to be grateful to her mother for. And almost immediately she felt a measure of guilt over the fact that none of her sisters had found suitable husbands. The life of an Irish spinster could be exceedingly lonely in this part of the world. But perhaps it was a problem that was common in all families with strong patriarchs. She had recently read a magazine article that stated that only one of General Robert E. Lee's daughters had married. The author theorized that it was almost impossible for eligible beaus to measure up to the qualities of a strong, confident father. But Matt did, and Annie recognized much of her father's personality in Matt.

Matt was a handsome and attentive man. He may not have had the upbringing and family experiences that were hers, but his keen perception allowed him to see the merits of an equal relationship where husband and wife shared the responsibilities of the family. Even so, Annie felt guilty that Matt had the greater burden. His ten to twelve hour days still left him time to have lunch and dinner at home, plus he did yard work and other chores around the house. While she ran the house and raised the children, she knew that she didn't have his stamina to deal with his many responsibilities. It was one of many things she found so amazing and attractive about her husband. Best of all, he had avoided the saloons and the social clubs even before Prohibition became the law. He claimed to enjoy discussing the day's events with her and the children much more than with the fellows he could find at a local tavern.

She didn't know what she had done to merit this wonderful man who had walked into her life when she had least expected him. But she thanked God each night in her prayers before she slipped into bed next to his sleeping form. And in the mornings, just like today, she prayed to the Blessed Virgin for their continued health and happiness.

Now it was time to leave their bed and prepare breakfast for her family. Then she'd get ready for church while Matt got the children dressed for Mass. They would have to get home quickly, as Father O'Brien had accepted her invitation to dine with them at their afternoon supper. Maureen would join them and help with the meal preparations.

Today Annie was determined to request an appointment with her pastor to discuss the church's position on sexual relations. She and Matt had abstained from their lovemaking sessions during her advancing pregnancy. However, that would mercifully come to an end in the next two months, and at some point, she would have to tell Matt about the doctor's advice. She knew that he would insist on ceasing their lovemaking out of concern for her health. But Annie felt that a sound relationship between husband and wife depended upon continued expressions of their love. She was not prepared to abandon such activities if they could be practiced without the complications of unwanted pregnancies.

As Annie sat up and moved to the edge of the bed, the sound and motion of the springs brought Matt to consciousness. "What time is it, honey?" he whispered.

"Close to seven," she whispered.

He rubbed his face and gave her an appreciative glance. "How's the baby this morning?"

"The little one has been stirring for an hour or so. And he or she was active during my last visit to the bathroom," replied Annie.

Matt reached over and took her hand. "Come close and hold me for a minute. We've had no time to snuggle this past week, and I miss it. I dare not embrace you in front of the family anymore, as you've become too big to get my arms around," he teased.

Annie moved closer and wrapped her long slender arms around her mate much as a swan enveloped her young with her wing. Matt rested his head on her chest and sighed his contentment. There were not many pleasures to be taken from the daily toils of life, but he seemed happy with the few he was granted through their marriage.

After a couple minutes of silent contentment, Annie felt the need to get up, and Matt instinctively left her embrace. "Thank goodness the Bible says that God rested on the seventh day," he commented. "If they had left that out, the Republicans would have us work every day of the year."

Annie chuckled as she put on her robe. "Since when did you pay attention to the Bible's dictates? You're always working, even when you're at home resting in your chair and reading the paper."

"Well, today I'll be on holiday. I'm sure Father O'Brien has no interest in the bakery. But he did mention to Maureen last week that he wanted to speak to us about a particular matter. Perhaps he'd like to arrange for a daily order of bread or pastries for the rectory. Do you think it's permissible to do business with holy mother church on a Sunday?"

Annie turned back from the door of the room. "I wouldn't know about such things, but if the good father brings it up, then I'd say that you're on safe ground in discussing it with him."

It was nearly two in the afternoon before Father O'Brien parked his car in front of the Conner home. His assistant, John Stevens, celebrated the early Mass this day, but Tom had performed the late service and talked with various parishioners afterward. He had also enjoyed helping the altar boys clean up and prepare the church for the two services that would be said the next day. He found few occasions to mix with the youngsters who served at Mass with such quiet, formal behavior. During the week they were rushing off to school or home afterward, but on Sundays there was time to relax and discuss what was of interest to them. Today, Jimmy Sullivan had initiated a most curious discussion about the blessed trinity and why the Holy

Ghost would take on the form of a dove in revealing His presence to mankind. Father Tom had enjoyed the banter with the two boys. He knew it was important to make friends with his younger parishioners. Too many priests lost touch with the children when they became older. Yet these young members of the parish needed love and guidance from him as much as from their parents.

The Conner house sat on Maple Street in the fashionable northeast quadrant of town. Tom recognized the design to be American Four Square with its box-like appearance and hip-roof dormer window in the attic. An inviting porch ran across the front expanse of the home. The house was made of brick except for the limestone foundation that reached three feet above ground. The homes here were formidable.

As he approached the front porch, his host opened the front door to greet him. "Good afternoon, Father," welcomed Matt. "We are so happy to finally have you visit our home. The ladies have prepared a large pot roast; so we're counting on your being hungry."

Tom was struck, not for the first time since his return to town, that this respectable family man may be one of the orphans whom he had encountered on his first day here so many years ago. He didn't remember the boys' names, but he recalled the name of the little girl for whom he had made arrangements to be raised in the convent. And he understood that this Maureen Conner had developed her baking skills at a convent.

"Matt, it is so very kind of you and your wife to invite an old priest over for supper. And it's doubly kind of you to do so after having to listen to one of my sermons just a couple of hours ago."

Matt took the pastor's hand and gave it a firm shake as he laughed appreciatively. "Nonsense, Father. Your sermons are easy to sit through. I especially enjoy them when you delve into the New Testament. I'm not much of a student of the Bible, but I do try to read the gospels when I have time."

"Well, that's admirable, Matt," said the priest. "I'll have to invite you over to the rectory to explore some of our Lord's teachings."

"I'd like that, Father. I've been curious as to whether some of my opinions square with those of real scholars."

"Well, I don't qualify as a Biblical scholar, but I'd be interested in talking to you about your opinions. Maybe we can meet next Saturday after you close the bakery," replied Father Tom.

The men entered the comfortable home where the rest of the family was waiting for them. The living room was dark and cool. The walls and furniture were shades of brown, and there was a gold carpet in the center of the room.

Annie came forward and took Tom's hands into her own. "Father, it's so nice of you to visit our home. You've met Matt's sister, Maureen, and of course our two children, Brian and Katy."

Tom embraced Maureen and then stooped to say hello to the two young ones. "It is my great pleasure to be with your family this afternoon. Are you children as hungry as I am?"

Brian's eyes widened, and he nodded affirmatively. "Yes sir, Father. I always get hungry when we have lunch so late."

The adults stifled polite chuckles, but Katy took this as her cue to let forth her heartiest laugh. At that moment, the formality of the occasion dissolved into a comfortable family dinner, and Father Tom O'Brien felt that he had found new friends with whom he could relax.

As the group sat at the dining table and helped themselves to the roast, mashed potatoes and gravy, fresh carrots and green beans, and, of course, fresh bread, the conversation included parish matters, the weather, children's games, and local politics. Even the children were allowed to offer opinions. Maureen and Annie took turns bringing dishes from the kitchen. Tom tried to control his appetite and was helped by the barrage of questions that kept him busy talking rather than eating. But he did find time to clean his plate and have a small second portion of everything.

Later, the men helped clear the table as Maureen brewed fresh coffee and stacked a platter with scones that she had prepared yesterday. When they were all seated, Father Tom raised one of the issues that had been on his mind this day. "I have been talking with some of my fellow pastors here in town, and we have plans for a weekly breakfast. I'll host the first one at the rectory."

"Now that's a bold step towards reconciliation with the Protestants, Father," exclaimed Maureen. Matt and Annie murmured their agreement.

"Well, it may be considered revolutionary by many," replied Tom, "but I have always believed Christians must embrace and express love and respect for each other. A good way to start is by having ministers, men with similar vocations, get to know one another and become friends.

"Besides, men of the cloth can share concerns with each other. In the large cities, there are enough parishes to enable priests to develop friendships with other priests. But we can't do that in small towns. Through these breakfasts, I hope that we can encourage such friendships among others in the same professions. And if we can develop some goodwill among our neighbors by the example we ministers set, then I think our Lord will look favorably on our efforts."

"You're not afraid that this action will be considered appeasement to those who have rejected the church?" asked Annie. "Does the bishop approve of your plan?"

"I have talked with his Excellency when I visited with him in Ft. Wayne. Bishop LeFranz has his reservations, but he's given me his blessing." Father Tom hesitated before he expanded on his idea. "The Catholic Church did some pretty bad things that led to the Protestant Reformation. I do not believe that we need to exclude the heirs of that unfortunate movement from our homes or our lives. It would be good to attempt some sort of reconciliation with our brothers. We can treat them as fellow Americans who deserve our respect. After all, we fought and died together in the trenches in Europe."

"I like your concept, Father," voiced Matt. "But I don't know that we will ever be able to put it into practice. Our neighbors barely tolerate us here in the community. They shun us more than we do them. When I walk home in my work clothes for lunch, they look on me like I'm a gardener. And when I head back to the bakery in a suit to do my business in the afternoon, they give me the same looks. It's rare that I get a wave or a greeting from my neighbors."

The priest had been eating one of the scones while listening to

Matt. He took a sip of coffee before he spoke. "I don't think it will happen overnight, but we have to make a start. I hope that these breakfasts will be such an initiative. And I would like you and your sister to make something special for us to serve to our guests. Perhaps a coffee cake or pastries . . . what do you think Maureen?"

"Oh, Father, it would be our pleasure," replied the surprised Maureen. She glanced at Matt, who nodded his approval. "How many will be present, and what else will you be serving these gentlemen?"

"We'll only be serving coffee and tea. I expect four or five, and we will have had our regular meal before we get together. Some of us have duties that require us to be up rather early. I'd like to serve them something different and memorable. I'm suspicious that my fellow clergymen don't think that a pair of bachelors like Father Stevens and myself are capable of making coffee, let alone anything appetizing to eat."

The adults at the table laughed politely. The children had finished their treats, and Annie gave them permission to leave and entertain themselves in the living room.

Father Tom looked at his hosts and then offered an afterthought. "Who knows, maybe we can generate some new customers for the bakery. And of course, I'll pay for everything myself at your normal prices."

Matt looked at Annie and smiled. "Father, I believe that we can meet your needs at a good price. I'm sure Maureen will spare no expense, but with a generous promotional discount, we'll be able to keep the bill to a reasonable level."

"Wonderful," exclaimed Father Tom. He was quite sure that this Irishman was making sport of him. Tom was prepared to pay for Maureen's efforts, but he probably would never see a bill.

"Annie, can I help with the dishes to earn this lovely meal you've let me share with you?"

"No, Father," replied his hostess. "Matt and I will clean up later. It's a chore that we like to do together. But before you leave, I'd like to schedule an appointment with you for this week. Can I visit you Tuesday morning?"

"Certainly," said her pastor. "I presume that you wish to schedule baptism plans for the new baby?"

"Yes," stammered the embarrassed young woman.

As the four got up from the dining table, Father O'Brien decided that it was time to satisfy his curiosity about his connection to this delightful family. "I noticed in the parish records that both Matt and Maureen were baptized in our church. I had the opportunity to administer Extreme Unction to a Bridget Conner when I first came here over twenty years ago. I was wondering if she might have been your mother?"

There was a moment of silence as the two women and the elder man looked at Matt. His face appeared to be gazing into the distance, or perhaps the past. "I remember a young priest who came to our home with the doctor on the night our ma died. He arranged for Maureen to be taken to the convent in Chicago. Was that you, Father?"

"Yes, my son. I apologize if I've caused you grief by bringing up a sad time."

"It's no trouble, Father," dismissed Matt. "That was a very long time ago, and our family has managed to survive."

The older man laid his hand on the younger one's shoulder. "I don't mind telling you that I'm as proud of you both as your parents would be to see how you've grown into such fine adults."

Maureen looked puzzled and then her face took on a look of comprehension. "Father, a couple of years ago I visited the convent, as I have on occasion over the years. After dinner and the normal gossip, I met with Mother Superior and asked her to accept a check as partial payment for the years they kept me. But she wouldn't accept the money because she said a woman from Indianapolis had paid my fee each year. Did you arrange for my care?"

Tom stared at his young parishioner for a moment and then closed his eyes, and his voice trembled as he spoke. "The night of your mother's death was my first day at St. Mary's. Later, I wrote to my parents about my anguish at not being able to take care of five young orphans in my first task as a priest. My father responded that I was not responsible for the care of all the poor and helpless I would encounter in my calling. He told me to do what I could and trust in our Lord to accomplish the rest."

Tom paused, opened his eyes, and looked directly at Maureen. "My mother echoed those sentiments, but I thought it curious that she also wanted to know where I had arranged for you to be sent and what it would normally cost for such care. I can't be sure, but from what you have learned, it's possible that my mother may have been your sponsor. She had a small inheritance, and this is the type of charity she was famous for before her death."

Tom smiled at the young woman and then a question intruded on his thoughts. "I'm curious, Maureen. What did you do with your money?"

Maureen stepped closer to her pastor and touched his sleeve. She lowered her voice to a whisper and said, "I made Mother take the money and use it to support some of the young girls that come into her care in the future."

Tears came into Tom's eyes as he smiled down on this admirable young lady. "You have made my mother's gift something special. I'm sure she's looking down on us right now and is very pleased." He embraced Maureen, and they both were overcome with emotion for a few moments.

The following Tuesday, Annie waited in the rectory office for her meeting with Father O'Brien. She wore a pink maternity dress, a gift from her mother and father. Her long dark hair was held in place under a cream-colored pillbox hat ornamented by white netting. The office was furnished in a rather Spartan style. There were three straight-backed black cushioned chairs on one side of the room between two large windows. On the opposite wall were two roll-topped desks with matching captain's chairs. The curtains were old and dusty, and the red knotted rug in the middle of the floor was coming unraveled. It was probably the perfect study for two bachelors who were not fond of worldly possessions.

Annie could hear Father Tom's foot steps as he came down the stairs and walked directly into the room. He wore his long cassock over his shirt and pants.

"Sorry to leave you waiting," said Tom. "I was changing from my suit that I wore earlier when I visited the hospital."

Annie rose from one of the chairs and let the priest take one of her gloved hands into his own. "It was no trouble to wait, Father. Mrs. Haney let me in and brought me a glass of water. I'm always thirsty these days."

"How do you feel? Is the baby giving you a lot of trouble?"

Annie sat down, and Father Tom pulled another chair close to her. Annie took a deep breath and another swallow of the cool water before speaking. "I'm fine, and I'm anxious for the baby's birth. Dr. Nash says it will be another eight weeks, but this little one is doing a lot of kicking around. I'm probably going to stay at home after my doctor's appointment this week."

Father Tom gave Annie a look of concern as he searched her features for signs of distress. "Annie, I'm surprised that you would want to make arrangements for the baptism now. Most women I've met want to wait until after the birth of their child. It's considered bad luck to make arrangements in advance."

Annie reddened and cast her eyes down at her lap. "Actually, Father, I'm not here about the baby."

"Oh," said the flustered priest. "I'm afraid I jumped to conclusions. You must forgive me."

"No, it is I who need to be forgiven," lamented the young women. "I was too embarrassed to correct you at dinner the other day. You see, I need some religious advice about sexual relations between husband and wife."

She looked up and waited to see if the priest was startled by her disclosure.

Father Tom had some experience in advising modern women about marital relations, and so he was prepared to help this new friend in any way he could. He perceived that this young mother needed the comfort and guidance so central to his calling. Some priests made great preachers, but he found his talents were better suited for individual counseling among his congregation. He smiled at Annie and patted her hands that were folded on her enlarged lap. "Why don't you take your time and fill me in on your situation."

Annie cast her eyes down to the floor and held a gloved hand to her chin. She took a deep breath and then blurted out her problem. "Father, I'm thirty years old, and the doctor says I'm getting too old to be having any more children after this one. He's afraid that there may be complications, and he's afraid of what may happen to me if I were to go through another pregnancy." She paused, apparently to see what effect her confession made upon him.

"Are you in any physical trouble now?" asked Father Tom calmly.

"No," said Annie. "It's just that I recognize that sexual contact between a married couple should be for the purpose of having children. If we can't have any more, then we should stop having relations. Giving it up is something I don't want to do. Am I being sinful to want more of the happiness that has been so good for our marriage?"

Tom knew he was dealing with a delicate matter. Most parishioners would not approach their pastor with such a personal issue. Tom admired the courage and assertiveness that Annie showed in coming forward with her problem. He instinctively knew to take time to further flesh out her concerns.

"I don't think that you are being sinful in wanting to continue to express the passion that you and Matt must have for one another. I don't believe we have a reason to adjourn to the confessional, yet. Tell me, what does Matt say about this matter?"

Annie reached for a handkerchief inside her purse and pressed it to her nose. She rocked back and forth in the chair as she composed herself. "He doesn't know about the doctor's advice. I haven't told him. If I did, he'd want to quit even hugging me for fear of my health, but I believe it's important to our lives together. I need to understand if there is a way to continue our relations after the baby comes."

Father Tom considered this information and then asked, "What advice did Dr. Nash give you about continued sexual relations?"

Annie shook her head negatively as she spoke. "The doctor said we should use some form of contraception. He recommended condoms. He said that they are fairly dependable these days. He also said that we could practice the rhythm method of abstaining from relations during the ten-day period of ovulation. But contraceptive devices are illegal. And wouldn't it be a sin to practice sexual activity and attempt to stop conception from taking place?"

The priest was amazed that he was having such a serious and personal conversation with a woman parishioner. Women were becoming more confident in the world outside their homes, and Tom thought it was an agreeable development.

"Well, Annie," he began, "condoms were made legal in 1918. You can find them in discreet pharmacies. However, the church considers them to be the same as other artificial forms of birth control, like douches and cervical caps. We do not believe in the use of any device or chemical to prevent the natural process of procreation."

"Then why has the government made them legal if other devices are still forbidden?" asked the puzzled young woman.

"Condoms are effective in preventing the spread of venereal disease. They became popular with the soldiers in Europe during the war. Our government has changed the law for hygienic purposes rather than for any moral stance."

"I suppose the rhythm method is also considered sinful, too?" queried a dejected Annie.

"That's not true," replied her pastor. "The abstinence from sexual relations during certain fertile days each month is considered permissible. You see, there is nothing artificial being done to block conception. The rhythm method is considered a natural form of birth control, and the church has accepted its use."

Annie didn't seem convinced of the merits of this concept. "But Father, I've read it has been very unreliable. I don't know that God would give us a means to avoid children that didn't work. Besides, wouldn't it be cheating to avoid sexual relations on those days when you thought it would produce children? Isn't that the primary purpose of the sex act?"

Father Tom slowly composed his thoughts. The discussion had

escalated from an instructional one to a far deeper theological deliberation. "First of all, Annie, the rhythm method has become much more reliable now that medical science has determined the ovulation period during a woman's cycle. Originally doctors thought that the safe period was in the middle of the cycle. They now know the midpoint of the cycle is actually the proper time for conception to take place. Also, a woman needs to have a regular cycle that she can monitor. If the cycle fluctuates or she doesn't track the days correctly, then sexual activity could occur on a day when conception can take place."

Annie was giving Tom her full attention; so he went on. "As to the moral issue of using such a natural method, keep in mind that God designed and created the reproductive process with all of His divine wisdom. I'm not an expert on this subject, but it appears to me that God developed this window of nonproductive sexual relations in order to control the number of people being born into this world. Perhaps this is God's way of regulating the numbers that can exist here. There are so many poor and starving around the world. I can't imagine the suffering that would take place if children were a product of every carnal union.

"Therefore, since God designed the process with this safety period built into it, then I see no problem with a married couple taking advantage of it. I don't think it is cheating to physically express your love with your husband while trying to avoid having children. If God wants you to have more children, then you will have them, even if it's by accident."

"I think I understand what you're saying, Father, but I still feel guilty about it."

"That's a fairly normal response, Annie," said the priest as he got up and moved across the room to his desk. "Let me read to you a passage of scripture that may help explain this concept. Are you familiar with the Book of Acts?"

Annie wrinkled her forehead and said with obvious embarrassment, "No, Matt is the Bible scholar in our family."

Father Tom found it curious that a layman would be considered a biblical scholar. He turned the pages to the section he had marked.

"Most people are unfamiliar with Acts. We rarely get to preach on it. But listen to this passage. St. Peter is explaining a dream or vision of certain forbidden types of animals being brought down from heaven to him. Jewish law held that some animals were unclean and even touching them was forbidden. They certainly could not be eaten as food.

"Here we are in Chapter 11. 'And I heard a voice saying unto me, Arise, Peter; slay and eat. But I said, Not so, Lord: for nothing common or unclean hath at any time entered into my mouth.

"'But the voice answered me again from heaven, What God hath cleansed, that call not thou common.'" Father O'Brien sat again in the chair across from Annie and sought out the intelligence he observed in her eyes.

"The religious point of this passage is that God creates all things for the benefit of mankind. Therefore, taking advantage of the reproductive process as God has designed it is not sinful. Does this make any sense to you, my child?"

Annie drew her eyes away from the priest and gazed at the far wall and the desks that dominated it. She held the handkerchief in her lap. "I understand that what God has created is good, so if we restrict our passion to safe periods then we will not have committed sin. But what if we make a mistake or my cycle changes and I become pregnant? Does that mean that we have done wrong? Will another child be punishment from God for daring to have relations when we should have abstained from such passion?"

Father Tom stood and placed his free hand on Annie's shoulder while he held his Bible in the other. "No, Annie. I believe that if you were to become pregnant again, then God will have deemed it proper. There may be health risks involved, but it will be part of God's plan."

Annie reached for the glass on the floor and took another sip of the water. She took a moment to compose herself while Tom replaced his Bible on his desk. Finally she spoke in a halting tone. "Thank you, Father. You have been very kind to discuss this extremely delicate subject with me. I have been so greatly upset about it, and you have relieved my concerns."

Father Tom had turned to face her as she spoke. "You have been very brave and quite correct in coming to seek guidance from me. I'm afraid many women of our faith would not have the courage to do as you have done. Their family life may suffer from their ignorance."

He put the tips of his fingers together as he contemplated this idea. Then he shook his head and returned to his parishioner's situation. "Do you want me to talk to Matt about our discussion?"

Annie smiled for the first time as she gathered her things and stood up awkwardly. "No, thank you, I'll talk to him. I appreciate your offer, but Matt and I communicate openly and quite frankly on family matters. It's only our finances that he keeps to himself. Men need something to have absolute control over, and for Matt, it is his business and our income. I'm quite happy to let him handle such things."

Tom raised his eyebrows and a slight smile creased his face. "I'm learning that you are a very formidable person, Mrs. Conner. I'm glad to have you as a friend."

"I'm happy that you've come to St. Mary's, Father. You will make Donegal a much friendlier place to live." She stepped forward and took his hands into her own. Her emerald green eyes gazed up and communicated deep sincerity to him. "Thank you, Father. You have been a great help to me."

CHAPTER 5

September 1922
Donegal, Indiana

Two days later Matt came downstairs after having tucked his two children into bed. He carried his tattered Bible, planning to read a chapter from the Epistle to the Romans. Annie had finished cleaning the kitchen and had taken a comfortable position on the sofa. She had reclined into a position that took the weight off her back.

"Matt, come sit next to me for a moment. I need to discuss something with you."

Her husband came over and kissed her on the forehead before dropping onto the other end of the sofa. "What is it, honey? Is the new little Conner already too much for his mother?"

"No," she replied. She paused, her eyes downcast. "It's about us . . . and what we do after the baby comes."

Matt became alert. Whenever Annie was hesitant to talk about personal matters, it was a signal the topic was something important to her and probably to him as well. He understood from past mistakes that it was better to remain quiet and let her proceed at her own pace.

Annie took a deep breath, raised her eyes, and focused on him. "Dr. Nash is concerned about our having any more children. He says my health will suffer if I endure more pregnancies. He thinks I'm getting too old to have babies."

Matt wrinkled his brow and frowned in puzzlement. "Are you in any danger now?" he asked worriedly.

Annie shook her head. "No, I'm fine, but I'm near worn out from carrying this one around. The doctor, with his modern theories, just doesn't think we should be having any more children."

Matt felt a tinge of regret at having to cease their lovemaking, but the relief that swept over him about his wife's current health overwhelmed it. As a practicing Catholic, Matt was used to the concept of denial preached by the church. He could readily accept abstinence from carnal relations as the price to be paid for his family's welfare. It had almost been sinful the amount of pleasure they had derived from their intimate moments in bed.

He moved closer, and Annie turned to allow him to embrace her. "Look," he said, "I know you wanted lots of children, but raising three will be plenty for us. I don't know that we can afford any more children."

Annie shifted on the sofa and glanced at the floor before returning her gaze to her husband. "I can accept having only the three children, but what about us? What if we have to put limitations on our . . . our passionate expressions of our love?"

Matt blushed at this frank talk. One of the things he found so attractive about Annie was the firm, direct way she dealt with private feelings they shared for each other. Matt was not nearly as good at initiating such discussions. "Well, I always thought that what we shared was too good to last forever. If the doctor thinks we're getting too old to behave in such a manner, then we need to be mature enough to accept the advice. It would be a terrible calamity if either one of us weren't around to help our children grow up. Trust me, dear, it's hard growing up without parents."

Annie inclined her head onto Matt's shoulder and reached out for his hand. "I know, but our moments of passion are important for our continued happiness. We need to find a safe way to be intimate without having children."

"You mean that I should start using condoms?" blurted out Matt.

"No," replied his wife. "I've consulted with Father O'Brien, and he says that such things are wrong."

"You went and had this discussion with the new pastor?" Matt asked, incredulous.

"Yes," said Annie. "He was most understanding about our situation. He told me that he wished more couples would come to him when this problem developed."

Matt rolled his eyes and then looked up at the ceiling. "I don't know what to think."

Annie went on. "Father O'Brien says that condoms or other devices are considered to be artificial birth control. It's sinful to use such things. But if we were to limit our intimate moments to times during the month when conception is not possible, then it would be proper. That would be natural birth control, and it is acceptable in the eyes of the church."

"How do we know which days are safe?"

"Dr. Nash gave me a pamphlet on the subject. It's called the rhythm method of birth control. We take advantage of the natural rhythm or cycle that my body follows each month. I have to keep track of the days when conception could occur, and we abstain from sexual relations during those days."

"Do they all occur at the same time?"

Annie beamed and caressed Matt's chin with her fingers. "Yes, silly man. There are ten days during the middle of my cycle when I could get pregnant. We just need to be careful."

Matt was not comfortable with this new complication to their married life. Yet he knew to trust Annie in regard to health and family matters. She had a much better education than he did on these topics. Matt had confidence in his knowledge of people and the activities that made up daily life. However, he knew that his meager education did not prepare him to deal with subjects such as science, medicine, or even history.

"All right," he finally said. "If the doctor and you are in agreement, then I'll go along with this idea. The only times we have for ourselves now are Saturday evenings. Just give me advance warning if it's the wrong day."

Annie looked relieved and adopted a demure look. "I'll let you know when the time is right for us. Just be prepared."

Matt chuckled at his wife's boldness. "The only thing I find strange is that Father O'Brien is in on this matter."

"You're going over to meet him on Saturday. Ask him if you need more assurance."

"No, I couldn't," whispered Matt. "I'd be too embarrassed to bring it up."

The following evening Lucas pulled his Chevrolet off the road and onto the dirt driveway that snaked up a hill to the Holmes farm. He took the right fork away from the main house and toward the large white barn. Tom Stewart sat next to Lucas holding a satchel that contained the paperwork for the new klavern. They were twenty minutes late for their meeting, but that was intentional. They wanted their recruits to get comfortable with each other before Lucas and Tom conducted the business portion of the gathering.

John Holmes had confided in Lucas that he was in dire straits. John had inherited the farm from his father three years before. He knew as much about agriculture as his father, but John had not made a profit in the three years he operated the farm. He had taken on greater loans each year when the bank had been in a generous mood. Now this year the bank wanted to see the debt reduced. But the commodity prices he was quoted for his corn and bean harvests would not provide the cash the bank required. He would need to beg his banker for a smaller payment. Lucas could tell John did not like to beg. He had joined the klavern the first time Lucas had spoken to him. He had even paid the full ten-dollar klectoken at his first meeting. That had surprised Lucas.

Lucas parked the car behind a couple of others that were off to one side of the barn's big double doors. The shelter was closed against the night air, but a lantern light streamed out of the crack between the doors. A clear night sky allowed the stars to shine distinctly. The cool temperature combined with a mild breeze signaled the approach of autumn. Dew was already settling onto the long reeds of grass that grew next to the barn. It could be a good evening to relax and enjoy the change in seasons. But it was also a good night to conduct the type of business that Lucas engaged in. Darkness gave an air of privacy to these gatherings.

Tom shoved open one door part way, and as he and Lucas entered, all conversation stopped.

"Good evening, fellow Klansmen," intoned Lucas. "Is everyone here?"

"We think so," replied John.

Lucas and Tom made their way through the gathering to the rear of the structure, where John had erected a table from two long boards and a couple of sawhorses.

"All right, we're sorry to be late," apologized Lucas. "Tom, would you start our gathering with a prayer?"

Tom put down the satchel and took a few steps toward the center of the group. "Our Father who art in heaven, we beseech you this evening to look favorably upon your noble servants. We ask your blessing upon our fight to bring justice to this land. We seek your blessing on our brave group, who desire only to return this country to the virtues that made America great during times past. We ask for your help in ridding our nation of the Jews, papists, and foreigners, who have crippled our economy and polluted our way of life. Give us the strength and courage to do your will. Amen."

A chorus of "Amen" came forth from the gathering.

Lucas moved into the center of the group. He counted twelve regular members and three new recruits. "Tom, take attendance of the members present. Any of you who need to make payment on your klectoken, please see Tom while he has the membership ledger out. Those of you who are new, we welcome you and hope you'll feel free to contribute to our meeting.

"Tonight we need to make plans for our first public demonstrations. But first, let's have Klansman Holmes go over old business. John, what's on your list?"

John Holmes rose from the hay bale he had occupied and picked up a piece of wrinkled paper lying on the table. "We need to move the date of the harvest picnic back a week. There is a conflict with the Baptist church. They're having a congregational meeting that Sunday. Is that good for everyone?"

There were affirmative nods from the group.

"Okay. Each person bring what they signed up for to the picnic ground by two in the afternoon. We'll have canoes for river rides and a horseshoe-throwing contest. Lucas, you're still going to judge the baked goods the wives make?"

Lucas grinned and thought for a moment. "I've decided to make Tom a fellow judge. I don't want the losing wives to be angry with just one bachelor when there are two of us to share the blame."

Tom Stewart looked up from where he was counting membership fees. "Damn," he exclaimed. "I get stuck with all the dirty work in this army."

There was some good-natured heckling from others before John went on with his notes. "Next, we need to set a date for the spelling bee that Bill is organizing. We can get the Grange hall most any night except weekends. Isn't that right, Bill?"

Klansman Bill Henry nodded and then cleared his throat before speaking. "I can get it free of charge so long as we clean up afterwards. If we can set a date before Thanksgiving, then we shouldn't have a problem with the other groups who want to use it."

"Let's try for November first or second," suggested Lucas. "It would be good to have it before Election Day so we can remind people of our duty to vote for the right candidates. It's important we elect the proper man for senator this time."

"I'll check it out and get back in touch with you, Lucas," replied Bill.

"The only other matter concerns our robes. Ed's wife has finished using the sewing pattern we have. Who still needs to have one made?"

None of the Klansmen present required it. The new men had ordered their robes from the Provisional Realm's offices in Indianapolis.

"Then I'll keep it," said John, "until another new member comes forward. That takes care of our old business."

As John returned to his seat on the hay bale, all eyes turned toward Lucas, who had positioned himself on the left side of the makeshift table. "What's the status of the cross?" he asked.

Jim Preston raised his hand and sought permission to speak. Lucas nodded in his direction. "I've got a couple of seasoned beams from a tree that died last fall," said Jim. "The big one is about twenty feet tall, and the cross piece will be eight feet."

Lucas looked around the cavernous structure. He wanted to impart a little drama with his next pronouncement. "All right, fellow members, next month's klavern gathering will be on the Deer Park bluffs across the river south of town. We'll meet in full uniform, and we'll burn that cross high in the night sky to show Donegal we are a force to be reckoned with."

There was general applause and approval from those present. Lucas noticed that even the new recruits appeared excited about the idea.

"But first," cried Lucas, "we are going to have some visitors come to town in a couple of weeks to help get our message out to our neighbors." Lucas waited for the comments and questions to stop before he continued. "I've been informed by headquarters that they want to have a little gathering at the county courthouse. They'll provide a speaker for what they call a political rally. We need to show up in our robes and lead them into town with a torchlight parade. We don't need to do nothing else but gather around and hear the speech. It's supposed to be a powerful display of our statewide presence to the community. So mark your calendars. We will all need to be present."

One of the new members, Tad Cochran, raised his hand. "Mr. Crawford, can I ask a question?"

"Sure," Lucas said.

"Do we need to go marching around in hoods and robes? Doesn't that suggest that we're bandits or crooks out to scare people?"

"It's tradition," replied Lucas. "The early Klan was a secret society, and we continue to be a secret organization. No one is allowed to reveal our membership to outsiders. When the federal government outlawed the group in the South, they found it necessary to limit their identities to only a select few in each klavern. Also, legend has it that one night a bunch of Klansmen were headed home from a meeting when they ran across a band of outlaw niggers. The niggers were prowling around the countryside robbing and stealing from isolated farms. When they saw the Klansmen ride up in full regalia, those boys thought they were seeing ghosts and goblins come to steal their souls. They ran off in all directions and never bothered folks again."

"Yeah, but we don't have that problem here in Indiana," said another young recruit.

"That may be true," conceded Lucas, "but we are a secret society. We can have a bigger impact on people if they don't know who makes up our klavern. You know King Arthur only had so many knights who sat at his round table. But when they patrolled the countryside in full armor with their faces covered, it must have seemed like there was a whole army of them.

"We want to present the same illusion. And we don't want anyone to know our membership. We've got enemies that we'll have to deal with. Those of us who are committed to improve our community need to be shielded from the people who have let things degenerate into chaos.

"We have got to make the big grain and corn brokers see the merits of paying farmers a fair price for our crops. We've got to turn out the politicians who have let the bankers run our economy into the ground. We need to take our country back to values that existed prior to 1900. The way of life our daddies and granddaddies had was best. Hell, even President Harding got elected on the slogan 'A return to normalcy.' It's going to take a great effort on our part to get back to that type of life. Secrecy will protect us from our enemies and from the many spineless men who won't join us. There are some good, decent folks who are too weak to stand up for our values. They won't go along with our methods, but they sure will be happy to share in our victory."

"What kind of methods are you talking about?" queried another recruit.

Lucas gave a conspiratorial glance around the barn. "Did you ever hear about the tobacco wars down in Kentucky?" When he saw some appreciative nods, he went on. "A group of farmers banded together and refused to sell their crops to the big tobacco processors until they got a fair price. Some of them went around as Knight-Riders enforcing the ban on farmers who wavered. We'll have to take similar actions to achieve our goals. That will require secrecy if we're going to avoid the law until such time as the law is on our side."

There was silence in the barn; not even the two dogs in the corner made a sound. Lucas knew he had gone far enough for this evening. It was time to loosen up the atmosphere. "Man, I'm thirsty from all this talking. Who brought along a jug of fresh apple cider tonight?" Lucas would have preferred a beer or a shot of whisky, but Klan orders were to enforce Prohibition. Liquor was no longer allowed at klavern gatherings.

A couple of men jumped up and headed for containers stored in their vehicles outside. John Holmes removed a cloth from a tray of cookies he had sitting on a workbench and placed it on the table. The men broke into smaller groups and began to chat among themselves.

John turned and whispered to Lucas, "I've got a flask of gin here. Should I get it?"

"No," replied Lucas. "Booze is illegal now, and we need to adhere to the law of the land. We'll soon be enforcing Prohibition within the community."

The following afternoon Father Tom visited with Matt Conner and Father Stevens at the rectory. He met Matt in the same office where Annie and he had spoken earlier in the week. Matt had avoided any reference to his wife's visit, and Tom took this as a hint that Matt was uncomfortable with the subject of sexual relations between a married couple. Tom kept their discussion focused on the origins of the scriptures.

He was quite surprised and impressed with Matt's knowledge of the New Testament. Here was a parishioner with only a grade school education who not only knew and respected the commandments, but also had keen insights on theology. They delved into topics regarding the origins of the four gospels and how Christ's coming had been the fulfillment of the Old Testament theology. Matt expressed his appreciation for John's Gospel and how he felt it was more complex than the others. Father Stevens explained that the other three were considered "summaries" of Christ's ministry and therefore not as detailed as John. The young priest's recent seminary education was more advanced than Tom remembered of his own. Tom made a mental note of the fact that he needed to study the recent theological publications as a way of keeping abreast of current Catholic views.

"Matt, I am pleasantly surprised by your scholarship of the Bible," Tom enthused. "It's quite unusual to find laymen who make a study of God's word on their own. What prompted your interest?"

Matt looked across at both priests from the black upholstered chair where he sat opposite them. "I've always had a fascination for the Bible. My mother used to read to us as children, and her Bible was my only inheritance when she died. I'd read it when I found the time as a youngster, and I focused a lot of my attention on the gospels. I felt that they were the most important part. Besides, they were a lot easier to understand. The Old Testament didn't have much interest for me."

"Matt, as a priest it helps me to know the problems our flock has with the faith," broached Tom. "Is there any issue that troubles you about our teachings?"

Tom watched as Matt looked at his shoes for a moment and played with the crease in his trousers. Then he looked up and spoke hesitantly. "I guess the one concept that I wrestle with is the devil and his influence on the world. I know the gospels mention Satan and the evil he creates, but I don't see it."

"Really," exclaimed Father Stevens. "How do you explain our Lord's temptation in the desert?"

Matt hunched over and placed his forearms on his thighs and clasped his hands between his knees. He looked up sheepishly. "To me the episode in Luke, Chapter Four symbolizes the decision Christ had to make to do God's work. If Jesus was both man and God, then he had a free will and could reject His Father's plan. I think it must have been a brave decision to accept his calling knowing the suffering and abuse he would endure."

"So, you don't think Satan came and tempted him to break his fast?" questioned Tom.

"I don't know," replied Matt. "Who was there to witness this event? Did anyone see them on top of a mountain or on top of the temple? It seems like the author was trying to explain Christ's decision to become the Messiah in rather dramatic terms. I don't necessarily believe the temptation took place that way. Still, our Lord must have been tempted to reject the plan to be the sacrificial 'Lamb of God,' as John's gospel describes it."

Tom shared a look with Father Stevens, and then Tom put forth the accepted position. "The church teaching would be that either our Lord explained this incident to one of His disciples or that the author was divinely inspired by God to record it factually. However, I'll grant you that it doesn't seem all that plausible to us living in our modern world almost two thousand years later. I appreciate your candor. It is something we need to reflect on for the good of our congregation."

"Well," Matt said, "if the church says we need to believe it happened, then I need to go along with it. But my experience has been that men create enough evil and bad things in life. I don't need to blame the injuries and sins committed by people on some magical force that moves invisibly around the world spreading havoc on us. I think the concept of witches and goblins is superstition and reflects ignorance. My education, such as it is, comes from my experiences in life, and I've found the sins we commit are due to our own selfishness."

Tom exhaled deeply. He stared at this tough-talking Irishman and saw an intelligence he did not find in most of his parishioners. He noted that it was past four in the afternoon, according to his vest pocket watch, and he didn't want to detain his visitor from his family.

"Matt, this has been a most interesting conversation, but we need to stop and let you get home. Perhaps we can do it again in a few weeks?"

"I've enjoyed it, and I've learned some things that will be helpful in my studies," replied Matt. "Next time let's meet at my house. Annie and Maureen may like to join us. Do you gentlemen have any problem with women being part of the discussion?"

"I don't have a problem with that," stated Father Stevens. "I don't know Mrs. Conner all that well, but your sister has become one of my favorite parishioners. I'm sure her convent training will provide us with some interesting ideas."

Tom along with Matt chuckled at the inference that convent positions on their faith may be different from their own.

"Then it's decided," Tom stated. "Matt, you will talk with Annie and give us a date that is convenient for you and your family. Let's not wait too long; your baby will be due soon, and after the birth there won't be time for such discussions for a long while."

Matt nodded his agreement. He watched Father Stevens go to the hall closet to retrieve Matt's gray fedora. He had walked over to the parish after work and now would get his exercise by making the twelve block walk to his home. He shook hands with the two men, and then he walked out past the church and down the steps to Olive Street.

The light was fading, and the trees that lined his walk cast long shadows. Matt felt guilty that he had taken time from his family. But he also felt good about deepening his understanding of his faith. Also, he now felt a stronger bond to these gentlemen, and Matt always had a need to cultivate friends in his life. He left the rectory feeling good about his day and life in general. He had tomorrow to rest and spend time with his family. There was a baseball game scheduled in Peru between the "Grays" and the Logansport "Ottos." He intended to drive over to the game with the kids. Annie planned to rest and visit with some friends, who were to stop by the house after church. Matt hoped that the dry sunny weather would continue for another day.

CHAPTER 6

October 1922
Donegal, Indiana

THE AIR WAS CRISP OUTSIDE on a sunny Friday afternoon. Faded green leaves gave way to a smattering of yellow and orange leaves that shimmered on the tall oak and maple trees lining the town's main streets. Inside, the bakery was pleasant with a warm, homey atmosphere and delightful aromas from the various products that had been baked during the morning. Matt Conner had finished measuring ingredients for tomorrow's production. It would be a typical Saturday. The store would be open only until early afternoon, but they would have as many customers as any weekday. Farmers who came to town on Saturdays would bring in much of the day's business.

Matt wore a three-piece suit of brown herringbone cloth he had purchased on a trip to Chicago last year. It felt good to wear the wool suits brought out of storage, even if the odor of mothballs had not yet dissipated. At thirty-two Matt enjoyed the feeling of success that a suit gave him. He didn't mind tramping around in work clothes in the early mornings while he labored around the hot ovens, but he preferred to be in a suit when he met with customers and conducted his business around town in the afternoons. Matt understood he was an uneducated orphan whose success was built on hard work and innate intelligence. He felt he had earned the right to display his prosperity to the community.

Davy and Maureen had left for the day, and soon Matt would take his receipts to the bank deposit box and drop off a few loaves of bread at the hospital and the police station. He also had one of Maureen's apple pies for Police Chief Johnson. Matt had learned certain public officials like the county health inspector expected cash gifts, but law enforcement people avoided such favors. The chief and his men appreciated small edible gifts, but Matt hoped the chief would take the pie home to his family. Such a grand dessert deserved a better fate than to be wasted on the inhabitants of the station house.

Matt was becoming proficient in baking some of the desserts Maureen had brought to the business. This batch of apple pies had actually been his work. The delicate pastries were the only recipes he had not yet attempted. He would have to spend more time with his younger sister in order to learn the secrets she possessed. While Maureen was a joy to be around, Matt felt guilty for having taken her away from her merchandising career and her friends in Chicago. She had found a temporary home in a good boarding house. The two siblings had agreed Maureen would return to Chicago at such time as both were certain Matt could bake her specialties without her help.

These specialty goods proved to be as popular as he had hoped. There had been a few experiments that were thrown out, but most of the desserts and pastries had been excellent and sold very well. The basic product lines of breads and rolls also increased in sales as more customers were attracted to the seasonal treats Maureen prepared. Matt considered sending a portion of the desserts to certain grocery stores for resale along with his breads. But currently, they were able to sell all their specialty items directly from the bakery.

Soon the fresh fruits would be out of season, and Matt would use the preserves Maureen and Annie had put up at the house to continue generating the level of sales and revenues he had come to expect from the extra efforts of the past few months. He had been able to pay Maureen a good wage plus make the expenditures required to create Maureen's specialties. Some of his fellow merchants around town thought he had taken a big risk in a poor economic period. Yet Matt considered it a wise decision. People would pay for simple luxuries in hard times to raise their spirits.

The bell over the door rang, and Matt could hear Mrs. O'Rourke offer a friendly greeting to a potential customer. "Matt," she hollered from the front store area, "Rip Riley is out here and wants to say hello."

Matt took off his apron and left his work at the wooden counter to walk into the front room. "Hello, Rip. You're off early from work today."

Rip was a small, well-muscled Irishman in his thirties who occasionally played cards with Matt and some other men from church. Rip swept the red hair out of his eyes and smiled modestly. "The boss let us go, as there were no more loads due for the day. The corn is pretty well picked for the year." He worked seasonally for a grain cooperative when he wasn't doing carpentry. There wasn't much need of his craft at the moment, but he was dependable and could always find work when such existed.

"How's Annie doing?" inquired Rip.

"She's doing all right," replied Matt. "She'll be glad once the baby arrives, but the cooler weather has helped."

Mrs. O'Rourke chuckled with the air of wisdom. "Don't I know she'll be glad to shed that bundle of joy and get out of the house. These last weeks are a trial even for a strong woman like Miss Anne."

Matt walked over to one of the tables, sat down, and gestured for Rip to have a seat. "Well, she hasn't complained much, but she has become more irritable with the kids. She's probably irritated with me, too, but I've been too busy to notice."

"Well, your time is coming," laughed Rip. "Once that wee little one drops into this world, you'll get the duty to care for it until Annie has rested up from the labor."

"Oh, go on with you," retorted Mrs. O'Rourke. "Miss Anne is a strong woman, and if she could hear you now, Rip Riley, she'd box your ears with a rolling pin."

Matt laughed at the picture of his pregnant wife chasing Rip around the shop with such a lethal weapon. "Rip, can I interest you in a fresh loaf of Italian bread today? We've made a pugliese with sliced green olives inside."

"That's why I'm here," replied the beaming Rip. "And would you have a good price on any leftover pies? Maureen told Hildy I should check your supply today."

Matt knew Maureen confided in Rip's wife and other women from church that there was always a discount on unsold items late in the week. Such a discount did not exist except for friends whom Maureen accumulated daily. "We've got a few apple pies left, and I can sell one for thirty cents. Would you like it for your Saturday supper?"

"That would be grand," said Rip. "I'll be tempted to have it tonight instead of the tuna Hildy is fixing." Catholics had to abstain from meat on Friday, and while it wasn't a great sacrifice, no Midwesterner liked the idea of dinner without meat.

Ginny O'Rourke took a loaf of the specialty bread from the display case and wrapped it in paper. She then took out the pie and wrapped it in similar paper and tied it up with thin string she doubled at the top into a handle.

When she was done, Rip and Matt stood and walked over to the cases, where Rip produced forty-five cents and gave it to Matt. "Thank you, Matt. I'm sure we'll enjoy this, and I hope to see your family at Mass on Sunday. Good day to you too, ma'am. Say hello to Mr. O'Rourke for me." Rip donned his cap, took his packages and exited, ringing the bell as he left.

Matt dropped the coins into the drawer behind the counter and logged the sale in his book. "I'm not going to get rich selling pies for that price," he said.

Mrs. O'Rourke patted his arm. "No, but you're bound to be a rich man in heaven some day, Matt Conner. The Lord takes notice of those who help out their neighbors."

Matt winked at the old lady to acknowledge a shared secret. Then he took out the deposit bag from the drawer and counted out the funds he intended to take to the bank. Moments later he retrieved his tan homburg and strode out of the shop with a smile and a wave to

Mrs. O'Rourke.

By four o'clock, he had returned from his appointments and sent Mrs. O'Rourke home with another of his apple pies. There were few customers this late in the day, so Matt had time to do small chores in the kitchen. The bell over the door alerted him whenever someone entered the store.

He was completing an inventory of his spices when the bell announced a late customer to the bakery. Matt shed his apron and walked into the front store area. He found a fellow merchant standing just inside the door. Jakub Miller was an eastern European immigrant who had moved to Donegal recently to escape the impoverished life of New York City. He and his wife and two daughters kept to themselves in a small shop at the edge of the town where Railroad Avenue and Broad Street converged to form the westbound pike. Jakub, older than Matt, was an experienced tailor who could make beautiful clothes out of bolts of cloth. Annie and Katy had pretty dresses made by Mr. Miller from the same blue fabric Annie had purchased at Stewart's mercantile store. Annie had shown Matt the material before she had the tailor work his craft. Matt had been stunned to see what this strange quiet man had created. The dresses were as stylish as anything shown in the magazines Annie and Maureen liked to purchase. Annie referred to her dress as the "Hollywood look," since it was of a style worn by some of the actresses seen in recent motion pictures. Matt and Annie enjoyed an occasional evening looking at the "flickers" at the Colonial Theatre in Logansport.

Matt was certain Jakub's family name was something more exotic than Miller, but the immigration people in New York always changed such names to something simple to spell on the government form. It would have been better if the unknown official had bestowed the name of Taylor on this craftsman.

"Good afternoon, Mr. Miller," began Matt. He came forward and shook Jakub's fine-boned hand. The wary man had gray hair and a craggy face and was clearly not comfortable with the language and customs of the rural town. Matt was sure that it hurt his business, and in sympathy Matt tried to make him feel more relaxed.

"Hello, Mr. Conner," came the stiff reply from the nattily dressed tailor. "I come to buy your good bread."

"Certainly, sir. I have either a sliced loaf of white bread or an uncut loaf of Italian-style bread. What can I get for you?"

"Please, I would take the Europa bread. It reminds me of home." The reluctant man reached in his pants pocket and produced a few coins he held in his delicate fingers.

Matt wrapped the loaf and then wrapped three sweet rolls in another piece of paper. He placed the bread on the counter and took three buffalo nickels from Jakub's palm. He then placed the second package on the counter to indicate that they were a gift. "Please take these to your wife and girls. I'd like them to try our little treats."

Jakub studied Matt for a moment and then nodded as he picked up the two items. Matt instinctively perceived that a proud man would not take charity as long as he had money in his pocket. But such men would not refuse gifts for their family. Mr. Miller shuffled to the door and turned back to Matt before he opened it. "Mr. Conner, I have nice material at my shop. I can make you good shirts if you need them."

Matt considered the unexpected offer for a moment. He was usually negative to solicitations brought to him, but this one had merit. "I'll visit you next week. I need new collars on two shirts, and you can measure me for a new one."

The man smiled for the first time, waved a goodbye and, departing through the door, headed down the street toward his home. Matt had once wondered why he didn't see the family going to church on Sundays but had concluded the family may be of Jewish heritage. Matt had met few practicing Jews in his life, but he found them to be good businessmen. He was sure he would pay more for Mr. Miller's work than he earned from a loaf of bread, but one didn't need new shirts as often as one needed to buy bread. Matt reflected the meeting had been a beneficial one.

Promptly at five o'clock, Matt turned off the lights and left, locking the door behind him. He placed a few unsold items in a tin behind the bakery. Some of the less fortunate would pick them up before long. Davy would return from his wanderings and dinner at the hotel café later in the evening. Matt was pleased to have Davy living at the bakery. Matt had a terrible fear of fire and had drilled Davy on how to sound an alarm and fetch water to put out small kitchen fires.

With this bit of security, Matt strolled away from his business and turned his attention toward his family. The baby was due soon, and Annie would need his help in taking care of the children. Brian was showing an interest in baseball, now that the World Series had concluded. The newspapers had made much of the New York Giants' second straight championship over the Yankees, and Matt and his son had discussed each game. Matt held John McGraw, the Giants' manager, to be the greatest Irishman in the country.

He recalled watching a young Walter Johnson pitch as an amateur in California. He still marveled at the speed that the then young man had generated with his pitches to the plate directly in front of Matt's seat. The now famous member of the Washington Senators had a relaxed sidearm delivery that disguised the velocity he imparted to the ball.

As a youth, Matt had very little time for sports, but he'd been good at a form of baseball played in the streets on the north side of Chicago. He recently bought a ball and bat so Brian and he could play. Brian was still too young to learn anything more than the basics of the game, but it was Matt's secret ambition to make Brian into a famous pitcher, like Walter Johnson. He hoped the secret lay in teaching the young boy that unique sidearm throwing motion.

As Matt turned the corner onto Tenth Street, he took note of the lawns in front of his neighbors' houses. The recent rains had perked up the grass. He'd have to get out his reel mower and cut the yard, most likely for the last time this year. Soon it would be time to rake up the fallen leaves and burn them in the alley behind his home.

As Annie prepared dinner, Katy bounded in from her room and displayed the new clothes she had found for her stuffed bear. The girl had Matt's brown eyes, but her brunette hair and high cheekbones came from Annie's side of the family. Annie took note of the time and the fact that it was already getting dark outside.

"Katy, dear, Daddy will be home soon. Why don't you go wait by the window in the living room and surprise him when he comes through the door?"

"Oh, Mommy. That will be fun." Off she ran to the front room, leaving Annie to finish cooking her white fish casserole and creamed corn side dish.

Minutes later she heard the front door open and Katy's peal of laughter as she overwhelmed Matt. Annie could tell from the giggles that Matt had picked Katy up and was busy exchanging kisses with his daughter. Katy squealed with delight. "Oh, Daddy, your whiskers hurt."

"Well, I just shaved a few hours ago. They grow back pretty fast, my little lady."

"Put me down, Daddy."

After a few moments of muffled conversation, Annie heard her husband's heavy footsteps come into the kitchen. She turned to greet him and was reminded once again why she fell in love with him. His light brown hair was parted off center over his high forehead. His brown eyes radiated affection that contrasted with the stern jutting jaw, the most notable feature of his face. He was so proud and masculine in his business suit. He held in his left hand the steel-cased pocket watch she had purchased for him from the Illinois Watch Company. He could no longer hug her because of her added girth, the baby about to enter their world. He smiled and kissed her on the lips.

"Hello, Honey. It's getting dark much earlier this week. How are you feeling?"

"I'm fine," replied Annie. "But this baby is getting heavy. I'm going to leave the dishes to you tonight."

"That will be fine by me. I'm hungry, and the casserole smells delicious."

"Take off your suit and wash up while I set the table. We'll eat in a few minutes," said Annie. Matt gave her a wink and turned to go upstairs to their bedroom.

"Hey, Dad," yelled Brian from somewhere upstairs.

"Hey to you, son" answered Matt. "Clean your hands for dinner."

"I will, but Dad, there's a police car outside."

Matt wondered if he heard Brian correctly as he headed for the hallway. Before he could get to the stairs, there was a soft tap of the doorknocker. Matt stepped to the entrance and opened the door to Chief Johnson. The tall police chief was dressed in his dark blue uniform and held his hat in his hand. "Hello, Paul. Was there something wrong with my apple pie?" Matt joked, but the policeman only frowned in response.

"No, the pie is at home waiting until I get back for a late supper. I've been visiting some of the merchants to alert them about a rally that's being held tonight at the courthouse. A man from Indianapolis came and got a parade permit this afternoon from the mayor's office. So we didn't have time to alert you." Paul Johnson was a good-natured man who was hired as head of the police department ten years ago. He had been recruited from the Logansport police and was well respected throughout the valley. Being a staunch Methodist, he was considered a fair man by the various factions of this small town. He spoke with a deep gravelly voice, which together with his thick eyeglasses made him appear older than his age of forty-three years.

Matt stared at the man for a moment as he assimilated the information. "What kind of rally?"

The chief looked at his shoes before he answered. "It's the Klan. I've been hearing rumors that they started a local chapter. They've apparently decided to go public with a torch-light parade into town."

Matt wasn't surprised. He had followed in the newspapers the rise of the Ku Klux Klan in the southern part of the state, especially in Indianapolis. He understood that they did not like Catholics, so he considered them a potential threat to him and his family.

"Will you be able to keep order, or will they cause trouble?"

The chief put his hand on Matt's shoulder. "I think we can control them. They have done this sort of thing in other towns, and there haven't been any problems. They gather and listen to a few speeches and shout for a return to the good old days, but no damage is done.

Their reputation probably helped get them the permit. Plus the mayor doesn't like to turn away potential voters."

"So you don't think there is a problem?" queried Matt.

"No, I don't, but merchants may want to be present to guard their property. In your case, I'd be concerned about how Davy will react to the commotion going on near the store."

Matt rubbed his chin and felt the whiskers Katy had complained about. "Thanks, Paul. I appreciate your warning. Can you drop me off at Mrs. Tilly's boarding house? I want to get Maureen to come here and stay with Annie. Then I can spend the night at the bakery."

"Sure, I'll run you over and bring you both back here before we head down to Broad Street. But I don't think you need to worry about spending the night at your place. This rally starts around eight, and they'll be gone before eleven."

"Let me get my coat and my work clothes," said Matt. "You're probably right, but I'm worried about what they'll do with those torches once they're through with them. I won't be able to sleep unless I know things are safe."

"All right, I'll start my car."

Matt went back to the kitchen and told Annie of his plan. "Will you be all right with Maureen here tonight?"

"Yes," said his clearly concerned wife. "Will you be safe?"

"I'll be fine. I'll stay inside and keep watch with Davy. Can you wrap some casserole for me and a little extra to share with Davy? I'll pick it up when I bring Maureen back in a few minutes."

"Yes, I'll call her and warn her to be ready and to bring her bed clothes," said Annie. She then placed her hands on her husband's shoulders. "Be careful, Dear. You are more important to your family than the bakery. We can always build a new store, but I can't live without you."

Matt smiled and leaned forward and kissed his beautiful young wife on the lips. "I'll be careful. I plan to grow old with you, and I want our children to grow up with a father."

After gathering some clothes, he rushed down the stairs and waved to Annie who was already on the phone in the hallway.

Annie had the receiver up to her ear as she spoke into the instrument mounted on the wall across from the stairs. "Operator, connect me to number 1246, please."

At ten minutes past eight in the evening, seventeen men gathered together outside of town at the Third Street bridge that crossed the Wabash River into Donegal. Each wore a white cotton robe girdled with a sash plus a separate cotton hood topped with a red string tassel. A white cross upon a red background was stitched below the left shoulder on each uniform. Lucas and Tom had colorful geometric decorations on their chests. All held makeshift wooden torches wrapped with a rag that had been soaked in petroleum.

Lucas stood in the middle of the group of men, and they waited for him to signal the start of the march. But Lucas was focused on the road coming down into the valley from the south. He had promised the group a guest speaker for tonight, and he looked anxiously for Mr. Clarence Carpenter to arrive from Indianapolis. These men didn't need to hear Lucas or Tom expound again on the merits of their cause. For a public celebration like this, a dignitary was needed. Someone from the capital city was required who would lend legitimacy to their efforts. A high-ranking official could signify to the group that they were part of a much bigger and powerful effort to take back the country for the white knights of democracy who had inherited the country from its founders. Mr. Carpenter had promised to come or send a capable substitute, and Lucas dared not start without them.

"Just a few more minutes, men," he intoned in his deepest, most authoritative voice. "We need to wait for our honored guest." He shifted from one foot to the other trying to increase his circulation and warm himself. The night air was turning cold, and the wind was intensifying again. Lucas's costume was a source of concern for him. He never felt comfortable with the robe trailing around his feet and the hood blocking his peripheral vision. But the feeling of secrecy the costumes imparted to the gathering was exhilarating. The silk embroidered insignia on his chest gave him the authority to lead these men.

They really were just like knights of medieval times, and the costumes were their armor and protection.

"Here comes somebody," hollered one of the assembly behind him. Lucas looked south to see a group of headlights coming over the crest of the hill about a mile out of town. If this was Mr. Carpenter, he had brought his own parade with him. Lucas counted four autos driving along in a procession that maintained a good speed on the two-lane highway sloping down into the shallow valley.

The caravan produced a chilling effect upon the group. They all sensed the strangers' arrival was the start of something extraordinary for this evening. "All right, Klansmen," intoned Lucas. "It's time to light these torches and greet our guests."

Matches were struck, and the small flames turned into large flickering beacons as the rags caught fire. The men spread out on both sides of the road moments before the cars braked to a halt on the berm in front of their own parked vehicles.

Four black-robed and hooded men stepped out from both sides of the lead vehicle, a Chevrolet, and moved directly to the second and third autos in the convoy. The men smartly opened the rear doors of both cars in unison. The second car was a gleaming four door Studebaker, but the third one was an expensive National Sextet Phaeton, a true luxury car. Lucas knew that such vehicles cost more than three thousand dollars.

Out of each car stepped two men in colorful orange or red robes made of shiny material. These were apparently the guests of honor Mr. Carpenter had promised Lucas for this first public gathering in Donegal.

The four dignitaries came forward. One of them, wearing a red satin robe and hood, approached Lucas and offered his hand. "Lucas?" he queried.

"Mr. Carpenter, sir, I'm glad you could make it. I hope your drive wasn't too long because we're ready for a big demonstration."

"The drive was pleasant enough; we did some planning on the way up here. Let me introduce you to our speaker for this evening. You and this klavern are in for a real treat tonight. Lucas Crawford, this is our leader for the Provisional Realm of Indiana, our King Kleagle, Mr. Henry Lampton."

A chubby figure of medium height garbed in rich orange satin, trimmed with military braid and silk embroidery, stepped forward from the other two who had held back a few paces behind Clarence Carpenter. "Hello Lucas," bellowed the hooded man. "I'm mighty glad to meet you. You have done good things up here in starting the Wabash Valley klavern."

Lucas was stunned at having the esteemed Mr. Lampton pay a visit. This man was the best known Klan official in the state. His picture had been in the papers, and quotes attributed to him were constantly making news around the state. "It's an honor, sir . . . to meet you," stammered Lucas.

"Thank you, son" replied the finely disguised head of the movement. "Now, let's get these proceedings under way. I've got a speech that will help double your membership and a woman waiting for me back in the city." His fellow travelers laughed and gathered around him.

Mr. Carpenter took charge of the proceedings. He had Lucas line up his Klansmen in two columns, one on each side of the road. Two of the guests who had accompanied the dignitaries led the way into town beating small drums in a cadence similar to one used by troops marching into battle. Lucas and Carpenter marched behind them, giving directions as the parade made its way across the bridge and east along Railroad Avenue. The colorfully robed guests followed in a line with four black-robed guards taking positions around the officials. These guards in front and behind carried torches, but the two stationed behind the dignitaries kept one hand hidden inside their robes.

The silent group with their torches held high passed the Wabash Depot and continued east to Twelfth Street, where they marched north three blocks to Oak Street. With only the sound of the drums and their shoes hitting the brick pavers of the street, they proceeded west through the residential areas and back down to Third Street. Then the small silent parade turned onto Broad Street and strode east the three blocks to the front of the county courthouse.

By the time the parade reached the courthouse steps, Lucas took note of the large group of townspeople who had come out from their homes to watch the phenomenon. Such a public display in the evening was unheard of in Donegal. While this was staged as a peaceful demonstration, the effect of the costumes and the torches seemed to create an uneasy mood among the citizens. Mothers and fathers picked up their children, and neighbors exchanged hushed questions and comments. In an attempt to dispel this fearfulness, the dignitaries called out for people along the march to come hear a major political speech.

The Klansmen formed a half-circle around the steps of the courthouse. The white limestone building glowed a golden yellow as the flickering flames illuminated the facade. Mr. Lampton and his group moved through Klansmen and ascended halfway up the ten steps of the government building. Several men from town gathered on the fringes of the costumed participants to watch the proceedings. A few women also came forward with their husbands. Lucas knew this was as much entertainment as could be found in this small farming town on a Friday night. He spotted Paul Johnson and his uniformed officers take positions on the edges of the crowd.

Included with the crowd was Matt Conner. Despite his promise to his wife to remain in the bakery, he felt it necessary to observe and hear the intentions of this gathering. He had been fearful of the group as it marched up Railroad Avenue just south of his building, and he and Davy had hardly breathed as they observed the parade from the front window. Matt worried that the march would return to Seventh Street, in front of his store, and one or more of the torches would be thrown through the glass and incinerate his business. But once they had passed on up the street, he ordered Davy to stand guard while he went out. Matt sensed there was relative security in mingling with the other townspeople who were just as curious as he was regarding the purpose of this display.

A tall man climbed a couple of steps above his colleagues and held up his hands to quiet the various conversations that were taking place below him. "Fellow citizens of the great state of Indiana, we are gathered here this evening to celebrate the establishment of the Wabash Valley klavern into The Invisible Empire of the Knights of the Ku Klux Klan. We are a fraternal order of free men descended from the great leaders who founded our country, and we are dedicated to returning it to the values and traditions that once made it great and will do so again."

The speaker paused, and a spontaneous cheer went up from the Klansmen at the foot of the steps. He let it die down before he spoke again. "Let us pray. God, our salvation in times of trouble, we humbly assemble here this evening to do your work. Give us the courage to stand up and champion our Christian values in this great Promised Land that you have so generously given to us. Amen."

There was a muffled agreement to the prayer from the hooded contingent present. The speaker cleared his throat and continued in a louder voice. "Tonight, we want to extend an invitation to the fine people here in the Donegal area to join us in asserting our rights to a free economy with fair prices for our crops and services. A fair wage for our labor is our God-given right, and the only way to protect this right and to obtain life's necessities is to band together and force the government to enact laws that will provide them."

There was another spontaneous eruption from the Klansmen.

The tall orator waited for almost a full minute before he again raised his arms and signaled for silence. "Here in Indiana, we feel so strongly about the lack of attention we've received from federal and state officials, that we've formed our own fraternity to procure our rights. And from among us has come a champion to lead our cause. This man knows of the suffering that takes place in our homes and on our farms, where costs go up but our wages stagnate and the prices of our crops spiral downward. He knows that the legacy of President Wilson and the policies of President Harding have led to the loss of ten percent of family farms in just the past year. He knows that the violent union strikes in the big cities last summer could have been avoided by state governments that weren't controlled by the factory owners.

"This leader has a plan, and tonight he is here to share it with us.

Klansmen and citizens of Donegal, let me introduce you to our leader and the hope for free men throughout this great country of ours." The tall man turned sideways and extended his arm towards the rotund man in the distinctive orange costume. "Ladies and gentlemen, it's our great honor to be here tonight to listen to Mr. Henry C. Lampton."

Again the Klansmen roared their approval, and along with them, some of the citizenry joined in the ovation. It was rare that Donegal hosted a famous person, and many of those present were appreciative of the moment.

Lampton bounded up three steps, waved both arms to the crowd, and allowed the applause to wash over him. He turned to his left and waved; then he turned to the other side of the steps and waved more. Finally, he faced the center and stood erect with his hands behind his back. When at last the cheering died down, he reached up and in one swift move pulled off his hood.

There was a shudder from the crowd, and someone exclaimed, "It's him!" Matt was surprised to see the face of a man whose photograph had appeared regularly in the newspapers.

Lampton leaned down and gave the hood to one of his companions positioned two steps below. Then he faced the crowd again. "Good citizens and fellow Klansmen, we wear these uniforms as a sign of our solidarity with one another. We are faceless knights trying to uphold the honor of our forefathers. But you know who I am, and I'm not afraid to face you."

Matt detected a murmur of approval from the crowd, and a few Klansmen voiced their agreement.

"Tonight we are here to recognize the Wabash Valley klavern as the newest branch in our fraternity. And we're here to let the people of Donegal and the surrounding area know that we are taking charge of the future welfare of this community.

"This great country is now in the throes of the worst economic depression to engulf our land since before the turn of the century. God-fearing Christian men and women, the descendants of those great leaders who established this country and held it together during the

Civil War, are crying out for a return to the values of times past. We want a return to a period of normalcy that President Harding only talks about while he sits in the White House or on his front porch in Ohio. It is up to us, the good Christian law-abiding populace of this country, to take back our sacred right to make an honest living from an honest day's work."

The crowd erupted into applause, and Lucas could tell that many in the crowd had caught the spirit. Lucas had trouble concentrating on Mr. Lampton's message. His thoughts turned to his good fortune at being here at the head of this movement. Soon he would be able to give up his position of kleagle and move into a management role. As the klavern took on more members here in the Wabash Valley, he hoped to be given greater responsibilities, perhaps back in Indianapolis. Surely Mr. Lampton and Mr. Carpenter would reward him for his successful efforts here. More applause brought Lucas back to the present, and he again focused his attention on Lampton's booming voice.

"The huge influx of new immigrants from Eastern Europe is destroying our society and our economy. These serfs from the war-scarred lands across the Atlantic are the castoffs of their own corrupt societies. They have no education and little intelligence. They come to our shores and work for slave wages and take jobs away from the honest native-born Americans who made this country great. If we don't force the government to stop this onslaught, we'll soon find all our farms and our factories are owned by greedy bankers and robber barons who want the rest of us to work for slave wages."

Lucas heard the crowd voice its anger, and Lampton nodded as he looked down into their faces, encouraging their protests. His face turned red as he worked himself and those present into a fit of anger.

"We need to elect government officials who will not only halt the inflow of these poor, stupid European serfs but who will enact laws that will force them to return to their native lands. They aren't welcome here." The crowd erupted in applause, showing its support for the concept.

"Let me speak plainly about modern society. Each race must fight for its existence and conquer the others. History has shown the world that the greatest progress for mankind comes when the white race is dominant over the others. This truth must be allowed to continue if our country is to flourish and become the great land envisioned by our forefathers. The pioneers of our nation, men like Washington, Jefferson, and Lincoln, bequeathed to us title to this land. Our mission is to perpetuate and advance what the country's founders began. That cannot happen if we let outsiders share in our heritage. American stock should never be polluted by others with inferior intelligence, morals, and customs."

Matt Conner had no trouble listening to every word spoken. He had stationed himself in the back of the crowd of onlookers but close enough to remain a part of them. He perceived that he was listening to his enemy, and he needed to know as much as possible about this menace to his family and his livelihood. He was more than a little nervous that the Klan's theories were being so warmly received by his neighbors. It had always been hard making a living, but until this moment, he had not understood that people could turn on one another as a means of improving their situation.

Lampton continued his case in his deep, authoritative voice. "The income tax cut was pushed through Congress by the Jewish bankers and stock manipulators in New York City. You and I won't see a dime of it. Only those rich Hebrews and those in their pay will get relief. It is now time for us to throw out the corrupt politicians and their Jewish paymasters. That's why we all need to vote for Samuel L. Ralston for senator next month. Sam Ralston is honest and brave, and he'll fight for us in Washington."

Matt saw the Klansmen on the steps erupt in applause, and they turned to the crowd, encouraging their support. Lampton continued through the noise. "All over this country, we are going to drive out the Jews, the Catholics, and those crooked politicians who have been bought by them. We're going to send them all back to where they came from. We're going to make this country safe and prosperous for the Christian people who own this fair land. Sam Ralston will help, and there will be others in Congress and within our own state. Your mayor, Lawrence Griffith, is such a man. And I hope we can all support him for reelection in two more years. He may even be considered for governor by then."

A cry of surprise emanated from the crowd, and Matt now discerned how the Klan had gotten their parade permit at the last moment. He saw a new potential threat in the mayor, and he wondered if Paul Johnson would soon be included on this list.

"It is time for action," thundered Lampton as he brought his fist down in a hammer motion. "We all need to go to our homes and consider what can be done to return America to its great heritage. If we are to move forward as a great nation destined to lead the world for the balance of this century, we must first return it to the values and ideas espoused by our fathers just a generation ago. Social decay must be rooted out of our lives. Good moral Protestant values must have dominion over our daily actions. Public intoxication, tobacco use by women, illicit sexual relations among our neighbors can no longer be tolerated. We need to return to the good Christian values that made us a great country and will do so again." Lampton stopped, nodded to the crowd, and received a hearty ovation from the majority of his listeners.

"Klansmen will be walking among you with applications. Take one and consider joining us. We have a wide range of activities such as monthly dinners that benefit all. Soon, there will be a women's auxiliary group to provide help for our wives and daughters. We are making plans to take control of the educational system statewide. We hope to have our own college available soon, to better educate your sons. Think over what you've heard tonight. Examine your family situation, and ask yourself if you don't deserve a better shake than you've been getting from the government back east. We're ready to change things for the better, but we need your support. Take an application home and mail it to our offices. Thank you, and God bless us all."

Thunderous applause broke forth from the hooded partisans in front and was picked up by others present. People turned to those around them and commented on what they had heard. Lucas Crawford stood on the steps looking out on a sea of faces that appeared galvanized by this speech. Mr. Lampton was shaking hands and accepting congratulations from the Klansmen who surrounded him.

Mr. Carpenter, still disguised by his hood and robes, slapped Lucas on the back. "This ought to help get things rolling for you, son. Nobody does a better job of explaining our mission than that man. He's a true crusader for the cause."

Lucas nodded. He now realized how deeply affected he had become from tonight's events. This was no longer a job for him. This was a religious and political movement he had become part of. It would require all of his energy and dedication to make it a success here in the valley. And Lucas vowed to himself to make the Klan a moral force people feared and respected.

The crowd was breaking up, and Matt knew it was time to depart. He mingled with a few of the townspeople who were moving away from the steps and toward Broad Street. Suddenly they came to a halt in front of two white-robed Klansmen passing out handbills that probably contained the applications Lampton had mentioned. The two men in front of Matt each took one, and Matt felt it would be safer to accept the piece of paper rather than reject it. As he held out his hand, another robed hand snatched the application before it reached him. Startled, Matt looked around at a tall hooded figure who glared at him with angry eyes.

The hooded man returned the handbill to one of the other Klansmen and said to Matt, "You won't need that, and you ought to consider closing that bakery." He wheezed in a raspy voice, "You sell the pope's bread, and pretty soon nobody will want to buy it. Why don't you go back to Ireland, where you belong?"

The man continued to stare at Matt, who kept silent for fear of provoking a worse situation. Matt lowered his head and walked quickly away from the scene. He trembled in fear as he strode up Broad Street toward the bakery, but he kept listening to see if anyone followed. No one did, but Matt thought he heard the laughter of men confident in their position of superiority.

Now that he was out of danger, one other piece of information registered with Matt. He had always been terrible at remembering the names of people. This caused him some embarrassing moments with customers at the store. Yet, he could identify many customers from back in the kitchen by the sound of their voice, while they made their selections in the front room. He could even recognize friends he spoke with on the telephone before they introduced themselves. As he reached the front of his business, Matt deduced that the Klansman who had threatened him was Tom Stewart, the injured soldier whose father owned the mercantile store. He recognized the raspy voice, a result of his gassing during the war. Matt considered that this information might be useful to him.

But the threat confirmed his worst fears. It was one thing for a stranger to rail against the Jews and Catholics who held positions of authority back east. However, it was something different altogether when a local man threatened you and your business in the midst of so many angry Protestant young men. Matt feared for his future, and the anxiety kept him awake the rest of the night. It wasn't until he began his workday with Davy that he managed to set aside his misgivings and concentrate on the day's activities.

Yet even as he labored through the early hours of the new day, a part of Matt's mind considered the implications of the events of the previous evening. He decided he would have to fight this menace to his way of life. He didn't have a plan, but he was shrewd enough to sense that a viable one would present itself if he remained alert to the problem and the possibilities.

However, he was not completely without options. He made one other decision and left the bakery a little early for lunch. He stopped by the Western Union office and sent a telegram to the railway union offices in Chicago.

CHAPTER 7

November 1922
Donegal, Indiana

Annie had left her bed for only short spells during the last few days. The baby was past due, and she was tired and frustrated over the delay in the impending birth of her third child. The weather outside her bedroom window was cool and dreary. A cold rain had fallen during the night. In another week such storms would bring snow to the brown landscape. She had prayed earnestly to the Blessed Virgin that the baby be born before inclement weather made the trip to the hospital dangerous.

It was mid-morning, and Joannie, Annie's older sister, was taking care of the children downstairs. Joannie had been sent by their mother to help during the last weeks of the pregnancy. Annie's other sisters had performed this duty during her prior pregnancies. Matt had taken their auto to work with instructions to hurry home when the time of delivery became apparent. Annie felt what she thought were contractions during the night, but they had ceased. She experienced the same sensations before Katy was born, and now the discomfort had begun again. Annie calmed herself and waited to be sure the contractions were real. It would be very embarrassing to alert Matt and Dr. Nash for what turned out to be a false alarm. After another few minutes, Annie wiped the perspiration from her face with her handkerchief. Her baby was apparently ready.

"Joannie," she called out. "Joannie, I need you."

A moment later she heard the patter of quick footsteps on the stairs. Joannie replied to her while still on the staircase. "Yes, Sis. Are you all right?"

"Joannie, it's time to go to the hospital. Telephone Matt and then Dr. Nash's office."

Her sister never reached the bedroom. She froze on the top step, then turned and hurried down to the phone in the hallway. Annie considered going to the bathroom but decided to conserve her strength until her husband arrived home.

In order to calm herself and to pass the time as she waited, Annie thought back on the births of Brian and Katy. Both of those deliveries had been normal, but Brian's birth stood out in her memory. She guessed most mothers felt that way about their firstborn. It was such an incredible experience for a woman that much of the entire pregnancy was fixed in her mind forever. Annie had to admit it was the same with other first time events in her life. The time her father took her for a ride in a locomotive or the first time Matt kissed her were occasions to cherish for life.

The children's voices brought Annie out of her reverie. Katy barged into the room in her usual direct manner with Brian in tow. "Are you going to the hospital to get my baby sister?" she queried. She came up to her mother's bed and let Annie wrap her arm around her.

"Yes, sweetheart," cooed Annie. "Your father is coming to get me, and then we'll leave, but Aunt Joannie will stay here with both of you. I expect you two to behave and help out until I return home."

"Okay, Mommy," replied the precocious little girl.

"Will you come home for dinner?" asked Brian.

"No, having a baby takes time. Mommy will have to stay at the hospital for a few days until the doctor decides that we're ready to come home. Hopefully, your daddy will be home before bedtime tonight to tell you both whether it's a sister or a brother."

"I want a brother," said Brian.

"But I want a sister," whined Katy.

"God will choose which it will be," intoned their mother. "And whatever He decides will be good enough for all of us. Both of you will need to love and take care of our new baby."

"Yes, Mommy," replied her two chastised children.

They talked awhile longer about matters important to mothers and their children. Then Annie became aware of the voices of her husband and her sister downstairs. "Give me some kisses and then go greet your father. You mind Aunt Joannie while we're gone. I'll be home in a couple of days."

Nearly four hours later Matt found himself in the private waiting room at St. Joseph's Hospital in Logansport. It was nice to have a Catholic hospital for the birth of their third child. The walls were a soft green, and a crucifix hung on one with statues of Mary and Joseph on tables flanking it on each side. Magazines and newspapers had been neatly arranged on tables near the chairs that lined the other walls. The room was a pleasant change from the open area in the Huntington hospital, where he had waited during the birth of their first two children. He hadn't thought of it as inconvenient; he had been happy just to have a hospital to take care of Annie. Matt didn't like the idea of having babies at home with only a midwife or doctor in attendance. He and his siblings had entered the world in such a manner, but Matt considered it to be risky and old-fashioned.

A nurse wearing a white uniform with a winged cap approached him. Her expression was formal but calm. "Mr. Conner, Dr. Nash would like to see you. Please follow me." She smiled and then turned toward the end of the suite.

Matt wanted to question her as to the reason for this unexpected summons, but she didn't appear ready to give out any additional information. She had him wait just inside the hallway that led to the operating rooms and then disappeared down the corridor. Several types of calamities went through Matt's mind as he stood staring at the featureless walls. It was probably no more than a minute before the doctor appeared. He wore a white surgical gown that revealed his shirt collar and the knot of his tie. A cotton cap covered his head.

"Mr. Conner, there is a complication with the baby. The child will be a breach birth, unless we do a Caesarian procedure. Your wife gave me her approval and has already been sedated. In such cases, I always seek assurance from the father before I proceed. Do I have your approval to operate?"

Matt thought for a moment. "Doctor, could the baby be delivered safely without the operation? I'm worried about the pain my wife will suffer."

The doctor nodded sympathetically. "There is a good chance the baby will be injured if delivered feet first. Hip damage is my biggest concern. Mrs. Conner will not suffer during the surgery, as she will be completely anesthetized. There will, of course, be quite an incision, which will cause her recovery to be longer. But a Caesarian section is a common procedure with very little risk involved. I've done this operation many times, and it's what I recommend."

Matt exhaled deeply. "All right, doctor, you have my permission. Is this one of the problems with childbirth in older women?"

Dr. Nash put his hand on Matt's shoulder. "No, a breach birth can happen to any woman. It's quite common, but there are other complications we worry about regarding pregnancies in older women. It really is an experience better tolerated by younger women.

"I've got to get back to the delivery room. Please return and wait for a nurse to take you to your wife's hospital room. It shouldn't take long now."

Matt went back to the waiting room and greeted another man who had arrived during his conversation with the doctor. They exchanged names, and Matt learned that the man was a resident of Logansport who had just brought his wife in for their first baby's delivery. Matt reflected that it would be a busy day for Dr. Nash.

Matt recognized that Annie had faith in the doctor's skills, but the man seemed a little cold to Matt. Maybe it was just his formal manner with patients. Matt made a mental note to get a bottle of Canadian whisky from his Irish source on his next trip to Chicago. He found illegal booze made excellent thank-you gifts and helped to endear him to people he did business with. It was important to show Dr. Nash that nothing was more valuable to him than the health of his family.

As the minutes ticked by, Matt found himself speculating on Annie's health. He had never contemplated life without her, but the thought of surgery alarmed him. He was not equipped to raise children. Annie was the caregiver in their home, and as such she could never be replaced. More important, his beautiful bride was the compass that guided him and kept him from the follies to which so many Irishmen succumbed. Matt expected he would make a valiant attempt to raise the children if she were to die, but he would never again find the happiness he shared with her.

Such thoughts were not helping his mood. He turned almost sheepishly to silent prayer. Matt had not prayed outside of church or home in a long time. He had stayed so busy that he neglected his spiritual life, and he knew he had no excuse for it. He wondered if God was punishing him for his lack of faith. His Catholic training had taught him to pray for intercession from the Blessed Virgin. If anyone had access to the Lord, it was the Holy Mother, Mary. He prayed she might protect his wife since Mary herself was a mother who knew the importance of a woman's influence on a family. After a few moments of reflection, Matt found he could do no more than to continue to pray the "Hail Mary" over and over again.

The other man's family came in and took seats around him. They talked in hushed tones, and they did not disturb Matt. He wished he had family, or even Annie's parents, here to stand vigil with him. He had insisted on moving her to Donegal in order to put distance between them and his father-in-law. Now he wished the hard old Irish engineer were here to sit with him. Plus, Annie's mother would be a strong positive presence to help him deal with his fears.

The nurse came quietly into the room and approached Matt. She appeared friendlier this time. Matt dared not get his hopes up.

"Mr. Conner, you have a lovely baby daughter. She and Mrs. Conner are doing well. I'll take you to see your new child, and then you can wait in your wife's room until she awakens."

Matt felt relief wash over him like a waterfall. He went to stand up, but his legs were suddenly weak. He felt tears form in his eyes. He took a moment to compose himself as he glanced over at the statues and gave thanks to the Blessed Virgin before he got up and let the nurse lead him to his new baby girl and his beloved Annie. The other expectant father rose from his seat and offered Matt his hand. Matt smiled, shook the man's hand firmly, and said, "Best wishes to you and your wife."

Later in the week, as the day drew to a close, a cold wind swept in from the west, and the temperature dropped as the landscape dried out. Winter was approaching, and Tom Stewart recalled Lucas's theory about needing to change their methods of recruitment. The farmers who made up the core membership would now have more time to spend on Klan activities. But the big events such as the torch parade or the cross burning would be curtailed until warm weather returned. A private Christmas program at the Holmes' farm had promise. In the past two months, membership had tripled, and Lucas did not want to lose momentum. Tom wished they could hold a big family event at a local auditorium, but the organization didn't have the acceptance necessary to go out in public without their uniforms. They would have to gain such acceptance from the community before they could dispense with the secrecy that protected them.

What was needed was a series of small demonstrations that kept the Ku Klux Klan in the news and confirmed its growing power. Men liked to be associated with causes and groups expanding within their community. As Lucas explained it, the key to approval across the valley required the Klan to establish itself as the moral authority in the area. Good Christian folk would be more attracted to membership if the group confirmed its religious foundation.

To that end, Tom Stewart had planned the first knight ride for tonight. Lucas was worried the plan might fall apart. But Tom was certain no one would get hurt because no guns were carried by the group of four he had selected for the mission. However, there was the risk that they could get caught, and Tom judged that they didn't as yet have the political clout to skirt the law. He knew Chief Johnson would arrest them all on assault and battery charges if they were caught. There would be a trial, and the group's reputation would be seriously damaged.

The possibility of arrest was one reason why Lucas delegated this action to Tom. The other reason was that Tom was a war veteran. He understood how to apprehend the target of the planned action.

At the end of town, Tom, Don Lester, and Clyde Harrow were huddled in Clyde's car behind a stand of trees that bordered a fallow field. Leon Grainger, the fourth member of the group, was sixty yards beyond in the darkness watching for their prey. They would each have to take one-hour shifts standing outside until the right opportunity presented itself. Tom had prepared the group for a long, tedious evening. He had warned them that, just as in the army, a successful martial action required hours of patience prior to a few quick minutes of action. Tom had trained to infiltrate enemy lines and capture prisoners for intelligence purposes. At long last his training would be put to use.

They had waited for two hours already, and the coals in the bucket on the floor no longer produced any warmth in the Dodge sedan. The windshield had to be constantly wiped clear to watch for the signal from their lookout.

When Leon lit the signal match a few minutes later, the others almost missed it as they fought off the cold and the boredom. But Clyde saw it from the driver's seat, and the other two members quickly put on their black hoods and left to join Leon.

The trio approached a privy that sat behind a small rented house on the edge of town. They carried rope and rags to bind and quiet their mark. Past observations had determined that the man they hunted made a late evening visit before going to bed. Tom was thankful that the house didn't contain a bathroom. He hoped to apprehend the man without alerting his wife and daughters to the action.

They crept to the front of the shed and waited. Soon the door opened, and Leon and Don seized the startled man by each arm. Tom stood before him with the bindings. In his most authoritative voice, he confronted his prey. "If you keep quiet and come with us, no harm will come to your family."

Their quarry, Jakub Miller appeared startled. He stood motionless, perhaps considering his options, and then nodded his consent. Tom stuffed a rag into his mouth, and the others held the captive's arms together in front of him as Tom bound his hands with the rope. Within a minute, they were marching him through the small woods that separated his home from the field that lay behind it. As they approached the car, Clyde slipped on his hood and turned over the engine of his black Dodge sedan. Tom had requested that Clyde be the driver for their mission. His three-year-old Dodge Model 30 was similar to the staff cars used by officers of the American Expeditionary Force during the Great War. To Tom the auto lent an air of military precision to their maneuver. Clyde waited until the others had piled into it before he lit the lamps, shifted into gear, and pulled back onto the road that led away from town.

Now that they were relatively safe, Tom turned towards Jakub, who was sandwiched between the two others in the rear seat. "We don't plan to hurt you, Polack, but we will if you give us any trouble. You don't belong here, and we mean to give you a reason to go back to where you came from."

After a ten-minute drive north, away from the river, the car pulled onto a farm and drove up to the barn. The farmhouse was dark. Tom stepped out of the front seat and pulled open the barn door to let Clyde drive inside. Clyde turned off the motor and jumped out and lit a lantern hanging on the wall next to him. Tom shut the door as the other occupants removed Mr. Miller from the backseat.

"We won't be bothered here, so I'll remove the gag," wheezed Tom, coughing to clear his chest. "You see this is the Denton farm. The bank foreclosed on them two months ago, and they had to pack up and leave. I don't know why a bank would do such a dumb thing. The Dentons had to move in with the wife's family downstate. But there's nobody here to take over and work the farm. The damn bankers should have found a way to let Steve Denton stay on and work off his loan.

"I think the bankers are all Jews. Are you a Jew, Polack?"

The captive man made eye-contact with Tom, but he didn't respond.

After an uncomfortable pause, Clyde Harrow blurted, "We'll just have to make use of this nice barn tonight."

"Yeah," answered Leon as he and Don continued to hold Jakub by his arms.

Tom looked at the two guards and pointed to a barrel that sat in front of the car. "Set him down and hold him so he can't run out." He then motioned to Clyde but didn't use his name. "Get the fire lit under the pitch bucket."

In a matter of minutes, a small fire crackled under a two-gallon bucket that held tar paint. The smell of burning hickory wood permeated the barn, but Tom noted the tiny fire provided little warmth in the cavernous structure.

"Make sure it doesn't get too hot," warned Tom. "We just need it to get warm enough to spread easily."

Clyde turned to Jakub, who watched the proceedings from his seat on the barrel. "Have you ever been to a tar and feathers party, Polack?"

Jakub only stared back at Clyde, but Tom thought he detected a growing alarm on the man's features. Tom wondered if this foreigner even understood what they were saying to him.

"Well, tonight you're going to be guest of honor," crowed Leon.

"Get him out of his clothes and tie his legs together," rasped Tom. Leon and Don hauled Jakub up to a standing position and yanked off his shoes and his trousers. Don produced a knife and cut through the man's shirt from the back as well as his undershirt. They had to cut through the sleeves to remove the garments from his bound limbs. They left on his long-leg underpants.

Jakub offered no resistance.

Don whistled as he examined Jakub from the rear. "He's been beaten . . . a long time ago from the looks of these scars."

Tom walked over and scanned Jakub's bare back. "What did you do to deserve this kind of punishment, Mr. Miller?"

Jakub straightened and glared at his hooded captors. "Where I come from, it is how they treat persons who worship a different God. They had other ways to scare us and keep us out, but sometimes they went mad."

Tom could only stare at his enemy. He didn't know if it was the scars or the proud defiant demeanor of this man that elicited sympathy from him. Finally, he offered what little consolation he could. "Don't worry. We won't hurt you. We're Christians."

Jakub's eyes crinkled and his mouth formed a wry smile. He stuck out his chin and replied, "So were they."

Tom blinked twice from underneath his hood, but he had no reply to his captive's challenge. Instead, he turned to address Clyde. "Is the tar warm enough to spread?"

Clyde bent down and patted the side of the bucket. "It's ready," he replied.

Tom glanced over and motioned toward Don. "Spread out the tarp." Don Lester unfolded a piece of worn canvas that had been on a shelf on a wall of the barn.

Clyde removed the bucket by the wire handle using a rag to keep from burning himself. He poured the black liquid in wide circles onto the tarp. Acrid steam rose up from the puddled fluid that spread out onto the canvas. Leon brought a large burlap bag over from a dark corner. They let the tar cool for a minute.

Tom held up his hand and stared down at their captive as he sat bound on the barrel. "By order of the Kleagle of the Wabash Valley Klavern, Mr. Miller, you are found guilty of trespassing on American soil. Your presence on our land is considered a violation of our rights to live free from foreign interference. Your punishment for your crime is to be tarred and feathered and to be held for public humiliation in the center of town. You are hereby ordered to leave our community after you have been released from your sentence."

Tom motioned to his helpers. "Get him by his hands and his feet. We need to roll him in it to get good coverage."

Leon and Don grabbed their captive's tied limbs and stretched him onto the ground in front of the tarp. Tom looked down upon the victim and then nodded to the two men who held Jakub. They in turn rolled the bound man onto the canvas into the tar and continued to turn him over in order to spread the black substance over his entire torso.

Tom noticed a release in tension of the prisoner's muscles as the slimy black substance coated his exposed skin. The tar apparently didn't burn or sting him. In fact, it may even provide a little warmth for the nearly naked man. Tom couldn't help but think this punishment was greatly preferable to the lash Mr. Miller had apparently experienced some time in the past.

They finished rolling him in the tar, but they held him down in the center of the tarp. Clyde stepped forward with an old paintbrush and began to wipe globs of the tar onto Jakub's head and his arms and legs. Then they let go of the man and stood back.

Tom barked out his next order. "Get up onto your knees, Polack."

The prisoner slowly obeyed. His legs quivered as he reluctantly assumed a position on his knees that left him defenseless against an attack.

Clyde Harrow stepped forward with the burlap bag and a large hunting knife. He grinned into the Polack's face as he fondled the weapon. The yellow glow from the lantern reflected upon the polished steel blade. Then Clyde moved around behind the prisoner and cut open the bag very slowly. The man trembled, and Tom knew the poor peasant had to be terrified about the kind of punishment that was about to befall him. Clyde hefted the bag over their victim, turned it over, and began to dump chicken feathers over the man. Many of the soft airy feathers stuck to the tarred prisoner in the penitent position. Many more fell onto the tar-stained tarp. Leon and Don began to laugh.

Tom stifled a laugh, but there was amusement in his voice. "Now get up and move about in the feathers. I don't want to see any of the tar on you. You need to look as white and pure as an angel sent by

God to show other foreigners the way to salvation."

There was more laughter from his companions. The tension of the night was broken, and it was replaced by a relaxed mood of accomplishment.

When Jakub Miller had finished squatting in the feathers, they led him out of the barn by a rope and secured him inside a cart that was then hitched to the back of Clyde's Dodge. Don rolled up the tarp and took it outside in the yard where it and the other supplies were set afire. The lantern and small fire in the barn were extinguished, and they quickly abandoned the site.

It was now past one o'clock as the Klansmen slowly hauled the two-wheel cart back to town. They encountered no traffic during the trip back from the deserted farm. Clyde stopped at the edge of town as they checked for activity. Tom saw nothing suspicious and motioned Clyde to proceed. They drove forward at a faster pace until they reached the courthouse at the center of Broad Street. Clyde angled the car and cart to a stop at the curb in front of the steps. Don got out and cut the rope that held the cart to the rear bumper. Leon brought out a sign that stated:

America is for Americans.
Foreigners get out!
KKK

He hurriedly lashed the sign to the side of the cart. Then both men jumped into the back seat of the car, and Clyde slipped the car into gear and accelerated down the empty street and out the east end of town.

Jakub took stock of his situation. He hoped his wife had stayed home, but he knew she would be sick with worry that he'd gone missing. He could call out for help, but he was afraid of creating a disturbance. He would be embarrassed by his predicament. He didn't know who would find him or if they would be willing to release him. He attempted to slip free from his bindings while he waited for the police. The night patrolman would be along soon, and he would release him. It would be best for the police to see the result of the criminal activity of this group that had captured him.

He pondered his future. He had been lucky not to be physically hurt by this assault. He didn't think he or his family would fare as well a second time. He resolved to leave this strange little town. He had believed it would be safer here than the ghetto they left in New York City, but he had been wrong. His feet were cold, and he tucked them under his legs.

Some three hours later, shortly after four in the morning, Matt Conner approached Broad Street on his way to work. He had not gotten his usual amount of sleep due to all the recent activity the birth of their new daughter brought. Brian and Katy were excited, and he had spent extra time with them, answering their questions and making plans for the baby's arrival home with Annie next week. The children were disappointed they weren't allowed to visit their mother and new baby sister. They didn't understand the hospital's policy, and neither did Matt. Many friends and fellow parishioners had stopped by to get news on Annie and the baby. Others, such as Father O'Brien, had visited with Annie and Matt at the hospital.

Matt had been worried about how much Annie had suffered from the surgery. But she was so ecstatic over the birth of their new daughter that she had few complaints regarding her condition. If his wife was in much pain, she hid it well from him.

Matt had walked almost three blocks on Broad Street before he sensed something unusual that brought him back to the present. He silently cursed his lack of attention to his present surroundings. He had learned as a young boy to be careful of his situation while on public streets in Chicago. He still remained alert to unusual conditions here in this small town.

What was it that brought him back from his daydreaming this early morning? There was no activity on the street, no movement or unusual noises. Then he realized that he had not seen Officer Harris on his rounds. It was the first time in memory Matt had not seen the young man making his presence known to Matt during the early morning. Perhaps he had the day off or was sick.

Matt was alert now with all his senses seeking out anything unusual. As he approached Seventh Street and the bakery, he wrapped his hand around the small revolver in his overcoat. He'd purchased the weapon two weeks ago from a fellow parishioner who had grown too old to use it. Matt had been frightened by his confrontation with the Klansman at the courthouse.

He had a clear path to his shop, but as he scanned down the street toward the center of town an object at the curb in front of the courthouse caught his attention. In the dark he could not identify it, but he knew it didn't belong there. It wasn't large enough to be an automobile, but perhaps it was a wagon.

Matt knew he should get inside to his work, as the strange object was too far away to menace his business. But he couldn't overlook bizarre sights in town; his curiosity always got the better of him. Besides, if there was criminal activity taking place and Officer Harris was in trouble, Matt was the only one up at this hour who could lend assistance.

Matt walked past Seventh Street and on down the main boulevard through town. He kept to the sidewalk and moved slowly and quietly. He scanned the street and the buildings in front of him and even stopped twice to check for activity behind him. As he came closer to the courthouse, he detected movement in what appeared in the darkness to be a hay cart. Matt stopped at the corner of Broad and Sixth, next to the courthouse and spent several moments surveying the scene. Someone or something was in the small wagon, but there didn't appear to be anyone else in the vicinity.

Matt drew out the pistol and held it at his side as he stepped into the street and proceeded forward to the side of the cart. He could read the sign, and he determined that the vehicle contained a strangely garbed individual who appeared to be held prisoner. Matt approached the cart and spoke in a low, soft voice. "Hello, are you in any trouble?"

The captive stirred slowly, as if from a light sleep. "Please sir, if you could untie these ropes, I could get out of the cold and home to my family."

Matt swallowed as recognition of the voice came to him. "Jakub Miller, is that you? It's Matt Conner. What's happened here?"

The man took a few seconds before he could reply. "Mr. Conner, I was taken prisoner by hooded men. They stripped me . . . covered me in road pitch. Please help me get free. My wife will be scared I've been taken and killed."

Matt went around to the other side of the cart and examined the rope used to hold the man. "It's all right, Jakub, I'll get you out of here." Matt put the revolver back into his coat and pulled out his pocket watch. There was a small pocketknife on a chain attached to the watch. The blade was small but sharp, and he cut through the rope quickly. Jakub moved slowly to the end of the cart. His muscles were most likely stiff from exposure to the cold night air. Matt helped him off the wagon, and as he stood, Matt got a good view of the ugly crime that had been perpetrated against the poor man. Matt placed a strong left hand under the man's arm to support him, and he felt the cold greasy tar that stuck to the man's skin. Matt had only read about tar-and-feathers parties; the reality of such abuse sickened him.

"You can't go home like this, Jakub. Let me take you to my garage. I've got gasoline there, and we can clean this off. I'll get you started, and then I'll go to your place, tell your wife, and get you some warm clothes." Jakub didn't argue. Matt guided him to the garage on the alley behind the bakery. Matt wondered if anyone was up to notice their progress down Broad Street, but he saw no lights in the windows of the buildings they passed.

It had been a most unusual morning for Matt. Jakub had removed most of the tar and scrubbed his skin with soap and warm water Matt had brought from the bakery. After putting on clothes that Matt had retrieved from Jakub's house, the older man had been led to the kitchen of the bakery, where he sat in the warmth and nibbled on fresh bread with butter and drank strong coffee that Matt always brewed for early customers. Jakub's wife came to help him home just after the sun rose on this clear cold morning. Winter certainly was present in the crisp air.

Maureen arrived before sunrise and curtailed most of her own baking in order to help Matt and Davy produce the staples needed for the day. Matt telephoned Chief Johnson at eight o'clock and asked him to visit the bakery in regard to the wagon parked in front of the courthouse.

Within the hour, the chief came over, and Matt led him into the kitchen area, where Davy was still at work. Maureen handled the customers in the front of the store.

"One of my patrolmen spotted that cart on his way to work this morning. I had it towed off before it became too big an attraction for the public. But what do you know about it, Matt?"

Matt frowned as he gauged the sincerity of Chief Johnson. He didn't know whom he could trust in this matter, but the big law officer had always been fair to Matt, so he decided to take the man into his confidence. He explained what had happened on his way to work and what he knew about Jakub's capture from the prior evening.

"He's at home resting now. I told him he could trust you and that you would be visiting him later to get details. I don't think he knows the identity of these Klansmen, but maybe he'll remember some details about the farm. He was pretty distraught when he was here. He's planning to leave town, and I gave him the names of people in Chicago who might help him settle there."

Matt watched as Paul Johnson finished taking notes in his small book and screwed on the cap to his fountain pen. "I'm shocked that this took place here in town. I received a letter last week from an anonymous citizen who wanted to report the drunken actions of one of his neighbors. The guy implied that if the law couldn't put a stop to the man's public intoxication, then the Klan would handle it. I didn't take seriously the implied threat. I just never had a clue that they were planning any sort of vigilante action."

"What can you do about them?" asked Matt.

The policeman removed his hat and wiped his brow with his handkerchief. Matt realized it was warm in the bakery's kitchen. "Nothing for the moment," replied the chief. "We don't know who represents the Klan. It's a secret organization, and I don't know that they were responsible for this crime. It could have been anybody posing as the Klan."

"Nobody has reason to attack Mr. Miller except these guys," growled Matt. "The Klan is on record as being against immigrants, and Jakub Miller qualifies as one."

"Well, I'll talk to him, Matt. But unless he can identify one of his attackers, I can't just go arrest any Klansman I find walking on the street wearing a hood and robe."

Matt nodded in reluctant agreement with the policeman. Then his eyebrows furrowed as he focused on the other man's eyes and the glasses that shielded them. "One other thing I don't understand, Paul. Where was Billy Harris last night? He should have found Jakub in that wagon long before I did."

"Billy got sick last night. He said he came down with food poisoning around midnight and spent his shift in the station house. He should have called me, but he said he didn't want to wake me up. Are you thinking he had something to do with this crime?"

Matt considered the question for a moment. "No," he said. "I just find it peculiar that this happens on the night we don't have any police presence in town."

Chief Johnson stood up from the stool on which he had been seated. He took off his glasses and rubbed his eyes. "Trust me, Matt, it's just a bad coincidence this crime took place on the night my man was sick to his stomach. I better get over to Mr. Miller's place. Maybe he can remember some details. It would be nice if he saw a license plate number from the car."

Matt walked the chief out to the street and shook his hand. "I hope you can catch these guys," said Matt. "The town doesn't need this kind of trouble. A lawless town is bad for everyone."

"I agree . . . and so does the mayor. He wants an explanation for that cart parked in front of the county offices, and he's not going to be happy about what I'm going to report to him."

"Why?" asked Matt. "Didn't the Klan get a parade permit for the cart?"

Paul Johnson frowned. Slowly he tipped his hat, climbed into his car, and drove off toward the Miller house. Matt watched him depart and considered what he had learned. The Klan was beginning to assert its influence in the community, and they knew how to avoid the law. He was willing to believe Officer Harris had been sick last night. But he also knew that the criminals would never have brought Jakub into town for a public display if they thought there was a chance they would be apprehended. Therefore, Billy Harris had to be in on the plan.

That was information Matt would save to use at the right time.

CHAPTER 8

December 1922
Donegal, Indiana

The wind whipped snow crystals around Maureen's dress as she hurried up the walkway to her home. She had been living at the Tilly boarding house, a Queen Anne-styled dwelling, for six weeks and had slowly grown to enjoy the camaraderie of the people living there. It was almost six in the evening, and Mrs. Tilly liked to serve dinner promptly to her husband and two boarders at the top of the hour. Maureen should have told her this morning that she'd be doing some Christmas shopping and might miss the evening meal. However, Maureen had thought she would be done and home before dark. She hadn't foreseen she'd become sidetracked shopping for toys for her nephew and nieces.

She climbed the steps to the gas-lit, spindled porch and used the broom to sweep the snow from her dress and her laced boots. She was cold, and the packages had made her arms ache. She was thankful to enter into the warmth of the hallway inside the big two-story house. Maureen looked into the dining room and spotted Mrs. Tilly arranging china on the table. "Hello, Mrs. Tilly. I am so sorry to be arriving at the last moment. I'll just be a minute getting my packages to my room."

The matron of the house looked up and smiled and then came over with a sly look on her face. She spoke in a whisper, as to a confidant. "It's all right, dear. We have a few minutes before supper. Take your time and freshen up from your day at work. We have a new boarder. He's a gentleman from Seattle who just arrived in town. He's not much older than yourself."

Maureen became amused as she deciphered the meaning of her landlady's information. Naturally, she would have to make herself presentable for dinner and her introduction to this new gentleman. But finding an eligible suitor here in Donegal was not a priority for her. Still, first impressions were important. "I'll be down before the soup gets cold," she whispered. She smiled, patted the sleeve of the housekeeper's sweater and hurried up the stairs to her room.

Ten minutes later Maureen descended the stairs in a clean lavender dress with her hair and makeup repaired as best she could in the time allotted. She entered the dining room in a slow, casual walk. "Please forgive me, everyone. My dress was wet from the snow, and I had to change before dinner."

"It's all right, dear," exclaimed Mr. Tilly in his authoritative voice. "We were just getting started. May I introduce you to Mr. Randall Madison, our new guest."

A tall man with dark features arose, walked around the table, and held Maureen's right hand lightly between his fingers. "Good evening, miss. I'm so happy to meet you. Mr. and Mrs. Tilly have been telling me about how Mrs. Floyd and you are such wonderful boarders and how hospitable things are here in the house. Now that I've had the chance to meet everyone, I just know that I'll be comfortable here."

Maureen took in the features of this tall gentleman. He had wrinkles around his eyes, which spoke of a hard life, but there was mirth in the eyes themselves. He was certainly older than she was by at least ten years. Yet his features were attractive, and Maureen found herself curious about the sudden appearance of a stranger to this small town. She met new people all the time in Chicago, but few people came to Donegal during the winter.

"Thank you for your kind words, Mr. Madison, and please be

seated. Welcome to Donegal. Are you visiting family here?" Maureen took her place and smiled at Mrs. Tilly seated at the end of the table and to Mrs. Floyd, who sat to Maureen's right.

Mr. Madison returned to his seat across the table before he replied. "No, miss. I'm from Seattle, although my family is originally from Virginia. We're supposed to be related to President Madison, but I've never met anyone who could prove it."

Mr. Tilly took it upon himself to finish the introductions. "Mr. Madison is an entrepreneur looking to start a new business in these parts."

"Actually, I'm a mechanic trained in the repair of gasoline engines," added the newcomer quickly. "I've worked for years in the shipyards in Seattle and lately with the motors that pump water from the ships' holds. I've come east to use that experience to start a business that will supply motorized pumps for wells and irrigation systems for farmers."

"How interesting," declared Maureen. "And what made you stop here in Donegal?"

Maureen noted a slight blush on the man's cheeks, perhaps due to her direct questioning of him.

"I took the Empire Builder east to Chicago. Along the way I found that they already had similar ideas in Montana and the Dakotas. When I had to depart my train in Chicago, I asked around town where was the best farmland in these parts, and more than one fella recommended the Wabash Valley. I was fortunate to find a position at the Sutton Garage, here in town. I can work there repairing automobiles while I promote my ideas to the landowners around the county."

"Are you a churchgoer, Mr. Madison?" asked Mrs. Floyd.

"Yes, ma'am," replied the newcomer without the hint of embarrassment. "I was raised a Lutheran, but I've been known to attend Methodist services in the last few years."

"How nice for you," replied Mrs. Floyd.

Maureen was somewhat disappointed. Her fellow boarder had extracted information Maureen was curious about, but the answer was not what she had hoped to hear.

"My husband and I both attend the Methodist church on the next block," added Mrs. Tilly. "You will find it an excellent place of worship. Mrs. Floyd attends the Baptist church on Wednesday evenings as well as Sundays. Miss Conner belongs to the Catholic church across town."

"Well, what a diverse group of Christians we have here," offered Randall as he spooned up the last of his soup.

Maureen picked up her spoon and began to partake of the soup, but she didn't really taste it. How strange, she thought, that she had been attracted to this stranger and so disappointed at finding out he wasn't Catholic. She had been away too long from Chicago, where there were so many eligible young men.

On Friday evening, Lucas was pleased to be present in the crowded barn of John Holmes. There were more than forty men in attendance in spite of at least half a dozen members who had stayed home to avoid the snowy weather. His recruiting efforts were beginning to flourish. The barn was warm and humid from all the bodies packed into it. A recent recruit, Bill Marshall, had delivered a strong prayer to open the meeting. Bill was a deacon in the Independent Christian Church and brought some professionalism to their prayers. John Holmes chaired the meeting, a job Lucas had delegated to him as host of the gathering. The discussion was centered on "old business," and Don Lester had commented that the recent Knight Riders mission had not resulted in the public display that had been intended. Billy Harris spoke next.

"Chief Johnson interviewed that Polack after it happened. It turns out that the mick baker, Matt Conner, found him and set him free early in the morning before anyone could see his tarred and feathered butt."

A few of the men offered curses for the bad luck that had partially spoiled their plan. Officer Harris continued. "But the old guy was pretty shaken up. He and his family left town by evening. He wouldn't even accept a guard that the chief offered to provide at his house that night." This brought forth a few cheers and some laughter from those present.

"Was the chief able to get any useful information from the Polack?" inquired Lucas.

"Nope," answered Billy Harris confidently. "He didn't recognize anyone, and he couldn't provide a license plate number since the plate had been removed. There are no leads in the case to follow." That brought a cheer from those present.

"We'll have to deal with that uppity Irishman," stated John Holmes. A few men seconded the idea.

Lucas held up his hand as a way to silence the discussion. "Mr. Conner is a papist. The profits from his bakery go straight to the pope in Rome. This practice is un-American. I believe a resolution is in order that we withdraw our support for his business and encourage others to refuse to buy his goods. All those in favor say aye."

There was unanimous support for the resolution.

Lucas went further. "There are two other local bakeries run by good Christians who could use our support. I will ask our membership committee to interview both of the other proprietors about joining our fraternity. If either or both decide to join us, we'll recommend them for future business. As for Mr. Conner, I advocate that we ask Tom Stewart and his committee to undertake action that will convince this papist he would be better off baking bread back in Ireland."

There was general agreement and a smattering of applause from the group.

"Any other old business?" asked Mr. Holmes. "If not, let's move on to new business. All Klansmen were empowered last month to investigate the morals of their neighbors. Has anyone anything to report regarding immoral activity observed on the part of people in the community?"

Lucas knew this was a new and delicate issue for the klavern. These men were raised to be self-reliant and private. As such, they were prone to stay out of each other's business and not to pass judgment on one another. There was great reluctance to air their suspicions about the lives of their neighbors. After a few moments of awkward silence, Lenny Thomas stood up to be recognized.

Lenny was a thin man who maintained a small productive dairy farm four miles east of Donegal. Lucas had heard Lenny was the third of four sons of a farm family who had good land adjacent to the Wabash River. His oldest brother, Thad, would inherit the property after his folks died. Lenny had worked hard to survive in the farm country around Donegal. After years of working as a hand for other landowners, he had benefited from a stroke of luck that had enabled him to buy the Simpson dairy farm from the owner's widow. The old woman wanted to move back east with her relatives and contracted with Lenny to take over the farm and purchase it through its profits over a five-year period. People said Lenny was grateful for his good fortune, but he still felt that he was due more. He had taken out loans over the last two years to buy new equipment for the farm and appliances for the home. But he had lost three cows over the past year to disease, and he was getting behind in his loan payments. His anger at this current reversal of luck was probably an impetus in his joining the Klan. Hopefully, the fraternity gave him a place to feel good about himself and pride in his position in the community.

Lenny spoke hesitantly at first. "My neighbor, John Hood, has had equipment for brewing beer or some kind of alcoholic ale for several years. I can tell he continues to make his brew in a shed he has at the back of his property . . . where it backs up to mine."

No one commented or challenged Lenny.

"Lately, I've seen him out walking the pastures staggering and hollering out curses like a drunk man. I fear that in such a condition he may harm his wife or two daughters."

Lucas looked around the barn for reaction, but few had the courage to look at him. If they looked up at all, it was toward the barn rafters.

Lucas took charge of the gathering. "Can anyone else verify this information?"

Officer Harris raised his hand. "It's pretty well known that John Hood brews beer. He's been doing it for years. But we've had no complaints about his drunkenness. Of course, he lives outside of town, and the county sheriff would be responsible for any criminal activity on his property."

Lucas looked at his members for about ten seconds while he thought about how to proceed. It was obvious that many of the Klansmen present had no wish to pursue this case further. But if the Klan's mission to be a moral leader in the community was ever to succeed, then action was needed on this initial case.

"We have a confirmed violation of the federal law against the production of alcoholic beverages. It doesn't matter that Mr. Hood has confined his drinking to his own property. His family may be suffering from his actions while he is intoxicated. Also he is a bad example to the community. We know Sheriff Grimes can't be bothered to uphold the law of the land. He doesn't support Prohibition, and he never will. It is my recommendation that a private letter be sent to Mr. Hood informing him that he must cease his brewing operation and dismantle his equipment. If we don't see evidence that he has complied with our anonymous request within seven days, then our Knight Riders will have to destroy it. All in favor, vote aye."

Less than half of those present voted affirmatively on the motion.

"All those opposed, vote no," challenged Lucas.

No one uttered a sound.

Lucas was satisfied that he had control of the situation. "The motion is approved. Tom, please send an appropriate notice to Mr. Hood. Lenny, if you see any further illegal activity by John Hood after one week, inform Tom Stewart, and he will proceed to phase two of our action."

Lucas stood up from his chair and walked out in front of the table set between the gathering and the leaders present. "We need to stand firmly for Prohibition. Public intoxication has been a plague on America. It is no longer legal, and it has always been morally wrong. The Bible finds it sinful, and we need to show our disapproval of all forms of booze. Therefore, anyone who knows the presence of any saloon or speakeasy that exists in the area must report it to us. We need to put an end to immoral activity wherever we find it. We must be a beacon of righteousness to our neighbors."

There was an uneasy silence in the barn until Tom Stewart coughed and cleared his throat. As many sets of eyes turned in his direction, he took the opportunity to speak. "The only drinking establishment in these parts is Higgins' Funeral Parlor. What are we suppose to do, shut down the only undertaker in town?"

The group broke into nervous laughter. Tom stared at Lucas, who gave him a tolerant look before returning his gaze to the men assembled before him. "If we are going to uphold the Christian values our founding fathers supported when they created this great nation, then we need to do so all of the time. There can be no exceptions. Our integrity cannot be challenged.

"I believe a demonstration at Higgins' Undertakers is in order. Clyde, make plans for a cross-burning ceremony next month. First we'll notify Chief Johnson by letter that he needs to close down their saloon. He won't take action, and so we'll bring the issue to the public's attention. We'll gather in force one evening and advise them to shut down their illegal operation. The cross-burning will signal the town that men of good character will no longer tolerate the Higgins' saloon. Fellow Klansmen are to be notified of the date once we've pinned it down. All in favor, raise your hands."

More than half the men present raised a hand in agreement with the action.

"I count a clear majority for this proposal," stated Lucas. "The motion carries. I'll take it on myself to organize the ceremony. John, what other new business is on the agenda?"

On the following afternoon, Matt Conner was visiting Father O'Brien and Father Stevens at the church rectory. The two priests had visited Matt and Annie in early November, and Matt found it a delightful evening talking about some of Christ's parables recorded in the gospels. It had been interesting to see which ones were the favorites among the group. As it turned out, the parables concerning The Good Samaritan and The Prodigal Son had been the most popular ones for discussion.

Today, the priests had talked with Matt about the construction of the gospels. He had long been curious about consistencies and differences that could be found from one to another. Father Stevens had explained that scholars believed one or more of the first three gospels had used one of the others as a source for its own account of Jesus's ministry. Since the authors were writing for different audiences, there was no conscious attempt to plagiarize the other's work. Yet differences could occur because each author had additional sources.

"Take the example of Christ's baptism," continued Father Stevens. "After Jesus receives the water, Matthew implies that God spoke to all those present. Mark and Luke state that the Father spoke only to Jesus. And John's gospel says that God spoke to John the Baptist. Are any of these recordings wrong? Perhaps they are all correct insofar as the witness perceived the event."

"That clarifies things for me," said Matt. "I'm afraid I am always looking for absolute facts in the Bible. I have trouble understanding that the authors may have their own interpretation of events. I was led to believe in religion classes that God would allow only absolute truths to be recorded as fact in the Bible. But I've often suspected that there was a degree of human interpretation or even error involved in the recordings."

Matt caught Father Tom's look of displeasure. "We don't like to dwell on errors in the Bible. It upsets those among us who believe that the Bible is the literal word of God. As pastors, we are taught to avoid that issue. As Paul states in Romans, we must let each member believe as he has the capacity to understand the faith.

"Unfortunately, there are some uneducated Christians and those of diminished capacity among us who commit sin in the name of God. Even right here in Donegal."

"Who? Are you referring to the Klan?" asked Matt.

Father Tom said nothing. After a moment he stood and returned his Bible to his desk on the other side of the office. "Not necessarily, but yes," he said as he made his way back his chair. He looked anguished to Matt.

"History is full of wrongful actions taken on the basis of religious belief. The Klan is merely the latest in a succession of misguided groups who hide their evilness under the cloak of righteousness. What they did to that poor man was sinful."

Father Tom paused and spoke again in a calmer tone. "I was proud to hear that you were brave enough to help Mr. Miller. He could have suffered a great deal of humiliation before the whole town if you had not come along when you did. Matt, you behaved like the Good Samaritan, and now I worry that your courage will get you into trouble with these hooligans."

Matt stared down at his hands. "I was already in trouble with these boys. Any Catholic who tries to better himself and his family is an enemy to the Klan. They don't want anyone to share in economic prosperity unless he has a robe and hood hanging in the closet."

Matt looked up as Father Stevens stifled a grin. The young priest took out a package of Camel cigarettes from his cassock. He offered one to Matt.

"No, thank you, Father. I smoke cigars at home when I have time to relax. I've never smoked cigarettes because I'm afraid I couldn't stop, and I don't want to give part of my attention to smoking. I need all of my concentration for my work."

Father Stevens lit one and spoke to Matt after he exhaled. "What can we do to combat this menace to our town, our state and to our society?"

Matt looked over at Father O'Brien, who nodded that he also wished to hear from Matt. Matt frowned and composed his thoughts.

"Finding Jakub Miller in that cart really scared me. I had hoped that the police would start an investigation of the Klan and try to ascertain who was behind this action. But Chief Johnson wants proof that they attacked Mr. Miller. Frankly, I don't believe he or the mayor is upset to have this group in town. As long as the KKK doesn't get caught breaking the law, they can go about their business just like everyone else. Since they keep their identities secret, the law won't touch them. I think all Catholics are at risk of being assaulted like Mr. Miller."

Matt scratched the back of his neck and paused for comments. Neither of his better-educated hosts spoke. Matt realized that the three of them were dealing with an issue with which they had no experience.

"It's hard to know when a man should take action against threats to him and when he should wait and let events run their course. I guess that's why it took President Wilson and the country so long to wage war on the Huns. How many more lives would have been lost or saved if we had gone 'over there' in 1915?"

Father O'Brien cleared his throat and spoke. "We must believe that God in his infinite wisdom has a plan for all of mankind. We do need to proceed cautiously and be governed by the laws established to regulate our activities in society. However, I also feel Father Stevens is correct. We need to take action to combat the Klan's activities. The Lord helps those who help themselves.

"I've read quotes attributed to Mr. Lampton in Indianapolis and from their Imperial Wizard in Atlanta. These men are promulgating false accusations regarding American Catholicism. No pope has ever tried to govern our actions in this country, and no church official ever will. What can we do here in Donegal to defend ourselves from these scurrilous accusations?"

Matt noticed Father O'Brien's cheeks were scarlet, and his hands trembled. The man sat back and looked to his colleague, Father Stevens. Then they both turned their eyes towards Matt.

Matt stroked his chin with his left hand and stretched his facial muscles while he considered what had been said. He had always been a quiet person, letting others like his brothers guide him through difficult situations. His brothers had also taught him to never let people take advantage of him. He'd given this problem much thought, and he was ready to act.

Matt leaned forward and said, "I've got a couple of ways in which you gentlemen could help. First, call a meeting of the men of the parish for the evening after Christmas. We need to gather as a congregation to consider what our options are to deal with the Klan. And it will be necessary for both of you to leave the meeting once it gets started."

Father O'Brien nodded in agreement. "We'll put a notice in the bulletin for next week, and we can announce it from the pulpit tomorrow." He looked at Father Stevens and said, "Naturally, we won't be able to disclose the purpose of the meeting."

"Then," said Matt, "suggest to your fellow ministers at your next breakfast that certain passages of scripture should be used on certain Sundays for sermons on common themes. For example, I think if each church had a sermon on the Good Samaritan on the same Sunday, it might do some good among neighbors here in town."

"That might work," exclaimed Father Stevens. "You've been giving this some thought, Matt."

"What else have you got planned?" queried Father O'Brien. "Matt, I must warn you against fighting with these men. The church cannot be a party to violence. It would be sinful to physically attack Klansmen in order to bring an end to their evil ways. Unless we are forced to defend ourselves from an assault, we must not injure others who are our brothers in Christ."

Matt didn't reply. After a moment, he continued. "I don't have any concrete plans yet. I do know that we need to get organized if we are going to stand up to them. There is strength in numbers, if only to get the politicians on our side."

Matt stood up and put on his suit coat as he faced the two men. "I promise that I will not take any violent action against these so-called pillars of virtue, unless it is to defend myself. And I won't allow any members of our congregation to commit such an action. But we've got to find a way to stop this group before they take over the whole town. There's no telling what could happen if this movement takes control of the legal system."

Father O'Brien stood and placed his hands on Matt's shoulders. "Very well, Matt. I trust you to do the right thing."

Father Stevens spoke as he exhaled smoke from his cigarette. "Matt, I agree with you that this madness can consume a whole town. The Indianapolis paper had an article about a near riot in Kokomo recently." He walked over to his desk and rummaged down through his stacks of paper. He turned and brought over a clipping he gave to Matt. "Someone started a rumor in Kokomo that His Holiness the Pope was on the train from Chicago. Pope Pius was supposed to be coming to Kokomo to take control of the city. People gathered at the train station and threw bricks and rocks as the train arrived, in an attempt to thwart the purported plan. Can you scarcely believe that people would put any stock into such a wild rumor? Bishop LeFranz has since issued a warning throughout the diocese denouncing rumors concerning actions by Catholics against local governments."

Matt stared at the other two men in disbelief. Then he took the clipping and read it before returning it to Father Stevens. "That's unbelievable, and yet I find it very interesting. If you come across any other articles that concern the Klan, would you save them for me?"

"Certainly," said Father Stevens. "But what do you hope to learn from them?"

"I don't know, but we can use all the information we can get on the Klan. The army would call it intelligence, but I'm just looking for news which can help us to understand them."

"With God's help, surely we can defeat this evil," stated Father Stevens.

"Sure we can," replied Matt. "But I don't really see the Klan as some unworldly evil force. This is a group of men who are trying to get ahead in this world. They're trying to eliminate the competition to improve their chances at success. It also helps to blame someone else for their troubles. It's been normal behavior for mankind since at least biblical times."

Father O'Brien furrowed his brow, glanced at Father Stevens and then said, "What are you thinking?"

Matt blushed, embarrassed. "I'm sorry, I was speaking about my own uneducated view regarding our Lord's death. I shouldn't have brought it up with men who are far more learned on the subject."

"I'd like to hear more about this view," said Father Stevens as he extinguished the remains of his cigarette. "We have great respect for your opinions."

Matt looked at Father O'Brien, who nodded his agreement. Matt drew a deep breath and exhaled. The mournful sound of a train whistle could be heard as it signaled its approach to a grade crossing somewhere in town.

"It's just that I've come to believe men are very selfish and always have been," stammered Matt. "In the first three gospels, Christ comes to Jerusalem and throws the thieves out of the temple. Those people worked for the priests and temple officials who profited from the money exchange and the purchase of sacrificial birds and animals. Therefore, Jesus in a very public display cut off a source of revenue for the Jewish religious officials. The gospels state it was then that the decision was made to have Jesus killed."

Father O'Brien turned and paced back across the room with his head down in thought. He turned towards Matt. "I never thought of it in just that way. Certainly, theologians consider the Jewish leaders of Jerusalem responsible for our Lord's death. The primary reason for their hatred was their fear of losing power and position to Christ. But their loss of income would also be of major importance to those leaders."

"I recall one of my professors lecturing us on the greed of the temple officials in charging exorbitant fees for sacrifices and for the exchange of money for Hebrew coins to use as proper offerings," explained Father Stevens. "It was this greed that Christ railed against when he cleansed the temple."

Matt continued. "I know that it was more complicated than I've just made it out to be. John's gospel says it was a more complex decision than one based just on economics. Yet even in John's gospel, the high priest implies Christ's death will benefit the status that he and others enjoyed in Jerusalem. My theory is that selfish men killed our Lord in order to preserve their privileged positions. And I think most of us would have done the same thing, if we were in that same situation. People have a tendency to make decisions based on their own selfish interests.

"The Klan we confront today is just another example of base human nature at its worst. They just want to keep more of the economic pie for themselves. The fewer people around with whom to share it, the more pie they get to eat.

"We need to find a way to make their efforts futile. Let me know if either of you gentlemen conceives of a way to stop this group. You're both intelligent and well educated, but I fear that it's going to take something underhanded to rid us of the Klan."

The two priests nodded as Matt prepared to leave. He shook the hand of each man and then thanked them for their guidance and their hospitality. "I'll see one of you at Mass tomorrow and both of you for Mass on Christmas." He strode into the hallway with Father Stevens, who retrieved Matt's coat and hat from the closet.

"Which service will your family attend on Christmas day?" asked Father Stevens as he helped Matt into his gray overcoat.

"We'll be at the late Mass," replied Matt. "I give myself a small present on Christ's birthday. I sleep in until the kids get me up."

Matt wrapped a blue scarf around his neck, put on his gray fedora, and headed out into the snow and wind for a brisk walk home.

CHAPTER 9

Christmas 1922
Donegal, Indiana

Annie Conner finished changing from her red wool dress she had worn to Christmas Mass into a comfortable frock and sweater. Now she was ready to prepare the turkey dinner feast that was a tradition in her family from the time she had been a small girl. She took a moment to study her precious baby daughter, Laura, as she slept in the crib positioned near Annie's side of the bed. She hoped Laura would nap a little while longer to allow her to get a start on the afternoon meal.

As Annie descended the stairs, she focused on the sounds of her older children playing with their Christmas presents in the living room. Annie peeked into the room from the doorway. Katy was quietly singing a nursery rhyme to herself as she combed the hair of a doll, a gift from her Aunt Maureen. Brian played with a wooden toy train Matt and Annie had purchased months ago from the Sears, Roebuck catalogue. He kept up a one-sided conversation with his father about the speed at which trains traveled along the countryside.

Matt gave him only halfhearted attention as he studied a newspaper he had received from Father Stevens after Mass today. Annie observed that her husband had been in a quiet, black mood for days.

He'd barely enjoyed Christmas with the family, an event that normally brought him great joy and contentment. Annie generally let these moods run their course, and Matt would recover from them in two or three days. If he couldn't resolve a problem in a few days' time, Annie knew to confront him. The act of talking over issues between the two of them would relieve Matt of some of his anxiety.

Annie tiptoed into the room and pushed some torn gift-wrappings under the Christmas tree with her shoe. She knelt down beside Katy and admired her new doll. "What a beautiful little doll Aunt Maureen gave you. Have you given her a name?"

"No, not yet," said Katy. "I just call her Dolly."

"That's a pretty name," said her mother. "Be careful not to comb her hair too much, or it may fall out."

Katy continued to focus on her toy but nodded her head in acknowledgement of her mother's warning. "Mommy, will you help me make Dolly a new dress?"

"Yes, dear, we'll make something later this week. But right now I need to start getting dinner ready."

Annie stood and made her way over behind the chair where her husband sat contemplating the newspaper. She leaned over and stroked the back of his neck with her index finger. She watched the hairs on his neck stand up, and his breathing slowed noticeably. "What did Father Stevens want you to read, dear?"

Matt grunted. "Nothing really. I asked him to save me any articles he found on a certain subject."

"Would that subject have anything to do with your mood lately?"

Matt folded the paper and turned his head to look at his wife. "What are you talking about, Anne? Can't I enjoy a quiet day off with my family?"

Annie smiled, as she knew she had gotten her husband's attention. She looked down on their son, who was still busy with his train. "Why don't we talk in the kitchen, where you can help me prepare dinner?"

Matt dutifully stood and followed his wife past the opened gifts that cluttered the floor and through the hallway to the kitchen.

As Matt brought the turkey in from the back porch, Annie confronted him. "Something has been bothering you for a couple of days. You have been surly and in that black mood that envelops you every time you have a problem to resolve. It's time for you to talk to me about it."

Matt placed the big bird in the sink, washed it, and then put the turkey on the cutting board. As he searched for pinfeathers, he began to unburden himself. "Mr. Schmidt from the hotel came in and paid off his bill on Monday. He said he was canceling his weekly order from us. He's going to use Daly's for his baked goods."

Annie was stunned. The Wabash Hotel was their biggest customer. Jackson Schmidt had told her that Matt's baked goods had increased his business from the day he introduced them at his restaurant. "Did he say why he wanted to switch?"

"No, he was vague and even embarrassed when he came by the bakery. But he implied that he needed to do business with a fellow Christian, but not a Catholic."

Annie stood holding a knife over the vegetables she was cutting for her bread stuffing. "Why would that make a difference after two years of doing business together?"

Matt looked deep into her green eyes. When the reason didn't readily come to her he stated quietly, "It's the Klan. I think I'm being ostracized for helping Jakub Miller."

Annie put down her knife as her mouth opened in surprise. "Jackson Schmidt is a member of the KKK?" she finally asked.

"I don't know," said Matt cautiously. "Sales were really down this week, especially for a holiday. The groceries here in town returned a lot of unsold bread. Yet sales over in Logansport remained good. I think someone locally, for some reason, has targeted our bakery. I never told you, but a Klansman confronted me after their rally at the courthouse. He advised me to pack up and leave. He said people would no longer want to buy 'Pope's bread.' I think the Klan heard I helped out Jakub and his family, and they want to punish me for it."

Annie went back to cutting her vegetables while she considered this information. Matt watched her as he basted the bird with butter.

She tried to think of something positive to say. On several occasions she had provided him with support and solutions not apparent to him. But no good ideas came to her now.

When Annie had finished preparing her stuffing, she filled the turkey and put the remainder into a baking pan. Then she cleaned her hands, came over behind her husband, and put her arms around him. "This place is becoming dangerous for us. Perhaps we should sell the bakery and move elsewhere."

Matt closed his eyes and allowed the warmth of Annie's touch to engulf him. "I've considered that," replied Matt. "But we couldn't get a fair price for the work we've put into the business. A Klansman would probably make a low bid, and no one else would try to top it."

"I can't think of a better idea than moving," reflected Annie. "I don't like the thought of just waiting to see if this nightmare goes away. This menace is getting stronger and bolder with each passing day."

"That's my conclusion as well," answered her husband. He placed his hands on her arms that still held him. "I think you and the children should go for a long visit to your parents in Huntington."

Annie pulled away from Matt, turned him around by his shoulders, and stared at him as she contemplated his intentions. "What will you do?" she finally managed to inquire.

Matt grasped her by her arms. "Honey, the reason I brought you to Donegal was because it was the only true home I ever had. Yes, I knew the town was perfect for my concept for fresh-baked goods, but I also thought that it would provide us with the right environment to raise a family . . . like the one I lost. Maybe I should have listened to you and settled in Huntington close to your family. But I didn't want to be that close to your parents and your sisters. I thought we'd do better out on our own where we'd have a degree of privacy."

Matt stopped. Annie just stared at him, her eyes searching.

"I'm not about to give up all our efforts and run. I've decided to stay and fight for our home. But I can't do it and protect you and the children at the same time. I need to know that the four of you are safe. Then I'll be able to devote my attention to defeating this peril."

Annie looked at her husband for a long moment and then motioned him to help her put the turkey in the hot oven. It was a Chambers automatic, and it would stay at the selected temperature. After she closed its door, she took his hand between hers and asked simply, "How will you stop them?"

Matt shrugged his shoulders and dropped his gaze to the floor. "I don't know yet. I promised Father O'Brien I wouldn't get into a fight, except in self-defense. I won't be a part of any militant action to run these characters out of the county. But I've initiated certain steps, and I'm gathering information that I hope will eventually evolve into a plan to put them out of business. The parish meeting for tomorrow night is my idea."

Annie suppressed a smile. This was the man she knew and loved. Matt would always admit when he didn't have an answer. And he moved cautiously and deliberately when trying to solve a problem.

"Who's in this with you?" she asked simply.

"No one at the moment. When and if I come up with a plan and recruit others, I won't be able to tell you about it."

"Why, don't you trust me?"

Matt looked again into her eyes and smiled. "Annie I trust you more than anyone, but the less you know the better. What I eventually decide to do may be illegal. Things may go badly, and I could be found out and even arrested. If you don't know anything about my plans, then you can't be charged. That's another reason why it would be better if you went away until this is over."

Matt stepped back and moved to the sink to wash his hands. As he stood there, he looked back at her over his shoulder. "If things work out for the best, maybe the ringleaders will get caught doing something criminal. Then I'm hopeful the law will put them in prison and the rest will disband."

Annie was scared, but she didn't want to leave her home and her husband for the safety of her parents' home. Curiously, she felt a strange relief at hearing Matt talk about such foreign ideas. She recognized the skill and talent her husband possessed in his analysis of the situation. They were the same gifts he utilized to plan their life here in

Donegal. This ominous, shapeless threat to their happiness had to be defeated. Matt would oppose it, and she was calmed by that realization. Her husband was really very good at solving problems.

"Will Maureen leave as well?" she inquired.

Matt dried his hands with a towel as he walked over to her. "I haven't asked her yet, but if we don't have a pick-up in sales I can't afford for her to stay. She'll have to return to Chicago sooner than we had planned. Still, I can protect her while she's in town, and she may be able to help me."

An uncomfortable silence hung in the air for several minutes. Matt turned his attention to the potatoes. He peeled them and cut them up before tossing them in a pot of water. Mashed potatoes were a favorite dish that he enjoyed making. Annie snapped the ends of her green beans and dropped handfuls into another pot of cold water. They didn't need to begin cooking for a couple of hours.

Annie fought the jealousy pangs she felt growing in her heart. There was a bond between Maureen and Matt that she didn't feel for her own sisters. As much as she rationalized that Matt loved his sister in a way quite different from the love he had for her, she couldn't help but compare herself to Maureen and feel slightly inadequate. She would probably never understand how that jealousy factored into her decision, but it did.

"I won't leave Donegal without you," she stated simply and calmly. "I can protect the children, and it will look better if we continue to lead a normal family life. If you wish, get me a pistol like the one you carry, and we'll be fine." She reached up and kissed her husband on the lips, glanced at the clock on the wall to ascertain the time she started roasting their turkey, and then walked out of the kitchen to check on her infant daughter.

At that moment Maureen entered the dining room at the Tillys' house to have a light lunch. She would be feasting at her brother's house for dinner and wanted a small meal to ward off her hunger until then. She found Mr. Madison already seated, having a meal appropriate for his size. He was intently reading a recent Zane Grey novel, *The Man of the Forest.* "Good day to you, Mr. Madison, and Merry Christmas, as well."

Randall Madison looked up in surprise, pushed away from the table and stood with napkin in hand. "Merry Christmas to you too, miss, and please call me Randall. I hope you've come to join me for lunch. Our hosts have already finished, and Mrs. Floyd is dining with friends for the holiday."

Maureen was hesitant to join the stranger, but she was curious about him as well. Her curiosity won out over her sense of propriety. She walked over to the sideboard to select some cheese and bread as well as Mrs. Tilly's homemade apple butter. "I'll be happy to join you, but I'm afraid that I'm having only a small lunch. I'll be leaving for my brother's home in a short while for a holiday meal."

"Well, now that sounds like a grand way to spend Christmas," exclaimed Randall. "I attended church with the Tillys this morning, but I'm on my own for the rest of the day."

"It must be difficult to spend holidays without family," empathized Maureen. "What do you do on such occasions?"

"Oh, I've been on my own for quite a while, and I have my ways for passing the time. Before Prohibition, I liked to play cards in the saloons. I never was a big drinker, mind you. And I never gambled for much money, but I enjoyed the social aspects. I hope that doesn't scandalize you, Miss Conner?"

"Hardly, Mr. Madison. I'm an Irish girl who is used to plain talk. What will you do now that the government has outlawed your social activities?"

The gentleman paused for a moment as he chewed a piece of bread. "I've had a chance to visit a private club that continues to provide the atmosphere of bygone days. There must be one in every town that isn't controlled by the anti-saloon league or a strong Baptist church."

Maureen laughed and had to hold her napkin in front of her face. "I don't suppose your private club would be Higgins' Undertakers?" toyed Maureen.

The man hesitated, momentarily at a loss for words. "I see you are familiar with the establishment. For a young woman raised in a convent, you are wise to the ways of the world."

"How did you know about my upbringing?" asked Maureen as she nibbled on some Swiss cheese.

"Mrs. Floyd mentioned it at lunch the other day. She has the scoop on everyone and was kind enough to share some of it with me. She wanted me to feel more comfortable among some of the people I would come in contact with on a daily basis."

"That was very thoughtful of her," replied Maureen sarcastically. "I fear Higgins' will not be open this evening. Perhaps I could call my brother and see if there's enough food for another guest."

Randall blushed and looked uneasy. He raised his hand in such a way as to ward off the idea. "Thank you, but no, miss. This holiday is for families, and I wouldn't feel comfortable intruding in someone's home. Besides, I'm not Catholic, and I might be a bit of an embarrassment."

Maureen frowned at such a concept. "My brother and his wife are very open-minded. Just last month, my brother came to the aid of that poor man who was tarred and feathered here in town. My brother helped the man and his family move to Chicago, where they'll be safe. They were not Catholic, but they were God's children and deserved better treatment than they got from some of the Christians here in town."

Randall stared down at his plate while he cut and ate another piece of ham. Maureen, sensing that she had gone too far, hesitated before she spoke again. "I apologize, Mr. Madison, if I upset you. As I mentioned earlier, I am used to plain talk."

"That's all right, miss, I'm not embarrassed, but you really need to be careful in bragging about your brother. I'm sure he is everything that you say, but such talk could get him in trouble."

Maureen looked blankly at the man as she gauged the import of his last statement. She decided it had not been meant as a threat, but rather as a warning. This man had a gentle streak in him, and she again questioned why such a stranger should come to Donegal. She thought there must be something in his past that had made him into such a lonely wanderer. She wondered what it could be.

"I really think that my family would be very happy to have you join us. They might even get a thrill in seeing me escorted to their house by a tall, dark stranger."

Randall looked up from his plate and took a sip from his coffee cup. "Again, thank you, but I do have plans for this evening. I have a tendency to go to bed late, and I've started taking walks around town in the evening. I made the acquaintance of your police chief and several of his officers. After all, I didn't want to be arrested as a suspicious character roaming the city looking to cause mischief. Well, now it has become part of my routine to visit the station house and swap stories with the men on duty. It is almost as much fun as relaxing in a saloon. There's a nice young policeman, Officer Harris, who even lets me go with him as he makes his rounds before midnight."

"What a curious idea," said Maureen. "Were you ever a policeman, Mr. Madison?"

"No, miss, but I've always been interested in police work. I guess I read a lot of pulp novels about lawmen and the Wild West." He tapped the Zane Grey book that lay open on the table.

"It's become a hobby of mine. Now I really must insist that you call me Randall. I would just be more comfortable if you did."

"Very well, Randall, and you must call me Maureen. Perhaps you will drop by the bakery in the near future. I could introduce you to my brother. I'm sure you would like him almost as much as your police friends."

"I'll be happy to come by and meet your brother. I'll even purchase one of your special desserts. Mrs. Floyd tells me that they are sinfully delicious."

The two sat quietly finishing their meal. Maureen felt they had taken the conversation as far along as was proper. She found Randall to be a very interesting older man. She thought it a pity he wasn't Catholic.

Just after eight o'clock the following evening, Matt along with a group of more than thirty men gathered in the basement of St. Mary's church. It was warm in the assembly hall, as the large room was next to the boiler room. This collection of men, who had come directly from work or after supper, made the atmosphere pungent. Matt realized most men held to the custom of baths only on Saturday evenings. Cigarette and pipe smoke further polluted the stagnant air. The men didn't mind the odors as long as they were protected from the cold winter night.

Father O'Brien asked for silence. He said a short prayer asking for the saints' help in finding a solution to their grievous problem. He then led the men in a recitation of the Lord's Prayer. There was a noticeable increase in volume at the last phrase, "deliver us from evil."

Then Father O'Brien addressed the men with Father Stevens at his side. "Gentlemen, thank you all for coming out tonight. It's cold, and I know you have families and perhaps holiday visitors who require your presence. You know that we have a grave issue confronting us, or you wouldn't be here. Father Stevens and I will do anything in our power, and in line with our office, to lessen the hostility and ill will that currently exists between the Ku Klux Klan and our church. We pray daily for a solution to the suspicion and mistrust that has evolved within our community in just the last year. We are hopeful that among you, the leaders of our parish, an effort or a plan can be developed that will halt this wicked, poisonous movement that pits neighbor against neighbor.

"However, we will not condone violence, and I must tell you that any assault on members of that organization will be viewed as a mortal sin. We must abide by the commandments and show love to our neighbors and also our enemies.

"But the commandments don't say anything concerning self-defense. As Catholics, we are allowed to take positive steps to defend ourselves from physical and psychological attacks. We have the right and the duty to stand up to these villains and force them to recognize our lawful title to our homes and our businesses.

"Recently, Matt Conner brought to my attention that these

Klansmen are not some evil force, but merely men gone astray. I understand that they tout the Bible as their book of instruction, but they have not read it very closely."

There was general laughter from the parishioners, and Father O'Brien had to pause to let the men quiet down.

"We'll have to find a way to instruct them as to its clear message that God alone is the judge of mankind, and He has vested that responsibility in His Son, our Savior. No man, or group of men, has the right to judge their fellow neighbors as worthy of salvation. Plus, in this country, all men are created equal. The law doesn't allow for any group of vigilantes to decide who can live here and have a chance to earn a living to provide for their loved ones."

Matt heard a verbal affirmation from many of the men.

"Matt Conner has asked that we bring you here tonight to consider what can be done about the Ku Klux Klan. He has requested Father John and I leave in order that you may speak freely among yourselves. May the Holy Ghost be with you in your deliberations. And be careful as you head home tonight. Matt, please lock up when you leave. Good night to you all."

Most of the men present called out their salutations to the priests as they left. Matt then felt the group turn their focus on him as he held his position at the front of the room.

He looked out at the men assembled and recognized them all as fellow parishioners. Some he was friendly with, while others were mere acquaintances. He looked down at his shoes and began to speak with some awkwardness.

"I don't claim to be a leader of this church, and nobody should interpret my standing here before you as an indication that I presume to become such a leader. But my business is suffering, and I believe the Klan is behind an effort to drive me out of town. Some of you may be experiencing similar threats."

There were nods of agreement, and a few men voiced their suspicions.

"I've lost a couple of roofing jobs recently, and there was no good reason for why the customers cancelled," called out Chris Worley.

Michael Kincaid, a conductor for the Wabash Railroad, spoke up in his deep authoritative voice. "I've got two crewmen who have worked for me for years, but now they've requested different assignments. The only explanation I get from the trainmaster is that they don't want to work for a Catholic."

Matt let the complaints run their course. As the noise level died down, he peered into the eyes of the men who looked towards him. Eventually there was silence in the stuffy room.

"I want to fight against these thugs. I believe that as a group we can defeat these so-called Knights for Christianity and get them to disband here in Donegal. I don't think we can stop them all over the state, but I hope we can shut them down here."

Rip Riley took a pipe out of his mouth and cleared his throat to get Matt's attention. "Some of us here have either been threatened or know someone who has been bullied by these hooded rascals. What's your plan, Matt? We'll help you beat these knights of the devil."

Other voices raised a chorus of support for the stocky carpenter. Matt could see only a few silent faces among those present. Clearly his fellow parishioners who came here tonight were prepared for action. Matt waited until the men quieted down again.

"I don't have a plan," admitted Matt. He let the silence permeate for a moment. "I promised Father O'Brien there would be no physical attacks upon these people, and that goes for every man who joins me. We can protect ourselves from attacks like the kind they sprang on Jakub Miller last month, but we can't do anything to provoke a fight."

Matt sensed many of those present admired him for the aid he had rendered to the immigrant tailor. No one spoke for several moments.

"Well, what's the point of bringing us all here if there's no plan?" asked Liam McNamara.

"We need to develop a plan and identify the men who will carry it out." Matt stated this idea flatly. But then he raised his voice, and his eyes brightened. "If we all give it some thought, someone will come up with a solid strategy, and someone else will think of the means to carry it out. We've got to find a way to threaten these Kluxers in the same way they're threatening us. I don't mean to abduct any of them, but we need to scare them into dropping their aggressive and militant behavior."

"What about the law, Matt?" called out Auggie Romano from one side of the room. "Why not get the police to arrest their leadership and scare the rest of them, too?"

"Yeah, let's do it," cried others, and then even more of the men began to offer comments.

Matt raised his hands and held them palms forward as a call for silence. "I've talked with Chief Johnson, and he can't arrest anyone unless he has evidence that they committed a crime. No one knows who tarred and feathered Mr. Miller. No one even knows if it was the Klan, just because it was written on a sign attached to the hay cart where they left him." Matt felt exasperated as he looked out at the men.

"So we need to trap them in the act of doing something illegal and hold them for the police." John Davis, a retired railway agent, stated this very evenly.

Matt looked at the old man and merely nodded his agreement. "Maybe we just need to discredit their actions and bring public rebuke down on them," added Matt.

John stared back and breathed deeply. "It's going to take one helluva plan to stop them. Matt, you seem the most likely candidate to direct our efforts. What do we need to do to help get things rolling?"

Matt heard several men voice their approval, so he finally decided to take responsibility for their combined efforts. "First of all, we need funds. I propose we each contribute five dollars to a kitty."

There were several moans and some grumbling, but Matt pushed forward. "Let's let Rip hold all the funds, but John Davis will get a list of everyone who contributes. He'll keep Rip honest."

The men shouted out good-natured protests about Rip's honesty.

"Anyone who has an idea should bring it to me either at the bakery or at my home. Once I believe we've got a workable plan, I'll contact those of you who can help carry it out."

James Collins, a successful lawyer in the county, raised his hand

and got Matt's attention. "Matt, it would be wise if you kept the overall plan secret. There would be less chance of being discovered by the Klan if nobody else knew exactly what we were going to do. Maybe different men could have separate duties, and no one would be asked to do something criminal. I would be most distressed if I were forced into representing some of you before the courts."

A mischievous smile played over the lawyer's face as he voiced this last comment.

"What if you're found out or something happens to you before things take place?" queried John to Matt.

Several others voiced similar concerns.

Matt scratched his chin. "I'll tell you what we'll do. I'll bring in one other person on the entire plan. None of you will know who that person will be, but he and I will agree on our plan of action. If I'm caught, then that person will step forward to take over. Whomever I choose, I'll trust with my life."

There was more discussion, but after several minutes, no objections to this strategy surfaced. Matt called for silence and then dismissed the group. "If you can raise the money in the next month, please get it to Rip and confirm your payment with John. Rip, you'll put the money into a separate account at the bank and verify all payments with John each Sunday. Don't talk about this meeting to your wives, and don't discuss it with anyone here or elsewhere. See me if you get any ideas or have any other questions. If needed, we'll meet again when things firm up. Lastly, if anyone has good reason to suspect a neighbor or fellow worker of being part of the Klan, I need to hear from you. That kind of information could prove useful to us."

The men gathered their scarves, overcoats, and hats and began to prepare for their trips home.

"One last thing," called out Matt. "As Father O'Brien said, pray to the Holy Ghost for inspiration and guidance. I'm not big on public prayers or wearing my religion on my sleeve, but we need all the help we can get. Good night and watch out for trouble."

As Matt pulled on his overcoat, James Collins stepped forward and poked Matt in the chest with his index finger. "I don't think there's much of a chance of trapping the KKK in some illegal enterprise, but I'm sure you're going to need some help. I'm not much of a soldier, but I have a keen mind for what we might call criminal activity. Stop by my offices any time you'd like to discuss your plans."

Matt took the man's right hand and held it in a firm handshake. "Perhaps you might know of some wealthy clients who would be willing to donate funds to our cause," offered Matt.

The lawyer smiled, and a twinkle came to his eyes. He set his black homburg on his graying head of hair and turned toward the door. Matt watched as the men filed out of the room. He was elated to have so much help in this impending conflict, but he also felt trepidation concerning the responsibilities he had accepted.

CHAPTER 10

January 1923
Donegal, Indiana

Heavy snow had been falling across the Indiana countryside for nearly two days. It was rare to have winter storms of such duration. Usually, snow would fall for six hours or less, producing heights of at most two feet. On this Wednesday morning, the snow depth was more than three feet high in front of Matt Conner's bakery. Davy had shoveled the sidewalk in front of the store twice, but still the snow pelted the street and beyond.

Matt was far from unhappy with the inclement weather. A steady procession of customers had made their way into the bakery and purchased everything Matt and his helpers could produce. As he labored over the ovens baking his third batch of bread for the day, Matt chuckled to himself over developments that would cause him to miss his normal lunch and midday nap. From information imparted to him from certain customers, he had learned that the other two bakeries in town had exhausted their supplies on Monday. They had not been able to replenish their inventories of flour and other ingredients because of the storm. Train service had been suspended early Tuesday, and the tracks were not expected to be open until later today. Until then, Matt had the only source of bread and baked goods in town. His inventories had been rather high because his sales had suffered for more than a month. In addition, he always restocked his supplies on Friday, and luck had been with him in this storm's timing.

The bakery was a warm contrast to the weather outside on the street. The aroma of the freshly baked goods brought people through the door just to rest and talk to neighbors. The roads were impassable, so Matt suspended deliveries to the grocery stores, but he had paid three young boys to carry sacks of bread to the stores open here in town.

Customers who had not visited the store in more than a month were stopping in to get their basic provisions in case the storm continued another day. Matt had required those who had not paid their bill for more than thirty days to pay off their debt along with their current purchases. He explained very politely that he could only offer credit to regular customers. He had no quarrel with anyone, and he was happy to serve all who came through the door, but it had to be on a cash basis. Ginny O'Rourke delighted in announcing this policy to former customers that she felt had betrayed them. Matt hoped this development foretold a return of his normal business when and if the Klan no longer had a boycott against Catholics. He no longer harbored any doubts the boycott was real. He had spoken with two other men of St. Mary's parish who had also experienced a downturn in their business. Many good Protestant families were part of this economic ostracism of him and other Catholics. He had learned there was a term for this action. Local citizens were calling it a "whisper campaign."

As the noon hour approached, Maureen came into the kitchen area and stopped in the small bathroom just long enough to check her hair and lip rouge. Then she approached Matt with her face flushed and excited. "My friend Mr. Madison, whom I was telling you about, has stopped in again. Take off your apron and come out and greet him. I've told him all about you and Annie. He'd like to meet you."

Matt gave his sister a condescending look and then began to untie his apron strings. He didn't feel comfortable meeting this man in front of his sister. He washed the dough from his hands and then followed Maureen out front into the store area.

Matt noted five customers waiting for Mrs. O'Rourke. That was high even for lunch hour. Maureen was talking to a gentleman dressed in a heavy winter jacket unbuttoned to display his overalls. He held a gray kangol cap in his left hand. Matt recalled Maureen had mentioned her fellow boarder was a mechanic who was working temporarily at Sutton's garage. Matt had his truck and automobile serviced by Jeremiah Sutton. This man was taller than Matt and older, as well. He had dark hair and deep creases around his eyes that told of a life spent out in the sun. Otherwise, there was nothing remarkable about him, and Matt was amused by Maureen's lively interest in him.

Matt approached and held out his hand as he caught the man's attention and peered into the stranger's eyes. "Hello, I'm Maureen's brother, Matt Conner."

"A pleasure to meet you, sir. I'm Randall Madison, and I've dropped by to see if you have any bread left for me to take to work. A few of us have come to enjoy having it with our lunch. There's little to do but eat while the storm continues."

The men shook hands, each testing the other's grip. "I'm glad to make your acquaintance, Mr. Madison. I'm sorry I wasn't here to greet you on your previous visits. We're having a very busy day, but we have some fresh bread available now, and I'll have more available at two o'clock, if more is needed."

"The one loaf will be fine for today, but you must call me Randall. You may need to visit our garage at some point in time, and it would be awkward for you to refer to me by my surname."

"Very well, Randall. I understand you have teamed up with Maureen for games of canasta against the Tillys."

"We have indeed, sir." Randall winked at Maureen and turned back toward Matt. "Your sister is much better than I am at cards, but I try to play a decent hand. Unfortunately, the Tillys are much better players than both of us. Do you play cards, sir?"

"No, I'm afraid I don't have much time for cards these days. I play poker with friends every so often on a Saturday evening, but my family keeps me pretty busy when I'm not at work."

"I completely understand," said Randall. "One of the joys of bachelorhood is having a few hours to yourself each day. Although I'm sure the happiness found with a good woman and your own children must be quite satisfying." Again Randall turned toward Maureen and smiled at her. She smiled back with a look of embarrassment.

Matt was annoyed by this turn in the conversation. Randall seemed to be patronizing him, and he didn't like it. He tried to cover his irritation by leading Randall Madison over to the display cases to make his purchase. Maureen excused herself to help Mrs. O'Rourke with some of the other customers.

"I've heard that you hope to start a business here in Donegal," continued Matt.

"Yes, I hope to offer well pumps to farmers in this area in the near future. I've got an engine supplier in Indianapolis, and I've talked to quite a few farmers about the concept when I can stop them at the garage. Some of these men have rigged their Tin Lizzies to their wells and pump their water with their autos. Times are hard right now, and very few are able to pay my price. But I hope to sign up one or two families in the spring."

"It sounds like a good idea," offered Matt. "As economical as Mr. Henry Ford's Model T has proven to be, people can't expect to keep one sitting around the barn just to provide them with water. You know, I've always made my money by being one step ahead of everyone else. I wish you good fortune in bringing your product to market."

"Thanks," said Randall. "Time will tell how successful I am. But in the meantime, I'm enjoying the fine hospitality I've been shown here." Matt felt this last statement was said for the benefit of Maureen, who had walked over to join the two men.

"Oh, everyone enjoys having you here, Randall," replied Maureen. "Mrs. Floyd may even become a Methodist in order to share your company on Sunday mornings."

Randall blushed, smiled wanly at this idea, and shrugged his shoulders. He produced two buffalo nickels from his pocket and gave them to Matt, who had finished wrapping the bread in white paper and was tying it up with string.

"It has been a pleasure to meet you," offered Matt as he took the money and gave the tall man his package. "Please stop in again, and I'll look for you the next time I need my auto serviced."

"Please do so," replied Randall as he turned toward the door and put on his hat, letting the side flaps settle over his ears. He buttoned his coat while holding the bread under his arm and then waved a goodbye to Maureen. On his way out, he held the door for a customer who arrived covered in a fresh dusting of snow.

Maureen and Matt watched him head up the street through the swirling winds and gathering snowdrifts. Maureen turned and asked expectantly, "What do you think of him? He's been rather nice to me."

Matt immediately became alarmed at his sister's tone of voice. He knew he needed to quell any amorous expectations she may harbor without upsetting her or ruining her friendship with the man.

Matt took his sister out of the range of hearing of others. "I like Randall," he offered. "He seems like a very decent sort of man. I think you could trust him to look out for you in an emergency, such as if the Tilly house were to catch fire in the middle of the night. But he's not a Catholic, nor does he seem to be the kind of man to settle down and raise a family. Don't give your heart away to this Protestant stranger passing through town."

Maureen froze and turned away from her brother. When she turned back, her anger showed. "I didn't introduce you to the man as my beau. He's just a friend, and I have few enough of those here other than the ladies at church."

Matt felt the sting of her rebuke as if he had been slapped. He gently placed his strong hands on his sister's arms. "I know it has been a sacrifice for you to leave Chicago. You have been extraordinary, but now this Klan business threatens to destroy all your efforts along with my own. I wish you'd return to Chicago. I can hardly afford to pay you anymore. Besides, I can make most of your sweet concoctions now. You'd be better off among your friends and away from the troubles of this small town."

Maureen stared up at her older brother and slowly let a smile return to her features. She blinked back gathering tears. "Someone needs to look after you, brother, when Annie isn't around. I know that you will have to deal with these hooligans, and I'm not leaving here until things are settled. Besides, I promised I'd give you a year to learn the various seasonal items we can offer here, and the year doesn't expire until this summer.

"Afterward, I'll be more than happy to return home and live with John and his sour-faced wife. I may even find a husband among all the eligible young men in Chicago. Until then, I'm here to help you, and you had best get use to the idea."

Matt wanted to cry and hug his sister, but he merely nodded his head and released her. He appreciated her love and loyalty, but he was embarrassed to show it. He walked back into the kitchen to check with Davy on the current batch of bread. His sister was more stubborn than their brother John was. Matt judged Maureen would be safe from harm. Perhaps she could be of some small help in his struggle to wreck the Klan.

Later, after the bakery had emptied of both customers and goods, Maureen had a chance to reflect on the busy day with Mrs. O'Rourke. At the right moment, Ginny brought up the topic that had been on her mind most of the morning.

"And what did Matt think of that nice Mr. Madison when they finally met today?"

Maureen's mouth turned downward as she pursed her lips. "Mr. Grumpy wasn't much impressed with him. He's not one to warm up to people whom he hasn't known all his life. He's suspicious of newcomers, especially if they're Protestant."

Mrs. O'Rourke came closer and laid her hand on Maureen's. "I don't think that's necessarily so," replied the older woman. "I've seen Matt charm many a new customer with his knowledge of politics, crops, and the economy. I've heard one or two lawyers tell him that he should run for a seat on the county commission."

Mrs. O'Rourke raised her head and smiled at Maureen. She lowered her voice as she added, "But most sons of Ireland are a little tight-lipped when it comes to their sisters and daughters. No man is ever good enough, but he'd better be Irish or at least a good Catholic."

Maureen turned and embraced her friend. As they parted, Maureen took the woman's hands and patted them between her own. "You are my good and wise friend. You're right, but you know a lady likes to have a conversation with someone besides another woman now and then."

Mrs. O'Rourke nodded in acknowledgement. She had come to think of Maureen as a daughter and relished their shared moments. "Mr. Madison is very good looking and so polite."

Maureen glanced knowingly at her confidante, but her tone of voice was wistful. "He's too old, and he's not Catholic. I don't know what it is, but I just feel comfortable with him. He strikes me as the type of man a woman could count on to protect her and their family. I think he would be a good provider."

Just then the bell over the door rang, and a woman bundled up against the storm entered the shop in search of a loaf to purchase.

Lucas Crawford had hoped the change in the monthly meeting place to the fellowship hall of the Independent Christian Church north of town would provide added legitimacy to his klavern. The idea and offer to use the large room had come from Deacon Bill Marshall, who had become an energetic new leader of the group. The location was Spartan, with white walls and pine benches and stools. Lucas felt the setting would bring a touch of moral righteousness to their cause. Yet he found himself going over tonight's agenda during the opening prayer. Deacon Marshall was gifted at presenting spontaneous prayers to God that reflected the hopes and concerns of the group, but Lucas could never seem to concentrate on the message of such prayers. To Lucas, God had always been a distant force stimulating fear in humans more than love and worship. The idea of having a personal conversation with the Father was something he was not prepared to do.

At last Deacon Marshall finished and turned the meeting over to John Holmes. Lucas thought John relished his role as chairman of the monthly gatherings. Most likely John was also pleased at the change in venue, as his barn was too small to comfortably hold the gatherings that had grown to more than sixty men. John was going over notes from last month in order to review issues and actions taken.

"In regard to the matter of Mr. John Hood and his illegal brewing site, what action has taken place?"

Lucas knew Tom Stewart was not present. He had a severe cold, and his doctor feared it could develop into pneumonia if he ventured out into the frigid weather that had settled upon the countryside. A few of those present knew his breathing was getting worse as his lungs deteriorated. In his place, Clyde Harrow stood to present the actions of their group.

"A warning was given to Mr. Hood to shut down his operation. He ignored it and was spotted making beer the last week of the old year. Apparently he was planning to ring in the new one with some homemade suds."

The remark brought a general chuckle from the crowd present.

Clyde turned and acknowledged the joke to various friends who surrounded him. "Anyway, we notified the sheriff of the situation, but he didn't do nothing. So as some of you already know, we staged a knight ride last weekend. Hood and his family were isolated in their farmhouse while we moved to the shed and busted up the equipment. We then set fire to the shed and a cross was planted by the front gate."

"I heard Hood tried to stop you with a shotgun," commented one of the other Klan members.

Clyde turned in the direction of the voice. "He came out onto his front porch with his gun, but we warned him that we had rifles trained on him, and he froze. Tom went right up to him and took away his gun. After that, the man just stood there and watched while we went to work."

Lucas noted in the silence following this report that the men present appeared impressed by the efficiency displayed in the knight ride. He'd be sure to compliment Tom on the planning and execution of this action. A demonstration of the Klan's organization and power was a good way to recruit new members. Lucas hoped it would embolden some of the more timid members to join tomorrow's mission.

The meeting moved on to other items. A widow and mother of two who lived in town was alleged to have allowed a gentleman to spend the night in her home. She would be warned by letter against immoral activity.

Several Catholic tradesmen were identified and marked to be boycotted. There were other Protestant craftsmen who deserved the business more than the papists. If the word were privately spread within the community to favor certain carpenters or plumbers over others, then perhaps those ostracized would leave the county.

Leon Grainger raised his hand as he stood next to a window that was dark except for the frost formed in the corners. John Holmes, who now used an old wooden hammer as a gavel, pointed it in Leon's direction. Leon straightened his posture and cleared his throat. "What's going on with the Irishman who runs the bakery? He's doing a pretty good business this week."

Lucas looked at Clyde Harrow, who shrugged his shoulders. Lucas turned back to Leon and then spoke loudly enough for all to hear. "We put out the word to shun Mr. Conner and his bakery, but some people prefer his bread over what they can get elsewhere in town. I know Tom Stewart has planned an action against this papist, but it has a lower priority than tomorrow's demonstration at Higgins' establishment."

Lucas paused and observed that his words were favorably received by the gathering. Lucas knew from his years in sales that a positive statement was the best way to close any conversation. He looked at Leon and then turned toward Clyde Harrow. "Clyde, make a note of the fact that Mr. Grainger would like to participate in any upcoming knight ride against this Conner fellow. It's conceivable that the mick may need to sell his bakery in the near future. Anyone looking to go into the business at a good price ought to scrape up some money."

The men were silent as they considered this, but slowly their faces registered an understanding of the message. Many turned and whispered to those seated around them.

The rest of the night's business was conducted fairly quickly. There were some questions and a discussion regarding the planned cross burning at Higgins' Undertakers, but even this matter was disposed of in a timely fashion. The men were anxious to get safely home on a cold night. However, Lucas had left one new item for the end of the meeting. As John Holmes prepared to close with prayer, Lucas stood and came over behind Bill Marshall. He waited until he had everyone's attention, and then he spoke. "Tonight we will ask each of you to contribute two bits or more to the plate on your way out. We'll ask the same thing of you at our next meeting. Then on the last Sunday in February, we'll have our first church visitation here at Independent Christian. Now Bill doesn't know about this yet, but the state officers in Indianapolis recommend it as an effective means of demonstrating our Christian moral values. The entire klavern will be expected to meet here on that morning, and we'll deliver our contribution to the preacher in front of the congregation."

Dennis Schmidt jumped to his feet, frowning. "How much money do we have to raise?" he called out.

"Not much," replied Lucas. "We'll tap the klavern treasury for enough to make a decent contribution. And we'll continue the practice at other churches in the area until each of your congregations has been paid a visit. We want people to know and respect our fraternity. And we want you to feel proud of your involvement in our noble cause.

"So contribute what you can tonight, and we'll meet again tomorrow at the rendezvous site at midnight. Now, Mr. Holmes, please close us with a prayer."

The group stood up, scraping the numerous bench and stool legs on the waxed pine floors as they did so. They took off their caps and bowed their heads. Then John Holmes began to pray for the success of these men and their efforts in the days ahead.

On Saturday evening, Matt Conner climbed out of his bath and dried off before putting on fresh underwear and his heavy cotton robe.

Annie had been very affectionate this evening. She had given him unmistakable signals of her intentions, and Matt intended to pursue her with overtures of his own. So Matt stropped his straight razor and stirred some shaving soap in his large cup before brushing it onto his beard. Normally he'd wait until morning and shave before church. But tonight, he wanted things to be perfect for his bedroom rendezvous with Annie.

Matt was embarrassed by frank talk about sex, but Annie had learned to leave him subtle hints. He had to admit he was attracted to her bold manner of confronting issues such as their continued sexual relations. Annie was a thoroughly modern woman. She had not demonstrated for the vote when the suffragettes had been so public a few years ago, but she was not afraid to speak up about things that were of concern to her. Although her high school education was more advanced than Matt's, she never put him down about it. Instead, she shrewdly used it to help him advance his knowledge of the world. Matt knew it and was grateful. He was a lucky man to have such a wonderful partner to share life with.

The razor's edge was sharp, and with practiced motions he quickly removed the stubble that darkened his features. During the week, Matt shaved before bed to save time before his early start at work. By mid-afternoon he had a deep shadow of whiskers.

He splashed cold water on his face to remove the remainder of the soap and to quell the razor's irritation. Lastly, he brushed his teeth with the paste his dentist had recommended. Like most people he knew, Matt had only recently begun to take care of his teeth. He hoped to avoid the need for false teeth as long as possible.

Upon entering the bedroom, he found Annie in a chair reading a newspaper next to the radiator. Laura slept soundly in her crib near Annie's side of their bed. Matt removed his robe and placed it at the end of the bed. He crawled under the blankets and quilt to begin warming up the sheets.

Annie looked up, and Matt caught a knowing glance. She looked over to the baby's crib and then whispered, "Father John brought these papers for you today. Most are from Indianapolis, but one is from Chicago. He's put an X by the stories he wants you to read. They're all about the Klan."

Matt squinted and ran his hand through his hair. In a low tone he inquired, "There looks to be about a half dozen papers you've got in the pile. Are there any articles that caught your interest?"

"No," Annie replied. "I'm amazed that these silly robed men can generate so much news. It appears the entire country is taking them as seriously as they do themselves. Is there anything new on them downtown?"

"Nothing has reached my ears recently." Matt sighed. "We've had our best week in more than a month, but I'm sure that it would be too much to hope for it to continue without another blizzard."

Annie looked across the bedroom from her chair to her husband's covered form. "Did the bakery make money this week?"

"Yes," he said as his features relaxed into a tired smile. "I'm not sure how much longer I can make the payroll, but at least for this week and next we'll be in the black. I made the loan payment to the bank from the week's receipts."

"Did you get Maureen to take her wages?"

Matt rolled his eyes before he answered. "It was a battle, but she finally agreed to take half of it. She says she doesn't need it, and I should save it for Mrs. O'Rourke and Davy. I convinced her our savings are adequate and that I had to pay her enough to meet her expenses. She offered to move in with Katy if it would help save cash, but I think we're all better off with her living at the Tilly place."

Across the room Annie slowly nodded her head.

Matt crossed his arms and thought for a moment as he gazed at the ceiling. Then he focused on his wife as he stated, "I will have to let go Mrs. O'Rourke in another month if business drops off any more. God help me, but I won't have any other choice. I need Davy more than I do either of the two women."

Being able to provide for his family and for those he worked with gave Matt a great deal of satisfaction. Yet at the same time it was a tremendous burden he shouldered alone. Matt never trusted in luck or divine providence. He always felt new opportunities would be garnered only through his own efforts, and all of his energies were devoted to seeking them out.

Annie lowered her head and looked again at the newspaper in her lap before she spoke quietly. "Before you let Mrs. O'Rourke go, you need to cut my allowance in half as well. We can make do on less money here at home. You need her at the bakery as much as she needs the job."

Matt stared at his wife and pulled himself out of his depression. "You know we're going to beat these knights with their fiery crosses, if for no other reason than because they are in the wrong."

Annie shook her head in frustration. "How can anyone justify trying to ruin decent people economically, and then they have the gall to attend church on Sunday?"

Matt had considered his wife's position many times himself. "They don't wear their hoods to church, but they do feel it's their ancestral heritage to claim superior rights over those of us whose parents were born in foreign lands. It really is all about money. Most of them don't have enough to pay their bills, so they want our money to make up for their shortfall.

"What's in those newspapers? Has President Harding become a Klansman, yet?"

"No, but there is an article that mentions he has proposed a law requiring the registration of all aliens entering the country. Klansmen in Georgia have come out in public support of the idea."

Matt shook his head. "I had heard about that story. If we elect many more Klansmen to Congress we'll end up with laws that divide the country into two classes. Only one part of society will maintain the rights that are supposedly guaranteed by the Constitution. Anything else catch your pretty eye?" he inquired.

Annie frowned as she dropped one paper and rummaged around for another from the stack at her feet. "There was this article from Indianapolis about how the Klan won a court victory over someone who wanted their membership made public. It was apparently a big case down in the capital city, but a judge ruled that the Klan was a private fraternity and did not have to divulge its roster for public scrutiny. So I guess they have power in the courts as well as in the legislature."

Matt didn't react to her facetious remark. Instead he pursed his lips. "I find it interesting that these noble fellows were willing to pay a lawyer to go to court to protect their privacy. If they have so much power, why do they feel the need for complete secrecy about their ranks?"

Annie got up from her chair and brought the paper over to her husband. He scanned the article while she stood next to him. Then he looked up and gazed at her face for a few moments.

"The bed has warmed up a bit," he whispered. "Why don't you abandon your reading for this evening and give me your undivided attention."

Annie smiled at her husband. She walked over to her side of the bed and checked on Laura as she began to unbutton her robe. "Perhaps they have an Achilles heel you can attack."

Matt set down the paper and then focused on his wife as she slid into bed. He moved closer to take her into his arms. "What does that expression mean?"

Annie smiled as she moved her fingers under her husband's nightshirt. "Achilles was an indestructible warrior in Greek mythology. As an infant he was bathed in a river that gave him protection from bodily harm. But the place on his heel where he was held during his dunking in the river remained unprotected. It was the one part of his body vulnerable to attack. Now can we set aside the Klan for a few hours?"

Matt undid the strings of Annie's nightgown as she kissed him on the neck. "We need to find such a heel or weakness with this group. We don't need to conquer them throughout the country or even across the state, but if they have a weakness here in Donegal, we need to exploit it and put them out of business."

Annie looked up at her husband whose attention was becoming focused elsewhere. "It's late," she said. "We really should concentrate on more pleasant things."

Matt slid his hand down and along his wife's hip and kissed her passionately on the lips. He then wheeled out of bed to turn off the electric ceiling lamp. Lastly he slipped out of his underwear and crawled back into bed. Annie's delicate smooth fingers found him before he could pull the covers over them again. Soon they would generate enough passion to ward off the cold of the long winter night.

Later that evening, five vehicles made their way from different points across icy roads to a gathering at the Holmes farm. Tom Stewart was still home in bed, fighting his cold. Lucas had decided to lead the knight ride against the Higgins' establishment. Everyone was present and on time. Don Lester had kerosene and torches stored in the back of his truck along with a twelve-foot wooden cross made from a long-dead pine tree.

Lucas gathered the men around him in the subfreezing temperatures for final instructions.

"We go into the parking lot in single file with the first two cars on the left and the next two on the right of the main building. Don pulls his truck up between us, and the riders gather the torches from the rear. As soon as your torch is lit, establish a position near the auto that brought you. The drivers need to stay in their seats with the engines running and the headlamps focused on the front doors. Is everyone clear on our initial positions?"

There was general agreement among the sixteen men present.

Lucas continued with the plan. "I'll lead the group up to the front door with everyone forming two lines behind me. I'll call out to the Higgins boys and any of the patrons enjoying their liquor inside. We'll demand they cease their illegal and immoral actions immediately. If they threaten us or try to start a fight, Leon and Dickey Taggert will cover us with their pistols. Until then, you men keep your weapons hidden inside your robes. I don't want to give anyone cause to start a fight."

Lucas looked over at Don Lester. "Who's riding with you?"

Don pointed to Bill Wolfe, standing next to him.

"Bill, you help get the torches lit and then pour some kerosene on the ground near the road out front. Light it to get the ground softened up for the cross. When we've spoken our peace to the crowd inside, we'll move back past the vehicles and set up the cross and light it up. I'll give the prayer invocation, and then we'll return to the cars and leave. The drivers will stay with their vehicles in case we need to leave quickly. Once we depart, we all return straight to our own homes. I expect we'll be hearing some talk about our action at church services tomorrow. It may even make the newspaper by Monday."

Leon Grainger spoke up in favor of the mission. "We need to talk this up with our neighbors and friends at work. It just isn't right to break the law of the land in front of decent God-fearing folks. We gotta let people know, if the police won't put a stop to these saloons, then righteous men will step forward and force them out of business."

Lucas smiled and patted Leon on the shoulder. It was heartening to see the shy, private farmer take on leadership abilities. Lucas hoped to turn over his duties to men like Tom and Leon soon and return to Indianapolis to a more important position in Mr. Lampton's organization.

"All right, men," cried Lucas. "It's getting cold out here. Let's put on our robes and perform our duty."

Ten minutes later the small procession of vehicles made its way north on Third Street to the outskirts of town and pulled onto the funeral home's property. The large white house had single-story wings on either side of the main section. An expansive gravel parking lot sat in front of the building, and it had been shoveled and packed down into a flat layer of ice. There were a few cars positioned at various spots on the lot, indicating some people were still enjoying the amusements offered at the mortuary early on a Sunday morning.

The arriving automobiles took up positions on either side of the truck with lights shining on the front double doors of the establishment. The knight riders exited their vehicles and proceeded to set fire to their torches and march silently up the front steps onto the wide porch.

Aniston Higgins must have been alerted to the intruders' presence by the flood of light coming from the hallway. He and his brother,

James had thrown open the two doors and barred the way into their facility. Perhaps a half dozen of their patrons stood behind them, trying to comprehend the meaning of this intrusion into their party. The white-robed Klansmen must have appeared surreal in the glow of the torchlights and outlined by the car lamps behind them.

Lucas held his burning torch high with one hand and pointed at the two brothers with the other. "It is a crime against the laws of God and those of this great country to serve beer and liquor to the public. It is even more of a crime to do so on the Lord's Day. The commandment says we must keep holy the Sabbath. You are hereby ordered by the The Invisible Empire, Knights of the Ku Klux Klan, to shut down your operation and return to a legitimate business within this premise. Will you comply with this order and return to the moral ways of God Almighty?"

Lucas knew Aniston Higgins attended the Methodist church in town. He probably considered himself to be a good Christian, and he certainly was on good terms with all the ministers in town. But the economic depression, along with Prohibition, had pushed him into his current situation.

Aniston placed his hands on his hips and spoke with courage in his voice. "You have no right to come onto our property and tell us what to do. The police enforce the laws in this town, and I don't see any badges pinned to your nightgowns.

"Unless you are the law and have a warrant to search the house, I'll ask you all to leave the property and allow me, my brother, and our friends to conclude our business here in private tonight."

Lucas was infuriated at the boldness of the man. To deny the validity of their moral position was intolerable. He knew the only business being conducted here at this late hour involved booze and card games and perhaps carnal activities.

"How dare you deny the sinful actions obvious to everyone here! We are the guardians of the moral authority of this community, and we demand your compliance with the laws established for the good of the public."

James Higgins stepped forward and swung his fist into the hood covering Lucas's face.

Lucas staggered backward from the poorly aimed blow to the side of his face. The two Klansmen behind him caught him and supported him while he recovered his balance. Both of these men then produced revolvers that they aimed toward the younger Higgins brother. The sight of the weapons made the man retreat toward the doorway where Aniston still held his ground. Behind them, men and women shouted and scattered in the direction of the interior of the house.

This attack and affront to his leadership further enraged Lucas. He didn't know what to do, but he perceived he held the advantage by having weapons trained on the two brothers. He needed to act quickly before someone inside found a gun and mounted another challenge to him. He walked along the left side of the porch to the nearest window. Breaking the glass, he thrust his torch through it, into the room inside. Shrill screams from both men and women rang out from inside the house. Aniston Higgins snarled a protest. Lucas then walked back to the doorway and took hold of Leon Grainger's torch. He glowered at the undertaker, walked over to the right side of the porch, and proceeded to smash the torch through the window. At this point, the Higgins brothers retreated inside to attempt to extinguish the fires.

The Klansmen stood in their two lines unsure of what to do next. Lucas gathered his emotions and addressed his men calmly. "Proceed to the cross, fellow knights."

The men turned and spotted Bill Wolfe standing over flames emanating from the ground back behind the headlights of the autos. They fell in step and marched away from the porch to the spot picked for their next demonstration. Two of them lifted the twelve-foot cross from the rear of the truck while three others gathered shovels to dig a small hole to plant their symbol. Lucas kept an eye on the flames through the windows on the front of the house. At first they seemed to intensify, and he could clearly see the shapes of the people fighting them. But then the fires grew faint as the occupants of the house gained control over them and extinguished the blazes before they could spread.

The cross was now erected at the front of the property. It had been doused in kerosene and brought to flaming life in the midst of the robed figures who surrounded it. Lucas raised his arms and shouted toward the heavens. "Our Father, bless our efforts to correct the sinfulness that we see corrupting our society. Grant unto these knights, Your faithful servants, the power to overcome the devil and all of his compatriots who attempt to degrade us and lead us into sinful actions. We ask Your help to sustain us through these troubling times. Give each of us a fair share of the good things on this earth that You have bequeathed to Your true followers and heirs to Your kingdom. All of these things we ask for in the name of Your Son, Jesus . . . our Savior. Amen."

Lucas lowered his arms and bowed his head. There was no noise among his gathered knights except for the sound of the flames licking up and around the wooden cross. After a few moments he began to hear nervous coughs and shoes crushing the snow as the men changed their stances. Finally, Lucas raised his head and beheld the cross. Then he looked at his gathered companions. "The mission is complete. Return to your homes and rest. Tonight we have done the Lord's work. Be proud and spread the word that we will not tolerate sinful activity in this community anymore."

The men raced for their respective vehicles. Torches were doused in the snow and, along with the shovels, were thrown into the bed of the truck. The men hurriedly piled into their cars and sped away from the scene as quickly as they could. Lucas was the last one to take a seat in the back of Leon's sedan. He pulled the door shut and nodded to Leon to drive away. Behind they left a flaming cross standing silently in front of a funeral home.

CHAPTER 11

February 1923
Donegal, Indiana

ON A LATE TUESDAY AFTERNOON, as the winter sun was setting beyond the Wabash River in the southwestern sky, two men entered a door in the middle of a two-story building on Broad Street. The Franklin Building had been constructed in the Italianate style typical of commercial structures found in small towns throughout the Midwest. The first floor of the red brick edifice was divided into four retail stores that housed a barbershop, haberdashery, bicycle dealer, and drugstore. The door used by Billy Harris and Randall Madison opened to a vestibule and stairway that led to a second floor. The men took off their hats and gloves as they climbed the stairs and strolled down the hallway to the right, past an assortment of rented offices, some with doors open. They stopped at an opaque glass and wood door at the end of the hall. Stenciled on the glass were the name "Lucas Crawford" and the perfunctory description "Insurance Agent." They knocked on the wood frame and entered after a muffled response from inside the office.

Lucas was inside finishing a report to Mr. Carpenter on the activity from the prior month. He sat in his shirtsleeves with a Camel cigarette between his lips as he stared at the typewriter on the side of his desk. He had been expecting Billy, who briefed him on the police activity every Tuesday before the deputy started his evening patrol shift.

Lucas recognized the stranger accompanying Billy as one of the mechanics who worked at the Sutton Garage on Railroad Avenue. He was dressed in his dirty overalls, but his hands were clean. The man apparently had put in his day at work and was on his way home. The fact that he should appear in Lucas's office with Billy was not surprising. In recent weeks, more and more of the Klansmen would stop by with friends whom they recruited for membership. Lucas welcomed them all, as each new member who paid his klectoken put money into Lucas's pocket.

Lucas stubbed out his cigarette into a large glass ashtray that contained several other butts. He rose and greeted Billy with a handshake and then welcomed Randall as Billy made introductions. "Have a seat, gentlemen," offered Lucas. "Officer Harris, grab that chair from the other desk and let Mr. Madison have the upholstered one, seeing as how he's our guest."

Randall took a seat in the green leather chair that sat in front of Lucas's desk. Lucas knew all recruits surveyed the office on their initial visit. They took in the faded gray walls and the insurance calendar on the wall next to the door. A pair of windows set into the wall opposite the door looked out onto an alley behind the building and the orange sunset. Lucas sat behind a large yellow oak desk in front of one of the windows, while a similar desk sat in front of the other window. The only other object of interest in the office was a floor safe that stood on the far wall next to the unoccupied desk.

"I didn't know what to expect when Billy suggested I accompany him on a visit to your headquarters. But I sure wouldn't have thought that you kept a regular office."

Lucas chuckled at the easy openness of the man. "I live in Peru, so I need to keep an office in town. Besides, I'm an authorized agent for an insurance company out of Indianapolis. There's nothing mysterious or magical about our organization, Randall. May I call you by your first name?"

"Randall suits me just fine, Mr. Lucas," replied the new recruit.

"Good," answered Lucas. "I would be obliged if you would call me Lucas. We're more comfortable with informal meetings. Isn't that so, Billy?"

Billy Harris smiled and nodded as he looked from Lucas to Randall. "I've told Randall that the Klan is the best thing to come to this town and that we do more good than the police and courts put together. Randall would make a fine addition to our klavern. He's got a real keen interest in the law. He goes with me on my rounds some nights just to keep me company. He doesn't drink or swear, and he's from good colonial stock."

Lucas straightened up in his chair and eyed Randall with added interest. "Is that right? Do you go out in this weather at night just to keep Billy company?"

Randall shrugged and looked out the window behind Lucas before he answered. "There isn't much to do in this town at night. I don't need much sleep, and I prefer a good conversation to reading books and newspapers. Spending time with Officer Harris and the other policemen is a good way to stay up late and stay out of trouble."

Lucas and Billy laughed at the self-deprecating manner in which Randall described himself.

"What brings you to Donegal, Randall?" inquired Lucas.

"I'm hoping to start a well water service for farmers once their business turns better. In the meantime, I'm making connections and learning about the area."

"Good," said Lucas. "Have you made many friends yet, and have you found a church to attend?"

"I've gotten to know some people from my job at Sutton's, and I've been visiting St. Mark's with the Tillys, where I have a room."

"He's sweet on that baker's sister who stays with the Tillys," interjected Billy.

"She's a swell girl, but I'm too old for her," muttered Randall. "Anyway, I think that she's got a rich boyfriend back in Chicago."

"She's a papist," stated Lucas. He purposely said this in a dismissive manner. "We have no use for people affiliated with Rome or any other foreign entity. Besides, I don't think she'll be around for very long."

"What's going to happen to her?" inquired Randall.

Lucas thought he detected sincere concern in the question.

"Nothing," he answered. "It's just that her brother's bakery is going to close up in the near future, and she'll probably return to Chicago."

There were a few moments of silence, and Lucas watched his visitors contemplate what had been said.

"Would you like to join our fraternity, Mr. Madison?" queried Lucas. "I promise you it will be at least as interesting as patrolling deserted streets at night."

Randall looked over at Billy and then moved closer to Mr. Crawford's desk. "Yes, I would like to join, if you'll let me."

Lucas smiled at the man facing him. "We'd be delighted to have you join the Klan, Randall. We are always looking for Protestant men with high morals and integrity. Billy vouches for your character. All we need to do is have you fill out our form and pay the ten-dollar klectoken. Since you don't have a wife, you'll probably want to buy a uniform from our supplier in Indianapolis. And if you don't have all of the money right now, you can pay it over a three-month period."

Lucas had a habit of trying to collect the dues quickly since his commission was a large part of it.

Randall Madison again looked out the window behind Lucas as he contemplated his decision. "Fine," he replied at last. "I can give you a fin now and the rest from my next two paydays."

Lucas looked at Billy and smiled his approval. He opened one of his desk drawers, pulled out a form, and handed it to the new recruit along with a fountain pen from his shirt pocket. "Please fill this out and print your information if you would."

Randall reached into his overalls and produced a worn leather billfold. He gave a five-dollar bill to the resident Kleagle. As he began to fill in the form, Lucas pulled out a ledger book from his desk and recorded the payment, and Randall's name was written next to number 143.

Lucas considered the newcomer to be a welcome addition to his klavern. Randall probably knew a lot about the local police department from palling around with Billy. So Lucas felt safe to question Billy about useful information the patrolman had picked up since last week.

"What's new with the Higgins situation?" began Lucas. "There's been nothing in the newspaper for a couple of weeks."

"The heat's still on the case from what I've heard," replied Billy as he moved forward in his seat. "Chief Johnson is mad as hell they didn't call in a fire alarm or report the confrontation until the next morning. He's in no mood to help the cheap gin peddlers who brought these troubles on themselves. But he's been getting some criticism from town folk about vigilante justice, and now the mayor has gotten a complaint from the Higgins brothers."

"The mayor knows who the loyal citizens are in this town," interjected Lucas.

Randall remained silent and continued to fill out the membership form.

Billy Harris scratched the top of his head. "Well," he finally added, "the chief did say that if we could just catch one Klansman, he'd sweat out of him who the leaders were and arrest them. The chief's treating the whole thing as an arson case."

Lucas found this information disturbing.

Two days later on a frigid dark morning, Matt Conner left his house and headed down Tenth Street for the bakery at the usual time. He wore his gray overcoat and blue scarf, and his favorite gray fedora sat on his head. He had bought the rakish gray hat because he felt it gave him the proper appearance. He was a young enterprising businessman. Homburgs were for older men, and derbies were for young men. He also had concluded that black was a color for lawyers and undertakers while brown was a color favored by politicians and shop clerks. Al Smith, the famous New York politician, wore a brown derby. But the color gray was reserved for bankers and businessmen.

Unfortunately, Matt's attire did nothing for his disposition. Sales were down again for the week, and Matt realized he need only produce about half the stock that he had produced daily just a few short months earlier. Matt was so depressed he had almost stayed in bed this morning, but he knew Davy would panic if he did not appear on time to inspect his labors. So Matt braced himself against the cold and trudged down the snow-bordered sidewalk toward Broad Street. Besides, he thought, Officer Harris would be disappointed if he didn't encounter Matt as he made his rounds.

Fortunately, Matt's survival instincts were still keen from years spent making his own way in the world. He noted the sound of an automobile engine coming to life a block east on Eleventh Street. This was something he had never before heard at this hour of the morning. He removed the glove from his right hand and clasped the revolver that had become a constant weight in the pocket of his gray overcoat. He moved slowly and cautiously down the street, past Oak Street and onto the next block. He needed to walk another two blocks to Broad Street and then three more to his bakery on Seventh.

As he approached the intersection of Tenth and Broad, he noted a car start forward from a block away at Eleventh Street. He carefully searched to his right and then surreptitiously looked over his shoulder to check behind him. There was no movement anywhere except for the car coming slowly toward him. The passenger side of the vehicle would be closest to him, which he knew would allow people to step out of both doors if it stopped in front of him. He thought about turning and running back up the street to his house and raising an alarm to awaken the neighborhood. But that would only postpone the showdown and perhaps embolden his opponents. It was best to confront them now while he felt he had the edge with his hidden weapon.

The car accelerated into second gear, and Matt thought it was going to pass by him. But then he heard the brakes engage, and the engine went to idle as it pulled even with him. The doors opened, and Matt saw two black-hooded figures emerge in front of him. Matt calculated that one or more knights might be up ahead, waiting for him to run in the direction of the bakery. He backed up a couple of paces and glanced behind him again as the two men from the auto approached.

"You need to come with us, Conner. We have some business to discuss before you go to work today."

The voice was calm, but there was urgency in the command, and Matt saw no weapons on either assailant. He also observed a hooded figure at the wheel of the large vehicle, an expensive Apperson Jackrabbit.

Matt wanted to throw them off balance, so he decided to act as if he was in control of the situation. "I don't think you boys want any part of my business this morning. So get in your car and go on back to your homes."

The two men looked at each other, and then the lead one moved in to grab Matt. As he took two short steps, Matt pulled the small revolver from his coat and extended his arm to point it at the man's chest.

The first man stopped a foot away from the gun. The second man had taken a slight angle to approach Matt from his left. He also stopped three feet from Matt as he spied the pistol.

"Get on your knees," Matt ordered. He moved the revolver back and forth between one attacker and the other, watching for either one to draw out a weapon. After a few seconds that seemed like minutes, both men dropped to the ground. The driver of the car now had a clear view of Matt and his pistol. He panicked and threw the car into gear and accelerated down the street with both open doors swinging back and forth on the passenger side of his vehicle.

Matt chuckled at the sight of the auto in full flight away from the confrontation. "Well, boys," he mused, "it looks like you've lost your ride home. Let's just head down to the police station, and I'm sure we can find you some warm beds to spend the rest of the night."

"You're the one who's going to be arrested," snarled the apparent leader. "If you take us in, we'll say you jumped us. It will be your word against ours. We were on our way home from helping a friend. You flagged us down and pulled that gun on us when we stopped. We can produce witnesses who'll say that's what happened. The police are sure to take our word over a mick who brandishes a revolver in public on the city streets in the middle of the night."

Matt realized he hadn't completely thought out his predicament. He didn't know whom he could trust with the police, but he was sure that the night patrolman, Officer Harris, was someone who would not accept his version of the attack. His frustration turned to anger. He knew to keep his distance from the pair to decrease the chance that they could jump him, but he wanted to fight back, especially since he had the upper hand at the moment. He took a step toward the man on his left and then quickly pivoted and swung his right arm down. He struck the other Klansman with the pistol on the side of the man's head at about the point where his ear should have been inside his hood. The shocked leader cried out and fell sideways dropping onto his hands to stop his fall. Matt backed up a step and repositioned the revolver on the other Klansman.

"So you think you own the law in this town. Who within the department is on your side?" Matt directed this at the second man, who had yet to speak, and he made no sound now. Matt took a quick menacing step towards him, but the Klansmen only held up his hand to ward off the blow. This only added to Matt's frustration. He felt guilty for becoming the aggressor instead of the victim. He did not like what was happening, and he knew the longer this incident went on the more likely that it could end badly for him. He looked at both men as he calmed himself and thought quickly on how to extricate himself from the situation.

"I suppose you'll claim that I put these fancy black sacks on your heads. Take off those hoods, now," he bellowed in his most authoritative tone. Again he moved the revolver back and forth between the men. The one on the left raised his hand and lifted the cotton cloth from behind his head until it cleared his face and dropped in his hand to his side. Then the man on Matt's right straightened up onto his knees and pulled his hood sideways from his head. In the dim street light, Matt recognized the leader as a farmer and former customer whom he had not seen in months.

Matt looked down at the leader and detected what looked like blood at the man's hairline near his temple. "You're Clyde Harrow, aren't you?" stated Matt.

"What if I am?" replied the defiant captive.

"You still owe me money on your account," replied Matt. "Have your wife bring it to the bakery by the end of the week. I'd ask for it now, but it wouldn't look too good taking money from you while I pointed a gun at your face."

Matt turned to the reluctant second attacker. He didn't recognize the face in the dim light. "What's your name and don't play me for a fool," he snarled.

This man lowered his head in resignation and muttered, "Thomas . . . I'm Lenny Thomas."

"Who owns the Apperson that brought you here?" asked Matt in a near normal tone. "I spotted the jackrabbit emblem on the radiator."

"Leon Grainger," muttered the subdued Mr. Thomas.

"He's got expensive taste," said Matt.

Matt backed up a step and scanned the street in both directions. He still thought someone might be waiting a couple of blocks closer to town. "Here's what we're going to do. You gentlemen are going to stand up and walk five paces in front of me until we get to Seventh Street. If any of your fellow kluxers are waiting up ahead, you need to call them out to join you. Because if anyone tries to jump me before we get to my bakery, I'm going to shoot you boys first. Do you understand?"

Both of the kneeling men gave brief nods of understanding.

"After I get to work, you can go on home."

The two would-be captors looked at each other with simultaneous expressions of incredulity.

"One more thing I want you to remember before we end this little meeting. I'm going to wire some money to people I know on the north side of Chicago. I'll ask them to use the funds to hire a certain type of unsavory character who lives and works up there."

Matt leaned closer to the two men and bared his teeth in anger. "If anything should happen to me or any member of my family. . . . I'll leave instructions that they come find the two of you and shoot off your kneecaps."

Matt let a few seconds of silence pass in the cold night air. "Of course, I can't guarantee they'll be sure to shoot that low. They might take an easier shot by aiming just a little bit higher."

Matt straightened up and moved behind the still-kneeling attackers. "Now get up and start walking slowly toward my bakery. Be sure to tell your friends about my warning. I'd hate to see you guys get hurt because some other kluxer didn't get the message."

Clyde looked behind to check Matt's position. He struggled to his feet, as did Lenny, who raised his hands in the air as a sign of his submission. Clyde grabbed Lenny's right arm for balance. "Put your damn arms down and help me to walk," he muttered in disgust.

The two men trod slowly down the sidewalk, and Matt kept step with them a few paces behind. They never did see anyone else on the three-block walk to the bakery, and Matt was relieved to get the door unlocked and slip safely inside. He had left the two men still walking down Broad Street in the predawn darkness.

Later that day after his lunch and nap at home, Matt attended a small private conference at the train depot. By now he was much calmer and even began to feel a bit more optimistic about his predicament. Several ideas were developed from this clandestine meeting. Before leaving the depot, he paid for a wire addressed to Sergeant John Conner of the Chicago Police Department.

A day later, Matt was back to his normal routine, and after lunch he visited with Rip Riley at the man's home off Seventeenth Street. His truck fit in well with the less affluent neighborhood. Later he stopped by the bank to make his deposit, and on his way back to the bakery, he parked in front of the police station after spotting Chief Johnson's Nash in the parking lot beside the station house.

Upon entering the building, he found the chief alone in his office to the left of the main waiting room. The big man gave Matt a smile and extended his hand for the customary handshake with which he greeted all of the citizens of his town.

"Hello, Matt, how's business going today?"

"Not so good, Paul."

The chief sat down behind his desk and motioned Matt to a chair opposite him. "I thought all those fruit pies my wife has bought from you and your sister had made you a rich man." The robust policeman smiled, but he looked tense in his chair. He apparently knew this was not a social call.

"Your patronage is greatly appreciated, Paul, but our business is suffering. The KKK is boycotting the bakery. I'm down to about half my normal sales since before Christmas."

The chief sat back in his chair and gave Matt a serious stare. "I've heard those boys have been getting bigger and bolder with their ideas about who should run this town. But are you sure you've been marked by the Klan?"

"I'm positive, Paul, and so have other Catholics here in town. I'm surprised you hadn't heard about their plot."

The lawman shook his head. "No one has come to me to complain about such a thing. But, you know, I don't think there's anything criminal in refusing to do business with someone because of their religion."

Matt gauged the sincerity of the policeman before he continued. "I agree with you on that score, but yesterday morning a couple of them accosted me on my way to work."

The chief jumped up from his chair and leaned over his desk. "What! Someone assaulted you yesterday, and you're just now coming in to report it? You're as bad as those undertakers who didn't call me about the cross burning until after they hid all their booze. Let me get a form from out front so I can take down your complaint."

As the lawman moved away from his desk, Matt held up his hand to stop him. "Sit down, Paul. I won't be making any complaint, because they're the only ones who got hurt."

The chief looked confused and then slid back into his seat. "Fill me in on what happened," he said with concern.

Matt explained what had taken place during the confrontation, including the part about striking Clyde Harrow. He told Chief Johnson that he had intended to bring the men to the police station, but Clyde implied the Klan had infiltrated the police staff and that the law would side with them on their counter-complaint. Chief Johnson's mouth dropped open at this revelation, but he remained silent while Matt continued his story.

Matt finished with a statement that he assumed would not be good news to the peace officer. "Before we parted, I warned them that if anything bad happened to me or my family, someone would come and get even for me."

Chief Johnson made no comment, but he knew Matt's older brother was a distinguished member of the Chicago police. The chief turned in his chair and gazed at some photos of his staff that hung on his wall. He sat there for almost a full minute before he turned to Matt and spoke.

"They're probably right. If you had brought them in with only their hoods as evidence, I couldn't have charged them. You had the firearm and without corroborating witnesses, it would be your word against theirs.

"Of course, I know what you were doing walking the streets of town at four a.m., but they'd have been hard-pressed to explain why they were out at such an odd hour during the winter."

The chief removed his eyeglasses and rubbed his eyes with his thumb and index finger. He took a deep sigh before he spoke again. "I don't want to believe any of my men are members of the Klan, but I can't rule it out. You were probably smart to let them go."

Matt nodded his acceptance of the man's analysis.

Chief Johnson continued. "However, now you have escalated the conflict with these vigilantes. If they come after you again, it will probably be with rifles. Maybe you scared them off, but I wouldn't bet on it. I've told the Higgins brothers the same thing I'm telling you. Be very careful because these boys could get violent. They seem to feel they are a law unto themselves."

"Can't you arrest Harrow and Thomas for the incident at the funeral home?" asked Matt.

"Oh, I'm going to go out and visit each of them, including Mr.

Grainger, but I doubt it will do much good. I need proof that they were in on the cross burning. Hell, I need proof that they're members of the Klan. But what I really need is for someone to tell me who the leader is who wears the funny emblem across the front of his costume. I can charge him with arson and force him to tell us who ordered the assault on you and the abduction of Jakub Miller. Then I can get the courts to send some of these guys up to the state pen in Michigan City."

The policeman stopped, but Matt sensed he was continuing to fume in silence.

Matt looked across the desk and finished the man's thoughts for him. "Cut off a snake's head and the rest of him is sure to die."

The policeman nodded his agreement with the adage.

The following Sunday dawned clear and cold. Lucas was nervous. There was a slight breeze rustling the bare walnut and hickory trees that dotted the Douglas Park landscape north of town. But a warm sun began melting snow and ice that had crusted on nearby rooftops, allowing icicles to form on eaves and downspouts as the water ran down the edges of the roof lines. Winter would soon be over.

At a quarter past eleven in the morning, Lucas and Tom Stewart had pulled into the park and met several other cars filled with their brethren. Otherwise the park was as vacant as could be expected on a Sunday morning during midwinter. Both men were aware of the failed knight ride against Matt Conner, and they were anxious to generate some positive news for their klavern. Lucas had moved up the church visitation to today, and he had taken two dollars and forty-five cents out of his personal funds to bring the offering for the Independent Christian Church to an even five dollars.

Lucas got out from the passenger side of the Chevrolet and started counting heads. He wore his robe but not the hood. He knew he took a chance in being discovered by a passerby, but he didn't care. It was just easier to move around without the tasseled head cover obscuring his sight as he walked to each car. Two additional autos arrived as he made his count, and he added the occupants to his total.

Finally he made his way back to Tom and reported the results as he shook off the chill in his body. "We've got thirty-four members present, thirty-six with you and me."

"That will be enough for our demonstration this morning," replied Tom. He put the car into gear and led the way out of town to their planned destination. Bill Marshall had assured Lucas and Tom that the church service would be well underway by half past the hour, and the doors would be open to the new arrivals. Lucas liked Bill and had told Tom that they would make Deacon Marshall the Kludd, or chaplain, for the group. Along with today's visitation, it would help lend dignity to their klavern.

The blacktop road leading north was wet from the melting snow. As the caravan approached the little church nestled next to a grove of poplar trees, the men donned their hoods. Cars were parked at various angles surrounding the sanctuary building, but a clear, open driveway led to the wooden front door. Tom stopped a few car lengths beyond the door, and the motorcade of vehicles halted in a row behind him. Each man moved quickly and silently to predetermined positions in the two lines that made up their procession.

Lucas in his white cotton robe, and Tom in his, mounted the four steps to the entrance. Tom took one look back to determine that the men were ready, and then he flung open the door for Lucas, who led the way into the whitewashed sanctuary.

The church members were in the midst of singing "The Old Rugged Cross," a hymn Lucas and Bill Marshall had selected for this moment in the service. The Klansmen marched silently down the center aisle between the two rows of dark walnut-stained pews. And as they moved forward, the singing died out until only the minister and the front row were left to finish the last chorus. Then there was total silence in the building. The pastor, Reverend Everett Jacobs, looked up over his hymnal and stared at the intruders much as he might have done if confronted by ghosts from now-departed parishioners. Words failed him as he stared at the group of silent men. After several seconds, Lucas approached the two-foot-high platform at the front of the church where Reverend Jacobs stood. With one great step he mounted the stage and approached the terror-stricken minister to stand beside him.

Lucas looked down upon the congregation before raising his arms, revealing empty palms to the congregation. "Brothers and sisters in Christ, we Knights of the Ku Klux Klan visit you today to honor your commitment to Christian principles and morality that is the backbone of everything good about our country. We are engaged today in a crusade to reform a community and, yes, even a nation that has gone astray. With God's help, we will return our country to the evangelical holy land our Lord has bequeathed to our fathers and forefathers. Your dedication and help in achieving our goals is a blessing to all, and we wish to show our appreciation through this small offering. Please accept it with our thanks and use it to continue the good works that pour forth from this holy place."

Lucas reached into his robe and pulled out the small white envelope that contained five dollars. He held the envelope up high for all to see and then he deposited it into the reluctant hand of Reverend Jacobs. He patted the man on his back, faced his knights, and motioned with his right arm for their departure. Silently, the Klansmen turned on their heels and marched back out through the rear of the church. Lucas followed. Tom had stayed outside to open and close the door and to keep lookout for any unexpected trouble. But the visitation had gone as planned. The men climbed back into their cars and dispersed for their homes.

The sixth vehicle, a Model T contained four men. In the rear compartment, Billy Harris removed his hood and turned toward Randall Madison, who sat beside him. "Well, what did you think of your first gathering? Was there enough excitement for you?"

Randall ran his fingers through his hair to flatten the locks that had been disheveled when he removed his hood. "That's the most interesting church service I've ever attended. I was nervous when we were going in, but it was fun watching all those people straighten up and turn white as these sheets. They must have thought the Last Judgment had come down upon them. Even the little kids sat as still as statues."

The two men in front laughed at the humorous comments of their new member.

Billy leaned forward to address the men up front. "I thought that old preacher was going to scream and run off when Lucas reached into his pocket and pulled out the offering. Did you ever see anything funnier than a preacher who didn't want to take your money?"

All four men laughed harder at this comment.

Randall fought back tears as he added, "It will be a miracle if the poor man can give his sermon today. And it will be a greater one if the people listen to what he has to tell them."

A "Faultless Conversion Top" that made the vehicle suitable for winter weather enclosed the old black Model T. Randall still shivered from the cold as the Ford approached the bridge that crossed over Stone Creek and back into town. They halted on the north side of the creek and shed their uniforms. There was no reason to parade around town during daylight hours in their armor.

Once their uniforms had been stowed into clothing bags, the group motored into town. Randall relaxed and enjoyed the conversation. It was approaching lunchtime, and he had worked up an appetite on this unusual day of rest.

CHAPTER 12

March 1923
Donegal, Indiana

A<small>NNIE</small> C<small>ONNER</small> <small>FINISHED SWEEPING THE FLOOR</small> of the kitchen as her last chore of the day. Matt had already helped her clean up the dishes from dinner, and now he was reading to Brian and Katy in the living room. Four-month-old Laura played on a blanket kept for her in the dining room. Annie knew that soon Laura would begin to crawl, and she would be forced to keep a closer watch over her baby girl.

The more immediate concern for Annie was her brooding husband. She understood Matt didn't want to involve her with his troubles at work or with his looming confrontation with the Ku Klux Klan. Yet over the course of the last few weeks, he had become more difficult and at times sullen. At other times, he appeared to be happy and optimistic about the crisis. It was bewildering to see how his temperament fluctuated almost daily.

Annie would leave him alone except for one new development. Matt had failed to take communion during Sunday Mass for three weeks in a row. Like her, he had fasted from food and drink as of Saturday evening, but he had stayed in the pew with the children when she had gone forward to the altar to receive the Blessed Sacrament.

Annie could only conclude that mortal sin was keeping her husband from participating in communion. Less serious or venial sins would not prevent him from receiving the communion wafer.

If Matt was in a state of sin, then Annie would not remain silent. To die and lose one's soul because of disobedience to God's commandments was a fate Annie could not accept for her husband. Tonight she would confront him and force him to tell her some of his troubles. They could not continue to live this way. She was fully prepared to pack up and move back to her parents' home, but only if Matt came with her and the children. Their family was more important than their bakery, or their friends, or their pride.

Annie put away her broom and dustpan, walked into the dining room, and knelt beside her youngest daughter. She held out her index finger for Laura to grasp and tug while Annie cooed to her. Then she gave Laura the wooden rattle that was a present from Annie's sister, Eleanor. She picked up the baby and took her upstairs to their bedroom to prepare the child for bed. As Annie climbed the stairs, she silently thanked the Blessed Virgin again that Laura was a healthy baby who now slept through the night except for her one feeding.

An hour later Annie descended the stairs after putting all three children to bed. Matt had come down a few minutes earlier and was reading one of the big city newspapers Father Stevens had dropped off earlier in the day. Annie came over to his chair and with her fingers began to caress the back of his neck. It wasn't long before she had his attention.

"I know something has happened that must be of grave concern to you."

Matt shook his head and frowned. "It's nothing to worry about, sweetheart," he retorted.

Annie continued. "I know that it is grave enough that you've stopped going to communion. Isn't your mortal soul something we should worry about?"

Matt looked down at the newspaper in his lap and then up into her eyes. Tears rose to his own eyes as he spoke. "I struck a man a few weeks ago and in doing so, I broke a promise I made to Father

O'Brien. I've been too ashamed to confess it."

Annie reached for Matt's hands and knelt in front of him as he sat. "What did the man do that would cause you to fight with him?"

"I was jumped by three Klan members on my way to the bakery one morning. I had my pistol and got two of them to surrender to me. I was mad as hell, and I hit one over the head because I didn't like what he had to say."

Annie was frightened, but she felt that she needed to give Matt encouragement and support. "Surely this was self-defense. You didn't do anything wrong!"

Matt gave her a wan smile as he held her hands. "Yes, I did. The men were on their knees in complete submission. I reacted in anger, and it was wrong."

The room was quiet as the couple contemplated the significance of this event.

Finally, Annie looked up into Matt's eyes and broke the silence. "Will you be charged with a crime? Will the Klan come after you again?"

"No," replied Matt. "I reported the assault to Paul Johnson, and he agreed that there isn't enough evidence to arrest anyone. And I threatened those Kluxers with bodily harm should anything be attempted against our family in the future."

"Then we should have some peace from these hooligans," uttered a hopeful Annie.

Matt looked warily at his wife. "I still have to put these boys out of business before they bankrupt us and our friends. It's become my responsibility, but I don't know if I'm capable of handling the task. Plus, I've broken my word to Father Tom."

"Oh Matt, why can't we just pick up and leave here tomorrow? We could close the bakery and sell what we can't take with us. Our children need to be safe. They deserve to grow up in the care of a mother and a father."

Matt stood and brought Annie up from her knees to hold in his arms. "I want those things, sweetheart. I know what it's like to grow up as an orphan, and I remember how bad it was when my dad was taken away. But people are depending upon me. I don't think I could shave in a mirror anymore if I ran out on my friends.

"Besides, this is the only real home I've ever known. I used to imagine a nice life here during all those years I spent traveling out west. It was one rough town after another, and the earthquake that destroyed San Francisco gave me nightmares for years. I can't even talk about the death and destruction I've seen. Here I get to sleep soundly at night."

Annie buried her face into her husband's chest and after a moment pulled back to arm's length. "Then fight them, Matt. But first, get to church after work on Saturday and confess your sins. Seek Father O'Brien's forgiveness. Then get your friends together and put an end to this madness. You shouldn't have to resort to guns or violence to beat these hooligans. They should be no match for someone with the cunning and guile of a true Irishman."

Matt looked fondly at her before drawing her back into his embrace. He probably knew she was putting on her best face and offering him all the support she could.

It drizzled most of the day the following Saturday. By early afternoon, Matt closed his shop but hosted a meeting in the kitchen to get advice from various church members who had attended the first meeting at St. Mary's Church. John Davis was very encouraging about what needed to be done, and Liam McNamara was very supportive. Sean O'Toole had an interesting idea about taking what information they could develop to the newspapers and getting it published. Perhaps they could win the support of the general public by documenting the abuse being meted out by these hooded knights. At four o'clock, Matt visited with John Collins in his law offices on Second Street. Matt was coy about the preliminary plan, but he solicited the lawyer's advice on the consequences from actions that might be taken by his group. The elderly barrister took time to explain his views on points of the law dealing with such matters as abduction, assault, and bodily injury.

Just past five in the afternoon, Matt made his way up the steps to St. Mary's. He left his umbrella standing against the wall in the vestibule. Once inside the sanctuary, he dipped his fingers in holy water before making the sign of the cross. He went forward on the right side of the building and knelt in a pew near the confessional. There were people in the front pews, and others kneeling at the altar, who were most likely doing penance for their confessed transgressions.

On the right side of the sanctuary, halfway down the side aisle, stood the confessional. Three booths comprised the wooden structure with a door for the middle one that housed the priest. Heavy black cotton curtains covered the openings for the other booths.

The door of the confessional was shut, and the curtain was drawn on the left side booth. The curtain on the right box was open. Matt could hear whispers emanating from the two closed boxes. He could tell Father O'Brien was the confessor for this afternoon. Matt said his standard prayer of preparation for the sacrament before entering the confessional and closing the curtain behind him.

After what seemed like a short minute or two, Matt heard the divider shut on the other box, and then the one between him and his confessor slid open. Father Tom began his prayer in Latin, and Matt knew the moment he had dreaded was upon him.

"Bless me, Father, for I have sinned. My last confession was six weeks ago. Since then I have struck a neighbor once . . . and I have broken my promise to a friend. I am heartily sorry for these and all the sins of my past, and I ask for forgiveness from Almighty God."

Tom changed his position as he analyzed this penitent. The voice was familiar, but he couldn't identify the parishioner with the iron screen blocking his view. The first sin was a grave one, but the contrition voiced with the second one made it seem more important. His instincts told him he was dealing with larger issues than those present in the confessional.

"Are you truly sorry for your actions, my son?" asked Tom as the representative of Christ.

"Yes, Father," replied Matt.

There was silence as Tom considered the situation. Finally, he made his decision to segregate the sins and confession from what lay behind them. "For your penance, say three Hail Mary's and one Our Father before leaving the church. Then I want you to go to my office in the Rectory and wait for me. Now please say your Act of Contrition." Tom said the standard prayer of forgiveness in Latin and ended with the usual refrain to go in peace and sin no more. He shut the divider quickly.

Half an hour later, when Father O'Brien entered the Rectory, Matt stood in the office doorway and gave his confessor a sheepish smile. There was no sign in the priest's features that he held any shock or ill will for Matt. God's forgiveness was total for this man of the cloth.

"I had wanted to see you, Matt, but with Father John out of town, I had postponed inviting you over until another time. How is your family?"

"Everyone is fine, Father. Little Laura is eating and sleeping well. Her brother and sister are growing and looking forward to warm weather."

"And how is the bakery?" asked the priest delicately.

Matt sat back down in a chair and fingered his hat. He looked up at his friend and could tell that Father Tom was trying to relieve his anxiety. "Sales are off by half of my peak levels. I'm just hanging on right at the moment."

Father Tom shook his head and curled his index finger to his lips. He pulled over a small wooden chair with a cane seat and sat down.

"I am so sorry about this bad business," he said. "I pray daily that God will give us the strength to see this through and to do His will. Now tell me about this fight you've had."

Matt gathered his emotions and began. "I had a confrontation with a couple of those kluxers. They tried to jump me, but I was ready for them. Still, I let my anger get the best of me, and I hit one pretty hard on the side of the head with my pistol."

Father Tom looked horrified. "What!" he exclaimed. He glanced at the doorway before continuing in a subdued voice. "These people have no respect for the law. Have the police investigated? Will there be any charges filed against you or the others?"

Matt breathed easier. Apparently Father Tom was willing to overlook Matt's transgressions.

"No, I spoke to Chief Johnson, and there are no witnesses to verify what happened. It would be my word against theirs. Plus no one has come forward to complain. I guess they don't want to bother the police."

"Do you know what they wanted?" asked Tom.

Matt was reluctant to discuss his confrontation, but Father Tom deserved to know why he had broken his promise. "I can guess," said Matt. "They had a car and were going to abduct me just like they did Jakub Miller. Remember, I came to his aid after they were done with him. They may have planned a tar and feathers party for me . . . or worse.

"Their whole campaign is to intimidate and scare people they don't like. If they can force us to leave, they get control of Donegal. It's a fight to see who gets to live and do business here and who doesn't."

Matt watched Father Tom smooth the material of his cassock on his lap. His hands were agitated as he used them to push back the gray hair on the sides of his head. Clearly, he was disconcerted by this information.

"Matt, this is getting dangerous. You must have been frightened for yourself and your family. Perhaps you should leave the area for a while. If our laws can't protect you, then you have no business standing up to this menace on your own."

Matt stared at the floor and ran his fingers around the brim of his hat. He didn't look up. "You'll probably find this strange, Father, but I've learned to deal with fear as a part of life. I've been through it before. I was much more terrified as a kid when I survived the earthquake in San Francisco. I saw and lived through some horrible things during the week after that disaster."

"It must have been an awful experience for you," sympathized Tom. "Seeing a great city toppled before your eyes would have been a nightmare. And you were just a boy roaming from place to place with your older brother looking for work."

Father Tom paused, but Matt was reluctant to speak.

"I remember hundreds died," Tom continued. "Did you know any of those killed or injured by the quake? Were any your friends?"

Matt looked up into his mentor's face and smirked. "Father, the mayor and the rest of the local officials covered up the truth. The quake may have killed hundreds when it shook apart hotels and people's homes while they slept, but it wasn't the worst part. Those were the lucky ones. What haunts me and tries my faith in a just God were the many, many more who were lost from the fires that followed. My brother and I were lucky to be staying in a dormitory at the rail yards. We were still awake, having worked the third trick, and ran outside when it started.

Matt hesitated, but Father Tom just nodded; so he continued. "We spent days trying to help dig people out of the rubble. Because of my small size, I would crawl into the pockets looking for people who were trapped. I'd bring them water, and Joe and other men would try to find a way to get them out. But the fires kept following us, and the heat and smoke gave us little time to save those poor souls. I was always scared I'd become stuck or another quake would come and entomb me. The smoke was awful, and the crying and moaning of desperate people was . . . hell. I remember thinking that it was a race against the devil, and we were losing."

Matt stopped and wiped his brow with the back of his hand. He felt feverish and lightheaded, but he knew he had to go on. "Father, I saw policemen and soldiers shoot people who were trapped rather than let them burn to death. I left people we couldn't rescue because the fires got too close. I could hear their screams as we moved on toward others who still had a chance. But the cries of those hopelessly trapped people haunt me even now."

Matt took a deep breath.

"I remember one woman was pinned by a large wooden beam in a cellar just a few yards from my reach. She cradled her baby who I think must have been dead because it never moved and never even cried out while I was with them."

Matt paused and swallowed slowly. "I couldn't get through the rubble down to where she lay. All I could do was lower a tin of water to her using some rope. She never spoke, but I could tell she was grateful for the drink. When the smoke got thick, I had to abandon them. I didn't have the courage to say goodbye, but I looked into her eyes, and she knew I was leaving."

Matt began to choke. "I should have gotten a gun and gone back to shoot her. But I was scared, and I felt like such a failure. We came back later, but there were just piles of charred bricks and stones left."

"I'm sorry, my son," said the somber priest. "You have truly visited a hell I've never seen."

Suddenly agitated, Matt sat forward and shook his head in frustration. "But you need to understand me, Father. I have doubts about myself, and I fear for my family. But the Klan can be stopped. They're just men like you and me, and they can be beaten. But am I the one to do it? You see, I'm afraid I'm not qualified to do this thing. Maybe God has decided I'm not worthy to lead a fight against them. I lost my temper and hit that guy. I broke my promise to you. A few nights ago I dreamed about that young woman I'd left for the fires. In my dream the woman was Annie and her child was Laura." Matt stopped too emotional to continue.

The priest rose from his chair and stood beside him. Matt hid his face in his hands, but he felt Father Tom's hand on his shoulder.

"Matt, do you remember how Peter denied the Lord three times on the night He was arrested?"

Matt breathed deeply and raised his head. "Yes, after he pledged his loyalty to the Lord. I like the version in Luke where Christ tells Peter that He has prayed for his salvation. I think the Lord was being sarcastic with that proud fisherman."

Father O'Brien smiled. "You also remember that our Lord forgave Peter after His death and resurrection."

Matt thought for a moment before he answered. "In John's gospel, Christ questions Peter three times about Peter's love for Him. I believe it was our Lord's way of mocking or punishing Peter, before He forgave him. I've thought it to be a great example of the combined humanity and divinity of Jesus."

Father O'Brien exhaled and shook his head. "Matt, you constantly baffle me. You show such great understanding in your study and interpretation of scripture, yet you can't seem to apply it to your own situation. Our Lord would never reject you for your real or imagined failures in life. He is like the father of the prodigal son whose love is so great He forgives any and all of our sins.

"Didn't you just receive the sacrament of confession? Don't you understand I acted as the Lord's representative in offering you forgiveness for your actions? And what kind of priest would I be if I didn't offer you my personal forgiveness for breaking your promise to me during a crisis?"

Matt looked up into his pastor's eyes. He saw sympathy. He thought he saw understanding in those eyes, too. But those intelligent dark brown eyes seemed to implore him to take action, and Matt realized he needed to focus on the task at hand.

Father O'Brien stepped in front of Matt and took Matt's right hand into his own hands and held it. "I believe God has sought you out to be his instrument of justice as he once did with Moses. My experience has taught me that God favors those who acknowledge their weaknesses. A man who recognizes his own faults will seek God's strength to help him find his way and overcome his problems. God never fails to provide us with the power we need to act on His behalf."

Matt's hand lay between his pastor's palms. Involuntarily he drew it up into a fist. "But can God support a man who must oppose his fellow man to gain peace?"

He hesitated and then continued. "Can our Lord support someone who is willing to break the law in order to obtain justice?"

Father O'Brien stepped back and considered the implications of these questions. "Do you have a plan?" he inquired.

"We're working on one," uttered Matt without thinking.

Moments passed in silence.

"Who else is involved with you?" asked Father Tom.

Matt showed his distress. "Father, I can't tell you. It will be best for everyone if you know as little as possible. But let me ask you this plainly. Do you think I should undertake actions that may be illegal in order to put a halt to the Klan?"

Father Tom closed his eyes and turned his face upward toward heaven. Then he faced Matt again. "Do you recall that St. Peter tried to defend our Lord when the soldiers came to the Garden of Gethsemane?"

"Yes," replied Matt. "Only John's account identifies Peter as the disciple who cuts off the ear of the temple servant. I've considered the incident to be fanciful and symbolic."

"Why?"

"I find it unrealistic that a fisherman would carry a sword even for an evening walk outside the city. But let's say he did. Would this fisherman have the skill to clip off a man's ear with one swipe? And how could he have the courage to put up such a hopeless defense, yet later cower before these same soldiers? I suppose it could have happened, but what defies credibility is the idea that the temple guards didn't arrest or kill Peter for his crime."

"Perhaps the guards were affected by Christ's presence," suggested Father Tom. "He did replace the severed ear."

"Yeah, I know," said Matt. "Regardless of what happened, all four gospels were intent on demonstrating that Jesus had the power to resist His fate, but He submitted to His Father's plan."

"Yes, I would concur with that idea," said Father Tom as he sat down again. "Matt, you should have become a priest. The best professors I had in seminary were the theologians who questioned everything. There wasn't any part of scripture they didn't examine. You would have fit in well with the current scholars at St. Meinrad's."

Matt grinned as he contemplated this idea. "My mother had hoped I'd become a priest. But then she died, and Joe wouldn't hear of it. It worked out for the best. God led me to find Annie, and she is the center of my life."

Father O'Brien stared past Matt and seemed lost in thought. After a few moments of reflection he returned his focus to Matt.

"The reason I brought up this incident of Peter's attack was to point out that Christ never rebuked His disciple for such violence. And He never required repentance for this supposedly unlawful action.

"My point is that Christ and His church have always sanctioned actions taken in defense of others or yourself and your family. You say that the Klan isn't evil; they're just being selfish. Maybe they are just trying to make a buck by driving off the good, hard-working Catholics here. But I think they've started a war, and men have a right to defend themselves from the fear and economic ruin that are the Klan's favorite weapons. If you have a weapon that can stop them without bringing needless bloodshed to the valley, then by all means you have the right to wield it."

"I can't guarantee someone won't get hurt," Matt mumbled weakly.

The bell from the Methodist church down the street began to peal the new hour. Father Tom looked at his pocket watch and stood, indicating their talk had concluded. "I can give you my blessing, Matt. I firmly believe the Lord will stand with you in your fight for justice. And if your plans require a little chicanery, then so be it. It may be the only weapon available to you. Perhaps some credit should be given to our Irish ancestors. After all, the Irish have survived for thousands of years by living on the edge of laws made by other men. My father used to call it Irish Justice."

Matt pondered the man's words for a moment and then stood and put on his gray overcoat. "Thank you, Father. You've lifted a heavy burden off of me. I think I now know what to do." He picked up his hat and scarf from a chair and turned back to face his mentor. They eyed one another, then shook hands. "I liked your sermon last month on the Good Samaritan. Did you get any good comments on it?"

"Why, yes," said Father Tom as he escorted Matt into the hallway. "And the other ministers in my breakfast group reported positive remarks from their congregations. However, I don't think it made any difference to our friends who wear the hoods with the tassels. Perhaps they don't attend church around here."

Both men walked to the front door at the end of the hallway.

Matt buttoned his gray herringbone coat and swept his blue scarf around his neck.

"Oh, I bet some of them attend church, but not a Catholic Mass!" replied Matt.

"We are going to each speak about the Sermon on the Mount in a couple of weeks," added Father Tom. "We sort of like the idea of different denominations working for a common purpose. Of course I'm not sure Bishop Allen would be pleased to hear I'm in league with my Protestant brethren. I have a feeling word will reach him in Fort Wayne some day soon."

"Well, I'll look forward to your sermon on the Sermon, and let's hope the good bishop stays in the dark," said Matt. He hesitated and found his umbrella in the stand next to the door.

"Would your group be willing to accept a recommendation from a poorly educated disciple like myself?"

Father O'Brien stopped short of his front door and looked seriously into Matt's eyes. "If you have a request, I'll be sure to put it before the other ministers."

Matt put on his fedora before he spoke. "I don't know the date yet, but sometime in the near future, it would be most beneficial if your group would offer a sermon devoted to St. John's gospel, Chapter 13, verses 34 and 35."

Father Tom nodded. "I'll bring it up at our next breakfast," he answered as he reached for the front door. "I won't let them in on its importance," he whispered.

He let Matt out and went back into his office to make a note of the reference Matt had given him. He then reached for his well-worn Bible and looked up the passage cited by his young parishioner. He was certain it was one of three that repeat the same theme prior to Christ's crucifixion. He found it and read it with great satisfaction.

"A new commandment I give unto you. That ye love one another; as I have loved you, that ye also love one another. By this shall all men know that ye are my disciples, if ye have love one to another."

On a late Tuesday afternoon, Lucas Crawford's office was crowded. The air was thick with cigarette and pipe tobacco smoke. Such foul smelling air was probably not good for Tom Stewart, who coughed and gagged during the meeting he had called with Lucas's agreement.

"Chief Johnson didn't get nothing from me," stated Clyde Harrow. "I told him I banged my head on a shelf inside my barn. He didn't get nothing out of Lenny either. Lenny was so scared that he's decided to pretend it never happened and that he's never been part of our group."

Clyde looked directly at Tom who sat at his desk with a handkerchief held to his mouth. "He was a poor choice for a Knight Rider. He was scared of his own shadow."

"Grainger wasn't any better," added John Holmes as he sat in the big leather chair, puffing on his pipe.

Leon Grainger stood up from his makeshift seat on the windowsill. "There wasn't anything I could do. The man had a gun, and he'd already thwarted our plan."

"Who'd have thought that the mick would be ready for us?" cried the exasperated Tom Stewart. "What do we do now, shoot him in the back on his walk home some dark night?" This last question was followed by more coughing and labored breathing.

Lucas stirred from behind his desk. "We're not going to shoot anybody, Tom. We're law-abiding citizens, and we need to stay that way."

Tom gave his old friend a remorseful look.

Agitated, Clyde Harrow continued. "Remember, if you hurt him or his family he's going to come after Lenny and me. We'd have to go to the police and demand protection. I'm not so sure Lenny wouldn't cave in to Chief Johnson and tell him what we done."

Lucas looked to Billy Harris, leaning against a wall in his uniform. He had a couple of hours before he started his shift. He had brought along his friend, Randall.

"Conner told the chief about his threat, and the boss takes it seriously. Apparently the chief met Conner's brother on a trip to Chicago a couple of years back. The chief figures an Irish policeman knows enough Irish gangsters to get the job done cheap and quiet-like. Matt Conner would have a good alibi when some gunman came to town."

"So what do we do now?" wheezed Tom.

"Why do anything?" answered Randall Madison, who was leaning against the door. The room grew silent as Lucas turned his attention to the newcomer, who had remained quiet up until now. Randall had not been invited, and his appearance, along with the unexpected absence of Lenny Thomas, had irritated Lucas.

Randall unfolded his arms and stood straight as he spoke. "Matt Conner is in trouble. His business is off plenty since the boycott of his papist bread started. His sister has been moaning about how they can't keep going like this for much longer. One of these days he won't be able to make his bank payments.

"I've been thinking of taking some of my capital and buying him out. If I can get Maureen to stick around for a while it could be a better investment for me than putting in well pumps."

Lucas had to smile. This was the first confirmation that his planned ostracism of the baker was working. Plus, the thought of another Klansman taking over the business, with the unwitting help of the Irishman's sister, was a splendid addition to their strategy. Mr. Madison had intelligence and initiative that could be useful to the fraternity.

"Do you think he'll sell to you, Randall?" inquired Lucas.

"If he can't get his revenue back up pretty soon, he's got to sell or go bust. I think he'd take a decent offer from someone who had an eye for his sister."

"Are you planning on marrying that mackerel snapper?" asked Billy.

"Maybe," replied Randall defensively. "But that's none of your business unless I ask you to be the best man."

"I'm not attending any wedding in a Catholic church," stated Billy adamantly.

"Who said it would be a Catholic wedding?" replied Randall.

The two men eyed each other suspiciously until the others started to chuckle, and then they all broke out into laughter.

Tom coughed again as Lucas slapped his hand on his desk. "Well then, that's settled. We'll let nature run its course and see if romance blossoms in the spring."

More laughter ensued before Lucas asked for order. "We still need to put pressure on the other Catholic and Jewish businesses and tradesmen who are stealing work and money from the good Christians of the valley. Tom, you need to direct our efforts toward those we have ignored up until now. Let's stick to demonstrations and boycotts. With warmer weather, we can picket in front of stores and bring shame on those establishments that should be closed down. Knight rides are getting risky and should be used judiciously.

"Billy, I want you to find out what the Chief would do if we staged another cross burning on the river bluff next month when the weather turns better. It's outside the town limits, but he may try to get the county sheriff involved. I've received a letter from Mr. Lampton. Indiana has been a provisional realm of the national organization for over two years. Our membership has grown to the point that the Imperial Wizard will grant us a charter soon. Then we'll have even more power and prestige, not only within the Klan but also within state politics. Mr. Lampton will become Grand Dragon of the Indiana Realm. He wants all klaverns to clean up their act. Obey the laws, and work with the local government to promote decency and Christian values. We have not always done that here, and I admit that I've been guilty of not controlling our actions. In my haste to promote our cause, I've cut corners and approved actions that broke a few laws. That's going to stop. Any knight rides conducted from this point on will be done within the limits of the law."

Clyde was sitting on the safe at the end of the office. "Does that mean that the Sharp mission is off?" he asked.

"No," answered Lucas. "But I'll expect Tom and you to plan it carefully. No bodily harm or destruction of property will be allowed. Mr. Sharp must be convinced peacefully to change his ways."

Lucas looked around the room for a challenge to this order, but none was forthcoming from those present.

"Also, we need to start another collection for our next church visitation, so spread the word before our meeting next week. And one more thing, Clyde. You go and visit Lenny and tell him to be at that meeting. He's got nothing to worry about so long as he remains loyal to the Klan. But we'll ruin him quick if he runs out on us. Now, let's adjourn this meeting. Tom and I have to plan a recruiting campaign for the spring and summer. We're going to branch out to some of the other towns in the valley this year. If any of you have friends or relatives within an hour's drive of here, let us know. Give it some thought and get back to us. No phone calls though. I'm leery of the switchboard operators listening in on us."

As the other men filed out of the office, Tom had another coughing fit that lasted for half a minute. Lucas eyed him with concern as he watched him going through a series of convulsions as he sat at the other desk. Lucas turned in his chair and opened the window behind him.

"You're sick, Tom, and your group has not performed well without you to lead them. Clyde isn't qualified to execute these tasks. He should never have let the baker pull a gun on him. We should have nabbed the guy the way you did with the Polack."

Tom coughed a few more times and then cleared his throat as the involuntary spasms subsided. "Well, you can't do it. Trying to burn down the Higgins place wasn't too smart."

Lucas wanted to reply but decided to accept the rebuke from his childhood friend. They were both making good money from the klectokens that had been paid by the new recruits. In May, Lucas would be given a promotion that would mean an added half-dollar to the four dollars he now received from each klectoken. From this fee Lucas gave Tom ten percent for his involvement. The money didn't mean as much to Tom as the recognition did. Tom still lived quietly at home and helped his parents run the store in the afternoons.

Lucas opened his desk drawer and pulled out several sheets of folded paper. "Along with the letter from Mr. Lampton was a report from Mr. Carpenter. Apparently, we have some sharp lawyers down in the Capitol City who've done some research for us."

"How could that possibly interest me?" asked Tom derisively.

Lucas scowled at his friend. "Just listen for a minute, and I'll explain it to you."

Lucas held up the sheets with his right hand and jabbed them with his left index finger. "There is a law on the state books called the Horse Thief Act, which was established after the War Between the States to control the gangs of veterans who roamed the countryside. It allows counties to establish volunteer constabularies of ten or more men to carry weapons and make arrests of those found to be in violation of state laws."

Lucas looked up from the document he was reading and found that he had Tom's attention.

"Mr. Carpenter is creating a statewide organization to be known as the Horse Thief Detective Association. It will authorize the formation of amateur police squads that can carry weapons and arrest lawbreakers within each county."

"So how does that concern us?" questioned Tom.

Lucas stood up, walked over to Tom and leaned onto his desk. "We can do away with the knight rides and the black hoods. We can conduct our actions in public with the support of the local police."

Tom Stewart looked up, and his face brightened. "The agency wouldn't even need be associated with the Klan. We could set it up as a separate group, and no one need know that all of the members were Klansmen."

"Of course," agreed Lucas. "The Klan could continue as the social fraternity we've developed, and the detective agency could be the enforcement arm to bring about the changes needed in the community. And the agency would be legal and aboveboard. Mr. Carpenter envisions the group conducting roadblocks and making arrests for liquor violations. I don't think we would be able to work within town limits, but we could operate legally in the rest of the county."

"I like the idea," Tom decided. "But what if somebody lobbies to remove the law from the state books?"

"It won't happen," answered Lucas. "We've got too much power in the statehouse. Plus, after next year's election, we'll control the governor. Mr. Carpenter wants the name of someone he can propose to head up the agency for Fairview County. I want you to be that man. He'll file the proper paperwork in Indianapolis to get things started."

Lucas decided to bring up an idea he'd been formulating during the earlier meeting. "We need to find you a good assistant to handle the field work until you get well. Of course, you'd still run things. When the weather improves, your lungs will get better, and then you could go out and direct things personally."

Talk of his illness depressed Tom. He looked across his desk at Lucas and almost whispered his reply. "My lungs are not going to get better. You should replace me. I told you once before that I didn't like running around trying to scare people. I only did these knight rides because it made use of my training in the army. God knows I didn't get to utilize it in France."

"We need you, Tom. You're the only man I trust to do things properly."

Tom paused and took a couple of breaths before he continued more calmly. "What we need to do is find another veteran or a lawman to handle the action. I don't think Billy can do it. He's too young and would fold in a crisis situation."

Lucas sat down at his desk and drummed his fingers, considering the information even though he already had his answer ready. "How about Randall Madison to back you up? He's older and pretty smart. He likes police work, always hanging around the station and going out on patrol with Billy. He seems like he would be pretty calm in a tough spot."

Tom was quiet except for his own raspy breathing. "Let me think about it. Maybe I'll take him along to the Sharps' and see how he performs."

Lucas sat silently and held his friend's gaze. He concluded that he had made his point.

"Fair enough," Lucas finally replied. "Let's figure out which towns we want to visit in the spring. Mr. Carpenter wants a schedule by next Friday, and you know the roads better than I do."

CHAPTER 13

April 1923
Chicago, Illinois

THE PENNSYLVANIA RAILROAD TRAIN came to a gradual halt on the covered platform behind Chicago's Union Station. Matt was very familiar with the train terminal and the city, and the normal anxiety he felt when traveling to cities away from home was never present when he went to Chicago. This big robust city was a second home for him. But he was nervous over the purpose of this visit.

It had been a pleasant trip from Donegal this day. Matt and Rip Riley had motored over to Logansport, where they caught the train to Chicago. Rip needed to be present for an unusual meeting Matt would have later today. Thinking about that meeting gave Matt a touch of anxiety. The two men made their way down the steps of the train car's vestibule and onto the concrete platform. They were at ground level, but the station was located up a long flight of stairs that brought passengers to the streets of the city. They each carried a small suitcase for the overnight trip. Normally Matt would stay with his brother, John, but tonight he and Rip would share a room in a small hotel on the north side of the city.

"All the smoke from the locomotives really fouls the air down here," commented Rip. "It's sure different from home, where the breeze sweeps the air clean."

Matt grinned at his friend and replied, "The air isn't very good up on the street either. Too many people and vehicles for such a small area can't be good for your health. That's why I prefer a small town even though there are more opportunities to make money in the cities."

They reached the end of the platform and climbed the steps up to the terminal's main floor along with the other passengers. While the ground level was impressive with all the tracks and train equipment assembled in one immense location, the main floor was less inspiring. The two came out onto an open expanse with throngs of people moving in all directions. One wall held ticket booths similar to any train station, and the other sides of the terminal held a variety of concessions, including a large restaurant.

Matt watched his friend take in his first view of the large waiting room. He knew a carpenter like Rip could probably appreciate the engineering that had gone into its construction better than he could. The two men stopped near the center and let the other passengers pass them by. Rip focused on the ceiling and the pillars that supported it. His mouth hung partially open as his eyes scanned the length and breadth of the building.

Matt couldn't contain himself and chuckled, which brought Rip's attention back to his friend. Matt gave Rip an indulgent smile. "There are at least a half a dozen train stations in this town, and they're building a replacement for this one. The new one can probably hold this one inside its main waiting room. It'll have marble floors, vaulted skylights, and huge columns that ascend almost a hundred feet from floor to ceiling. We'll go over and look at it once I've had my meeting here."

Rip's eyes were large and filled with wonderment. "This depot is bigger than any place I've ever seen. I don't know how they could build a bigger one, but it must cost a fortune."

Matt put an arm around his companion's shoulder. "It has been paid for by the many passengers and freight customers who have to ante up the tariffs charged by the railroads. They can afford it, and they like us to know it. The new terminal would have been finished by now except for the shortages in material brought on by the Great War."

Matt guided Rip to a vacant corner and a richly stained wooden bench with a high back. He had Rip seat himself between their two suitcases positioned on the floor. "Stay here and look around for a while," said Matt. "I'll probably be thirty minutes if my contact is available. Then we can go to Little Italy for lunch and conduct some business. I'll show you where I order the best ingredients for my Italian breads."

Matt had advised Rip that his initial meeting was secretive because there was security for both of them if Rip knew as little as possible about Matt's plans. Matt's caution had been taught to him by his brother, John. His impending clandestine meeting was with John, and it was better if no one knew about it.

Matt strode across the waiting room and exited the big red brick building onto Adams Street. He walked to the steel lift-bridge that crossed over the Chicago River. The early spring winds coming off the frigid lake were harsh. The foot traffic was heavy with lunchtime crowds of office clerks moving along the sidewalks. Matt spotted a familiar figure dressed in a suit and topcoat much like his own. John was apparently not on duty and had wisely dressed in civilian clothes. The large steel girders that held up the bridge deck loomed over his head. He was leaning on the bridge railing, gazing south at the river below him. Matt stopped next to him and held out his hand in greeting.

John turned and shook Matt's hand while he scanned the traffic behind his brother. There was no embrace, and each man acted as if they were greeting a casual acquaintance from work. After exchanging news about their families, both men turned and gazed out at the river that stretched south between various buildings that lined both sides of it. The river itself was devoid of traffic. Too much ice still clogged the waterways for the barges to operate freely.

As the older brother, John initiated conversation regarding the reason for their rendezvous. "Does your friend, Rip, understand why we're keeping him in the dark?"

"I think so," replied Matt. "He's a good man, and he's willing to take orders from me."

John nodded his approval. "He needs to sit in on your meeting with Mr. Smith in order to document the expenditure from the fund. Come up with a phony name for him. Smith thinks he's meeting a Mr. Jones and his assistant."

"Anything special I should know about Mr. Smith?" asked Matt.

"He's Irish and has been retired for several years. He never did time in jail, but he was questioned on several occasions. That's how I knew about him. He now has a shop near my home where he does watch and clock repairs, but his own home is nicer than what one would expect from a watchmaker. He must be living off of his savings from his days spent on the other side of the law."

"Was he ever part of the O'Bannion gang?" asked Matt.

"He may have been associated with them at some point, but I think he was pretty independent. That allowed him to quit when he'd made enough to want to stop taking chances."

Matt leaned over the bridge railing and stared at some wood drifting in the water. He turned and looked at his brother. "John, do you trust this old-timer? Can he do the job and keep it quiet afterward?"

"I trust him, Matt. I think he's the best man we're going to find. If he screws up or fails to deliver for you, then he's smart enough to know I'll be looking for him. He wouldn't want to come home if he failed on this job. Plus, he's been quiet about his past jobs. He's not the type to be bragging about his exploits over a few beers at the local speakeasy."

Matt returned his gaze to the river as a fresh gust of wind blew on the brim of his gray fedora. "This is a big step. We've got it planned out, but the risk is more than I bargained upon."

Matt watched seagulls swoop down the river from his left.

"Maybe I should come down a couple days beforehand and help you out. I've got some experience with underworld activities," offered John.

"No," stated Matt emphatically. "I don't need to get any more

Conners involved in my problems. I wish Maureen would move back to the safety of your house." Matt paused a moment and recognized his brother's generous offer to relieve some of the strain Matt was feeling. "I appreciate your suggestion, but we've got a good plan and some good men to carry it all out. It's just that the farther we go, the more risk I see. If we get caught, I'll need you to look out for Annie and the kids. Her parents will take care of her, but she may need some protection from the Klan. They may control the whole state after the election next year."

John straightened up and faced his brother. "Nothing will go wrong; we've thought out all the angles. But I'll be sure to take care of your family, and I'll get you a good lawyer, if you need one."

John reached into his suit coat pocket and withdrew a slip of paper. "Here's the name and address of the restaurant. Ask for Mr. Smith. He'll have a table in a back room, and he'll be wearing a green tie as insurance that you've got the right man. I offered two hundred dollars, and don't let him go higher. And don't pay more than sixty up front."

"I won't," replied Matt.

"Do you have the details he needs to prepare for the job?" asked John.

"Yes, and it's written down so we don't have to discuss it in front of Rip," replied Matt.

"Good," answered John. "Call Rip 'Mr. Lane,' and use your new names for the rest of the day. It will be good practice before the meeting. Also, make Mr. Lane the contact for Mr. Smith when his train arrives in Logansport. Don't let Mr. Smith take a connecting train to Donegal. The fewer people who see him, the less chance of trouble."

"That makes sense," said Matt. "Thank you, John. You've been a lifesaver to pull this all together for me."

"Forget it," replied his brother. "You've designed a good plan. I've only helped refine it. I should be the one taking on these hooligans, but I respect your decision. Things should work out fine as long as everyone does his part. But you need to be ready to improvise if something goes wrong. You're smart, Matt. Everybody has confidence in you. Just do your part."

Matt nodded and held out his hand for a parting handshake. He wanted to hug his brother, but it wasn't something that they ever did, and this was not the place to start showing affection. After an exchange of smiles and a quick handshake, each man turned and walked in opposite directions from the middle of the bridge.

Later Matt took Rip to Little Italy south of the train station. They visited two commercial warehouses, and Matt and Rip were warmly received at each of them. Matt was on friendly terms with each proprietor, who took time to talk with them about the news locally and elsewhere. They were served coffee and pastries before being led into the storage areas, where Matt inspected different flours and spices. Hard but cordial negotiations took place before Matt placed his order at each stop. The vendors were reluctant to give him bulk prices on the reduced quantities he now requested.

Before returning to the train station to retrieve their luggage, Matt led Rip into a small restaurant, where Matt was treated as a visiting relative. The proprietor greeted them and ordered for them. There were no more than ten tables situated in front of two large windows. It was early afternoon, and only two other tables were occupied. A young waiter in a white shirt and black bow tie brought pasta and red wine to their table.

Rip looked surprised and confused by the reception they'd received. "Does everyone get treated so grand around here? I feel like I'm some millionaire with lots of servants to cater to my every wish."

Matt laughed and took a small sip of the wine. "The Italians are nice people, but they don't trust strangers. I got to know the area when I worked for Mr. Caggiano in his bakery. He established his store north of the river because he wanted to get away from all the competition. That's how he ended up using Irish kids like my brother John and myself. He'd bring us down on his wagon every week to get supplies. The people we met earlier know me from when I was a kid working for pennies. Stefano, whom we visited first, used to help load our wagon. He's our age."

Rip managed to get a bite of tortellini and red sauce into his mouth. He was trying his best to keep the white napkin tucked under his chin clean. He chewed slowly, savoring the rich sauce. "This is wonderful," he exclaimed. "How do they make this stuff, and how can they get away with serving wine here?"

Matt finished chewing a piece of warm bread as he scanned the mostly empty dining room. His eyes warned Rip to be more discreet.

"They import grain from the old country. Italy is famous for its wheat crop. In the hands of a great cook, they can make fabulous meals. They've been doing it for hundreds of years. As for the wine, the Italians have always had their own set of rules for the community. They're not much different from the Irish on the north side of town. The Irish are more open and will do business with everyone, but the Italians and Sicilians keep pretty much to themselves. The coppers who patrol Little Italy play by the rules that benefit everyone here. But it's not something you want to discuss too loudly."

Rip took a sip of the wine and frowned. "I don't suppose I could replace this with a cold beer?"

Matt smiled at his friend and shook his head. He motioned for the young waiter and asked for a glass of water.

"Whatever happened to that bakery where you worked? Is it still there? Can we visit it?"

Matt consumed a large bite of the rich pasta as he considered the questions. He swallowed the food and chased it with another sip of the dark red wine before dabbing his mouth with the corners of the white napkin stuck into his shirt collar.

"That bakery has been gone for years. The building burned down, and I think an apartment house now stands in its place. Mr. Caggiano was killed before that happened. He ran into trouble with the Black Hand here."

Rip's eyes widened, and he leaned across the table and whispered, "What's the 'Black Hand'?"

Matt sipped a little more wine and grinned at his frightened associate. He leaned forward and lowered his own voice.

"The Irish aren't the only ones who have underworld gangs. The Italians have had criminal elements inside this community for decades."

Matt broke off another piece of bread and dipped it into the sauce before taking a bite of it.

"A lazy way to make money is to offer protection from personal injury to those who can afford it. At one time it was common to send a man an extortion letter requesting funds for protection. The letters were signed with just a handprint dipped in black ink. I don't know if there was one organization that practiced this type of theft or several smaller gangs."

"What happened if you couldn't pay them?" asked a subdued Rip.

"They killed you," answered Matt. "That's what happened to Mr. Caggiano, or so I was told. I'd already gone west with the railroad by then. Apparently he thought he was far enough removed from Little Italy to be protected by the police. He was wrong."

Rip stared across the table at Matt and absently took a large gulp of the wine from his previously neglected glass. "My God," he said. "These guys are worse than the Klan. At least the kluxers leave you with your life. They just want you to get out of town."

Matt nodded and had another bite of his meal. He reflected for a moment before he replied. "Our clan is no better. Do you think the Irishman we're going to see this evening isn't capable of cutting our throats? The gangsters who run the north side of Chicago are just as deadly as the people here. That's why we've come to Chicago. There's an old saying I picked up out west: It takes fire to fight fire. The Klan is actually humane compared to some of the truly criminal organizations that exist in this country. This is a mean world we live in; everyone is trying to get ahead on the backs of their neighbors. If you want peace and contentment, go to confession and hope a truck hits you as you come out of church. Because happiness doesn't exist in this world, but hopefully we'll find it in the next one."

Rip turned and looked out the window at the street traffic that passed by. After a few minutes, he picked up his fork and finished his meal. When he was finished, he looked over at Matt, who was still sipping his wine. "Does the 'Black Hand' still operate around here?" he murmured.

"I don't think so," answered Matt. "From what my brother has told me, it isn't all that profitable. These days, Canadian whiskey and locally brewed beer keep the underworld busy. Prohibition is going to make the Irish and the Italians successful. They don't have to hurt anyone or make enemies within the neighborhood. What other country provides crooks with a good way to get rich?

"And we'll each be taking a couple bottles of Canadian spirits home with us tomorrow."

That night at seven, Matt and Rip left their hotel and took a taxi to the Pearl restaurant on Division Street. Matt knew the location to be far enough removed from John's neighborhood to be safe from acquaintances of both Mr. Smith and himself. Once inside the taxi, Matt gave the driver the address of the restaurant and then he added a comment. "Take Western Avenue, please. I want to take a look at my old neighborhood." Matt had never lived this far north in Chicago, but he knew the local taxi drivers were notorious for taking visitors on detours to increase the fare. Matt was in no mood to have a confrontation over a bloated cab fare this evening.

The restaurant was situated above street level and reached by a series of ten concrete steps. Steps on either side of these led to merchants who had stores below street level. Inside the restaurant, the men noticed the frayed wall coverings and worn upholstered chairs. The tables were covered with white cloths, and the bar area was deserted except for a waiter who served presumably legal beverages. There were few diners out this evening. The depression had hit the big cities almost as hard as the rural parts of the country. But those patrons present appeared disturbed by their arrival. The atmosphere was decidedly unfriendly.

An elderly hostess approached them, and Rip mentioned they were here to meet a Mr. Smith. The old lady arched her thin eyebrows and then directed them to a small private room off the hallway that led to the kitchen.

Matt knocked on the door and opened it without waiting for an answer. A portly man dressed in an ill-fitting suit stood up from his seat at a table and waved them inside. The man was balding, and what little hair he still possessed was gray. He also wore a long green tie. "Come in, gentlemen. My name is Mr. Smith, and I understand that you have a business proposition for me."

Matt moved to the table as Rip closed the door and followed behind him. The room was sparsely furnished with a sideboard cabinet along with the table and four chairs. The restaurant apparently accommodated few private parties, and those they did cater probably had no need of fine furnishings. Most likely, the room hosted poker games on weekends.

Matt shook the man's hand and waited for Rip to do the same. "I'm Mr. Jones, and this is my assistant, Mr. Lane. Mr. Lane is not privy to all of my business activities, and it would be better if we spoke guardedly tonight."

Mr. Smith looked at Matt, and then at Rip, before he nodded his agreement. He then sat down and motioned his two guests to do the same. "I appreciate your caution, Mr. Jones. I prefer to deal with a man who is private with his business matters."

Matt poured himself a glass of water from a pitcher on the table. He passed the pitcher to Rip before he spoke. "Our mutual acquaintance speaks highly of your reputation, Mr. Smith. He believes you have the expertise we need to execute our plans."

The older man looked at his two guests, and Matt sensed hesitation on his face. "What do you do for a living, Mr. Jones?"

Matt was taken aback by the question, and he wasn't sure he should answer it. "Why do you need to know?" he asked.

"I'm risking my life by taking on this assignment. I need to be sure I'm dealing with competent people. So I'll ask you again, what is your line of work?"

Matt breathed deeply and exhaled slowly as he looked over at Rip. He feared his background made him completely unqualified for the project at hand. "I run a bakery in the town. I've worked for railroads and highway contractors in the past."

The man nodded and stroked the top of his bald head. "And what do you do, Mr. Lane?"

Rip looked eager to accommodate the mysterious gentleman. He likely remembered Matt's warning about how this gangster could cut their throats. "I'm a carpenter, sir . . . when I'm not working for Mr. Jones."

The portly man relaxed and smiled as he reached for his glass of water. "I apologize if I've been rude with you. I normally work alone, and I'm uncomfortable entrusting my safety to others. I've taken the time to research your town and the surrounding area. It's surprising all of the information one can obtain from the Chicago library. Still, I'm used to casing a town weeks before hand, and I won't get that opportunity in this instance.

"Do you have the information I requested?"

Matt pulled an envelope from his suit coat and passed it over to Mr. Smith.

The older man tore open the envelope and pulled the sheet of paper from it. He studied the paper for only a moment before he folded it and put it in his vest pocket. "I'm familiar with Swanson. They've been in business a long time. I think they're headquartered in Indiana."

He smiled and placed his hands on the lapels of his jacket. "Their work is good, but I'm better. As for the hardware, it won't be a problem. I'll be able to fulfill my side of the contract."

Matt was relieved, although he tried not to show it. If this man turned him down, the entire plan was in jeopardy. He could charge them five hundred dollars, and Matt would need to pay it. "Do you still have the equipment needed for the job?" Matt asked.

"Yes," replied the little man. "Everything will fit neatly into a small carrying case."

"Good," said Matt. "Our mutual friend will inform you of the scheduled date three days in advance. Plan on taking an afternoon Pennsy train to Logansport. Mr. Lane will meet you after five o'clock and escort you to his home. I'll pick you up in the evening to take you to the target. After we have completed our business, we'll return to Mr. Lane's home, and he'll get you safely back to Logansport the next morning for your return trip."

Mr. Smith placed his hands on the table. "It sounds like you have a simple but carefully constructed plan, Mr. Jones. The fewer people I have to deal with, the better it will be for all of us. I presume your accommodations are somewhat secluded, Mr. Lane?"

Rip looked startled and cleared his throat. "Why yes. I live in a quiet neighborhood. My wife, Hildy will be there . . . she makes a grand beef stew." Rip abruptly stopped as if he realized he'd said the wrong thing.

Matt wished he'd kept quiet about Hildy, but Rip had been caught off-guard.

Their host lowered his head, but Matt caught the wide smile his mouth now formed. He wondered if this man was as dangerous as he feared.

Mr. Smith now turned his focus back towards Matt. "Now, is my fee acceptable to you?"

Matt folded his hands together and placed them on the table. "Yes, I am prepared to give you sixty dollars now and the remaining one hundred, forty dollars when we return to Mr. Lane's home after you have finished your work."

The older man looked into Matt's eyes for just a moment before he nodded. "Your terms are acceptable. I'll even pay for my own train tickets."

Matt was pleased, but something the man said bothered him. "I must tell you," added Matt, "that there is a chance you'll be introduced to one other of my associates." Matt hesitated, afraid he might say the wrong thing. "We have a man who handles our security."

The small man looked to Matt first, then to Rip. His face gave no clue as to his thoughts. "You are taking measures to deal with the local police," reflected Mr. Smith. "I have no problem with being seen by one other person. As I said before, I appreciate a man who takes proper precautions in his business dealings." The man stretched his hand across the table. "We have a deal then, Mr. Jones."

Matt took the other man's right hand and gripped it tightly as they shook on their agreement. He then turned to Rip, "Mr. Lane, please give Mr. Smith the sixty dollar advance on his contract."

Rip reached into his vest pocket and pulled out a roll of paper currency. He quickly peeled off three twenty-dollar bills and placed them in front of the man opposite him.

Mr. Smith scooped up the money, folded it in half, and placed it in his shirt pocket. He quickly rose and picked up his coat from the back of his chair. "Gentlemen, I must be on my way, but please stay and have dinner in the front dining room. I've already paid for your meals, and I heartily recommend the rainbow trout. It's trucked in to a local market from Minnesota, and it's superb this evening."

He then leaned across the table and whispered, "It's not a good idea to have dinner together. The coppers have many sets of eyes in this part of town."

Matt was unnerved by the abrupt action of the man. He wondered, not for the first time, if he was being set up for a robbery or a shakedown by some coppers who uncovered his plan.

The portly stranger must have guessed at Matt's concern. He placed a hand on Matt's shoulder as he came around the table. "Don't worry, Mr. Jones. You're safe with me. I've never been caught, and I'll do what you require. Hell, I'd be willing to kill a few of these Kluxers if that's what it takes to put them out of business."

Mr. Smith chuckled, apparently amused with himself.

"Enjoy the rest of your evening. Mr. Lane, it was nice meeting you, and I look forward to our meeting again in Logansport."

The man put on his overcoat and left the room. Matt stared at the table and replayed in his mind what had just taken place. His plans were coming together, which brought him much-needed relief. But he could still get caught. Would his family suffer the consequences of his crusade?

Finally Rip broke the silence. "He seems like a swell guy, but he scares the hell out of me. I'm glad you know what you're doing, Mr. Jones. Now let's go have dinner; I think we've earned it."

CHAPTER 14

April 1923
Donegal, Indiana

The day had begun cool and damp. A dense fog, fed by the river, had blanketed the town and the valley. But by noon the clouds had dissipated, and a warm sun had burned away the mist. The afternoon had been pleasant and signaled the arrival of spring to the Midwest.

The dining room at the Tilly house was warm and stuffy that evening. Mr. Tilly had a fire smoldering in the fireplace though it was not really needed for the supper gathering. Mrs. Tilly moved back and forth from the kitchen, removing dinner plates and returning with dessert plates that contained slices of one of Maureen's chocolate chiffon cakes. Mr. Tilly sat describing to his three boarders the new improvements of the ReVere sedan he had seen parked on Broad Street that afternoon. The ReVere Corporation was a local success story, but few could afford their hundred horsepower cars that sold for five thousand dollars. The sleek white automobile drew a crowd who appreciated the contrast it made to the black touring models and sedans that surrounded it. Randall Madison appeared interested in the news, and Thelma Floyd was also attentive.

Try as she might, Maureen found she had no interest in the conversation. She did not know if it was the heat in the room or the events of the day, or perhaps her health, but she was irritated and did not care to hide it. Betty Tilly complimented her on the cake, but Maureen was unresponsive to the praise.

Betty recognized her mood and probably sought to comfort her. "What's wrong dear? Are you ill?"

"I don't really know," responded Maureen. "It's a little warm, and we didn't have a good day at the bakery."

This exchange caught Randall's attention. "How is business down at your brother's bakery?" he inquired.

The question brought a halt to Mr. Tilly's discourse, and all eyes turned toward Maureen. She composed herself and clasped her hands before answering. "Things are fair, but we don't have the customers we used to see last year." No one replied, and she felt the need to downplay her concerns. "We need more loyal people like the Tillys to keep sales up," she hurriedly added.

Mrs. Floyd was moved to respond. "When the fresh fruits come back in season, you'll have to beat off the pie lovers with a stick. Sales will boom then, you'll see."

Mr. Tilly was more guarded in his assessment. "The Klan has ostracized all Catholics in the area. I've heard Joe Matichak complain that potential customers won't visit his butcher shop because of a whisper campaign by the Klan. A lot of otherwise decent people are frightened off when anything bad is said about a merchant. It may take some time before the community gets beyond this problem."

"Is that why the Conner bakery is having trouble?" asked Randall. Everyone looked at Maureen as tears welled up in her eyes. She lowered her head and nodded.

Mrs. Tilly moved to her instinctively. "Poor dear, things will work out. God has a plan, and we must have faith in Him." Maureen let the woman put her arms around her, but her fears were not calmed.

After a few uncomfortable moments among the gathered diners, Randall Madison spoke. "Maureen, I think your bakery is a grand business, and it would be a shame if your brother was forced into ruin by these troubles. Do you think he might sell it for a fair price to someone like myself? It would be a way to recover his investment."

Maureen looked up with shock on her features. Her back went rigid, and she felt Mrs. Tilly release her hold. Why was this stranger offering to take over their business? How could he possibly hope to do better than her brother?

"What do you know about baking, Mr. Madison?" she queried.

"Nothing," he stammered. "I would have to find someone like yourself to bake the goods, and I would be left to manage the business side of things."

Maureen and the others looked at the man, who was starting to become flushed. "I assure you I have only the best of intentions. I'm having trouble getting farmers interested in my plans for motorized well pumps, and I thought perhaps I should think about investing my capital into an established business. I've been impressed with your brother's operation, and possibly I could help him out of a bad situation."

Maureen looked coldly across the table at her fellow boarder. "I don't think my brother would sell the bakery to someone he hardly knows, Mr. Madison. Are you certain you could do better than we have by changing the ownership from Catholic to Protestant?"

The man looked crestfallen. Maureen knew she had verbally slapped him in the face.

"I had hoped I could prevail upon you and the other employees to continue working," answered Randall.

Maureen stared incredulously across the table at this man she thought she understood. There was something hidden behind his gentle demeanor that scared her. She didn't know what to say to his proposal.

Randall seemed to grow uncomfortable from her stare and the silence that engulfed the dining room. "Well, would it be all right with you if I stopped in some day to discuss it with him . . . directly? I wouldn't do so if you didn't want me to approach him."

"You are certainly free to do whatever you wish, Mr. Madison. I'll tell my brother tomorrow that you plan to call on him regarding your proposal. I'm sure he will give you a fair hearing."

Maureen abruptly pushed back her chair and rose from the table. "Please excuse me, everyone. I'm afraid I do not have the appetite for even my own baking. I must retire to my room."

The men stood, and all four diners watched as the young woman made her way out into the foyer and up the oak stairs. When everyone had taken his seat, Randall concluded the discussion by expressing his viewpoint. "I should think there are a few smart businessmen who would be willing to sell out rather than remain in a town where they are not wanted. There may be some excellent opportunities coming available in the near future, and astute men should be ready to seize them."

Betty Tilly balanced a bite of the chocolate cake on her fork. "Mr. Madison, I don't pretend to understand business or what's considered proper out west. But around here people treat their neighbors with respect, no matter what their religion may be. Be careful that you're not viewed as taking advantage of other peoples' problems, because you won't fare any better."

The next evening Matt was holding a conference with Liam McNamara, Boyd Phelps, and Andy O'Neill in the living room of his home. Matt had requested the help of these three fellow parishioners because he knew them to be hard workers and good providers for their families. They also held clerical jobs and were good typists, which were critical skills to completing phase two of his plan.

Matt sat in a straight chair he had brought in from the dining room. Liam sat to one side in Matt's favorite reading chair. The other two men were positioned at either end of the sofa located in front of the window overlooking the porch. Matt had laid out their task and was now going over the details. "You don't need to know who will be bringing you the package. A stranger will knock on the door of the church office and give you the signal 'Love thy neighbor' before he hands it to you. He'll pose no threat to you. Also, he'll tell you where to take the package when you've completed your work."

"But you think we'll deliver it to Chief Johnson's home?" clarified Liam.

"Yes," said Matt. "But I don't know for certain until I've reviewed it. You may need to deliver it to Fred Sloan. I don't want this matter to get into his newspaper, but we may have no other choice."

"What time should we expect the package?" asked Boyd.

"The three of you need to be ready by midnight. You'll already have finished waxing the floors. Remember that's your excuse for being out so late. You came back to finish the job that you left to get supper."

"But the floors will already be done," stated Liam. "So when we come back we need to set up the equipment and have everything ready ahead of time."

"Correct," said Matt. "I figure you'll have until four to finish your work. Andy will drop the envelopes in Peter's garage on his way home. Boyd will wrap up and deliver the package to the proper location. Make sure the note is displayed on the top of the package and don't get caught. If you do, your story is that you found it on the steps of the church as you were leaving and meant to deliver it to the person specified in the note.

"Liam can stay and clean up. Don't leave any materials behind. Nothing should suggest that the church, and especially our pastors, were part of this plan."

"Are they in on the plan?" asked Liam.

"No," replied Matt. "They will be told to stay out of the church after confessions because of the fumes from the shellac that will be used on the worn spots of the floor. That's your alibi, but you won't have time to varnish any spots. Don't let anyone inside once you boys start on the floors. That way no one will know when you actually finish. Leave the Under Repair sign on the door when you go home for supper. When you return, prepare the church for morning Mass and then set up for your other task."

"And after we're finished with our other work, we just mosey home and pretend that it's just another Sunday morning?" inquired Boyd.

"That's right," replied Matt. "Peter's group will take care of phase three and deliver the envelopes to the list I developed with some other plan members. This list started out to be fairly small, but it's grown to more than a dozen names. That's why we need men with good typing skills. Using carbon paper, I hope you can produce all the copies in three hours.

"Of course one set will be delivered to the Weinberg Brothers store, and they plan to produce and distribute more copies."

"Why are we getting involved with the Jews?" groused Andy. His features twisted into a sour expression.

Matt studied his young recruit and chose his words carefully. "They've lived and worked in this town longer than most of us. They've received hate mail, and they've been threatened just like us. They want to help, and I say we should let them. Besides, their lawyer is our own Mr. James Collins, and they gave him twenty bucks for our cause."

Andy O'Neill considered this information and shrugged his shoulders.

Matt's eyes softened at the young man's acceptance of his decision. He shifted in his chair and surveyed the others present in the room. "I don't know about the rest of you, but I plan to buy my next suit from the Weinberg Brothers store."

"I'd still like to know what we're making at such an odd time of the night?" said Boyd.

Liam spoke for the others like the wise Irishman that he was. "The less we know, the less chance the wrong people will find out about it."

Matt added, "You'll understand when you see the package. Until then, just pray that we don't get caught and that what we're planning has the desired affect."

There were a few other items they explored, and then the men rose to leave. After Matt had shown them out, he headed upstairs to see his family. Laura was asleep in her crib in his and Annie's bedroom. Soon she would have to move in with Katy, and Matt looked forward to regaining marital privacy. Yet he enjoyed having the baby sleeping next to him when he went to bed early in the evening before

Annie. The baby's presence calmed him and helped him drift off to sleep faster.

Laura was breathing easily, and Matt took comfort in the fact that she had made it through her first winter. With luck she would grow strong and healthy through the coming warm weather and be prepared for the various illnesses she would be exposed to next winter.

He found Annie and the older children in Katy's room. Annie was sitting on the floor reading from *Winnie the Pooh* while Brian and Katy lay across the bed peering over her shoulders. Annie stopped at Matt's appearance and looked up at him with apprehension.

"My guests are gone," he said simply. "Let me listen while you finish the story. It's a favorite of mine." He smiled at their children, and they returned his gesture. He sat down on the floor to share in the simple pleasure of a children's story they had all heard many times before.

But as Annie returned to the place she had left off, Matt found himself thinking about matters much different than children's stories.

On Saturday, Randall Madison was once again out on patrol during the early evening. Only this time it wasn't in the company of his friend Officer Harris or even with Chief Johnson. The chief had invited Randall along for company twice when he was making evening patrols. He said he enjoyed the common sense approach Randall applied to community life in Donegal. Chief Johnson told Randall that had he the funds, he would have offered Randall a position on his staff.

But tonight Randall was the guest of Tom Stewart, who had approached him to take part in the knight ride Randall had heard about during the small gathering he attended last month. It was obvious Tom was not in good health, and he had no business participating in physical outdoor activity. However, Tom was supposed to be good at planning these actions and for preparing for contingencies. He sensed trouble and knew how to avoid it.

Tom had briefed Randall on his role, and Randall understood he had a major part to play. He concluded that the Klan needed someone who could relieve Tom of the physical demands of these demonstrations and leave Tom to handle the planning phase. Randall figured he was being tested to see if he could take on the duties Tom could no longer perform. The idea had some appeal for Randall.

Tom explained to him that the Knight Riders were self-appointed morality police, having determined it was their duty to correct the actions of those they deemed had gone astray. There was little need to hurt anyone, but people needed to be shown the proper way to live in the community. It was the Knight Riders' job to put the fear of God into neighbors who needed corrective measures.

Tad Cochran pulled his Model T to a halt under a bare old elm tree on the side of the road. The fields were too wet to drive across, so this isolated spot on the sparsely traveled farm road was as close to the Adam Sharp farm as they could get. Don Lester pulled on his black hood and silently left the front seat to begin this evening's action. Don would sneak into the Sharp barn and release the animals from their stalls. His job was to coax two or three milk cows out into the night with a minimum of noise. Tom was sure Adam or one of his family would notice the problem, and it was hoped Adam would come outside to gather up his livestock. Tad's car was parked in such a way as to note the flare of a match that would be Don's signal if Adam Sharp came outside. Randall positioned himself in front of the Ford and held a black hood in his hand.

In a little less than an hour, Randall observed a small commotion coming from inside the Sharp house. Then someone with a lantern was seen moving in the yard. A few moments later the spark of a match appeared by the side of the barn. "There's Don's signal," whispered Tad. Randall spun the crank, and the car's engine sprang to life. He jumped into the rear passenger seat as Tad shifted into gear to move toward the farm's entrance drive. Tad drove up the level driveway but kept his headlamps off until he sighted the farmer holding onto one of his dairy animals. Then he illuminated the scene in front of them.

"We got him by surprise," exclaimed Tad.

The terrified Mr. Sharp released his cow and turned to flee to his house from the apparent danger. It was too late. A hooded Don Lester blocked his way with a shotgun leveled at the man. Adam Sharp stopped and raised his hands while still holding the lantern. He looked like a cornered animal as he turned back toward the car that braked to a halt on the gravel in front of him. Wearing black hoods, Tom and Randall got out of the rear seat and calmly approached their quarry.

"Where's the rest of your family?" scowled Randall.

"The boy's here by the barn," interjected Don. "The rest are inside."

"Have your son come toward the light, Mr. Sharp," ordered Randall. "No one will be hurt if you do what we tell you."

Adam Sharp looked scared, and he didn't have time to think of a way out of this predicament. He turned toward the barn and squinted into the darkness as he cleared his throat. "Come here, Josh. Don't be afraid, boy."

A young boy in overalls with a blanket covering his shoulders stepped tentatively into the light provided by Tad's car.

"Hello, son," said Randall in a polite tone. "I need you to go inside and bring your mother and sister here. Tell them they need to hear what we have to say to your daddy. Do you understand that, Josh?"

The boy nodded.

"Is there anyone else inside?" asked Randall.

Josh shook his head.

"Then go quickly and tell your mom to grab a coat and come here. Tell her she doesn't need to bring a gun or anything. It would just cause problems for your daddy."

The boy took a few tentative steps toward the house and then ran inside once he got past Don. Don followed to the porch and waited for the family to appear. Tom Stewart had already determined that the farm did not have a telephone so there could be no calls to the police. The Knight Riders had all the time necessary to complete their mission.

Adam Sharp seemed nervous. Randall was concerned that Adam would consider running off now that Don's attention was diverted to the house. Randall took a step closer to him, and when Sharp tried to move backward, Randall grabbed his wrist and in one motion twisted the farmer's arm behind his back. "Get on your knees," ordered Randall while he applied more pressure to the man's arm.

Mr. Sharp was a strong man, but Randall was bigger and had leverage. The man resisted momentarily, but then his knees buckled, and he lowered himself to the ground. The lantern dropped from Sharp's hand landing upright beside him. Randall released his hold on Sharp and walked around to where he could face the man.

The door of the house squeaked open on its worn hinges, and a woman walked out slowly with her two children in tow.

"Please come forward, ma'am," requested Randall while motioning with his left hand. "We have something to say to your husband, and everyone needs to hear it. It will only take a minute. Then we'll leave you to get your rest."

Bundled against the cool night air, Mrs. Sharp and her son and daughter reluctantly came forward into the light. Don stayed a few yards behind, watching the barn and the house for any unanticipated visitors.

Tom looked at Randall and nodded his approval to proceed. Randall approached the subdued man in full view of his family.

"Adam Sharp, the good people of this community have observed the poor way you treat your family. You have mistreated your wife and kids on more than one occasion on the streets of town. Your children have been seen at school with bruises on their bodies, and your son had a broken arm last year."

"Those were accidents," objected Adam.

Randall just stared down at the man before continuing. "In addition, your wife left church one Sunday with pain so severe she had to be administered aid by her fellow congregants." He stopped and waited for further protest, but Sharp wisely remained silent.

"You are known in these parts to get angry and violent for no good reason. You are hereby ordered to mend your ways. The

Knights of the Ku Klux Klan will no longer tolerate your bad behavior within our community. You must repent your sins and seek God's forgiveness. Do you understand what we are telling you?"

"I didn't do nothing wrong. I got a right to discipline my family," replied Adam Sharp bitterly.

Randall smiled beneath his hood. He now had the confirmation he wanted before he passed judgment. "No you don't," he said quietly. "You lost that right by being mean spirited and causing physical harm to these fine Christian folk. If any further accidents should befall your wife or children, we'll find out about it. And then we'll be back with horsewhips."

Randall leaned down and whispered into the man's ear. "You won't be able to milk those cows for a month, and I myself will castrate you."

Adam's head whipped around, and he raised his fist in anger, but Randall had anticipated the man's angry reaction. He grabbed Sharp by his hair and pulled him off balance while he also placed his foot on the farmer's ankle, pinning it to the ground.

Adam Sharp yelled in pain while his arms flailed out in frustration. He looked like a puppet on a string as Randall continued to hold him by his hair. After a few moments of grunting by the captured man, Randall released his grip of the quarry and stepped away quickly.

Sharp fell onto his hands and knees, breathing heavily.

Randall turned his attention to the woman and two children who stood transfixed in fear. "Mrs. Sharp, if your husband ever hurts you or comes after you or your children in a threatening manner, you go to the police or your neighbors. They may not be able to do anything, but we'll hear about it, and we'll come for him. This man must never again be allowed to harm a living soul."

Randall motioned for Don to come forward, then took a few paces back toward the car's headlamps. He turned and waited for Mr. Sharp to look up at him. "Repent of your wicked ways, Adam Sharp. Or else you'll suffer the consequences here on earth and forever in hell."

Randall turned and proceeded to the left side of the car while Don Lester and Tom Stewart opened the doors on the right side. The canvas top was folded down, and Don was able to stand with one hand on the windshield, the shotgun resting in his other hand and on his arm. Tad Cochran shifted into reverse and proceeded backward to the road. There was no traffic as he stopped, shifted into first gear, and accelerated toward town.

CHAPTER 15

May 12, 1923
Donegal, Indiana

THE FRESHLY MOWN GRASS SMELLED LIKE SUMMER as Matt drove his Ford one-ton truck through the residential streets to Rip Riley's home. It was past ten on a Saturday night, and he worried that the noise of his truck would bring unwanted attention to him. He could not have been more self-conscious if he were strolling down Broad Street in a nightgown at high noon. He found that his senses were fully alert even as his anxiety grew. The dew covered the ground, and even in the darkness, Matt could make out the muted colors of flowers and tree blossoms against the dark green foliage that surrounded them. He often enjoyed his predawn walks to work in the springtime. The sight and smell of the new blooms invigorated him, but not tonight.

Matt had been working since supper at the bakery with Davy to clean the kitchen and overhaul the ovens. Matt did this necessary dirty task two Saturdays a year after the coal fires had burned out. But tonight, Matt was leaving most of the work for Davy, who was excited to have such responsibility bestowed upon him. Matt was more than willing to let Davy handle the majority of the project since Davy had earned his trust. More important, Matt had other duties this evening, and Davy would unwittingly be Matt's alibi, if necessary.

The young loyal assistant thought Matt had taken the truck home to pick up a pair of new racks for the ovens. But the racks were already in the truck as Matt drove to Rip's place. It was a blessing that Davy was not very good at keeping track of time.

Earlier in the day Matt had been visited separately by Liam McNamara and Peter Sullivan, who were in charge of phases two and three of tonight's plan. Now they were ready, and they would gather at the appointed time for each group. However, everything depended upon Matt successfully completing the first phase, the one that could land him in jail or worse. The final piece of the plan had been set in place at noon today. Matt had taken Maureen to one side of the kitchen and requested she have dinner with him and Annie this evening. Afterward, she would take Matt's Elcar sedan home to the Tillys' and gather some things to spend the night at Matt and Annie's house. She would explain to Mrs. Tilly that Annie needed some help with the children while Matt worked late at the bakery. Now Maureen knew why Matt had been so eager to teach her to drive the car. She'd been shocked and was deeply troubled by what he had told her.

Matt slowed as he approached the Riley residence on Seventeenth Street, noting with relief the light shining through the front window of the modest bungalow. This was the signal that there was no trouble present. Hildy Riley had already paid Matt a visit at the bakery earlier in the afternoon. She casually mentioned during their conversation that Rip had met a certain Mr. Smith in Logansport who had revealed he was acquainted with Matt.

Matt stopped the truck in front of the Riley home and turned off his lights. As soon as the light went off in the house, Matt slipped the truck into gear, proceeded down the street, and parked again near the intersection at Oak Avenue. Two minutes later, Mr. Smith opened the passenger door and entered the vehicle carrying a small valise.

"Good evening, Mr. Jones, it's nice to see you again."

Matt turned on his lights, shifted into gear, and put the truck into motion before he spoke. "It's very good to see you as well, Mr. Smith. I've been anxious about whether or not you would make the trip."

"You need to have more faith in your kinsman," replied the man. "We Irish have so few pleasures in life as we get older, we have to embrace those infrequent exhilarating experiences that come our way."

Matt turned toward his companion and smiled in appreciation of the man's humor. "I hope you've had a pleasant trip so far," offered Matt. "Are you ready to earn your fee?"

"Yes indeed," answered Mr. Smith. "Just deliver me to our mark and watch and learn. I guarantee you it will be more exciting than the latest carnival or magic act to play your quaint little town."

Matt made his way back to Broad Street and his rented garage. "For some reason, I just don't feel as excited as you do," he said.

Mr. Smith lowered his voice as he became serious. "My only concern is with your local police. Are you quite certain that the law will be kept at bay for our little operation?"

Matt's felt his lips stretch into a tight grimace. "We think we have neutralized the police. There is only one officer on duty this evening, and he will have completed his rounds by now. He won't make another patrol until five in the morning. There is a risk he could receive an emergency call from someone during the night. We can't rule out a disturbance that might take place during this evening. But we'll have someone watching the streets for us."

The visitor looked across at his host and then turned his gaze to the view in front of them. The streetlights illuminated the commercial district, revealing a light fog rising up from the river. "Fair enough, Mr. Jones. Your brother said I could rely on you to cover all contingencies. But remember that I'm the only person who can tie your brother to this plan. You don't want me to be arrested and questioned by the coppers."

The two men drove on in silence as Matt contemplated the role each would play in tonight's drama.

Matt braked to a stop in front of the garage, got out, and folded open the doors before driving in and shutting off the engine. Only after he closed the doors did Mr. Smith exit the vehicle. Matt checked the entrance once again and found no one stirring outside. He opened one of the doors just a foot and slipped out onto the street. Mr. Smith joined him momentarily, and they proceeded up Seventh Street to the bakery. Mr. Smith lingered outside while Matt let himself in to check on Davy and to offer an excuse for the delay in bringing the new racks.

Within five minutes Matt returned, and the two men made their way quietly up to Broad Street and then west toward the center of town. They saw few people out at this late hour. Fortunately, Prohibition had brought an end to Saturday evening parties in the small farming towns of the Midwest.

As they approached the Franklin Building, they slowed their pace and surreptitiously scanned the street in both directions. No one was present when they stopped in front of the door that led to a staircase inside the middle of the building. Matt looked up at the dark brick edifice and was pleased that the lights were off on the second floor above them. In the gloom he saw the structure as a dangerous fortress that had to be breached.

Mr. Smith pulled a small ring of keys from his suit coat. Each key had cloth on it, apparently to muffle any sound that would be made by contact between the various metal probes. He squatted in front of the door and observed its hardware in the muted glow of the street lamps. He then stood and selected one key, removed its wrapping, and inserted it into the door's lock. Matt stood watch, praying that the blanket of darkness hid them. After a few slow thrusts, Mr. Smith twisted the probe hard in a counterclockwise motion and turned the handle to open the door. The two men quickly entered the building and proceeded to lock the door from the inside.

"How did you know to have the proper key?" inquired Matt.

"Each key is filed down to the point that it fits most of the locks designed by its manufacturer. I only need a couple for all of the locks made by a company. I guessed right on this one. That's a good sign."

Matt shook his head in astonishment and took the lead as the men proceeded cautiously up the dark stairway to the second floor of the building. There was a light for the stairs, but they knew better than to turn it on. It was best to have the security of the darkness even though it inhibited their progress. They walked down the hallway quietly, feeling the walls to guide them. No lights or noise came from any of the offices. Matt worried that someone would be sleeping in one of the rented spaces, but he heard nothing. At the far end of the hall, he pulled a candle and matches from his cotton jacket. Mr. Smith held the candle as Matt struck a match and lit it. The hallway was suddenly aglow. The light seemed far too bright to be coming from such a small candle.

Matt snuffed out the match, and the older man handed over the candle. Mr. Smith then peered at the lock below the stenciled name of Lucas Crawford. "Different lock maker than for the front door," said Mr. Smith. "That's typical for office space that gets rented out to numerous enterprises over the years. Fortunately, the information you provided me has been correct."

The older man pulled out his ring and selected a key with which he was able to unlock the glass door in a matter of moments. Once the two men were safely inside the small office, Matt began to feel relieved. He had been very apprehensive about their ability to get into the Klan's lair. Their success to this point emboldened him to believe they could finish their task productively.

At that moment, Randall Madison was walking up Fourth Street from the river. He was enjoying the spring weather and the serene stroll along the banks of the Wabash. The sounds of the birds and the nocturnal insects were like music to him after the long winter of silence. His only complaint was the noise from passing trains that rumbled along the river even in the late evenings.

Once he crossed the tracks and walked toward the center of town, the shrouded night grew quiet. The only sound he identified was the hum of electricity passing through the wires strung above the sidewalk. As Randall approached Broad Street, he glanced up at the back of the Franklin Building, which occupied the corner. A dim light in a pair of windows caught his attention. It moved and flickered like candlelight. He was aware that the windows were to the offices of Mr.

Lucas Crawford, Life Insurance Agent. Randall stopped in the gloom and stared more intently at the two windows of the corner office. Why would anyone try to conduct business by dim candlelight?

Madison realized thieves must be at work, and he quickened his pace as he approached Broad Street. He crossed over to the other side and headed east in front of the building while furtively scanning the street for unusual activity. When he walked past to Fifth Street, he turned left and ran up the block to police headquarters.

Randall hastily turned the knob of the massive steel and oak door to the police station and was thankful that it opened for him. If the evening patrolman had gone out, then the door would have been locked. He stepped inside and was relieved to find Billy Harris looking down at him from the high desk that commanded the view of the entrance to headquarters.

Billy's face brightened into a smile at the appearance of his good friend, but it quickly turned to one of alarm. "Hey, Randall, you look like you've just seen a ghost. Did you run into trouble down by the river?"

"No, I'm okay," answered the breathless visitor. "Is anyone else here with you tonight?"

"Nope. We've got nobody locked up, so there's no need for a second officer."

Randall approached the tall desk, removed his hat, and rubbed his fingers across his forehead. "Billy, it may be my imagination, but I thought I spotted a light in the windows of Lucas Crawford's office on the back side of Broad Street. All the electric lights were turned off on the second floor, but I'm sure there was some sort of flame burning in the office. And I saw some shadows move against the ceiling as I looked up into the windows. What would anybody be doing up there at this hour of the night?"

Billy Harris stared down at his friend as he absorbed this information. He turned his head and stared out the barred windows into the black night. The only things visible to Randall were the outdoor lights at the top of the county courthouse across Fifth Street. Billy turned toward Randall again before he spoke. "They keep money in that safe in the office. Lucas likes to have some ready cash available. It just may be a burglary in progress. I better call the chief and have him come down to investigate."

"But what if I'm wrong?" questioned Randall. "Besides, you know Lucas doesn't want any attention called to his presence here in town. That's why it's set up as an insurance agency."

"Well, we can't just let some burglars make off with his money just to keep things hushed up," replied the police officer angrily.

Randall stared up at his friend and then scratched his chin, turned and walked to the window. He stopped suddenly, pivoted, and snapped his fingers as he looked up at Officer Harris.

"Let's go over and set up an ambush. I can back you up, and if I'm right, you can nab them when they come out of the building. You'll be a hero for catching the scoundrels, and Lucas should be very appreciative that you saved him his money."

Billy Harris sat and thought for a moment while he inhaled the smoke from a cigarette that had been smoldering in an ashtray on the high desk. "That's not a bad idea, Randall. And if we don't find anything wrong, then you don't look the fool for raising a false alarm."

Randall was slightly annoyed at the playful rebuke from his friend. "Just get your hat, Officer Harris, and let's go do your job."

In the Crawford Insurance office, Matt and Mr. Smith were hunched in front of the Swanson safe at the far end of the office. According to Matt's pocket watch, they had been in the office for ten minutes, but the safe was still locked. Matt's anxiety increased as Mr. Smith spun the dial and started once again to attempt to decipher the combination. After a minute of turning the dial and listening for noises, the older man stood up and moved to the side of the window. He took a deep breath and stared out into the darkness.

"I thought I hired a safe-cracker, but now I'm not so sure," stated Matt in a low monotone.

Mr. Smith turned, and his eyes met Matt's. "My hearing is not as good as it was ten years ago. Plus I have to relearn the feel of the tumblers through the dial. I've broken into this type of safe before, and I can do it again. Be patient, Mr. Jones. I'll deliver what I agreed to do for you."

Matt stood and returned some papers that he had been reviewing to the desk drawer where he had found them. Smith had unlocked the desks before he began work on the safe. Matt had gone through the drawers looking for Klan intelligence but found only insurance correspondence. A couple of letters were requests regarding membership data from an insurance company in Indianapolis. Matt suspected they could be coded Klan documents, but they did not give him the information he needed. He was sure that it was in the safe, locked up for the weekend.

Matt regretted his comment. He needed to be calm and to keep his companion calm. They were running out of time, but patience was indeed called for at this critical hour in the timetable. Matt sought to take their minds off the problem at hand.

"Why did you retire from the bank robbery business?" asked Matt. "Did you make enough money, or did the law start to close in on you?"

"Neither," replied the older man. "Modern inventions put an end to my prior career. But you are mistaken. I never robbed anyone or any bank. Robbery is committed against persons who have reason to fear for their lives. I burglarized certain banking institutions late in the evening when no one was present. I didn't even take all of the money. I preferred to take just enough to meet my needs but not arouse suspicion right away. Sometimes, the bank never did go public about the theft. I never understood if it was because they didn't want to admit to the loss or they simply couldn't account for all of their deposits."

Mr. Smith walked over and sat on the edge of the desk nearest the safe. He looked at it, and then turned to Matt who had taken a seat in the big leather chair. "My world changed, Mr. Jones, with the invention of burglar alarms and especially time locks. It became much harder to get into banks and more so into safes after the close of business each day. I could have learned to blow them open, but that would have been noisy. I never liked to alert people to my presence in their fair community."

"So you retired and became a respectable business man." Matt said this with a chuckle and appreciation for a fellow Irishman who had become successful in a world that did not provide many advantages to men like themselves.

"Yes, I've been quite fortunate to make a new career for myself," said the old watchmaker. "Now days robbers invade a bank with customers present and the vault open. They scare the daylights out of everyone with shotguns and the big revolvers they wave around. People could get hurt, and besides, it's too risky. It's just not a good way to make a living.

"But a fine old safe like this one reminds me of days gone by and the exhilaration I once felt for my craft. And now it's time to get the job finished so we can get on with the rest of your plan, whatever that might be."

The retired safe-cracker moved over to the steel enclosure and sat down on the floor next to it. He put his ear near the door and began to manipulate the dial in slow movements both clockwise and counterclockwise. Matt sat quietly in the big green chair. He wanted to pray, but his conscience told him it would not be proper under the circumstances. He listened for noises and was reassured when he heard nothing.

Matt kept track of the time by holding his pocket watch open to the candlelight. He noted that another three minutes had gone by since they had spoken. To Matt the time seemed more like three hours. In another five minutes, they would have to quit. People would be waiting for them. Mr. Smith sighed, then dropped his hand from the dial. He got up and stretched his back and then he smiled. He looked across the room at Matt as he bent down and grasped the handle of the safe. With a quick motion, he snapped the handle into a horizontal position and pulled open the door. He then backed away from the coffer and motioned Matt to come forward.

Matt could hardly move. He rose slowly, his legs feeling wobbly. He crossed the room as if in a stupor. Up until now, all his energy had been focused on getting inside the Klan's offices and getting access to their papers. In a moment, he would know if his plan would bear fruit or if he had risked jail or injury, even death, for nothing.

He took the candle and peered into the safe. He noted a small stack of cash held together by string and a large revolver on the upper shelf. The bottom contained some papers and a canvas-bound book. Matt reached for the book and opened it. His hands shook in anticipation. Inside were seven pages of names written in ink with occupations and addresses appearing on the same line with each name. To the right side of each line were a series of numbers that Matt presumed were payment entries. The first name on the list belonged to Tom Stewart. Matt knew he had his prize, the membership roster of the Wabash Valley Klan.

Mr. Smith peered over Matt's shoulder at the book. "That's what we came for?" asked the semi-retired thief.

"Yeah," breathed Matt as he scanned the pages, recognizing many familiar names. He found the name of Mayor Griffith and two county officials plus a judge. Curiously, there were no payments registered for them. But most important to Matt, he did not find the name of Paul Johnson.

Matt exhaled deeply and smiled. "This is it; we can lock up and go now."

"What about these other things in here?" whispered the older man as he stepped around Matt and pointed into the safe.

"No," said Matt with a wistful glance. "We didn't come here to steal anything. We're just borrowing this book for a few hours."

"Suit yourself," said Mr. Smith. He knelt down and swung the door closed on the safe. He turned the handle down into its original position and spun the dial back and forth for a few seconds. He then stood, and taking the key ring from his pocket, he went over to each desk and closed all of the drawers taking care to lock them.

Matt moved to the door, clutching the book and listened again for any noise outside the office. He watched Mr. Smith make one last sweep of the office looking for anything that might be out of place. Satisfied that they had everything, Mr. Smith picked up his valise and the candle. He motioned to Matt, who grabbed the doorknob as the older man snuffed out the light.

Outside, Billy and Randall had taken up positions in the alley on the east side of the building. They had scouted around in back and seen the candle light from the two windows on the corner of the second floor. Randall had armed himself with a small coal shovel he found leaning against the rear cellar of the barbershop.

Billy was in charge, and he warned Randall to stay behind him. He probably feared that Randall could get hurt in a fight with armed burglars. "Just watch for anything suspicious behind me. I'll jump these boys as soon as they come out onto the street," he whispered as he drew his gun.

Randall was alarmed at the sight of the drawn weapon. "Damn, Billy. We don't know who they are yet. Put your gun away until we've had a chance to confront them. What if they turn out to be Klan members on a knight ride?"

Billy nodded to his friend and pulled his finger free from the gun's trigger. But he still held the weapon pointed at the doorway, mere feet from their position.

Inside, Matt and Mr. Smith had made their way to the staircase and down to the interior vestibule at street level. Matt had the lead, and he waited until his hired companion was next to him. "We wait here until we're sure that it's safe to leave," whispered Matt.

Mr. Smith nodded his agreement as Matt slowly turned the knob of the lock and just as deliberately rotated the handle of the big glass and wood door until the latch had been fully withdrawn. Cautiously he pulled the door open and heard it squeak on its hinges. He hesitated for a moment and then pulled it open further while holding up his other hand, which held the prized book, to keep his accomplice from moving past him.

Billy heard and saw the door open, and he stepped forward and settled into a crouch with his attention focused on the entrance before him. Randall stepped up behind the policeman and raised his shovel in order to render his opponent senseless.

Randall peered into the darkness to be sure the doorway was open and then he brought the flat part of the shovel down hard onto the crown of Billy Harris's bowler. The powerful swing stopped abruptly upon making contact with the policeman's skull. Randall heard a loud thud followed by a reverberating metallic ping as he pulled the shovel back for a second blow. But none was required. Officer Harris collapsed into a heap on the sidewalk in front of the building. Randall looked around, afraid that the noise would alert someone who may be out late this evening. He saw no one, so he put the shovel down and removed the pistol from the unconscious policeman's hand. He then dragged Billy back into the alley and began to undress his victim.

Matt heard the sound of the shovel and waited a full minute, but he heard nothing further. "I believe that it is now okay to leave," he told his companion. "Lock the door behind you and follow me into the alley. There's someone we have to meet."

Matt tiptoed around the corner, where he saw the prostrate form of Officer Billy Harris lying in the alley with Randall Madison leaning over him, buttoning an old wrinkled shirt onto the man's torso. "Is he going to live?" asked Matt anxiously.

"I think so," replied Madison. "But we need to get him tied up before he wakes up. Help me lift him onto my shoulders so we can get the dungarees on him."

Matt grabbed the man from behind as Randall grabbed Billy's hands and pulled him up, hoisting the policeman onto his shoulder. Then Matt grabbed the trousers laying next to the policeman's uniform and slid them up the limp legs of their victim. He turned to find Mr. Smith staring at them from the edge of the sidewalk.

"I see you've taken care of the local law," deadpanned the older man. "I don't know that our mutual friend in Chicago would approve of such actions."

"It was partly his idea," chuckled Matt. "He said that we needed someone to blame for the theft. Allow me to introduce you to another one of my friends. Mr. Smith, meet Mr. Madison."

The two men merely nodded to each other in the darkness. Randall lay Billy down, found the patrolman's shoes, and began to lace them onto his feet.

"You must be the security liaison for this operation," stated Mr. Smith.

"I guess so," acknowledged Randall. "Actually, I'm the spy on the inside. Was the information about the door locks and the safe helpful?"

The question surprised Mr. Smith. He stared at the back of the man, who took some rope from his pocket and began to tie up the now-groaning policeman. Finally the safe cracker replied, "Yes, the model number of the Swanson safe was very important. It would have taken me a lot longer than it did to crack it without your help. I'm beginning to understand why my contact told me that this would be an easy job."

Randall looked over his shoulder while still securing the bindings around Billy's legs. "Tell him I said hello when you see him."

Mr. Smith could only stare at the scene before him and shake his head.

Matt had gone up the alley and disappeared behind the building. He now returned with a wheelbarrow that moved silently on a rubber bicycle tire. Randall and Matt loaded the bound Billy Harris into it as he groaned again. Matt brought out a bottle of Canadian whiskey from his jacket that he had picked up along with the wheelbarrow. Randall took it, opened Billy's mouth, and began to slowly pour some down his throat. Billy opened his eyes, choked and coughed and spit out a great mouthful of the alcohol. But Randall persisted, and Billy ended up swallowing more than he lost. Randall backed up and watched his captive settle down into a stupor.

Randall replaced the cork and put the bottle in his jacket. "None of it's wasted on him. He should smell just about right for whoever finds him. I'll keep the rest to help me sleep on our trip west."

Matt looked at the comatose policeman and sighed in relief. He picked up the shovel and loaded it into the wheelbarrow. "Mr. Smith, would you be so kind as to push our friend to the back of the alley? I need a minute alone with Mr. Madison to review plans."

"I'll be happy to oblige," said the older man. "We'll wait for you at the rear of the building." He placed his valise on top of the policeman and began pushing the load back down the alley.

Matt checked his watch and waited for the old thief to get beyond hearing. "It's getting close to midnight. Remember to seem remorseful when you drop off the book. It looks to be a complete list, including the mayor and some other prominent citizens, but there's no mention of Crawford in it."

Madison considered this information. "He's probably on the payroll in Indianapolis and doesn't qualify as a dues-paying member. In any case, the note from Billy will tie him to the group. I'm going to drop it and Billy's uniform off at the station before I take the book to your friends at church."

Matt nodded. "Address the other note to Chief Johnson and tell Liam to deliver the book to Paul's house. He's not listed as a member, so I think we can trust him to make good use of it."

Matt shifted his stance from one leg to the other. They were running out of time. "Mr. Smith is a good guy. John was right about him. He shouldn't have a problem guarding Billy in the garage while I help Davy finish up with the ovens. Then I'll deliver Billy to you at the freight yard around three. I told Maureen to look for you at our kitchen door around one. She's got your things from your room."

"How'd she take the news about me?" asked Randall.

"It shocked her at first, but then she recovered enough to get mad at both of us."

"Maybe we should have kept her in the dark," ventured Randall. "I never liked the idea of getting her involved with this scheme."

Matt put his hand on his older brother's shoulder. "We went over this before with John. It wouldn't have been right to not let her have a proper visit with her long lost brother. She'd have been mortified to find out you'd been living in the same house watching over her for months and we'd never told her the truth about you. It's time to get moving, Joe. This isn't the place or the time to debate strategy."

"I know, Matt, but I'm scared to face her." Joe Conner's eyes twinkled, and a broad smile broke out upon his features. The big reserved man patted his younger brother on the cheek. "I'll see you at the freight yard. Keep your lamps off and look for me on the side of the road." He again patted Matt's face, gathered up the police uniform and the Klan roster, and headed down Broad Street toward the police station.

Matt watched him go and felt sad. He had spent very little time with his brother during the past few months. They had been very cautious during their clandestine meetings. But Matt knew beyond a doubt that he would miss his older brother's presence and wisdom.

CHAPTER 16

May 13, 1923
Donegal, Indiana

Joe Conner approached the police station cautiously. Except for his assault on Billy, the next few minutes would be the most dangerous moments of his evening. He felt like a fearful urchin stealing candy from a Woolworth's five-and-dime store. He had been a regular visitor to police headquarters for months and knew the office routine well. If anyone found him inside, he hoped he could explain his presence by declaring he had found the building unlocked and unoccupied. However, he'd just as soon get in and out of the office without being spotted.

A quick walk past the front entrance and a leisurely stroll around the building convinced him the station house was deserted. Using Billy's key, he let himself in through the front door and walked around behind the big desk. He deposited Billy's folded uniform and hat on the desk along with his pistol and holster. Lastly he placed a folded note on top of the uniform.

Joe had given Billy a bad time about his penmanship several months back. He had convinced Billy to switch from a cursive style of writing to the use of block letters. This method was easier to decipher, and Billy had adopted it as a practical improvement for his daily reports. This style was also much easier for Joe to copy, making the note concerning Billy's resignation from the force easier for Joe to pen. In it was Billy's admission to being a member of the Klan, his remorse over it, and his theft of the membership book from Lucas Crawford's office.

Joe quietly let himself out the front door and quickly locked it with the key he had removed from Billy Harris's key ring. He walked at a regular pace for a block west on Broad Street and back past the Franklin Building, before turning up Fourth Street toward St. Mary's Church. Here, he accelerated his pace. It was just past midnight, and Joe had one more act to perform. The deserted stores along Fourth Street seemed cold and sinister, and he longed to be relieved of the prized book that he carried. As he approached Olive Street and the church set on a small rise, he voiced a short prayer to himself. "Sweet Jesus, please let this work. You know I'm a disgraceful sinner, but I ask only for Your help for the good people here who need it."

He climbed the church steps and walked along the east side of the sanctuary. Even in the white mist, his large frame stood out against the white limestone exterior of the building. Any other soul out for a late evening stroll would notice him. But the plan called for him to avoid the west side of the church, where he could be seen from the rectory. The two priests had to be evaded. At the rear he saw the light from the offices in the basement. He knocked on the large wooden door and stepped back to see who greeted him.

Several long seconds later the wise old visage of Liam McNamara peered out from the partially open door. "Can I help you, sir?"

"Yes, you can," replied Joe. "My name is Randall Madison, and I'm a concerned citizen of this town who believes strongly in the Christian motto to 'Love thy neighbor.' A friend of mine, Officer Billy Harris of the police department, has come into possession of a book containing the names of all the members of the Ku Klux Klan here in the valley. I regret to say that our names are in it."

Liam stared at Joe as if he could see through him. Joe admitted to himself that his sudden appearance probably resembled a ghost from the spirit world. And he brought the membership roster of the Klan!

No wonder the elder gentleman seemed at a loss for words.

"Anyway, Officer Harris and I feel real bad about our behavior. We've decided to leave town and make a fresh start of things. Officer Harris arranged with one of his friends from your church to leave the membership book here. I believe you know what to do with it before it can be returned to its rightful owners. I've been instructed to tell you to deliver it to Chief Paul Johnson's home before daybreak."

Liam nodded, opened the door further, and reached out to take possession of the book. "Thank you, sir. I don't believe I know you, Mr. Madison. How can I be sure that this is a true roster of the Klan membership?"

Joe wasn't prepared for a challenge to his credibility. He scratched the back of his head while he thought things through. "You'll have to take my word for it, sir. But you can trust me the same as if I was your Irish brother. A pleasant evening to you and your friends. There's still work to be done this night." Joe tipped his kangol cap to the man, turned on his heel, and left the way he had come.

A waning moon had risen above the trees and its silvery beams of light penetrated the fog. Joe started to make his way across the lawn to Olive Street in the direction of Matt's house. The dim light cast by the moon revealed movement in the shadows of a stand of fir near the street. He stopped, and to cover his surprise, he bent down to retie the laces on one of his shoes.

Could it be that someone was following him? Had someone spotted him at the Franklin building or the police station? His biggest worry was that Chief Johnson would have become alerted to their activities.

Joe stood up and quickly made up his mind that he would have to confront this new threat. He had to find out if the plan had been compromised, and if so, he'd attempt to control any opposition to Matt and the others. He moved at a deliberate pace to the sidewalk, but instead of crossing over onto Oak Street, he turned right and walked toward the trees quickly. There was the movement again. And now a figure in dark clothing stepped out into the light. Joe tensed his arm muscles as he prepared to defend himself.

"Hello, Joseph," called the stranger in a calm voice.

Joe halted, unsure of what he had heard. Who could this be? And while he stood puzzled, the man stepped toward him.

"You don't remember me, but I celebrated Mass at your mother's funeral. I'm Father O'Brien."

"How . . . how did you know who I was?" blurted out the exposed Joseph Conner.

"The Conner family is special to me. And when I learned some months ago that a strange man had come to town and was paying attention to Maureen, I became suspicious. I'll confess that I've kept an eye on you, and I've been waiting here tonight to see who'd be making a visit to my church."

"But Father, how did you know that I'd come back to help Matt?"

Father O'Brien stepped closer and held out his hand. Joe took it and shook it hesitantly. He suspiciously wondered if the priest was here to thwart their plan.

"I've had spies of my own, Joseph," commented the priest. "Some of my parishioners kept tabs on your wanderings about town. On one occasion we followed you from a distance down by the river. You had a clandestine meeting with someone who turned out to be Matt Conner. That's when I realized who you really were."

Father O'Brien paused and then added, "I'm a much older man, but I still remember people who have been in my prayers since I was first ordained."

"You're quicker than we gave you credit, Father," mused Joe as he shoved his hands into his coat.

"Tell me the truth, Joe. Is everything okay?"

Joe looked into the shadowed features of the priest. He had made it a habit never to lie to a priest. "Yes, Father. The hard part is over, and the final scenes will take place before dawn."

"But something could still go wrong," blurted out Father O'Brien. "What if the police discover you? Or worse, what if the Klan should be out and pick you up?"

Joe smiled and put his arm around the priest's shoulder. "You should go to bed, Father. Nothing's going to happen that we can't fix.

Tonight, I'm watching over the Conner family. Go get your rest before church tomorrow."

Father O'Brien turned and faced Joseph Conner. He reached for the younger man's right hand and gave it a hearty shake. "I'll be saying a Mass for all of the deceased members of your family on Tuesday, Joe. Maureen requested it. I don't suppose you'll be in town, but it would be nice if you could attend."

"I'll be long gone, Father. But I'll remember to say a prayer of thanks that morning."

Joe looked again at the man with new respect. "Good-bye, Father, and thank you for all of your kindness to my family."

The priest turned and walked to his rectory. Joe watched him for several seconds before he started again for Matt's house. With every step, he felt the tension of months of living a lie fall away from his shoulders. He was going to visit with family, and before dawn he would leave this town for good. He was ready to go home.

Inside the church basement, Liam opened the book to the first page and noted the names written on the numbered lines. Tom Stewart's name was next to the red number one at the top of the page. "All right, let's get started. We'll put the book between the two of you, and I'll call out the names, addresses, and occupations while you two type. Since Boyd is the better typist, I'll watch over Andy's shoulder to make sure everything is correct. If we make a mistake, we throw out the sheets of paper and start over."

"This is going to take more than a couple of pages even single-spaced," worried Boyd. "We'll never get done on time."

"We'll do the best we can until four," stated Liam. "Once we have a complete set done including the carbon copies, I'll use the third machine and type an additional set. If we can get twenty copies of the list done in three hours, we'll have accomplished enough."

Andy had already begun to type the heading for the list. The top of the page read "Ku Klux Klan Membership for the Wabash Valley." He looked over his shoulder at Liam to confirm that he was proceeding correctly. "The list will be pretty embarrassing for some of the men on it. I wouldn't want to face people in town after this news hits the streets."

Liam just smiled and motioned for Andy to proceed with the first name, that of Tom Stewart.

Matt's neighborhood around Tenth Street was quiet, and there weren't any streetlights for the residential area. Joe feared that he would arouse a barking dog, but so far he had managed not to stir even a night owl. Matt lived in a fancy neighborhood. Joe realized the neighbors wouldn't leave pets out, even in good weather. Probably, most refused to have pets for fear of soiling the rugs. He walked across Maple Street on Tenth until he reached the alley that ran behind Matt and Annie's house. He proceeded down the alley until he was behind the garage at the rear of the Conner property. He avoided the trash barrels that stood on one side of the garage and tiptoed to the kitchen door of the house. He reflected that it was a hell of a thing to introduce yourself to your family at one o'clock on a Sunday morning.

There was a light on in the kitchen, and Joe could make out the forms of two women through the lace curtain that covered the glass pane in the door. He tapped lightly on the glass and heard footsteps in response.

Annie Conner pulled away the curtain and stared out at him. She nodded to Maureen, who stood by the sink, and then Annie opened the door to admit him.

Joe stepped inside as Annie closed the door behind him. He took off his hat and self-consciously smiled at the two women who took up positions opposite him.

"Where's Matt?" asked Annie. There was fear in her voice.

"He's fine, ma'am," replied Joe. "He's out of danger now. He just has to finish his work at the bakery and then drop off a couple of packages. Then he'll come home, and his involvement in the plan will be over. If things work like we hope they will, the police and the good churchgoers of town will take up this sorry business for us."

Annie stepped back, moved to her Chambers oven, and placed a hand on the edge as if to steady herself. "Am I to understand that you are my long lost brother-in-law?"

Joe could feel his face blush. "That's correct, ma'am. I'm Joseph Conner, late of Sacramento, at your service . . . at least for another couple of hours."

"Have we met before, Joe?"

"Yes, we have, ma'am. Matt brought all of you into Sutton's Garage a couple of months ago. He wanted me to look at the tires on your sedan. But it also gave him a chance to introduce me to you and the children.

"He's very much in love with you, Annie. He's been bursting with pride at the family that you have made with him. He hasn't known such happiness since he was Brian's age."

Joe's eyes teared as he looked at Annie and then Maureen. "I'd like to thank you for being so good to my brother. You've taken care of him better than I could."

Annie continued to stare at him as if she were appraising a piece of furniture. "You don't much resemble Maureen or Matt," she stated flatly.

"No, that's true. I favor my da, while the two babies resembled our ma." Joe returned Annie's stare, desperately wanting her acceptance. He feared she blamed him for deceiving Maureen and forcing Matt to play this dangerous nocturnal game.

Finally she walked over, took his hand and looked over at Maureen before she addressed him. "Thank you, Joe. It has been good to finally meet you, and I appreciate all of your help. I'll let you and Maureen visit alone now. I'm going to get ready for bed and check on the children. We've ham and rolls plus some coffee we brewed. Be sure to take along provisions for your trip."

"Thank you, Annie. I hope to meet you again under more normal circumstances. I'm going to visit John in Chicago next fall. Perhaps you can get Matt to bring your family up for a proper reunion."

Annie squeezed his hand and then let go. "I'd like that, Joe. Good night to you, and I wish you a safe trip back to your home."

As Annie left the kitchen, Joe turned his gaze on Maureen. He watched her features harden, and he marveled again as he had many times over the past year in her resemblance to their mother. "Are you upset with me, lass? Has our little charade angered you?"

Maureen folded her arms and looked at the man she thought had been her friend, who now had become her estranged brother. "It did upset me. You could have taken me into your confidence. Instead, you befriended me and deceived me with your play-acting."

Joe lowered his head and scraped the floor with his shoe. "I'm sorry, Maureen, but it was too dangerous to bring you in on the plan. If anyone found out my true identity, I'd probably have ended up in the river with a bullet in my head."

"So why did you move into the Tilly house?"

"Matt was worried about your safety. He felt he could protect the family here, but he fretted about you. I had to get close to you and gain your confidence. If things got ugly, I was responsible for you."

Maureen's features softened. "So you became my guardian angel."

Joe took Maureen's arm and steered her toward a chair at the kitchen table. He sat down next to her. "In a way that's true," he said. "I promised ma on the night she died that I would take care of the little ones. I haven't been around to keep my promise. Paul came to love the bottle, and it cost him his life. I let John and Matt go off on their own, and I didn't even write you one letter in the past ten years."

He hung his head and stared at the top of the table. Emotion choked off his voice. He took a deep breath and reached for his sister's hand. She in turn stroked his hair with her other hand. Their eyes met and communicated their love for each other.

"Oh, Maureen, I've been ashamed of my failings. But when Matt wrote to me of his troubles, I saw it as an opportunity to redeem myself. I knew it was time to honor my promise."

"How did he find you?" questioned Maureen.

"When Matt and I split up in San Francisco, I told him that I would never give up my railroad union membership. He knew he could always track me down by going to the union. When he wrote to me about the Klan, I sold my half of an automobile garage to my partner and headed for Chicago. I took over your old room at John's house while we considered what to do."

"John is also involved in this plot?"

"He had a small part in the planning, and his contacts with gangsters proved useful."

Maureen sat up, her eyes widened, and her lips puckered in alarm. "What have you done, Joe? What kind of trouble will Matt and John be in for breaking the law here in town while you go back to California?"

Joe backed away from the table and put up his hands in defense. "There will be no trouble, Maureen. What we've done involved a few illegalities, but nothing serious. And it was not my plan. Brother Matt concocted most of tonight's shenanigans. John and I added a few things to make it work, but Matt is the leader. You don't know me, but surely you trust Matt not to do something foolish."

Maureen ran her index finger along the checkered cloth that covered the table. She seemed to calm herself before she looked up into his eyes. "I trust Matt, and I trust you as well. But Matt has been under a lot of pressure with the loss of customers. He has been very worried about his bank loan, and desperate men will attempt desperate measures."

"Yes, we will," replied Joe. "But tonight, we pulled a fast one on those white-robed vigilantes. And in the morning they're going to learn that we also pulled their hoods off while they slept."

Joe relaxed and smiled at his sister.

"I'm hungry," he said. "I could do with some of that ham. And could you show me my belongings that you retrieved for me?"

Maureen stood, went to the counter, and brought out a loaf from a tin breadbox. "I'll make you a sandwich and some others for the trip. You'll find your clothes packed in your canvas bag in the dining room. When's your train due to depart?"

Joe had stood and took a step toward the adjoining room before he stopped and looked back at her. "I'm not taking a regular train, but sometime before daylight, I've got a private car reserved for me and my reluctant companion."

Maureen raised her eyebrows. "I don't follow you, Randall . . . I mean Joe."

"We've still got railroad connections here in town. Mr. Fitzpatrick, who used to work with our da, had an empty freight car pulled off into the maintenance yard for hot brakes. When they replaced the journal box they also cut a trap door into its floor. It's scheduled to make the trip to St. Louis as part of the westbound freight that will be made up in the yard this morning. My companion and I will be safely locked inside, but we can get out through the floor when the time comes. Like I said, it's our own private car."

"How many people are in on this plan?" asked Maureen.

"Maybe a dozen. I don't honestly know for sure. Matt confided just enough information to me in case I had to take over for him. He has a genius for delegating small roles to various people. In that way no one knows the entire plan, and most people are only involved with minor jobs that can't be considered dangerous or illegal."

Joe retrieved his bag and set it down next to the kitchen table. He located a cup in the cabinet over the sink and poured himself coffee from a pot on the stove. "Do you have any sugar for this coffee? You should know by now that I don't like it black."

Maureen looked up from the counter and found her brother smiling down at her. She began to understand how the stranger, Randall Madison, had been so interesting to her. He had reminded her of her brothers.

Shortly before three in the morning, Matt made his way out of his garage and drove down Railroad Avenue. The fog shrouded the streets in a white mist, making it necessary for Matt to navigate using the street lamps for direction. His fellow burglar, Mr. Smith, rode with him in the cab, while Billy Harris remained tied up in the truck bed. A minor concussion and an alcohol-induced sleep kept him silent. Matt passed the Wabash Depot, lit and alive with activity. An eastbound passenger and mail train would arrive from St. Louis within the hour. Matt drove four blocks east to the dark freight yard. The streetlights did not penetrate into the complex. He stopped at the drive that crossed over the main line and led to the switching and maintenance tracks that hugged the narrow strip of land between the river and the rail line. He listened for unusual sounds, but everything was normal. The running lights of a switch engine signaled that it was grouping cars at the far end of the yard. He spotted movement from the lanterns of perhaps a half dozen men who worked the third trick at the yard.

Matt turned off his lights as he proceeded over the tracks and onto the first road that went east alongside the tracks. He traveled slowly and silently cursed the noise made by his Model T truck. The only good thing about the vehicle was it looked like it belonged in the yard. In fact, there were a couple of similar one-ton trucks owned by the railroad and based here at the yard. Near the end of the drive, Matt made out the dark form of his brother standing in the middle of the dirt and cinder road.

Matt pulled to a halt, shifted out of gear, and set the parking brake. He left the motor running as he stepped out to greet Joe still standing in front of the truck. "Sorry to be late, but Davy needed some help before we could put the ovens back together."

Joe smiled as he shook his brother's hand. "We built some extra time into the schedule. We're still in good shape. How are our guests holding up?"

"Mr. Smith is fine," replied Matt. "He seems to be enjoying himself. Billy has been quiet, but I think he'll recover. Mr. Smith had to pour some more whiskey down his throat about an hour ago."

Joe was still holding his brother's hand. He took his other arm and wrapped it around Matt's shoulders. "It's time for me to go and for you to get home to your family. I hope our efforts will succeed and bring back your business."

"Regardless of how things turn out, it's been great to see you again, Joe. We couldn't have done any of this without you. I wish you could stay."

Joe backed away and looked into Matt's eyes. "I wish I could, brother, but I need to disappear.

"I told Annie that I hoped to get together with the two of you in Chicago before the end of the year. In the meantime, I need to go home and take care of some things. There's a nice lady I have been courting for several years. Frankly, I've been afraid of marriage, but you've shown me that it can be a great thing."

"It is," said Matt. "When you find someone to love it makes life pretty good."

"I guess I've always ducked responsibility," confessed the older brother. "I saw ma and da struggle and leave behind a bunch of orphans. I've been afraid of similar problems. It can't be easy trying to raise a family."

Matt shook his head and stuffed his hands in his pockets. "It is the hardest thing I've ever done. I've worn out sets of sheets tossing in bed at night and worrying where the money would come from. But when I get home each day and see Annie and the children, I know that I've found my true purpose in life."

"Ma would be pleased. She always thought you would become a priest, but she'd be proud of what you've made here."

Matt hugged his brother one last time. Joe broke off the embrace and steered Matt toward the rear of the truck. "Help me hoist Billy over my shoulder and then get out of here."

They dragged their victim from the bed of the Model T and onto Joe's sturdy frame. As he came around the side of the truck, Joe peered into the passenger side of the cab. "It was nice to meet you, Mr. Smith. I hope to buy you a beer in Chicago sometime."

"It would be a pleasure, Mr. Madison. Maybe we could share information on what took place here tonight."

Joe tipped his cap, turned, and headed across several sets of tracks with his bundle slung over his shoulder. In a matter of seconds he vanished into the cloud that hung over the facility. Matt slowly turned the truck around, clicked on his headlamps, and drove cautiously back out of the freight yard.

Minutes later, he pulled to stop at the intersection of Seventeenth Street and Maple Street. They had driven past the Riley house and noted the light in the front window. Matt shook the old crook's hand. "Mr. Lane will have the rest of your fee and will get you to your train in the morning. It has been a pleasure doing business with you, sir. I hope you have a safe trip home."

The older man beamed back at his young accomplice. "Thank you, Mr. Jones. It has been an exhilarating evening. I've enjoyed it more than I can express to you. Might I just add that you are a wonder, sir. You truly are."

Matt smiled and then watched the man climb out of the truck with his valise and disappear into the darkness behind him. Matt took a deep breath. He was finally in the clear. He shifted into first gear, turned onto Maple Street, and drove home.

Matt parked his truck in the driveway in front of the garage and turned off the noisy engine. At last he could return to his normal life. It was near four in the morning. Soon the men would be done at church, and then the last act of tonight's drama would begin. Everything was now out of his control, and he offered a small prayer to the Blessed Virgin for the continued safety of all involved. But he didn't feel right praying for the success of the mission.

Once inside his kitchen, Matt took off his jacket and unbuttoned his shirt. He drank a tall glass of water. It was his first refreshment in six hours. He reflected on how all bodily functions came to a halt when one is consumed with absolute terror.

He heard Annie come down the creaking stairs. He turned to greet her as she entered the kitchen. She was dressed in her white robe. Her dark hair was down around her shoulders, and her face showed lines of worry. Her green eyes questioned Matt about the status of his evening.

He got another smaller drink from the tap. "I'm finished. The bakery is ready for business on Monday."

The lines of worry were still present in her features. She came over to the sink and put her arms around her husband's neck. "Is it really over?" she asked.

Matt put his arms around her waist and bent his head down to touch her cheek. Suddenly his body shook with convulsions, and his emotions overwhelmed him. Annie held him close, and he heard sobs emanate from deep inside him.

She stroked his hair and whispered to him over and over, "It's okay, it's okay."

He composed himself and then pulled back in order to look at her face. He cleared his throat, and the words tumbled out of him like water cascading down a waterfall. "I was so scared, Annie. I was afraid of being caught. I wouldn't have cared going to jail, but I didn't want to cause you any suffering or embarrassment. It would have been bad enough to be taken away from you, but I couldn't have dealt with you and the children being exposed to shame and ridicule. We'd have lost the bakery and the house, and you'd have had to move back to your folks' home. The trial would have been a circus, and we'd have had the Klan following us wherever we settled in the future. I'd never have been able to make it up to you and the kids. The release of all this tension has just overwhelmed me."

Annie hugged him and caressed the back of his neck. "Come to bed, my love," she whispered. "We can hold each other until it's time to get the children ready for Mass."

Matt released his grip on her and took tentative steps toward the hallway. She kept pace adding support under his right arm. She punched the off button on the ceiling light fixture, and they headed for the staircase in darkness.

CHAPTER 17

May 13–14, 1923
Donegal, Indiana

THE SUN SHONE BRIGHTLY, and though the morning had been cool, there was little breeze. It would be hot in the afternoon, the first uncomfortable day of spring. John and Ruth Stewart and their only child Tom were in their regular pew at First Presbyterian Church for the eleven o'clock service. The church, bright with white walls and white pine pews, was large and sparsely decorated in the manner of the denomination. Tom knew his parents were glad to have him join them for the first time in weeks. He had been ill for most of the spring. The cool damp air had not been good for his damaged lungs, but the promise of warmer weather had brought him relief from the constant struggle to breathe.

Reverend Miles Carter had just finished the New Testament reading from John's Gospel, Chapter 13. Tom watched him close his Bible and look down at the congregation.

"Today's sermon was prepared several days ago. It is based on the scripture lesson you just heard concerning Christ's admonition to His disciples to love their neighbors. This is the third such lesson done in conjunction with our neighboring churches here in town. At the time it was chosen last month, this topic seemed to be very appropriate for people of different denominations who have been looking to find common ground in our shared belief in Jesus Christ as our one true Lord and Savior."

Reverend Carter took a small drink of water from a glass that he kept on his pulpit. "Almost three hours ago, this subject became very personal for the members of our congregation. I received this morning information that has made me abandon that sermon and instead speak to you from my heart.

"I find myself, standing before you here today, asking how people can be true to the commandment to love one another when they search out certain members of our community for ridicule and harm. I'm speaking of course about the Ku Klux Klan and those other secretive fraternities that not only bar certain people from membership but also plot to banish them from our midst. Their tactics involve sudden appearances in the middle of the night with torches and masks to cover the evilness they perpetrate on unsuspecting families at rest in their homes. They also make use of boycotts and malicious rumors to drive men out of business and exclude others from a fair chance to work."

Tom Stewart could feel his blood chill in his veins as he listened to his minister attack the Klan. He felt lightheaded, and he was certain that Reverend Carter had looked directly at him with scorn in his eyes. Tom was not really listening to the content of the sermon anymore as other thoughts and questions crowded into his brain. Why had the churches banded together against them? Had they been found out? Did someone get caught on a mission that he had not sanctioned? Were the police waiting to arrest him at his home?

Tom was having trouble focusing on what was being said, and yet it felt as though the message was being directed specifically at him. He heard the minister lower his voice and pause for a sip of water before he went on.

"Earlier this morning someone left a list under the door of my house. I understand that prominent citizens in town have received other copies of this list. The list purports to be the membership of the local chapter of the Ku Klux Klan here in the Wabash Valley. The list runs four pages, and six men from our congregation are among the one hundred and sixty-four names in this document."

There were gasps and then a low murmur from the people present. Tom felt as if he had gone deaf. He knew Reverend Carter was still speaking and that his sermon was a condemnation of Tom and his behavior. But Tom didn't really hear what was being said. He sat next to his parents and thought of the embarrassment that he was about to cause them. He was sick to his stomach. Fear gripped him worse than when the shells began to explode over his head in the small French town at what had been the start and the end of his brief military career. He wanted to get up and leave this place in shame, but fear and shock immobilized him. He would wait until the sermon was over and then seek to excuse himself because of illness.

He straightened his back and held up his head. If he had been caught, then he would bravely accept responsibility for his actions. The diminutive gray-haired minister was getting worked up. His cheeks had turned red, and the veins stood out from above his temples. Tom focused on the man and his words of condemnation.

"What would our Savior have to say if He returned to earth and observed our behavior? Would He be proud of the way we divide into small groups of like believers and exclude those who do not come from the same background? Would He be happy with the way we pray for His mercy on Sunday and then seek to remove our neighbors from their homes during the week? Would He have any sympathy for those of us who pray at the foot of the cross here in His Father's house yet burn cheap imitations of it in the night sky to frighten and intimidate people who do not live up to our ideals of Christianity?

"Who made these self-righteous vigilantes the defenders of our faith? Who designated them the new crusaders with responsibility for searching out and banishing the heretics from our land? Who gave them the authority to punish the sinful in our midst?

"I am not aware of anyone who gave such authority or power to any self-chosen group of individuals. I can think of no church doctrine that would allow such a group as the Klan to assert their right to dictate who lives among us and who is not worthy to be here. The creeds and confessions we rely on to establish our rights to God's abundant grace say nothing of our right to condemn others of different faiths or nationalities. Therefore, I say to you, the good people of our congregation, and to those wayward few in our midst, that no one individual or any self-declared knights of the faith have the right to decide who is and who isn't worthy of acceptance within our community. The Knights of the Ku Klux Klan do not have any power to condemn those among us as sinful and deserving of punishment. Their efforts to uphold Prohibition and to promote moral behavior are noble. But they have no authority to enforce their beliefs on others, and their tactics are just plain wrong. Vigilantism is not acceptable to men of Christian faith."

The minister paused and looked down from his pulpit at his congregation. He seemed to take time to compose himself and judge the impact of his remarks on those in attendance.

"I ask again, what would Christ say if He were to visit among us and critique our actions? I confess that I have no business trying to anticipate the words of our Savior. But I believe that His comments might include the following admonition. 'Whatever you have done to these, the least of My brethren, you have done unto Me.' As Christians, we need to show love and kindness to each other. Not just to those present here in our sanctuary, but to all people who are struggling toward salvation just as surely as we are here today."

Reverend Carter stopped. His hands trembled as he reached once again for his glass of water. After a moment he uttered his standard closing. "Let us pray."

Tom Stewart leaned over to his parents and motioned that he was ill. He rose from his seat and walked ponderously up the center aisle in his neatly pressed brown suit and out the rear of the sanctuary. He looked at no one, but he felt as if all eyes were focused on him.

Once outside the church, Tom stopped on the front steps to catch his breath. He was exhausted from expending so much energy and attention on the simple act of breathing. Always short of breath, he gulped down extra ones in order to get the proper volume of air into his lungs. He couldn't stop feeling like a failure so much of the time.

Nobody congratulated him on his war service. Even his government abandoned him after they released him from the hospital. And now his neighbors, who had shown him only pity, would dismiss him as a fool. He would be a great embarrassment to his parents.

Tom walked down the steps and along Oak Avenue until he reached Third Street. The sun shone brightly, and there were few people out. Many would be in church until the top of the hour. He absently wandered south on Third Street until he reached Broad Street. There was auto traffic on Broad and a few people out walking in their spring finery. Tom couldn't help but think that everyone who passed him was viewing him as a pariah, a criminal soon to be imprisoned. He tipped his hat to a woman who rushed past him holding the hand of her daughter. The woman appeared frightened of him. Tom walked on, fighting a combination of paranoia and depression. Without realizing it, he found himself standing in front of the doorway of the Franklin Building.

Reaching for the keys in his pocket, he let himself into the vestibule. Slowly he climbed the stairs to the second floor. His breathing remained steady. He felt as though he were walking in a dream. Natural light pierced through the frosted glass of the doors and transoms as he proceeded to the end of the green hallway. Lucas rented an apartment in nearby Peru to expand their connections to the east part of the valley. He seldom came to Donegal on Sunday, so the office was empty this morning.

Once inside Tom looked around for telltale signs that they had been burglarized. Nothing seemed out of place, but his minister said that a membership list had been published. How could anyone have gotten access to such information? He bent over the safe and dialed the combination. The brass handle turned smoothly, and the door opened quietly. Inside everything was in order, even the small stack of cash was present.

But there was more vacant space than usual. With alarm Tom understood what had disappeared. The klectoken register was missing. Yet he had seen Lucas deposit it into the safe when they finished their work on Friday. Lucas would never take it with him because it was their only record of who had paid their dues. It remained here in the office except for those meetings when Tom needed it to record payments received by the Klansmen who attended.

It was not here now. Tom went over to Lucas's desk and unlocked it. He pulled open one drawer after another in a hopeless search for the vital record of their klavern. He walked over to his own desk and opened all of the drawers, noting nothing of value. Finally, he sat down and accepted the inevitable. They had been exposed as surely as if someone had come along and taken away their hoods, tassels and all. Once more Tom felt the sickness of failure in his stomach. Surprisingly, it no longer seemed as bad as it had in the past. He was becoming inured to it. He looked at his desk for a long time before turning his gaze out the window and looking south toward the single story Wabash rail depot, where a train had pulled up to the platform. Its clanging bell had shaken him out of his thoughts. Perhaps he should try to catch the train and leave this predicament behind him, but he had no place to go. His precarious health kept him a prisoner in his own body.

Instead, he swiveled in his chair and pulled out a piece of stationery with the insurance agency logo embossed at the top. Tom sensed a return of the deep, dark despair that plagued him as he lay in the hospital in France. But he also felt resolve, and using his pen, a gift from Lucas, he began writing an emotional letter to his parents. He poured out his sorrow at any hurt he would cause them. He thanked them for their patience and help, but he said it was only a matter of time before his lungs failed. It would have been better had he died with his comrades on the front lines. His one request was to be buried in the family plot at First Presbyterian.

Tom folded the letter and placed it in an envelope addressed to his parents. Now committed, he picked up the old Colt revolver he had borrowed from his father's store as security for the office. There were four bullets in their chambers, and his fingers rotated the cylinder until the first bullet was next in position. If it misfired, the second chamber would be ready before he lost his nerve. Gazing through the window, he assumed a comfortable position in the green leather chair in front of Lucas's desk. Tom didn't really blame Lucas for his troubles, but it was appropriate that his old friend find him first.

Tom placed the barrel of the revolver into his mouth and took a deep, wheezy breath. Asking for God's forgiveness, he pulled the trigger.

Lucas Crawford overheard a discussion at a restaurant in Peru Sunday evening about the Klan being exposed in the valley. Alarmed, he put in a long distance phone call to the Stewart house. Anne Stewart told him that Tom had left them at church and had not returned home. She and her husband had become distraught when the police came by the house looking for Tom. Tom's name was at the top of the list they had heard about at church. She tearfully inquired of Lucas as to whether he had seen her son, and he told her that Tom might have gone to Lafayette to visit friends.

Lucas spent a couple of hours trying to understand what had taken place. He put in a call to the Donegal Police Department and asked to speak to Officer Harris. He was politely told that Officer Harris had quit the force. Next, Lucas put in a call to Clarence Carpenter's office in Indianapolis, but no one answered on this Sunday evening. Lucas was alone, and he wasn't sure what action he should take. Finally, he put most of his personal things into his old suitcase and drove over to Donegal. If the situation was as bad as he feared, he wouldn't be returning home.

The police chief's car and the hearse from Higgins Undertakers were parked in front of the Franklin Building with a patrolman stationed outside to keep a few curious citizens from getting in the way. Lucas drove past and turned onto the next block. He decided to stop at the train station, where he might be able to get some news. As Lucas had expected, the brown and yellow depot was alive with activity. Although there had been no mention of the Klan in the Sunday paper, the depot agent and some travelers provided enough information to confirm his fears. He learned a roster had been distributed around town, and various people listed as members had denounced it as false. However, the police were thought to have proof of the list's authenticity.

One of the waiting travelers told of the police investigation into a dead man found upstairs in offices on Broad Street. The traveler claimed to have been told the body was that of a disgraced Klansman. Lucas knew only Tom and he had keys to the insurance office. Nauseated and struggling to comprehend what had happened, Lucas concluded that his one true friend was gone. He couldn't understand how all of this had taken place on a quiet spring weekend. It all seemed so surreal. He pulled out and lit a cigarette from a pack of Camels tucked inside his suit coat and sat down with a copy of the Logansport *Pharos-Reporter*. But he quickly lost interest in the written news.

Instead, he caught bits and pieces of more conversation on the day's important events. The local churches had denounced Klan activities, and the mayor, denying his membership, was calling for a general repudiation of the Klan. The police were investigating the situation and hoped to arrest those responsible for the arson at the Higgins funeral home and the assault on a Jakub Miller who had previously lived in town.

Lucas sat quietly with the others until the ten-ten St. Louis-bound train arrived, and then he returned to his car when the few patrons emptied out of the depot. He sat morosely in his car and hoped he was living a bad dream. As midnight came and went, he walked past the police station, but as he feared, Billy Harris was not on duty. Another officer manned the desk in the main room. He wandered back down Broad Street, now deserted. The Franklin Building was closed and dark, but fear prevented him from visiting his office.

Lucas had no place to go. He had remained aloof from all except Tom during his recruiting drive in Donegal. Without his friend, he felt alone and once again a stranger in the small town.

Returning to his car at the train station, Lucas considered what to do next. The night was clear but damp. Only the noise from some passing freight trains interrupted his thoughts. He spent the next couple of hours anxiously considering his options. Finally, he decided that he'd wait until the bank opened and empty his account before driving to Indianapolis to visit Mr. Carpenter. He needed the support and connections from the capital city to reestablish himself.

As he sat through the night, it occurred to him that there was one item of unfinished business that he could manage before dawn. Shortly before four in the morning, Lucas drove his Chevrolet sedan away from the station and pulled up to the curb on Seventh Street near the front of the Conner bakery. He could see lights on in the rear of the building, but he knew the normal workday for the proprietor. He waited for the only man who had been able to challenge his plans over the past year. If anyone had a hand in thwarting his ambitions, it had to be this clever baker. Lucas judged that it was time to meet his nemesis and confront him regarding his hand in this catastrophe.

The night was damp as Matt made his way down Broad Street to work. While the heat from yesterday had dissipated, the humidity lingered. The blossoms on the shrubbery in front of his neighbors' homes scented the night air. Matt was in a good mood. He was eager to see that the ovens were working properly and was hoping his business would improve after the events of the weekend.

He had met privately at home yesterday with friends who had participated in the operation. Boyd Phelps had tripped on the steps leading up to Chief Johnson's house and was afraid the noise would awaken the household before he could drop off the Klan's book and escape. But no one stopped him. Peter Hayes had come by and reported that all the lists had been delivered by dawn to the appropriate locations, including one he personally nailed to the door of the county courthouse. One last copy had been saved for Matt to keep. Rip Riley had made the eleven o'clock Mass after getting Mr. Jones safely onto the Chicago-bound train in Logansport.

By late afternoon, Father O'Brien and Father Stevens stopped by with word that several ministers had called to offer their help in repudiating Klan practices within the community. These preachers stated that their sermons had been well received by their congregations. Father O'Brien had surprised Matt with a bear hug and tears of joy when he departed from Matt and Annie's living room. The depth of feeling that the priest had for Matt was disconcerting. Matt had never had a close relationship with a priest before. He smiled, thinking his mother would be proud that he had a close friend and a father figure in this dignified man of the faith.

As Matt turned and crossed Broad Street at the intersection with Seventh Street, he noted a dark sedan parked in front of the bakery. He felt inside the pocket of his jacket for the small revolver. It wasn't there; he'd left it locked in his tool chest for the weekend, as was his custom. In all the excitement, he had let down his guard and failed to retrieve it this morning. Matt stood on the sidewalk for a moment. He could retrace his steps to get the pistol, but he might be intercepted before he could get home. He could run to the police station a couple of blocks away, but the officer on duty might be out on patrol. Matt grew angry with himself. He decided that he was tired of being afraid. He strode deliberately down Seventh Street to his shop while his fingers felt for the right key in his pocket. He didn't bother to look inside the ominous black auto.

As Matt was unlocking the front door, he heard the car door open in the quiet of the still dark morning. Matt held his breath and turned to meet his opposition. One man walked toward him in a wrinkled black suit. A solid gray wool tie hung loosely below the collar of his white shirt. He was not wearing a hat, and his hands remained by his sides.

"Mr. Conner, I thought it was about time we finally met. I'm Lucas Crawford."

Matt scanned the street for others but found Mr. Crawford to be apparently alone. Matt opened the door to the bakery and held it open. "Come in, Mr. Crawford. We're not yet ready for customers, but we can talk privately for a few minutes if you wish."

The man nodded, but he did not offer his hand in greeting. He simply brushed past Matt and strode into the store. Matt followed, then led Crawford to a chair at one of the tables.

"Let me take off my jacket and tell my assistant I'm here," said Matt. He walked back into the kitchen and hastily greeted Davy. He retrieved the shotgun from the rear corner of the building and placed it near the doorway to the store area.

He returned to his guest with two mugs of coffee Davy had brewed earlier. Sugar was on the table. "Even when the weather turns warm, I like to start the day with hot coffee. I'm sorry, but we don't have any cream this morning and nothing yet to eat. It must appear strange for a bakery to be out of food, but nothing is left over from the weekend."

"Black coffee will be just fine," replied the subdued guest. "You're very kind to see me at such an hour and without notice." Lucas took the coffee and smelled the rich aroma before he took a tentative sip. He took a second sip before he set down the cup and stared across the table at his host and adversary.

"Mr. Conner, I believe you know who I am."

Matt nodded and waited for the man to go on.

Lucas placed his hands on the table. "It would seem that our cause has received a severe setback over the weekend. One of my best friends has apparently been killed, and I'll have to regroup our forces and perhaps start over in another town." He stopped to see what reply his comments might evoke, but Matt remained silent while he stared at his visitor.

Lucas went on with his thoughts. "I believe you may have played a part in the events that have transpired, and I wanted to let you know you have not brought an end to our cause. We'll return in greater force with public and political support that you cannot imagine. We will prevail in our efforts to return this great nation to the Christian values we inherited from our forefathers. You and your friends may think you have won some kind of victory, but our cause will ultimately sweep across the land, including here in this valley."

Lucas stopped and took another drink of his coffee. His eyes never left Matt's face, but Matt kept his emotions in check. This apparently angered his visitor.

Lucas raised his voice, and his hand balled into a fist, pounded the table once. "It would be better for you and the other foreigners here to leave our shores and return to your native countries. You will not be able to pollute our society much longer."

Matt held his coffee with both hands. It was hot, and he preferred to smell it for a few minutes while it cooled. He took his first drink and let the hot liquid stimulate his throat. He no longer needed it to help him wake up this morning. He was alert, and he was evaluating the threats that were being made to him. He was angry, but he saw no reason to show it. He was in control of the situation.

"Mr. Crawford, if it's all right with you, I'd like to give you my point of view regarding our differences."

"Certainly, sir," replied Lucas. "It is only fair and polite for me to hear your position on our disagreement."

Matt took another sip of coffee and continued to hold it, thinking he might need it as a weapon. "Mr. Crawford, I understand from talking with people yesterday that you were born in this area and that you were raised and educated here."

Lucas warily stated that this was true.

"Well, I was born here as well," added Matt. "Unfortunately, I had to leave town at an early age due to the death of my parents. But like you, I've always considered Donegal to be home."

Lucas made no reply.

Matt continued. "You know we're really a lot alike. We both believe in Christ as our Savior. We consider ourselves to be loyal citizens of this great country. Our fathers left us with nothing but their proud name. We're in the prime of life with our health and the ability to earn a good living. The difference is that I try to provide a product that people need and find beneficial. You try to make a living by taking that right away from me and others. I live and work within the bounds of the law and the Constitution that grants me the right to worship as I deem fit. You have lived and worked outside the law and wish to deny millions of us our legal rights."

"That's not true," replied Crawford. "We are law-abiding citizens."

"Abduction, assault, and arson are criminal acts, Mr. Crawford." Matt took another sip of his coffee as he held his adversary's eyes with his gaze. "You may be able to take over the state and pass new laws that favor your point of view, but the courts will strike them down. From what I've seen here, the good people of our country, the voters, will not continue to support you. Your ideas are just not fair, and law-abiding citizens cannot consciously condone your efforts. Over time you are bound to fail. In the meantime you'll only bring misery and suffering to many innocent people."

Lucas frowned but remained quiet. Matt sensed he was powerless to take action this morning. Instead, he took another sip of coffee.

"I'm sorry about the death of Tom Stewart," Matt continued. "I understand he left a suicide note for his parents. They are two more people who have suffered from your efforts. I'm sure there is nothing I can say that will stop the Klan from attempting to gain power throughout the country. But I believe that it's really just a different way for certain people to attempt to get rich. You and your leaders want to keep all the business for the few people who fit your definition of Americans. So far, all you've done is make a lot of money off of your recruited friends, and now you can't deliver on your promises.

"So when you go back to see your associates in Indianapolis, please warn them that there are a hundred or more former members here who want their money back. And anybody who they send back here will have to deal with that fact.

"As for yourself, Mr. Crawford, I wouldn't spend too much time here in town because your former friends will be looking for you. You were supposed to guarantee the confidentiality of your fraternity, and you failed. And, the authorities will probably have an arrest warrant issued for you before noon. Chief Johnson has evidence that you started the fire at Higgins Brothers." Matt paused, wanting to emphasise his next point. "That warrant will be good throughout the state."

Lucas slowly put down his coffee cup and looked through the window to the darkness outside. Matt knew Crawford wanted to issue his rebuttal to this appraisal of him and his cause. But he was scared, and his position was doubtful. He probably felt like a card player holding a pair of deuces while his opponent merely smiled and raised the bet.

Finally, in exasperation Lucas Crawford spit out a futile challenge. "You may have won this battle, but our cause is just. I promise you we'll be back, and next time we'll have the law on our side."

Matt stood up, signaling that the meeting was over. "I believe it is time for you to go, Mr. Crawford."

Lucas took a long swallow of his coffee and stood up. He buttoned his suit-coat and eyed Matt for a moment longer. With nothing more to say, he turned and left the store. Matt watched him get into his car. His visitor started the engine, shifted into reverse, and pulled away from the curb. Lucas drove past the window, never looking back. Matt took note of the Chevrolet's white numbers on the brown license plate. The car hesitated briefly at the intersection and then turned west onto Broad Street. Matt locked the front door before he wrote down the license number on a piece of wrapping paper. He would call Chief Johnson about his meeting with Lucas Crawford in a couple of hours. He really didn't want to see Lucas again, and so he'd give the man a head start.

At last Matt turned toward the kitchen to help Davy. He found his friend and assistant near the door holding the shotgun. Matt gave Davy a look of concern. The young man set the gun down against the wall where Matt had left it.

"I . . . I thought there may be trouble, and I was protecting you," stammered Davy.

Matt was moved by the act of kindness and smiled at his loyal assistant. He shook Davy's hand. "Thank you, Davy. We're getting behind in our work. Let's get some bread baked."

Shortly after noon Matt took off his apron, thanked Davy for his help, and went out into the store area, where Maureen and Mrs. O'Rourke were busy helping customers. It had been a good morning, and Matt and Davy had baked two extra batches of bread while Maureen had stopped work on her fresh strawberry pies in order to help out with sales. Three grocers had telephoned in large orders for delivery this morning. Later, as Matt gathered up the day's receipts to take to the bank, Mrs. O'Rourke put her arm around him and reached up to peck his cheek. Matt looked down, surprised, but said nothing.

Mrs. O'Rourke's eyes sparkled; strands of her gray hair were out of place from her labors this day. Matt noticed Maureen smiling behind the elderly woman. "I think you've saved the day, Matt," gushed Mrs. O'Rourke. "Old customers have been coming back, and new ones have been in as well. I can't recall such a day."

"I hope it lasts," muttered Matt. "But there's been nothing I did to bring back these customers. I think that the sermons preached yesterday have had a great effect on people and their consciences. Time will tell if it continues."

Mrs. O'Rourke turned toward Maureen and rolled her eyes. Then she sighed and put her hands on her hips as she turned back to her employer.

"Oh, Matt, I suppose the leprechauns were the ones that snatched that list from the Klan and arranged for all those church ministers to preach on love and generosity toward their neighbors."

She sternly shook her head at him. "You can't fool an old woman like me. Besides, some of the boys from the parish have had a hard time keeping their mouths shut. Now you go home and get your rest. But I know that your dear sainted mother would have been so proud of how you stood up to these hoodlums."

Matt smiled and kissed a clearly startled but pleased Mrs. O'Rourke full on the lips in front of Maureen. He then kissed his sister on the cheek, put on his cap, and with a wink toward them, left to conduct his business.

Ginny O'Rourke looked at Maureen and realized that she must be blushing. Maureen looked back at her in obvious amusement. "It has been some time since a handsome young man stole a kiss from me like that. We best not let on about this to Mr. O'Rourke. He'd feel obliged to come down here and punch your brother in the nose. I wouldn't want to be the cause of such a row."

She suppressed a laugh, grabbed a broom in the corner, and began to sweep the floor behind the counters.

When he got to Broad Street, Matt turned left, away from home, and went to the bank. He had called Annie and told her he would be late for lunch because of the extra bread they had baked that morning. Annie had prevailed upon him to finish his work for the day and come home. She had insisted on substituting for him that afternoon, helping Maureen complete the day. Matt was to come home to rest and spend the balance of a nice spring day with their children.

After making the deposit, Matt stopped by police headquarters. Chief Johnson was in his office sipping coffee and eating a sandwich. He waved Matt into the office when he spotted him.

"You were right, Matt. The Logansport police found Crawford's car at the Pennsylvania depot. How did you know he'd abandon it instead of driving to Indianapolis?"

Matt took off his hat as he sat down in one of the two wooden chairs the policeman kept in front of his desk.

"I didn't know which way he would head, but I knew that it would be smarter to get lost on a train than to risk detection on the roads. I wouldn't bet on his heading to visit his bosses in Indianapolis, either."

"Where do you think he's going?" asked the policeman.

"I haven't a clue, Paul, but most likely it will be out of state."

"So he's running to avoid prosecution for attempted arson," concluded the chief.

"He's running for a lot of reasons, but it would be bad for him to wind up back here to face a criminal trial. It would also be bad for the town. We need to put these events behind us. It won't do any good to play them out in the county courthouse. It would just stir up people and cause more trouble."

"So you think I should halt my investigation?"

"I'm not saying that, Paul. You do your job, but I wouldn't push too hard to bring criminal charges against any of the men on that list. There's a spirit of forgiveness going around today, and with luck it might just continue for a while."

The chief took off his glasses and cleaned them with his handkerchief. "How long have you known that this Crawford fella was leading the Klan here in town?"

Matt hesitated; he knew where this question would lead. But Paul Johnson was a friend, and the police chief deserved as much of the truth as Matt could share with him. "I've known about Mr. Crawford for two or three months."

The chief drew a deep breath and looked across his desk. "Why didn't you come to me with this information?"

Matt gazed back at his friend and told him the truth. "I wasn't sure I could trust you. I knew Billy Harris was a part of their gang, and I feared you might be also. As you know by now, the mayor and a few other officials were on that list too."

Paul Johnson donned his glasses and scowled at his visitor. "The mayor says he accepted a free membership to get some votes. He never attended any meetings. I'll admit he did ask me to go slow with my investigation of the Higgins incident. But I never did anything to intentionally help the Klan."

An acute silence lasted for several seconds, and the two men understood that this matter between them was now closed.

The policeman changed the tone of his voice as he moved on. "I've had more than a dozen men come in today and admit that they were Klansmen just like it says in the book Billy left me. Of course, they deny doing anything criminal. They all claim it was a secret group led by Tom Stewart. But I've got more than a hundred names left to go visit, and someone may just be scared enough to confess to being at the Higgins place with Crawford in their white robes."

"How did you find out about the Stewart boy's death?"

"Billy left me a letter as well as the book. He said he stole it from Crawford's office. We found the door unlocked and Tom Stewart dead inside when we went to investigate."

"Have you heard anything from Officer Harris?" inquired Matt.

The chief nodded and reached for a telegram on his desk. "I got this from a railroad police captain in St. Louis. They found Billy sleeping near an interlocking tower this morning. He claimed to have been abducted by thieves who took his uniform."

"Is he coming home?" asked Matt.

"He better not. His name is in the Klan book, and I'll arrest him for lying to me and being part of criminal activities. I sent a wire back to St. Louis telling him as much.

"But you know, his friend Randall Madison didn't show up for work today and his room was empty over at the Tilly house. He's also listed as a Klansman. I figure the two of them had something to do with this. Billy isn't all that smart, but Madison could have talked him into making amends and then running off. I never trusted that drifter."

The policeman rocked back in his chair and eyed Matt suspiciously.

"What I don't understand is how all those copies of the membership list got distributed. Those two boys would need a lot of help to do all that work over the weekend."

"Maybe they had been working on it for several weeks," offered Matt. "They could have stolen the book and typed up one list before they put the book back. Then they could have made extra copies before they were ready to steal the book again and make it public."

Paul Johnson rubbed his chin and looked across his desk at his friend. "You think like a copper or a crook, Matt. Are you sure you didn't have anything to do with this? Because I'm wondering why Lucas Crawford came to visit you before he left town."

"Chief, let's just say things couldn't have worked out better for me if I had planned it all myself. This mysterious chain of events answered my prayers and those of a lot of other people, including yourself. Let's just leave it alone and be grateful for our good fortune."

"Well, I'm going to continue to investigate this little mystery," said Johnson. "But I don't think it's going to lead to anything criminal. As you said, it's probably not a good idea to stir up any more trouble. I've been getting a few calls from newspaper reporters concerning the list and the arrest warrant for Crawford. I've told them that an investigation is active. But I don't think they've got much of a story. It would be foolish to let them snoop around and make up one. The only news is Tom Stewart's suicide, and it would only hurt his parents for the truth to be dragged out in print. I just hope the Klan stays out of the valley."

"I think they will," said Matt.

Matt got up from his chair and put on his black casual hat. He was uncomfortable out in public without a business suit. "I'm headed home for the day. We've been too busy for lunch, so Annie wants me home early. She's going to replace me this afternoon at the bakery."

"You and I are lucky men to have such good women to take care of us," drawled Paul.

"Yes, we are very lucky," replied Matt. "This is a hard, selfish world we live in. Without the love and support of such women, life wouldn't be worth living."

Matt waved to his friend and departed from the station house. A feeling of euphoria welled up inside him as he strode along Broad Street. He had reclaimed his right to live and work in this town. It had been a good week, and it was only Monday.